When Bad Feels Good . . .

Unlike most of the men at the bar, Shane had eschewed the resort uniform of khaki shorts and a golf shirt. Instead, he was dressed in a pair of well-worn jean shorts, flip-flops, and a white linen shirt unbuttoned to reveal enough skin for Carly to know he spent a lot of time outdoors. Sun-kissed brown hair curled around his collar, one stray lock hanging in front of eyes so dark she couldn't make out their color. A hint of stubble along his jaw gave just the right amount of danger to his look. His presence was . . . intoxicating, to say the least. And he was focusing all that dark, brooding intensity on her.

Strong arms held her against his tall, athletic frame and she sighed softly as his chest came in contact with her breasts. His lips brushed her hairline; the beginnings of his beard gently rubbing against her skin sent shock waves to the pit of her belly and below. He smelled of shea butter and soap. Clean and sweet. Definitely not the words most people would use to describe Shane Devlin, the Devil of the NFL. He shifted her against him again and she felt the heat and strength of his arousal.

Carly thought to herself, *Okay, this was definitely a bad idea . . .*

Game On

TRACY SOLHEIM

BERKLEY SENSATION, NEW YORK

THE BERKLEY PUBLISHING GROUP
Published by the Penguin Group
Penguin Group (USA) Inc.
375 Hudson Street, New York, New York 10014, USA

(Penguin logo)

USA | Canada | UK | Ireland | Australia | New Zealand | India | South Africa | China

Penguin Books Ltd., Registered Offices: 80 Strand, London WC2R 0RL, England
For more information about the Penguin Group, visit penguin.com.

GAME ON

A Berkley Sensation Book / published by arrangement with Sun Home Productions, LLC

Berkley Sensation Books are published by The Berkley Publishing Group.
BERKLEY SENSATION® is a registered trademark of Penguin Group (USA) Inc.
The "B" design is a trademark of Penguin Group (USA) Inc.

For information, address: The Berkley Publishing Group,
a division of Penguin Group (USA) Inc.,
375 Hudson Street, New York, New York 10014.

ISBN: 978-0-425-26663-2

PUBLISHING HISTORY
Berkley Sensation mass-market paperback edition / May 2013

PRINTED IN THE UNITED STATES OF AMERICA

10 9 8 7 6 5 4 3 2 1

Cover photo by Claudio Marinesco.
Cover design by Rita Frangie.
Interior text design by Laura K. Corless.

This one is for the home team.
Thanks for not laughing
when I said I was writing a book.

ACKNOWLEDGMENTS

This book would not have been possible without an abundance of encouragement and dedication on the part of so many wonderful people in my life. Oh, and luck. It takes a little luck now and then to make dreams come true.

Thanks, first of all, to Melissa Jeglinski, for agreeing to represent my books even after enduring eight hours stranded in the Shreveport, Louisiana, airport with me stalking you! (See what I mean about luck?) Your patience and guidance, as well as your friendship, are appreciated.

Cindy Hwang, thank you for believing in this book and those yet to come. It is an honor and a privilege to work with you and all the wonderful people at Berkley.

To the four beautiful fellow authors who have shared this journey with me these past several years—Christy Hayes, Susan Sands, Laura Butler, and Laura Alford—thanks for gifting me with not only your talented critiques, but your friendship.

Thanks to my steadfast college buddies, Diane, Melanie, and Deanne, for always agreeing when I beg for beta readers. Well, okay, two of you do, but the other one brings wine and lets me drive her convertible when I'm in the throes of writer's block.

To Allison, Chris, Dana, Donna, Jeanne, Kathy, Maureen, and Megan, my friends in the Talking Volumes book club, thank you for cheering me on and, no, we don't have to discuss this book in detail. Unless, of course, you really, really want to.

Thanks also to my wonderful small group. Your prayers are always helpful. Peace.

Finally, thanks to the three people who never doubted this book would get published—even when I did. Greg, Austin, and Meredith, your unconditional love and support—not to mention the endless supply of cupcakes—mean the world to me. I love you!

One

"Well I'll be doggone! Ain't this a small world or what?"

Shane Devlin looked up from the screen of his cell phone, shaking his head slightly to readjust his thoughts. He'd been so focused on the text message he was reading, he'd tuned out everything around him. A lizard darted through the dahlia bushes bordering the bar's patio where Shane sat. The ocean churned quietly beneath an inky night sky. Music and laughter from the nightclub drifted out amongst the strings of twinkling lights before being carried away to the sea by a quiet breeze. All in all, it was a travel agent's dream night on the Mexican Riviera.

"Kitty, get over here with the camera. I gotta get a picture with him to show the fellas at the rotary club."

Or it would be if not for the loud, obnoxious bar patrons. Shifting uncomfortably in the plastic resin chair, Shane glanced around for an escape route as the heavyset, balding man with the booming voice lumbered toward him, a wide-eyed Kitty in tow. Both looked harmless enough: a middle-aged couple dressed in typical tourist garb, complete with sparkling white sneakers on their feet.

"Mort, I don't think we should disturb him," Kitty whispered as Mort rummaged through the oversized, leopard-print bag on her shoulder, presumably looking for a camera.

Ahh, so Kitty with the bouffant hair wasn't as impressed by a down-on-his-luck NFL quarterback as hubby Mort. Perhaps it was the stay-the-hell-away-from-me vibe Shane was putting out. After all, he'd escaped to Mexico to lie low for a few days while his agent negotiated a new contract for him.

"Honey, do you know who this is?" Mort asked as he pulled a small digital camera from the depths of the bag.

Here it comes. This is where Mort tells Kitty she's looking at the idiot who, in the final minutes of the last game of the season, threw the winning touchdown—except the guy who caught it was wearing the other team's jersey. Shane felt his jaw clench as he shifted his six-foot-three-inch frame to a more defensive position, not an easy feat considering the small chair. Wringing her hands in front of her, Kitty shuffled her feet as Mort's pudgy fingers struggled to turn on the camera. From the look of panic on her face, she knew exactly who Shane was—or more important, who the tabloid press made him out to be: the Devil of the NFL. Nothing aggravated him more than fans bringing up that botched game or his even more botched-up personal life.

"This here is Shane Devlin, the son of a football legend. His daddy was one of the best players in the game," Mort said reverently. "Heck, if his old man hadn't been injured, he'd be in the Hall of Fame for sure."

Okay, *that* actually aggravated him more. Shane reached for the bottle of beer he'd been nursing all night, not sure whether he wanted to drink its warm contents or smash it over something. Being compared to his father never failed to make him angry. Or to remind him of how his plans had been derailed. Shane was a man with no team to play for next season. At thirty-one years old, he was at his athletic peak. Yet one ill-timed interception—along with several highly publicized scandals off the field—was enough for the San Diego Chargers to send him packing.

But Shane wasn't ready to hang up his cleats. It wasn't money he was after; he'd saved enough to live well after retirement. No, it was the records he wanted. Records set by his father—Bruce Devlin—when he'd played pro football. The same father who'd abandoned him. Shane would be damned if Bruce Devlin's name graced any NFL record books. No, he intended to break them all himself.

Several teams out there were looking for a veteran quarterback, but Shane couldn't afford to just stand on the sidelines. He needed a starting gig. Hoping another player would blow out a knee tripping over his dog wasn't exactly good karma, but Shane was running out of options. And tonight, sitting in a bar in Cabo San Lucas after thirty-six holes of golf with a few sponsors, his luck may have just turned. He glanced down at the text on his cell phone again, the message on the screen his talisman:

Blaze QB out 4 season. Working on a deal now.

Shane sucked in a lungful of air to calm himself as Mort edged closer. Stuffing his cell phone in his shorts, Shane stood, squaring his broad shoulders and puffing out his chest. The move had the desired effect; Mort stilled in midmotion.

"Um, you don't mind if the little lady snaps a photo of us, do you?" Mort asked, apparently finally finding his manners.

Hell yes, I do! Shane almost shouted. He bit it back, though, not wanting to listen to another lecture from his agent about playing nice with the folks who filled the stadiums, thereby funding his paycheck.

Shane grabbed the beer bottle, discreetly tucking it behind his hip. "Why not?"

It was all the invitation Mort needed. With a facesplitting grin, he handed the camera to a still leery Kitty and sidled up next to Shane, stretching up on his beefy legs so as to almost reach Shane's shoulder. The camera flashed twice, and while Shane's eyes recovered from the assault,

Mort pulled up a chair to the table and sank down into it. Kitty dropped her oversized bag into another chair and dragged it toward Shane's table.

"Thanks, buddy. Let me buy you another beer and you can catch me up on what your old man's been up to lately." Mort flagged down a waiter.

No way was Shane sitting with Mort and Kitty to "catch up" on anything, much less his dear old dad, whom he hadn't spoken to more than a half dozen times in the last twenty years. Shane scanned the patio for possible options to exit gracefully. He really wanted to head back to his room to wait for his agent's call. With any luck, he'd be signing with a new team tomorrow.

Peals of pleasant laughter drew his attention to a table next to the bar where two women sat sharing a pitcher of margaritas. He'd run into them frequently throughout the weekend since they occupied one of the VIP bungalows near his. According to the resort's golf pro, the dark, vivacious one was a famous wedding gown designer. She'd brought along a dozen or so Victoria Secret model–wannabes to shoot a photo spread of her gowns at a nearby ancient Spanish church. Shane had steered clear of her, figuring any woman who touched wedding gowns—much less designed them—clearly had fantasies of wedding bells in her future. His game was football, not serious relationships.

Avoiding her completely had become impossible because Shane was fascinated with observing the antics of the designer's assistant. She'd spent the weekend shuffling between the church and the resort's business office, all the while with a cell phone that, when it wasn't glued to her ear, chimed the theme to *The Wizard of Oz*. The taller of the two, she was also much fairer, her skin glowing a soft pink after several days in the sun. Her hair blew in long, chestnut waves, shimmering softly under the moonlight. But it was her eyes—the exact color of the blue Pacific waters caressing the sand along the Mexican resort—he found most interesting.

Too bad they weren't as warm as the ocean they reflected.

Every time he tried to start up a conversation with her, he was treated to a cold brush-off. Twice he'd offered to buy her a drink, only to get a polite—but chilly—refusal. The situation was a novel one for him. He was a professional athlete, for crying out loud. Wherever he went, women fell all over him. But not this woman. He wasn't used to having to work to get a woman to pay attention to him, and he was surprised at how much the effort seemed to turn him on.

The magazine photographer joined the two women at their table, chatting in rapid-fire Italian with the designer. Laughing, he pulled her up and off to the center of the patio where couples danced under the stars. Shane took advantage of the opportunity for a speedy escape.

"Thanks, but my friends are waiting for me at another table." Shane clapped Mort on the shoulder, forcing him to stay in his seat. Nodding to Kitty, he tried to look casual as he dodged between the dancers and other patrons, finally sliding into the chair the designer had vacated.

Cool blue eyes framed by long, dark lashes fixed on him as he set his beer down on the table. Dressed in a sleeveless floral blouse that wrapped around her waist and a short denim skirt that accentuated long, lean, sun-kissed legs, she shifted back in her chair. Any surprise she might have felt by his abrupt arrival was quickly covered with an abundance of poise. Casually she flung her hair over a shoulder, slowly crossing her bare legs. If the move was meant to be provocative, it worked.

"Don't panic. I'm not staying," he said, leaning back in the chair, crossing his own long legs at the ankles so as to present a relaxed image in case Mort and Kitty were watching. "I'm just avoiding that couple at the table back there."

Before he could stop her, she whipped her head around to look back across the dance floor at Mort and Kitty. Mort gave him a thumbs-up sign just as she turned back to Shane. *Ah, hell.* He took a long pull on his beer to buy some more time. It was nasty and warm, but he was heading for his room, so no point in ordering another one. The silence stretched.

"Shane Devlin," he said, finally.

She said nothing, continuing to stare at him, her full lips forming a brief, patronizing grin. Shifting in his chair, his gaze zeroed in on her smile, and he couldn't help wondering what her mouth might taste like. Forcing his eyes up, he noticed the constellation of freckles crossing her nose. His perusal stopped as his eyes met hers, still incredibly blue, but with a slight twinkle that Shane hoped wasn't a result of the bar lights. Other than a slight lift of her brow, her face revealed nothing.

"And you are?" he persisted, trying to remember if he'd heard her speaking English at any time this weekend.

"Allergic to jocks." A hint of an accent wove through her crisp voice.

Shane bit back a grin, finally relaxing in his chair. So she knew who he was and decided to play hard to get. The game just got a lot more interesting. Maybe not as easy as he'd like, but he lived for a challenge. Besides, this was a lot more fun than waiting on his phone to ring back in his room. Why not stay and chat her up, seeing as how she'd shot him down all weekend.

"How 'bout I just call you Dorothy?"

Both eyebrows arched in question. Shane nodded toward the ever-present cell phone lying on the table. She laughed softly and he felt it all the way to his groin. Leaning forward, she rested her arms on the table, giving him an excellent view of a silver chain dangling between two pert breasts. A dusting of perspiration glistened on her skin, courtesy of the humid evening. Her breasts were no rival to the silicone boobs adorning the models circulating the bar, but he didn't care. Suddenly, he wanted them in his hands. In his mouth. *Whoa there, buddy! Just killing time, here. Harmless flirting and nothing more,* he reminded himself.

"So, what is it you want tonight, Mr. Devlin?" She lifted her margarita glass to her mouth, flicking a piece of salt with her tongue. The simple action made him hard.

What did he want? Apparently, if he was listening to the plays his body was calling, he wanted her. But he'd be damned if he could figure out why. She was nothing like the women he normally found attractive. Nonetheless, she'd captivated his attention since he'd first laid eyes on her lounging beside the pool. Surrounded by a bevy of enhanced female perfection, she somehow stood out from the models. She was real.

Shane wasn't sure how to handle real.

His entire life, people had been sucking up to him, first to meet his famous father, then to meet him. It was one of the reasons he kept to himself. He trusted no one. Sure, he could turn on the public persona when his contract called for it, but for the most part, Shane was a private man. The women he got involved with knew the rules up front. They used him for publicity and he used them for sex. Simple. Or at least it had been up until recently.

Perhaps Dorothy's unpretentiousness attracted him. He couldn't say. All he knew was he was enjoying himself for the first time in many weeks. Nothing could come of it. He had a score to settle, a team to pursue, and records to break. His game plan didn't allow for the strong attraction he immediately felt for a strange woman in a bar.

"I just thought we could get to know each other better." The line sounded corny even to him. He was definitely rusty in the flirtation department. And she wasn't going to make it easy for him. In spite of that, Shane felt a slow smile spread across his face.

Rolling her eyes at his adolescent attempt, she fiddled with a strand of hair and leaned back against the chair.

"You jocks are all alike." She fingered the chain around her neck. Shane took a slow breath. The gesture was more erotic than her licking the salt off her glass. "You think any woman will be flattered by your attention."

"You could flatter me with a little of yours."

His lines were bordering on pathetic, but at least she didn't break out in hysterics. He thought he saw the beginnings of a real smile, but before she could say anything, the fashion designer and photographer returned to the table. The designer's eyes went wide as she noticed him sitting there. The photographer recognized Shane immediately.

"Hey, you two do know each . . ." Before he could finish

his sentence, Dorothy grabbed Shane's arm, yanking him up from the table.

"Let's dance." Her warm fingers manacled his wrist as she dragged him to the other side of the bar.

She didn't have to ask him twice. As luck would have it, the jazz trio was playing a cover of a John Mayer ballad, allowing Shane to gather her close. So close he detected the citrus scent of her shampoo. She smelled good enough to eat. Her soft, bare arms glowed beneath the twinkling patio lights. He stifled a groan as her hips swayed against his groin.

"Aren't you afraid of an allergic reaction?" he teased. She shivered as his breath brushed her neck. He took it as an invitation to lean in closer and trace his lips along the shell of her ear.

"I'll risk it." Dorothy breathed against his chest.

Carly March looked behind the gorgeous hunk of athlete she'd dragged to the dance floor to where her friend Julianne Marchione was waving frantically at her.

What are you doing? Julianne mouthed.

Good question, Carly thought to herself as she stepped into Shane Devlin's arms. What *was* she doing? She knew she shouldn't be touching him, much less dancing with him. But Marco had almost blown it back at the table and could have let it slip who she was. She didn't think about the consequences before rushing off with Shane. Clearly, the testosterone oozing out of his pores was wreaking havoc on her normally solid common sense. That and a weekend spent Googling everything ever written about him. Carly had stared at his photo so many times in the last few days, she dreamt about him at night. Now her dreams had become reality. And the real thing was oh so much better. She shivered as his mouth grazed her ear. Oh God, she needed to keep a hold of her senses and remember who she worked for.

Shane Devlin was no random stranger at a resort. Anyone who followed sports knew he was an out-of-work NFL quarterback looking for a team to play for. Up until a day or two ago, his prospects had looked bleak. But then, Gabe Harrelson, the record-breaking young quarterback for the Baltimore Blaze, broke a hip and a femur hang-gliding in Australia. As assistant to the team's general manager, Carly knew Shane occupied a spot on the team's short list for replacing Harrelson.

The search for a replacement quarterback had encroached on her getaway since the day she arrived at the beach resort. She'd tagged along with her best friend, Julianne, to rest and relax for a few days during the team's off-season. Instead, the only surfing she'd done was on the Internet. The dossier she'd compiled about Shane Devlin could fill a tabloid magazine. In fact, that's where she'd gotten most of her background on him. His play off the field was as notorious as his play on the field. Despite the fact that most of the reports about his behavior outside of football looked to her to be rumor and innuendo, she didn't think Blaze management would see it that way. Hank Osbourne, the team's general manager, was a stickler about his players being role models for the fans. If you played for the Blaze, you must be above reproach. The same could be said for those who worked for the team.

Earlier in the day, Carly made a strong case to management via a conference call that the exploits reported by the media of Shane's "extracurricular behavior" had been greatly exaggerated. One woman's claim that he was the father of her child had been easily refuted a few weeks later with DNA testing, but the stigma of his playboy reputation still lingered. A more recent claim by a San Diego Charger's employee that Shane had sexually intimidated her was never substantiated. However, the stink associated with both incidents was a red flag for Blaze management.

The tabloid press was notorious for blowing things out of proportion—Carly knew this firsthand. *They even turn on their own.* She felt a kinship for anyone crucified by the paparazzi, and it was one of the reasons Carly felt she needed to defend Shane against the sensational articles.

Heck, she'd stuck her neck out for Shane this morning. The same neck his lips were skimming over right now. Oh, this was not good. *It's just a dance,* she told herself as he moved her slowly around the patio. Unfortunately, her body wasn't listening to what her brain was saying as she pressed dangerously closer.

The photos on the Internet didn't do him justice. He wasn't glamour-boy gorgeous, but his dark, intense looks definitely drew the attention of most of the women at the resort. And when he'd smiled at her a few minutes earlier, she'd been lucky to be sitting because she was sure her legs had turned to jelly. Unlike most of the men at the bar, he had eschewed the resort uniform of khaki shorts and a golf shirt. Instead, he was dressed in a pair of well-worn jean shorts, flip-flops, and a white linen shirt unbuttoned to reveal enough skin for her to know he spent a lot of time outdoors. Sun-kissed brown hair curled around his collar, one stray lock hanging in front of eyes so dark, she couldn't make out their color. A hint of stubble along his jaw gave just the right amount of danger to his look. His presence was . . . intoxicating, to say the least. And he was focusing all that dark, brooding intensity on her.

Strong arms held her against his tall, athletic frame and she sighed softly as his chest came in contact with her breasts. His lips brushed her hairline; the beginnings of his beard gently rubbing against her skin sent shock waves to the pit of her belly and below. He smelled of shea butter and soap. Clean and sweet. Definitely not the words most people would use to describe Shane Devlin, the Devil of the NFL. He shifted her against him again and she felt the heat and strength of his arousal.

Okay, this was definitely a bad idea, she thought to herself. Letting a player kiss you would likely be frowned upon by management. Anything more would probably lead to dismissal. Carly really liked her job. She didn't want to jeopardize her position with the Blaze in any way. It gave her an excuse to live in Baltimore where she could help take care of her sister. Besides, she was through with jocks. With all celebrities, for that matter. If she was going to have a fling, it had to be with an accountant or podiatrist. Someone who didn't have paparazzi hiding in his bushes.

If she were being honest, though, it was nice to be held in a man's arms again. She hadn't realized how much she'd missed it these past months. Shane had been watching her all weekend—either through the pages of a magazine or in person. She couldn't help but be flattered by his attention, especially with twelve bikini-clad models running around on the beach.

If he were any other man, she'd be tempted to let her inhibitions run wild for one night of sex. Judging by the attraction humming between them, she knew it would be an interlude she'd not likely forget. She wished the team had already picked someone else so she could let him have his way with her on the makeshift dance floor. Or on the beach. Or in his bungalow.

But he was who he was, and she'd been down this road before. Carly couldn't let this get out of hand.

Shane had somehow maneuvered them off the edge of the patio to a dimly lit alcove beside the pool. She looked up into his shadowed face as a lock of hair fell past his left brow. Intense gray eyes blazed with hunger as his hands gently rubbed her back, one hand roaming lower to lightly skim her bottom. Her body continued to betray her as Shane's potent chemistry wore down her defenses. When he nipped at her collarbone, heat ricocheted through her belly and beyond.

Maybe just a kiss. Surely she could stop at one?

"What is it you want, Mr. Devlin?" she asked again, lifting her eyes to meet his.

"I want whatever you'll give me," he whispered, lowering his head.

She closed her eyes as her stomach quivered in anticipation, waiting for his lips to make contact.

But they never did. Instead, the *Wizard of Oz* ring tone grew louder. Julianne emerged from the shadows somewhere behind them, Carly's ringing cell phone in her hand. Carly leaped out of Shane's arms, a wild jumble of nerves, nearly bowling over her friend.

"You told me not to let you miss a call." Julianne handed her the phone.

"I've got it!" Carly said, annoyed that her friend seemed to be enjoying the moment a little too much.

Julianne failed to hide her grin, and, offering Shane an elegant shrug, retreated back into the shadows.

Carly turned to Shane, who stood, hands on hips, that single lock of hair obscuring an eye. Aside from his breathing being a little ragged, he stared nonchalantly back at her.

"I'm sorry, but I have to take this call." She spoke softly, embarrassment warming her cheeks. "I really have to go. Good night."

He said nothing, his lips compressed in a thin line. Quickly, she crept away before she changed her mind.

Mortified by her behavior, she felt a tinge of guilt for leaving him in a state of potent arousal. But as she glanced at the text message on her phone, she breathed a deep sigh of relief. She'd just dodged a bullet. Shane Devlin was her team's new quarterback.

Now all she had to do was find a way to avoid him altogether once he arrived in Baltimore.

Two

Carly dug the heels of her Steve Madden boots into the carpet as she maneuvered the wheelchair through the hallway of the Blaze headquarters building, all the while trying not to jiggle the chair's occupant too much. The Baltimore weather hadn't been welcoming after the sun and warmth of Mexico. Despite the fact it was nearly the end of April, winter still had the mid-Atlantic in its grip, complete with gray clouds spewing icy drizzle. Dressed in a sleek, gray wool pantsuit and silk pink blouse, Carly was beginning to regret her choice to dress for the weather as sweat began to pool on her neck, the result of wielding the bulky wheelchair for what felt like miles this morning.

"I can't believe you busted up your knee skiing, Asia." Carly tried not to sound as out of shape as she felt. "One would have thought you'd be a bit more graceful, being an All-American college basketball player and all," she teased.

The going got easier as they entered the cafeteria with its linoleum floor, and Carly pushed Asia Dupree, media relations director for the Blaze, to a table near the row of coffee urns.

"Yeah, well, college was a few years ago, Carly. And all this sitting behind a desk hasn't helped to keep my old body in shape."

Carly slid into a chair on the opposite side of the table, reaching over to adjust the pillow cradling Asia's injured knee. She smiled at the statuesque African American beauty. "Thirty isn't old." Carly gestured to the coffee bar.

Asia nodded. "Yeah, well, it's the last time I celebrate my birthday with a ski vacation."

Carly carried over a steaming cup of coffee, placing it on the table near Asia before going back to grab a handful of sweetener packets and a container of creamer. "Ah, but you did get rescued by a handsome hero. Seriously, if you wanted to get a certain director of security's attention, wouldn't it have been easier to break a heel here at work?"

Asia shot her a glare that turned to a smile before taking sip of coffee.

Laughing, Carly poured herself a cup of tea. "Next birthday, head to the beach. Cabo is beautiful this time of year," she said.

"Oh Carly, I'm so sorry that my accident ruined your vacation. I should have been the one vetting our new players, not you. But I was pretty hopped up on the painkillers. I feel bad you didn't get to relax yourself."

Carrying her own steaming cup to the table, Carly gently squeezed her friend's shoulder before taking the seat next to her. "Don't be silly, Asia. I had a great trip." She gave her friend what she hoped was a reassuring smile as she blew on her tea.

It was true; Carly did have a nice time in Cabo. Especially the brief time spent in Shane Devlin's arms. Putting down her tea so Asia couldn't see the slight tremor caused by her thoughts of Shane, Carly winced inwardly at the way she'd left him. It was childish. She should have just come clean in Mexico. Instead, she now faced an awkward situation when they first ran into one another at work. He was arriving today for a press conference and meetings with the coaches. A three-day player mini-camp was scheduled for the rest of the week. Maybe Carly would seek him out to explain why she'd abruptly left the dance floor. Maybe they'd both laugh about it. *Yeah, maybe.*

"But you really needed some downtime after all you and your family have been through these past few months," Asia persisted, forcing Carly's thoughts back to the present.

"Asia, I gave my sister some bone marrow, not a kidney. I'm fine. Besides, I'm just glad I could help you and Hank out. It made me feel useful."

"Useful? Carly, you were amazing!" Asia said. "Your contacts are unbelievable. I never would have been able to ferret out some of that information about Shane Devlin."

Carly took a sip of tea. "Well, one tends to become great friends with those slimy paparazzi when they were picking through your garbage."

Asia gave her a look tinged with pity, slightly shaking her head at Carly's self-deprecating humor. Carly steeled herself with another swallow of tea.

"Do you miss it?" Asia asked softly.

"Having total strangers hound your every move?" Carly shuddered.

"No, the sophistication and glamour of living as a European socialite."

"Never," Carly answered firmly. It was true. She hadn't asked to grow up in a fishbowl of European paparazzi. Her mother, Veronica March, was a media heiress, traveling the world as a correspondent for a cable news channel. Carly was ten when Veronica had been murdered by terrorists. She'd never known who her father was. It was the media who broke it to her. "Darling Carly," as they'd dubbed her, was Veronica's "love child" with a married American news anchor. Unfortunately, Carly's existence was news to her father as well. It made for great fodder to sell tabloids—including those owned by her grandmother. It was *not* a pleasant way to grow up. But her childhood couldn't prepare her for how the media treated her later in life. Carly refused to think of Max right now. Lifting her gaze, she locked eyes with Asia.

"No, Asia. I don't miss it. Like I said, I love my job here. I feel useful." Her voice was steely, she knew. But Asia boasted not only a national championship in NCAA basketball, but an MBA from the Wharton School's business program as well. Carly knew Asia appreciated toughness.

"Good," Asia said, her voice sounding just as determined as Carly's. "Because I'm going to need a little more help in the next few weeks."

"Of course. Whatever you need. I'm sure Hank won't mind."

"It was Hank's suggestion, actually. It's going to be difficult for me to carry out the media blitz we have planned for our new quarterback with this bum knee." Asia gestured to her leg, which was encased in a brace. "Someone needs to babysit him on his media outings while I'm still immobile. Both Hank and I thought you'd be perfect."

Carly took too big a swallow of her tea and nearly choked as the hot liquid burned down her throat. She wasn't sure if it was the hot drink or the shock of having to spend time with Shane Devlin—more than just sharing a laugh over her humiliating exit in Cabo—but she couldn't seem to find words to respond to Asia. Not that Asia was waiting on a response.

"I can handle today's press conference, but my knee is going to need surgery once the swelling goes down. Then there's physical therapy . . . Carly, are you okay?"

"Yeah, yeah. I'm fine," Carly reassured her friend. "Just feeling bad that you have to go through all that." It was a lie. Not that Carly wasn't feeling sorry for Asia; she was. But she was trying to figure out a way to deal with Shane Devlin without her hormones going haywire.

"Hmm. I'll be suffering and you'll get to spend time with a gorgeous bad boy," Asia said. "Who knows, maybe you two will hit it off."

Carly stared at Asia, trying desperately not to let her mouth gape open, all the while wondering if Julianne had broken her promise not to tell a soul about her close encounter with the Devil of the NFL.

"He's not my type." A girl could lock lips with a guy who isn't her type. It happened all the time.

"No one's your type," Asia said sarcastically before taking a swallow of coffee.

"I wouldn't say that," a male voice chimed in from behind them. "I'm sure there are a few guys who could be the perfect type for Carly."

The hairs on the back of Carly's neck stood on end as she recognized the voice behind her. *Great.* It was Joel Tompkins, one of the team's beat reporters. She'd made the mistake of having coffee with him several weeks ago and he'd been pestering her for a date ever since. Lately, he'd been popping up everywhere she went.

"Tompkins, you know media aren't allowed in this part of the building." Asia pinned him with the haughty voice known to cause grizzled sports writers to back down.

"I know," Joel said, his eyes glued on Carly. "I need to get my parking pass updated."

"Mary handles that up front and you know it," Asia replied. "Either find your way back to the press room or find your credentials revoked for a week."

"She's such a buzz kill," Joel said. Leaning his hip against a nearby table, he slowly eyed Carly from head to toe. "How was Cabo, Carly? You're back early. You must've missed me."

Carly was too stunned to respond. Only a handful of people knew where she had gone on vacation, and she would swear on her life that none of them would tell Joel. The guy was really starting to creep her out. Before she knew it, Donovan Carter, director of security for the Blaze, appeared out of nowhere and had Joel by the arm.

"Tompkins, I thought you and I had already talked about staying in your side of the facility," Donovan practically growled. Joel cowed quickly, intimidated by the stocky African American former Marine.

"Just checking on my best girl," Joel said as he yanked his arm out of Donovan's grasp. With a jaunty salute, he sauntered toward the hallway. "I'll see you later, babe," he called over his shoulder.

Best girl? They had coffee together. Once. Carly was certainly used to overzealous reporters, but Joel's fascination with her was a little over the top.

"That guy's ick factor just went way up," Asia said.

Donovan stood with his hands on his hips until Joel was out of sight. Hooking one foot around a chair leg, he pulled it toward their table and sat, offering a smile to Asia.

"He still buggin' you?" Donovan focused his eyes on Carly. She was always amazed at how a man so imposing could have such beautiful eyes: warm chocolate with a genuine sincerity that always managed to put Carly at ease.

"All media bug me, Donovan," Carly quipped, taking another sip of her tea.

Donovan leaned forward, putting on his best interrogator's voice. "I mean, is he still leaving little gifts in your office or waiting for you at your car at night?"

Carly shivered at his intensity. "Yes and no," she hedged.

Donovan made an incoherent sound before Asia subdued him with a hand to his arm. "Carly, don't mess with him. If Joel's being a worm, you'd better give us the details," she said.

Sitting back in her chair, Carly released a sigh. "*Yes*, he's still leaving flowers, candy, and notes on my desk. As far as I know, he hasn't disturbed anything in my office, though. *No*, he doesn't wait at my car anymore, but that's because I always find someone to walk out with. I think he's getting the hint."

"It didn't sound to me like he got the hint," Donovan snapped. He waved a finger at Carly. "If he gets in your face again, you're to come tell me right away. Got it?" He was so intense, Carly was surprised steam hadn't started to rise from Donovan's shaved head.

Carly smiled at him before giving him a smart salute. She wanted to grab him up in hug because, despite his ferocity, she knew his actions meant he cared. Sure he was responsible for the security of the team and its staff, but his protectiveness made her feel as if she were a part of something. Someone was willing to run interference for her with the media and it felt good. Until recently, she hadn't experienced that feeling too often.

Nonchalantly leaning back in the plush conference room chair, Shane watched as his agent, Roscoe Mathis, charmed a young woman into bringing him some coffee. Shane shook his head and chuckled softly as the receptionist offered to bring them donuts, too. Roscoe's grandmother used to tell Shane that Roscoe could charm the habit off a nun. He'd seen the effects of that charm too many times to argue with his friend's grandmother.

The two men had met when Shane was a freshman in college. Roscoe was in law school, working as a tutor to raise extra money. Determined not to make the same mistakes as his father, Shane did everything he could to earn the degree the football scholarship offered—even if it meant working with a tutor. By the time Shane was picked in the first round of the NFL draft, Roscoe was working as a junior attorney with a sports management company in New York. The relationship was lucrative for both of them. Shane trusted very few people in life. Roscoe Mathis was one of those very few.

Thin rivers of rain zigzagged down the glass of the huge windows surrounding the conference room. The cold, nasty weather was definitely a shock to Shane's system. Dressed in gray slacks, a black cashmere crewneck sweater, and loafers with no socks, he felt the chill seep through him. With the exception of games played on the East Coast and two weeks spent each summer at a cabin near the town in western Pennsylvania where he grew up, Shane managed to avoid living in the East. Southern California had the sun, the beach, and a laid-back lifestyle that allowed him to cultivate the "devil may care" attitude people expected of him. He never intended to return East. It was too close to Bruce Devlin and his new family. Yet here he was, practically groveling for a chance to play another season or two of football in Baltimore.

Several people entered the conference room, jarring Shane from his thoughts. He stood as Roscoe shook hands with a tall gentleman sporting a buzz cut who, were it not for his Brooks Brothers suit, looked as if he were commanding a battalion of troops in the Middle East. The middle-aged man turned and thrust his hand at Shane, his bright blue eyes twinkling behind wire-rim glasses and an easy smile on his tanned, weathered face.

"Shane, allow me to introduce you to Hank Osbourne, president and general manager of the Blaze," Roscoe said. "Hank's known around the NFL as the Wizard of Oz."

Shane returned the handshake with a nod. But, with the mention of the Wizard of Oz, his mind drifted back to the dimly lit bar on the beach in Cabo a few days earlier. Try as he might, he'd been unable to banish the image of Dorothy. Days later, he was still frustrated. If he'd been smart, he would have invited one of the models to his bungalow and lost himself inside her nubile body. Instead, he stayed by the pool trying to get a handle on his desire. When he returned to the bar, the Italian fashion designer had rounded up all her charges and sent them along to bed. Alone. Shane had spent the rest of the evening listening to Mort and Kitty talk about their grandchildren—they'd cornered him as he'd tried to escape across the patio to his bungalow. He kept telling himself he'd made a narrow escape. She obviously was one of those women who liked to tease. One minute, she was giving him the cold brush-off; the next, she was dragging him to the dance floor, grinding her hips against his. Yeah, it was a good thing she left when she did. He'd had enough psycho chicks to last a lifetime.

"This new guy, Carl, you hired has been a pleasure to work with—even it has all been by email," Roscoe was saying, bringing Shane out of his reverie.

Hank chuckled and stepped aside to reveal a young woman stacking papers on the conference table.

"It's *Carly* and we enjoy working with her, too," Hank said with a smile.

"Wow, he's a she." Roscoe turned on the charm as he

reached across the table to shake hands. Shane would have
rolled his eyes at Roscoe, but he was transfixed by the woman
in front of him. She lifted her head and their eyes met.
Almost as if he had conjured her up in his mind, Dorothy
stood before him. Her once wild hair was pulled up in some
fancy knot. A conservative pale gray pantsuit and pink blouse
covered up the soft glowing skin he remembered. Shane's
pulse rate shot up as her cool blue eyes stared into his. He
wasn't sure, but he thought he saw a look of wariness pass
through them before she quickly looked at Roscoe and
smiled. *Don't smile at him! The guy's happily married with
twin toddlers at home!*

"Shane Devlin, this is my assistant, Carly March," Hank
said. He placed his hand on Carly's shoulder to propel her
forward.

Shane waited to see if she would own up to having met
him before. When she didn't, he raised an eyebrow at her.
She lifted up her chin, offering her hand.

"Nice to meet you."

Her soft, precise speaking voice unnerved him. Two can
play at this game—whatever it was. Taking her hand in his,
he brushed his thumb over her delicate wrist. She barely
flinched before pulling her hand away quickly.

"Likewise, *Miss March.*" He carefully enunciated her
name.

They took their seats around the conference table, and
for the next hour or so Shane barely heard a word as the GM
and Roscoe went over the final details of his contract. Mem-
bers of the coaching and training staff came by for introduc-
tions, but Shane couldn't remember a single name or face.
His mind was racing as he stared across the room trying to
figure out what Dorothy was up to. Or Carly. Or whatever
the hell her name was. She'd known who he was all along.
Christ, he'd been nuzzling her neck! He'd spent the last
several days in a constant state of sexual frustration, ready
to hunt down a certain fashion designer who'd ruined the
evening. Shane should have felt relieved that he'd managed
to avoid breaking a fundamental rule he had: don't screw

with the staff within the team's organization. He'd learned that one the hard way.

But he wasn't relieved. The sexual tension was still there, sitting between them in the room like a giant linebacker. It was all Shane could do not to break out in a sweat. History was *not* going to repeat itself. He'd been falsely accused of sexually harassing the daughter of the San Diego Chargers' owner, when the truth was, it was she who'd been harassing *him*. In her capacity as the team's travel coordinator, she'd constantly made sure her room adjoined to his when the team stayed in a hotel the night before each game. When Shane had rebuffed her advances enough times, she cried foul, claiming he'd been doing the harassing. The problem was, he didn't feel a breath of the attraction to her that he felt for Dorothy. If she came on to him, he wasn't so sure he could resist.

"I think that does it," Hank was saying. "Asia Dupree, our media relations director, suffered a little mishap on the ski slopes last week and tore her ACL. Despite that, she's put together a fairly intensive media campaign to help turn you into a household name here in the Baltimore area."

"Ahh, damage control for my image." Shane leaned back in his chair defensively.

"Are you suggesting your image couldn't use a little public relations help?" Hank challenged.

Roscoe answered before Shane could damage his image further. "He's suggesting nothing of the kind," his agent said as the heel of his shoe made contact with Shane's shin beneath the table.

"Good," the GM replied, leaning back in his chair, one ankle propped over the other knee. He peered over steepled fingers at Shane. "We take our responsibilities for encouraging proper values in the community very seriously. Every member of the Blaze family is expected to adhere to a certain standard of conduct both on *and* off the field. You've had some very negative publicity with your off-the-field antics lately. You also have a reputation of bucking the team's system when it comes to dress codes and curfews. Everyone on this team follows our rules, Devlin. No exceptions."

Shane resisted the urge to squirm in his chair, instead maintaining an insolent slouch. He'd spent years cultivating his renegade reputation. Most of it was an act; a shield to keep people from getting too close. Best of all, his so-called bad behavior helped to wipe a bit of the sheen off the Devlin name. Shane meant to bring down his father any way he could.

Hank lectured on: "As a team, we believe we have everything in place to win the Super Bowl this season. Gabe Harrelson's little honeymoon mishap may have been unexpected, but there are still a few months until the season starts. Time enough for you to learn our system and lead us where we need to go. You're smart. You're talented. And you're here because everyone in this organization believes you can do the job. Leave the bad-ass behavior on the West Coast and come here to play and we'll be fine. Are we clear with this?"

"Well, of course," Roscoe said, again not giving Shane a chance to speak. "Gabe Harrelson was well liked by folks in the area. Shane wants to do everything he can to earn the respect of all the Blaze fans, too." Roscoe finished his sappy speech by shooting Carly his Boy Scout grin, which was beginning to piss Shane off.

"Excellent," Hank said, placing his hands firmly on the table in front of him. "Asia will put the wheels in motion. While she's recovering, Carly here will accompany you on the press tour around town." With that declaration, Hank Osbourne stood, putting an end to the meeting.

Shane was still reeling over the fact that not only was he going to have to pander to the media, he'd be doing it with Dorothy by his side. Not a good scenario. Sure his image wasn't the most pristine. He'd been wild in his younger days. But lately, he'd managed to stay out of trouble, just not out of the tabloids. Thanks to his celebrity, every move he made, every relationship he had, was chronicled at the supermarket checkout lanes, further fueling his bad-boy image. He hadn't done much to refute that image. It hadn't mattered to him what people thought.

Until now.

He wanted to tell Dorothy and the Wizard of Oz exactly where they could shove their image makeover; he would do his job as the team's quarterback, and they could leave his moral compass the hell alone.

But they had him where they wanted him. Shane knew if he wanted to play football, he'd be expected to adhere to the prescribed "values." Otherwise, he was screwed. He needed the Blaze as much as they needed him.

Roscoe quirked an eyebrow at him, but didn't say anything. They'd known each other too long for Shane not to know what he was thinking. He'd get the speech about being reckless and disrespectful later. He'd heard it so often, he could probably give the speech to himself. Still, he was peeved and he needed some breathing room.

"Well, I guess that covers it," Roscoe said, clearly wanting to get out of the room before someone on the Blaze changed his mind about Shane.

They all stood to file out of the conference room. Carly hung back to gather her documents. Slender fingers stacked and restacked them into a neat pile. Shane leaned in as he passed her and murmured, "We'll catch up later to discuss my world tour, *Dorothy*."

He wasn't sure, but he thought she flinched as he brushed by her. *Good.*

Carly let out the breath she hadn't realized she'd been holding and quickly collected her papers. *That didn't go well at all!* She was still mortified by her near encounter with Shane in Cabo. It didn't look like he was going to go easy on her, either. She'd wanted to come clean to him before the meeting, but there hadn't been time. It would have been awkward to do it during the meeting. Sure, maybe she and Shane would have laughed about it, but Hank? Probably not. She needed to apologize to Shane and clear the air. He probably thought she was some crazy tease. Not that she'd blame him. Maybe she could catch him before he got to the training wing.

As she hurried through the door, she collided with a broad, muscular chest. Strong arms enfolded her in a tight hug and she let out a squeal.

"Hey, gorgeous. Where's the fire?"

"You mean the fire*works*!" She buried her face against his fleece Blaze sweatshirt, her body beginning to relax after the meeting she'd been dreading for two days.

Two strong fingers brought her chin up and she looked into the smiling green eyes of the Blaze head coach, Matt Richardson. A former NFL player, Matt was tall and well built. His sandy brown hair was damp from the rain. He was dressed in his "uniform" of white athletic shoes, khaki pants, and a gray sweatshirt. The trademark smile he greeted Carly with had, at one time, endorsed everything from soup to athlete's foot cream.

"I take it my new quarterback was a bit of a hothead?" Matt released her, taking a step back to get a better look at her. "I hope that's sunburn making you so red and not Devlin's bad attitude."

"No, he was fine. I'm sure we'll have no problem working together." At least she hoped there wouldn't be a problem.

"Good." Matt pressed a kiss to the top of her head. "Because if he gives you any trouble, he'll have to answer to me." He gave her arms a gentle squeeze before releasing her fully.

"Can you still get away this afternoon?" he asked softly. She nodded.

"Great. I'd better get over to the training facility and meet our new addition. I've got some ground rules I want to lay down as well." He walked toward the conference room door, but before leaving, he lifted his hand to gently brush her cheek. "You're sure you're okay?" he asked. "I feel really bad Asia's injury cut into your trip. You needed the rest."

"I'm fine." She tried to infuse as much reassurance into her voice as she could.

"All right then. I want to hear all about Mexico over dinner. Deal?" he called over his shoulder as he walked out the door.

"It's a date," she replied with a smile, knowing full well she wasn't going to tell him *all* that went on in Cabo.

Sighing, she picked up the last of the paperwork. She'd barely made it out of the conference room before colliding with another hard body. This time, she looked up into the stormy eyes of Shane Devlin.

"Shane, Coach is on his way to the training facility to meet with you." She took a step back, clutching her paperwork to her chest.

"Yeah, I forgot my umbrella. It belongs to the car rental company and I wouldn't want to read in the tabloids I've taken to petty theft." Efficiently using his large body, he maneuvered her back into the conference room, quietly closing the door behind them.

She rolled her eyes at him as he circled the table to retrieve the umbrella from the floor beside his chair. Laying her papers back on the table, she took a deep, fortifying breath. It was time to clear the air.

"As long as we have a moment of privacy," she began, "I want to apologize for the other night in Cabo. I . . ."

"Save it, Dorothy. I caught the tender moment between you and the coach. Your friend the wedding planner did us both a favor back there in Mexico." He stood inches from her. "What's the matter? The coach's wife is recovering from her cancer, so you figured before he dumped you, you'd make the moves on the future quarterback? Is that how it went?"

He was so close she could see the black rings around his gray irises. His eyes were sparkling with anger. Confused, Carly tried to gather her breath.

"Wh-what are you talking about?" She braced her hands on the table, hating the way his menacing stance affected her.

"You know exactly what I'm talking about." He stepped even closer. "Chicks like you are all over this league. Playing hard to get, always trying to find the best deal for themselves.

Well, news flash, honey. I'm not playing. If the coach wants to dip his stick into you, that's his business, not mine."

What? She was no longer confused; she was incensed.

"That's disgusting!" She reached up to push him away, but he was already at the door.

"Save it, sweetheart. What you do is your business. Just don't let me hear any rumors about you and me in Cabo because *nothing* happened. Thank God! You try to say something did and I'll rat you and the coach out to the Wizard of Oz in a heartbeat."

He stormed out of the conference room before she could get a word in. Standing there with her mouth gaping open, her hands once again braced on the table, she was unsure whether to laugh or cry. Carly had had worse things said about her. The press—and people she thought she trusted—had certainly bested Shane Devlin's accusations. But that didn't mean his words didn't hurt.

Hank's secretary stuck her head in the room, startling her out of her shock.

"Gabe Harrelson's wife is on the phone again. She's not happy Gabe's signing bonus is revoked because of his fall. Hank asked if you could reason with her."

Great. Now she had two irrational people to deal with.

Three

It was still drizzling several hours later when Shane walked from the practice facility back to the main office complex of the Blaze. Earlier, he'd managed to endure the press conference, followed by a meet and greet with trainers and coaches who hadn't been paraded through the conference room that morning. Fortunately, Roscoe had taken off shortly after the media session. But not without a lecture.

"I know it's asking a lot, but try to play nice, Shane," Roscoe had chided him. "Smile for the media and suck it up. And, Hank's assistant is off-limits, if you know what's good for you."

There was no way Roscoe could have picked up on the sexual tension between Shane and Carly. It was just typical Roscoe, practicing damage control. But Shane knew enough to steer clear of her.

"Don't worry, I learned a valuable lesson in San Diego," Shane said. Roscoe just grunted, slapping Shane on the back before heading to New York.

Locating his locker, he unpacked the few things he'd brought with him on the plane. A three-day mini-camp began in the morning, and he'd finally get an opportunity to let his arm do his talking. Shane was always more comfortable dealing with adversity on the field than off.

The drizzle cooled him off as he walked. Next on his schedule was a private meeting with Coach Richardson. Something he was not excited about. Up until this morning, Shane had been looking forward to playing for the man. Richardson had been a pro-bowl player in his day and had evolved into a top-notch coach, one who was known and respected for his fairness and integrity. That image was destroyed this morning.

The guy was married to a woman with cancer, for Chrissakes. Shane shook his head in disgust.

The same disease that had taken Shane's mother's life some twenty years ago. Thinking of the coach's three children, he grew angrier. That anger certainly had nothing to do with the fact that the coach's hands had been all over Carly. No, he was upset that both Carly and Coach Richardson had somehow disappointed him.

Shane was someone who expected very little from people. Most people betray one another. It was a fact of life he'd grown up learning the hard way. It was the reason he didn't let anyone close to him. Let them in, and they'd just screw you over later on. He didn't want to delve too deeply into the particular reasons for his disappointment with the coach and Carly, however. That would only lead him to admit to feelings he didn't want to feel. He needed to forget about the Blaze's sexy siren and concentrate on learning the team's system so he could play football.

Stepping into the main office building, he combed his fingers through his hair, trying to dry it. Not knowing where the coaches' suite was located, he stopped to ask at the security office just inside the front doors.

"Shane Devlin, as I live and breathe," a voice called from the back of the office.

Shane looked up to see a shiny-headed African American man striding across the office, smiling with his hand extended in greeting.

"Donny Carter?" Shane smiled his first real smile in a long time. "What are you doing here?"

The two men clasped hands and then leaned in to tap each other on the back.

"Been here for a year now. You're looking at the head of security. So watch your ass!" Donovan teased.

Donovan Carter grew up in the same small Pennsylvania college town as Shane. Donovan's father had been the chief of police back then. Chief Carter probably had done the most of any adult to keep Shane from ending up in jail—or dead. In return, Shane let little Donny shadow him around the football field, picking up all the right moves to earn a commission to the Naval Academy as a tailback on its football team. His senior year, Donovan blew out his knee in a game against Michigan, ending his dreams of playing in the NFL.

"I told you I'd make it to the pros somehow." Donovan smiled as he leaned his hip against the desk behind him.

"What were you doing before this?" Shane was a little ashamed that he had lost touch with Donny over the years. But then again, Shane had put much of his past behind him.

"Oh, I did my stint in the Marines, working for Naval Intelligence. And before you say anything, I've heard all the jokes about me not having enough intelligence for the job." He put his hands up and laughed.

"How are your parents?" Shane propped a shoulder up against the wall, relaxing for the first time that day.

"Mama's good. She's already called this morning. It's all over ESPN about you signing with the Blaze. She's sending a box of cookies later this week. She made me promise to share."

"I always knew I loved your mama. How about your dad?"

Donovan's smile dimmed a bit. "Oh, he passed a few years ago. He had a heart attack in his sleep. Mama was just glad he died peacefully and not by a bullet."

Shane felt his chest tighten as his shame grew. Donovan and his family had been a lifeline for him while growing up, and Shane hadn't even bothered to keep up with them after going on to college. He should have. But that was his father's hometown now. Not Shane's. He didn't *want* to know what was going on there.

"I'm sorry." The words sounded hollow, even to Shane.

"Hey, he's in a better place." Donovan jumped off the desk, quickly changing the subject. "You got a place to stay? I've got a two-bedroom condo I just bought down in the warehouse district on Federal Hill. You're welcome to crash there 'til you find some place."

"Thanks, man, but I think the brass wants to keep an eye on me. They've leased me a place in some gated community a few miles from here. I'm sure it's a good distance from any decent nightlife."

"Yeah, that may be a little tame for a player like you, but I guess you gotta do what you gotta do, right?" Donovan teased.

They both agreed to catch up over dinner and a few beers at the end of the day. Donovan pointed him toward the coaches' suites in the other wing of the building. Shane made his way to his meeting with Coach Richardson feeling a little better about his day.

The feeling was short-lived, however.

"Coach Richardson had some pressing commitments outside the office this afternoon, but he'd like you to meet him at his house," the coach's secretary told him. "It's only about ten miles from here, hon. Here's the address. Just plug it into the GPS in your rental car and you should find it without a problem. The guard at the gate knows Coach is expecting you."

Shane could only imagine what the coach's pressing commitment was this afternoon. Getting down and dirty with the GM's assistant. His gut clenched again at the thought. He was just about to ask if he could reschedule the meeting for the next morning, when a young woman he'd seen hovering outside the conference room earlier in the day raced into the office.

"Amy, what've you got there?" the coach's secretary asked.

"Has Coach left for the day?" Nearly out of breath, she peeked into the coach's darkened office.

"Yeah, hon, he has."

Amy swore, then colored brightly as she saw Shane standing there. She turned back to the coach's secretary.

"Carly left these forms and she needs to review them and send them off to the commissioner's office first thing in the morning. I was hoping Coach could give them to her. I know they're getting together tonight."

Jeez, did everyone on the team know they were having an affair?

"No problem." She plucked the envelope from Amy's hand and handed it over to Shane. "Shane is headed to Coach's house. He'll take it."

Was she kidding? Take something for the coach's girl-friend to his house? Where his wife and kids lived?

Shane was about to tell them both what they could do with their envelope when his agent's parting words from earlier echoed in his head: Play nice. *Right.*

These people were just a means to an end, Shane reminded himself. So what if they weren't who he desperately wanted them to be. Nobody ever was. Wasn't that the main reason he kept to himself and trusted no one? The only thing he should be focused on was playing every game and breaking every one of his deadbeat dad's records.

Flashing both women his most charming Devlin grin, he took the envelope and headed for what would certainly be an interesting encounter. On his way out, Shane stopped at Donovan's office and left him a note rescheduling dinner for the next night. There was no telling what was waiting for him at Coach's house.

Twenty minutes later, Shane pulled into a long driveway that wound back behind a massive stone home. The plush front lawn was meticulously manicured, lovingly kept up as if the Blaze were going to play their opening game on it. He pulled back behind the house, toward the three-car garage. A carriage house stood farther back, with a basketball court and a swimming pool beyond that. The Richardsons lacked for nothing, it appeared. Shane parked the car in the round-about in front of the garage. One of its doors stood open, revealing a veritable sporting goods store: bikes, scooters, Rollerblades, hockey sticks, and every type of ball imaginable were strewn across the floor.

The windshield wipers squeaked to a halt as Shane turned off the ignition. Getting out of the car, he noticed a large, dark-haired woman, dressed in jeans and a chamois button-down shirt, standing at the trash cans just inside the garage. Her hands went to her hips as she greeted Shane with a smile that seemed to encompass her entire face.

"You must be the new guy," she called out. "Come on in out of the rain. Your California blood can't be used to this cold." She waved him through to a door in the back of the garage. Shane followed her into the garage, not bothering to dispute her assumption he was Californian by birth. What did he care what these people thought of him. He just wanted to get this meeting over with as quickly as possible.

"I'm Penny, the housekeeper," she prattled on, her back to him as she led the way. "Coach said to expect you. He and his family always like to welcome the new players their first night in town. The Richardsons are good people."

He thought Penny might be singing a different tune were she aware of the coach's fling with the GM's assistant. But, Shane figured it wasn't his place to burst that bubble. They entered the house through the mudroom. A row of floor-to-ceiling cubbies similar to those in the training facility were lined up along one wall. Each contained assorted jackets, more sporting equipment, backpacks, and shoes. Stepping over a pile of hastily discarded shoes scattered about the doorway, he carefully dodged two umbrellas drip-drying on the floor.

The conflicting aromas of garlic and freshly baked brownies greeted Shane when they stepped into the kitchen. The room was massive but homey, richly adorned with stainless steel appliances, granite countertops, and warm walnut cabinets. CNN droned on a flat-screen TV mounted above a gas fireplace, lit to ward off the chill brought on by the spring rain. A bulky sofa and two chairs took up the area in front of the fireplace, while a large farmhouse table occupied the spot in front of a huge picture window. Three teenage girls were spread out at the table, a laptop and notebooks covering its surface. They giggled as Shane walked in.

"Ignore the coven over there," Penny said, her tone admonishing the girls. "They're supposed to be working on a presentation for school."

Penny motioned for him to have a seat on one of the stools parked along the island at the kitchen's center.

"Coach will be here any minute. He just ran out to pick up some softball cleats for his youngest," Penny said.

Shane suddenly felt uncomfortable being in the coach's house, surrounded by his family. He knew what the coach was doing and he didn't think it had anything to do with cleats for his kid. He remained standing in hopes of making a quick exit as Penny set a plate of brownies on the counter, still smiling at him. She took another plate over to the table where the girls were seated.

"Where'd Emma run off to?" Penny asked.

"She's in the other room printing," one girl managed to get out before shoving an entire brownie in her mouth.

The garage door opened as Penny headed for the back stairs. "Shane, I'll be right down. I'm going to check to see if Lisa is awake. I know she wants to meet you."

Shane could feel his palms begin to sweat. He had to get out of there. He had no intention of meeting the coach's wife. The warm domesticity of this house was suffocating him. With the exception of his buddy Roscoe's house, Shane didn't do the family thing. It was all too unnatural for him.

He turned toward what he thought was the back door, only to collide with a teenage girl—Emma, he assumed. Papers she'd been holding went flying across the floor and she quickly bent down to retrieve them. Wavy strawberry blond hair hid her face as long, slender fingers efficiently snapped the papers off the floor. He was reminded of Carly and her long fingers passing over her reams of paperwork earlier that morning. God, he had to get out of there! He felt as if the pocket was closing in around him.

"We're hooooome!" a young girl's voice sang out.

Emma looked up at the same time. Shane felt as if he'd been blindsided and thrown to the turf for a loss. Blue eyes eerily similar to the ones that captivated him in Cabo San Lucas stared at him. A soft, shy smile adorned a face with a familiar smattering of freckles across her nose.

"Sorry," Emma said. "I didn't see you standing there."

Shane felt the air leave his lungs as they both found their feet.

"Look, Em," the younger girl cried. "Daddy got my ruby red cleats! Aren't they the bomb?" A pixie version of the coach danced around the kitchen, bright green eyes shining as her ponytail flounced behind her.

"Molly, your uniform is bright orange. Have you no fashion sense at all?" Emma practically wailed at her sister.

"Who cares! I like 'em. I'm going to go show Mom. I know she'll love 'em." Molly bolted for the stairs, grabbing a brownie as she went.

"Dad, how could you? She'll be a fashion don't!" Exasperation adorning her face, Emma stood facing her father.

Matt Richardson smiled, leaning down to kiss his middle child on the forehead—much as he'd done with Carly earlier in the day. Shane's gut clenched even tighter.

"I pick my battles where I can, sweetie pie. Red cleats are a fight I don't care about winning."

Clearly Emma didn't agree with her father, letting out a huff as she walked back over to her friends.

"Welcome to Camp Chaos." Coach grinned, extending his hand to Shane.

As the two men shook hands, the back door crashed open and loud footsteps thundered into the mudroom.

"Get off my case, Aunt Carly!" a male voice yelled. "You're not my mother!"

And there it was. Confirmation that Shane was an ass. Carly March wasn't fooling around with the coach. They were related somehow. He'd fumbled the play. Badly. Hell, he never should have pushed her buttons earlier in the day. He couldn't decide if he was relieved she *wasn't* having an affair with the coach or scared shitless about how and when she'd reveal the accusations he'd hurled at her. Right now, he was having trouble just getting a breath into his lungs.

A blur resembling a large teenage boy raced by.

"Hey! Christopher James!" Coach yelled. "You get back here and apologize to your aunt!"

Carly entered the kitchen, her shoulders slumped. Shane tried to blend into the wall behind her. She'd changed from her uptight power suit into designer jeans that, from Shane's vantage point, fit her to perfection. A fuzzy sweater jacket in a soft shade of lavender hugged the rest of her body. Her hair was loosely pulled back and tied with a ribbon. The kitchen, boisterous only moments before, was now silent as the girls stared at Carly.

"It's my fault, Matt," she said softly, dropping her keys on the countertop. "I overstepped where I shouldn't have."

"I don't care *where* you stepped," Coach bellowed, making his way toward the stairs. "He has no right to speak to you that way."

Clearly sensing an impending explosion, the girls at the kitchen table silently packed up their things.

"Devlin, make yourself at home while I take care of this," Coach called out as he stormed after his son.

Carly tensed at the sound of Shane's name. Slowly, she turned to face him. He was prepared to see anything in her eyes except the sadness that emanated from them. *Man, he had totally misread the situation.* Forcing her chin up, she grabbed her purse and keys off the counter.

"I'm out of here," she said to no one in particular.

"Aunt Carly! You can't go," Emma cried, throwing herself in her aunt's path. "You promised to help me pick out what I'm wearing to the Spring Fling, remember?"

"Look, I'll go," Shane said. "You should stay and be with your . . . family." He stepped past her and headed toward the door. The sooner he got out of there, the better. The fact that he was still standing told him Carly hadn't mentioned his earlier accusations to Coach. But that didn't mean she wouldn't rat him out now. He needed to get far away from her.

Besides, the woman was making him crazy with her multiple personalities. One minute, she was a sexy siren in a Mexican bar. The next, she was a chilly, uptight professional. And right now, she looked as if someone had just killed her dog. The vulnerable look in Carly's eyes was something he couldn't deal with. He didn't *want* to deal with the feelings it was stirring up in him. If he stayed, he wasn't sure he'd be able to stop himself from gathering her up in his arms and holding her until the look of sadness left her beautiful face.

And he'd never done that before.

"No one is going anywhere," a female voice called from the top of the stairs.

Despite being pale and thin from months of chemotherapy, Lisa Richardson was beautiful. Dressed in black yoga pants, a light pink cashmere V-neck sweater, and a pink batik scarf covering her head, she slowly descended the stairs. Shane was struck by the drastic difference between how the coach's wife handled her disease compared to how his own mother had.

Ovarian cancer had overwhelmed Marie Devlin at twenty-nine. She'd been an eighteen-year-old townie when she got pregnant by the local college's star quarterback. Bruce Devlin was only twenty. They were children with a child of their own when they married. The first few years of their marriage had been a whirlwind. Bruce won the Heisman trophy and signed with the Philadelphia Eagles. Shane had fleeting memories of those early, happy years. As Bruce became a superstar—leading his team to a Super Bowl championship—his eye and heart began to roam. Marie became despondent as the relationship unraveled. Her diagnosis with cancer kept Bruce in the marriage, but not at home. Not that it mattered. His injury and subsequent drug addiction rendered him useless in encouraging her to fight the disease. In the end, not even her ten-year-old son could coax her to fight. *To live.*

Lisa was different, Shane realized right away as she stood in front of him. Her lips were brushed with a shiny pink gloss, and a crisp, clean perfume permeated her skin. It was obvious that she'd chosen to fight her disease. For her husband. For her children. And for herself. Shane wanted to hate her for it. But one look into her big brown eyes and he knew he couldn't.

She smiled the same soft smile Emma offered him earlier.

"Welcome to Baltimore, Mr. Devlin."

Shane took the hand she offered as her husband appeared at her side.

"Lisa, honey, you should be resting." He wrapped his arm protectively around his wife's shoulders.

Shane felt like an idiot. It was clear he'd jumped to some very wrong conclusions.

"Don't be silly, Matt, I'm fine." She trailed a finger down her husband's chest. "I'm just going to have a cup of tea by the fire and let the girls practice their presentation on me. After that, Carly and I need to catch up on her trip to Mexico. She's been home for two days and I haven't heard the juicy details."

Shane sensed Carly stiffen beside him.

"Li, I've got a pile of paperwork I left on my desk that I need to have finished by the morning. Can we get together for lunch tomorrow?" she asked.

"Actually, I have your papers in the car." What was he thinking? He'd just blown the chance to get her out of the house before she could fill in Coach on his earlier wrong assumptions.

Carly turned to him, blue eyes wide and blazing. The look she threw at him should have shut him up. Except it didn't.

"Your secretary asked me to bring them," he babbled on. Crossing her arms beneath a pair of very nice breasts, she contemplated him for a long, silent minute. If he were smart, he'd stop provoking her. Except he really liked provoking her. Clearly, he had a death wish.

Finally, her eyes broke contact with his and Carly turned to her sister with a smile. "Bring on the lasagna," she said cheerily. Too cheerily. Shane was left to wonder when she might let the axe fall.

"Good. It's all settled then. Shane, you and Matt can have your meeting, Carly can do her paperwork, and afterward we'll *all* enjoy a nice family dinner."

Whoa, family dinner! No way!

"Oh, I couldn't impose, Mrs. Richardson," Shane back-pedaled. He'd rather be tackled by a three-hundred-fifty-pound defensive lineman than sit through a meal making nice with the coach's family.

"Nonsense. Penny has made her famous lasagna. It's tradition to have a new player over for dinner. Surely you don't have other plans already?" She eyed him carefully. It was the second time today he'd misread the play. He looked at the coach, who simply raised a brow at him.

"No, ma'am." Shane sighed.

He wasn't sure, but he thought he heard Carly cover up a snort as he followed Coach out to his office in the carriage house.

Four

Carly reviewed and signed off on the league policy changes and faxed them to the commissioner's office, crossing off one task from the pile of work waiting for her in the morning. Afterward, she and Emma went through the girl's closet to select the perfect outfit for the eighth-grade dance the following week; Emma persuaded Carly to loan her a Vera Wang shawl and matching shoes. Now, Carly stood at the breakfast bar slicing two loaves of crusty bread as Lisa carefully mixed the olive oil and the spices on a plate to dredge the bread in. She'd managed to satisfy her half sister's curiosity about her trip without giving her any details about meeting Shane there. Not that he deserved her silence, but she had played a part as well, and the less her family knew, the better.

"So it was fun spending time with Julianne again?" Lisa asked.

"Things are always crazy with Julianne." Carly tossed the bread into a basket.

"Do you miss working with her?"

She and Julianne had been roommates at boarding school.

They were like sisters. For seven years, Carly had worked as Julianne's publicist, working to get her designs noticed. She'd been living in Italy with Julianne when she learned Lisa had cancer and needed a life-saving bone-marrow transfer. It was the only time her father had ever initiated a phone call to Carly.

Carly didn't hesitate. She moved to Baltimore—and away from the media circus that was her life—to help care for Lisa's kids during the busy football season. While Lisa endured several rounds of chemotherapy to get her body ready for the transplant, Carly worked for the Blaze.

"Why? Are you trying to get rid of me?" Carly asked a little defensively. It was the second time today she'd been asked if she missed her old life. She didn't. She liked having a family to care for. Friends who cared for her. A job where she actually felt useful. But if she'd worn out her welcome . . .

"No, I am not trying to get rid of you," Lisa said, taking Carly's hand in hers. "I just want you to be happy. I don't want you to feel you have to stay here in Baltimore if you don't want to."

"I'm where I want to be," Carly said. "Besides, we both know Italy is not the best place for me right now."

"Carly . . ." Lisa started.

"No, Lisa. I get you have a PhD in psychology and you want to get in my head, but I'm fine. My life is fine." At least, Carly would be fine if a certain sexy quarterback wasn't looming somewhere in the house, but she didn't need her sister probing her right now. She just wanted to get through dinner and get this crazy day over with.

"Okay." Lisa looked away as she began to toss the salad. "So I hear you'll be taking over for Asia while she's recovering. Will that be difficult for you?"

Carly studied her sister. Did she already know about her encounter—er, *encounters*—with Shane? How could she?

Lisa looked up to stare at Carly. When she didn't immediately answer, Lisa asked: "Dealing with the press? Will it be difficult given what they've put you through?"

"No." Carly mentally breathed a sigh of relief. "It'll be mostly mainstream media, and besides, my celebrity, such as it is, is pretty much confined to Europe." Dealing with Shane Devlin, on the other hand, might be a problem. But she didn't dare tell her sister that. She no longer intended to apologize for her behavior in Cabo, given the accusations he'd made earlier. Both incidents should be something two adults could laugh off, but her reaction to Shane wasn't humorous. Even now, she could feel the hum of the attraction between them. She'd never felt such a pull toward a man—not even the man she'd intended to marry. She just hoped she could get through the next few weeks without making a fool of herself.

"Okay, change the subject. Tell me what I want to know. Has Julianne finished with my gown for the gala in June?" Lisa asked as she carried the dipping sauce into the dining room.

Following Lisa, Carly placed the salad and the bread on the large, oval table. She spied Shane standing against the wall looking like he'd rather have a root canal than sit down to dinner. After his outburst this morning, she wasn't exactly overjoyed to have to sit with him around the dinner table, either.

"She's making one for me, too, right?" Emma asked as she carefully set a pitcher of water on the table. "You said we all get to go to the gala for your new charity."

"Yes, Emma, I did say that, but I don't think we all need to be wearing designer gowns." Lisa caressed the top of her daughter's head in consolation. She looked up at Shane. "I've started a foundation for children whose parents are severely or terminally ill. After spending years as a couples' therapist, cancer has served as a little midcourse correction for my life," she explained.

Shane still had that deer-in-headlights look about him, but he managed a gracious nod.

"You lost your mother to cancer, did you not?" Lisa was no shrinking violet when it came to fund-raising. Smiling at her sister's tenacity, Carly glanced back at Shane. If possible, his face had gone even more ashen.

"Yes, ma'am," he said softly.

"Perhaps you'd be interested in hearing about our little endeavor sometime?" Lisa made it sound like a question when everyone in the room knew it wasn't.

"Go easy on him, honey," Matt said as he carried a steaming pan of lasagna into the room. "Let's just see if he makes it through dinner."

Hah! Matt's prophetic statement brought a smile to Carly's face.

"Shane, you sit here next to me." Lisa pointed to the chair beside her as her children clamored into the room, plopping into their chairs. The chairs filled quickly, forcing Carly to sit between Shane and C.J.

C.J. eyed her warily, still obviously holding a grudge about their earlier argument. When she'd picked him up after practice, she'd walked in on him shoving a package of condoms in his gym bag. Typical of a sixteen-year-old boy, he declared they were for someone else. Carly knew she walked a fine line with her nephew over the matter. The sweet little boy who'd played Thomas the Tank Engine trains with her had morphed into a hormonal teenager practically overnight. She didn't want to destroy the trust between them, but she figured that Matt would be better able to handle the situation. She'd figure out whether or not to speak with Matt later.

Right now, Carly had bigger problems. Like the solid muscle of Shane's thigh that kept brushing against hers. If the heat building inside her was any indication, she'd need a long run in the drenching rain after dinner.

Matt blessed the meal and everyone began to talk at once while Penny served the lasagna. Shane was tense beside Carly. Carly snuck a glance at him from beneath her lashes. For a guy who defined arrogant, he sure seemed apprehensive about having dinner with Matt's family. Carly thought back to the things that she'd read about him. Every article she'd unearthed depicted Shane as a loner. His childhood had been almost as dysfunctional as hers. Obviously, he wasn't used to breaking bread with a bunch of rowdy tweens and teens. Carly almost felt sorry for his discomfort. *Almost.*

After his behavior this morning, she should be stabbing his hot thigh with her fork. She smothered a chuckle at the thought and dug into Penny's lasagna. Shane shot her a look out of the corner of his eye. She smiled and enjoyed her dinner. The males on either side of her would just have to sweat it out wondering whether or not she'd be telling tales to Matt.

"I hear Gabe Harrelson is protesting the forfeit of his signing bonus," Matt threw out from his end of the table.

"Actually, he's having his bridezilla do his begging," Carly joked. The kids at the table snickered along with her.

"Serves the Valley Boy right," Penny said between bites of pasta. She'd been with the family for more than ten years and they were immune to her lack of political correctness. "What'd he need a television crew following him around on his honeymoon for anyway? That's supposed to be a private time between a man and his wife. You'd think they'd have better things to do."

Shane managed a chuckle beside Carly. She thought she heard C.J. mumble an *amen* under his breath.

"I think Gabe can't decide whether he wants to be a movie star or a quarterback," Lisa chimed in.

"I'd want to be a movie star," Molly said from her seat beside her father, a dreamy look passing over her face.

"Really, princess? Why's that?" Matt asked her with a grin.

"Because movie stars *rock*." Molly had spent her life around jocks. She was definitely jaded.

"Hey, Shane, you've dated a bunch of movie stars. What's that like?" C.J. leaned in front of Carly to peer at Shane.

Shane's fork stopped just short of his mouth. The look on his face was so comical, Carly nearly laughed.

"Well . . ." Shane stalled.

"Oooh, have you ever dated Elise Wages?" Molly interrupted. "She's my favorite."

"Gross, Mol, she's barely sixteen," her brother said. Carly gaped at the boy, but he ignored her and tucked into his salad.

"Yeah, but if he dated her, it would be like he'd dated Carly." Molly nearly flung her lasagna at her brother in an effort to make her point.

Shane choked on his bread as the rest of the table admonished Molly. Carly watched as he took a gulp of his water before staring blankly around the table.

"Elise Wages played Carly in the movie about her mother." Emma—ever the diplomat—offered an explanation to Shane.

Shane looked even more confused as everyone else stopped eating to stare at him.

"You know, *Death in a Sandstorm*." Emma leaned forward in her chair, enunciating each word as if he were hard of hearing. "It's always on one of the cable movie channels."

When he turned to Carly, both eyebrows raised in question, Emma continued in exasperation, obviously thinking Shane had spent too much time on the turf.

"It's about Veronica March, Carly's mother, who gets beheaded by terrorists. Elise Wages plays Aunt Carly when she was a kid."

"Emma, you know how I feel about everyone trivializing Carly's mother's death," Lisa softly chided her daughter.

Carly always admired the way her sister defended Carly's mother, a woman she'd never met.

"I'm sorry Aunt Carly." Emma sank back in her chair.

"No offense taken, sweetie." Carly sent her a reassuring smile across the table.

Shane was still gaping at Carly. He really was starting to resemble a concussed idiot.

"Wait!" He put his fork down and gestured for quiet. "You mean your mother was that famous war reporter? The heiress to the World Media? That means your dad"—he turned to look at Lisa—"is Hugh Delaney, the news anchor."

"The one and only." Lisa grimaced.

"That means you're . . ." Shane turned his head back to look at Carly. Could he really be that slow? Carly waited for the pity to show up in his eyes. "You're *Darling Carly*." She cringed. The moniker the media had dubbed her with as a young child always had the same effect on her.

"Wow," he said. "You were a child celebrity. Everyone's favorite orphan. The press used to follow you everywhere when you were young." His voice was almost reverent, as if Carly had enjoyed those long, lonely months when the media couldn't get enough of her pathetic story. She knew what was coming next. Twenty years later she'd once again been in the eye of the media storm, but not in a positive way. Somehow, she was no longer the darling, but the spineless woman who couldn't hold on to her sports star fiancé. Carly set down her fork, her appetite gone.

Fortunately, her nephew spoke up before Shane could even go there. "You know, that sleazy reporter who's always following you around the training center and leaving stuff in your office has the hots for Elise Wages," C.J. said, startling nearly everyone at the table.

Matt's fork stilled in midair as his gaze shot from his son to Carly. "Some reporter is hounding you at the complex?" he asked, his tone lethal.

"Yeah," C.J. answered before Carly could. "He probably thinks if he hangs around Carly, he'll meet Elise or something."

"Is this true?" Lisa asked, exchanging a worried glance with her husband.

"Donovan's got it handled," Carly assured them both. "Besides, the guy's pretty harmless." *I think.*

"Anyway, Elise Wages is pregnant," C.J. mumbled as he reached for a second helping of lasagna. Okay, Carly was grateful for the subject change, but she was definitely mentioning the condoms to Matt.

"Well, at least we know her baby's not yours, Shane," Molly blurted before her father could shove a piece of bread in her mouth.

Now it was Carly's turn to choke.

They managed to navigate the dinner conversation to safer subjects so that everyone finished their meal without necessity of the Heimlich maneuver. Carly slipped out before dessert, claiming that she had over indulged in Mexico and she needed to cut some calories. What she really wanted was to get away from the menacing presence seated next to her at the table. Despite all the embarrassing dinner conversation, Shane had eventually managed to relax and join in the banter. Not Carly. She'd had enough verbal confrontation for one day.

Shane took the stairs two at a time. It was Saturday and the Blaze corporate offices were empty. His flight back to San Diego was in two hours, but he needed to take care of something first. He hadn't signed off on the team's plan for his "image makeover." Mini-camp had kept him busy the past three days, giving him a convenient excuse to avoid Carly at the same time. Since Carly was a big part of carrying out the plan, he'd pushed thoughts of it—and her—off until the last possible moment. He needed to apologize for the dumb-ass assumptions he'd made the other day, but that meant he'd have to actually be face-to-face with her and he wasn't sure his body could handle it. The sexual tension between the two of them definitely interfered with his common sense. He needed to be focused and rational to get his job done. So, his plan was to sign the plan—provided he could find a pen on one of the secretary's desks—and slip it under Carly's door before his flight left.

What he hadn't counted on was Carly being in her office. As he rounded the corner, he came to an abrupt stop. The object of his obsession was pacing before a picture window, the spring sunshine streaming in behind her. A pair of running shorts showed off lean, muscular legs; her T-shirt strained against firm breasts. Damn, she was cute and his body was doing crazy things just watching her. Her ponytail bobbed as she paced about, having a conversation with someone on speakerphone.

"I can't believe you told Matt you saw condoms in C.J.'s bag." The woman on the phone had trouble containing a laugh.

Whoa. So that's what C.J.'s temper tantrum was about the other night.

"What was I supposed to do, Jules?" Carly plopped down in her chair, resting her sneaker-clad feet on the desk. She twirled a red rose in her fingers as she spoke. "Wouldn't you tell your brother if your nephew had condoms in his gym bag?"

"Jeez, Carly, my nephew is ten! If he had condoms it would probably be for some locker-room prank!"

Carly laughed. Shane sat down at one of the reception desks and tried to tell himself he was looking for a pen, not eavesdropping.

"Seriously, Carly, you're getting way too wrapped up in these people."

"*These people* are my family, Julianne." Carly stood and began pacing again, slapping the rose against her thigh. "And you of all people should know they are important to me. They're all I've got and I like that they need me."

There was silence on the other end of the line.

"I appreciate that you care, though, Jules." Carly moved out his range of vision, but from the sound of it, she'd stopped her pacing.

"I just wish you wouldn't equate personal happiness with feeling needed, that's all," Julianne finally answered. "And I wish you'd come to Italy with me!"

"I can't go back to Italy, Julianne. The paparazzi are too intense. Besides, I really don't want to have Max's happiness thrown at me day in and day out. It still hurts too much." The last statement came out as a whisper.

"So you're hanging around with American football players, now?" Julianne sounded appalled. "Like one of them won't propose to you and leave you for his Baby Mama."

Huh? Shane was having trouble keeping up with the conversation. Had some guy actually done that to Carly?

"Jules, I'm not hanging out with the players. I'm working for the team. For the first time in my life, I actually feel useful. I know Hank hired me as a favor to Matt, but Lisa is doing better and Hank has all but said the job is permanent if I want it," Carly said. She moved into view again and he watched as she dropped the rose in the trash and picked up a picture frame from the credenza behind her desk. "Besides, jocks are off-limits, remember? I'm not hanging out with anyone who lives their life in the public eye. I want quiet and ordinary."

"You want boring!"

"Hey, accountants or podiatrists aren't always boring." Carly's voice was laced with humor. "Now, can we get back to the business at hand, and talk about you finding me a dress for Lisa's black-tie fund-raiser? This is really important to her. She wants to raise enough money to start a counseling center for kids here in Baltimore by year's end. Wouldn't it have been nice to have a place to go when you lost your mom? A place where other kids could relate to what you were going through?"

Julianne paused before answering. "Boarding school took care of that for both of us."

Carly released an exasperated sigh. "Julianne, are you going to find me a dress or not?"

"Yeah, sure. But I don't know why I even bother. You won't wear any of the ones that I think you should wear."

"Then pick something out you know I'll wear, not something skimpy that belongs on the cover of *Cosmo*." She put the picture back down on the credenza a little too roughly.

Shane bumped his knee against the metal desk at the thought of her wearing one of those sexy dresses that always taunted him in the checkout lines. He was unable to stifle a grunt, and the sound alerted her to his presence. Snatching up the receiver, she quickly ended her phone conversation and came to stand in the doorway of her office. Crossing her arms beneath her breasts—a move that further tortured him—she leaned against the door frame. Shane cleared his throat and jauntily leaned on the two back legs of the desk chair.

"I was looking for a pen." He flicked through some papers on the desk, unsuccessfully trying to keep his eyes off her very pert breasts perfectly displayed in a T-shirt

proclaiming *Smart is the new skinny.* Shane tried not to
think about how sexy it looked on her.

"I guess the Pen Fairy took 'em all because there aren't
any out here," he joked, gesturing to the desks in the reception area.

Mumbling something sounding awfully close to *smart-
ass,* she pushed away from the door frame. He stood and
followed her into her office. Probably not a good idea on his
part, seeing as how he was already in the beginning stages
of arousal. Being in the close confines of her office would
only make it worse.

He took his chances anyway.

Her office was warm and welcoming, adorned with pictures
of her nieces and nephew. A large spider plant crawled from
its container down to the floor. Soft jazz music played over her
computer speakers. She rounded her desk and picked up a
Montblanc pen, then turned and nearly speared him with it,
he was following her so closely.

"I didn't want to leave town without signing this." He
held up the media plan between them.

"Of course not." She backed up a little to put some space
between them. "I was beginning to think you'd forgotten."

"Nope." His voice took on a husky timbre as he took a
step forward. She moved farther back to the wall. "You didn't
rat me out to your brother-in-law the other night. Why not?"

"Oh, well . . . now I have something to hold over you.
You know, when you start telling everyone how I attacked
you in Cabo," she quipped.

"Touché," he said, a smile breaking out across his face.
"Smart, pretty, and devious. Who would have thought?"

She tried to stifle a laugh, but one escaped anyway. Soft
and breathy. Somehow, she'd backed herself against the wall.
He stood inches in front of her. She wasn't a psycho chic,
he'd finally decided. Just a woman. A woman who he continued to be incredibly attracted to for reasons he couldn't
quite understand. If Shane was smart, he'd leave her alone.
Except his brain and his body weren't working from the
same playbook.

"About that night in Cabo . . ." he started off.

"Let's not go there." She shook her head from side to side.

He breathed in her scent—she smelled like Florida sunshine—as he moved his body closer. "You know, Dorothy, if your friend hadn't interrupted us, what do you think would have happened?"

She stared at him, her clear blue eyes wide as saucers, something between panic and passion beginning to build in them. Her breath was coming faster, fanning the skin at the base of his neck.

"Nothing." The waver in her voice—almost a whisper now—betrayed the firmness of the statement.

"You sure?" he asked softly as he tossed the document and pen onto the desk behind him. "Not even just a kiss?"

He knew he shouldn't be pursuing this. She was not only the GM's assistant but the coach's sister-in-law. If Coach found out, he'd probably string Shane up by his balls. But he couldn't seem to deny his body. Not now. Not after waiting a week to finally kiss her. Something about her pushed Shane over the edge. He had to know if it had been a fluke in Mexico. Maybe they'd both had too much to drink that night. Maybe he was the one who was a bit psycho. Either way, he wasn't leaving until he found out. He leaned his body closer, pinning her to the wall.

Again, she shook her head. The tight T-shirt showcased her aroused nipples. While her mouth was saying nothing, her body was definitely giving him the green light.

Lifting both hands from his sides, he carefully placed each one against the wall on either side of her head. Slowly, he leaned in further, his lips a breath away from her mouth. Never before had he used his body to intimidate a woman. He'd stop now if she put up any resistance, but her body was pliant against his.

Her tongue darted out to lick her lips. Definitely a green light.

"This isn't a good idea," she started to say.

He took advantage of her open mouth and swooped in.

Sealing his lips over hers, he let his tongue plunder her luscious mouth, stroking it along hers, making her body quiver. Any resistance she might have offered disappeared within seconds as she returned his kiss with a hot, eager one of her own. The way she kissed him back surprised him, spurred him on. He angled his head to the side to deepen the kiss and she responded by gently sucking on his tongue. A slow burn began in his gut, and he knew one thing for certain: the attraction that started on a beach in Mexico was no fluke.

He also knew he might not get enough of this woman.

With a soft gasp, she leaned in to deepen the kiss. It was nearly his undoing. Reluctantly, he broke it off, lifting his lips away from hers by a fraction. Leaning his forehead against hers, he tried to catch a breath. Her lips were puffy and damp, her eyes wild with passion.

"Damn," Shane muttered, taking his hands off the wall. Repositioning them to caress the sides of her face, he pulled her in closer so his mouth could take possession of hers again.

Carly's brain had ceased to function. She really should be telling him to stop, pushing him away. And she would. *In a minute.* Instead, the hands braced on his chest to do the pushing away slowly snaked up the black T-shirt that covered a finely sculpted torso before ending up wrapped around his neck. His skin was soft underneath her fingertips. She reached farther up to run her fingers through his hair, pulling his head deeper into the kiss. Their tongues were doing a passionate dance that had her stomach ready to fall out. She swayed against him as his hands reached down to cup her bottom, lifting her to sit on the credenza. He stepped between her thighs, allowing his erection to grind against her most sensitive area. The feeling was so overwhelming, she threw her head back and moaned. He took advantage of her exposed neck, nuzzling his way across her collarbone. When she wrapped her legs around him, he returned the groan before taking her mouth in a hard, demanding kiss. She nearly melted from the heat of it.

Carly had been intimate with more than a few men. But never like this. Never in her own office. On her desk. She'd never been so deeply aroused by another man—not even the passionate Italian she'd been engaged to—that she could lose control so easily. She'd definitely never been one to experience the toe-curling orgasms that she'd read about in magazines.

Until now.

She was on the verge of coming, and she was still fully dressed with just Shane's tongue in her mouth as his hard body rubbed against her. She wanted him naked and inside of her. Now.

"Yo, Devlin. You up here?"

The sound of Donovan Carter's voice was like ice water being dumped on her. With strength she didn't know she possessed, she pushed Shane off her and jumped to her feet. They both struggled to catch their breath. She forced her eyes to meet his. The heat and passion she saw reflected there made her shiver. With his hair tousled, his lips swollen and red, and his erection straining his already tight jeans, it was impossible to mistake his intentions.

"Oh God," Carly whispered. What had she almost done?

"Shane!" Donovan called again, his voice drawing nearer.

Shane continued to stare at her. Donovan was about to walk through the door. One look at Shane, and he'd know exactly what they'd been up to. Carly quickly turned to the window, her back to the door.

"In here," Shane called out, his voice a low growl.

She said a silent prayer that he would at least sit down before Donovan arrived.

"Hey you two . . ." Donovan's voice trailed off as he entered her office.

Neither one of them replied. Carly didn't dare turn around, sure that her neck and her nipples still showed the effects of their encounter.

"Everything okay in here?" Donovan's tone had an edge

to it now. He was no fool. The man had been a criminal investigator. Carly felt her face redden at the thought.

"Everything's fine." Shane's voice held a challenge in it. Just what she needed: two alpha males ready to duke it out over her honor.

"Ohh-kay," Donovan said slowly. "I'll just wait out here. We need to leave right away if you want to make that flight, Shane."

All she could manage was a wave over her shoulder as Donovan left the office. Mentally, she braced herself for Shane to say something, do something. Instead, she heard the scratch of the pen on paper and then it being flung back on the desk. He left without saying a word.

Leaning her forehead against the glass window, she took a deep breath. She debated with herself which was more mortifying: the fact that she had almost given it all to Shane Devlin, or that they had nearly been caught by the head of Blaze security. Shane didn't seem like the type to kiss and tell. She only hoped he could keep Donovan from spreading gossip. Two things she knew for sure: Shane Devlin had the power to overwhelm all her sensibilities, and she needed to avoid being alone with him at all costs.

Five

A fat bead of sweat trickled down the back of Shane's neck, adding to his already soaked T-shirt as his feet pounded the pavement. Despite a light breeze, the late afternoon sun and a brisk five-mile run combined to produce a sheen of sweat all over his body.

"I swear, I've never seen anything like it in my life, man." Donovan let out a little huff as he kept pace beside Shane. "She looked like a chick from one of those lip-syncing girl bands, only not so hot, you know? She stood there in this funky pink outfit—I mean nauseatingly pink—with big, bug-eye sunglasses on, and blasted poor Carly. Not that she was much of a threat. Jeez, she's all of five and a half feet tall in her spiked heels. She looks a lot taller on TV. Dude, she even had a dog in her purse! Damn, that thing was ugly." Donovan's whole body shook at the thought of the dog.

Shane laughed at his friend's antics. Apparently the arrival of Gabe Harrelson's new bride provided quite the side show at the Blaze offices earlier in the day.

"What's she so fired up about anyway?" Shane asked as they jogged through the neat residential neighborhood.

Small brick condos lined up uniformly behind pristine, postage-stamp lawns.

"Money. Isn't that what women are always fired up about? That and shoes," Donovan joked as he matched Shane stride for stride.

"Last time I checked, Gabe made some pretty good cash." Shane swerved to avoid a small sinkhole in the pavement.

"Dude, a woman like that can *never* have too much money. Their wedding alone had to cost a fortune. They held it on a beach in Kauai with nearly five hundred guests. Those people partied for *three whole days!*" Donovan checked his stride to look for oncoming cars before crossing a side street.

Shane paused to look at Donovan quizzically.

"You know this *how*?" he asked as they took off at a jog again.

"*TMZ. Access Hollywood.* Hell, they had a four-page spread in *People*. You didn't see that?" Donovan looked at him incredulously.

"Nope." Shane shook his head. "It's not my preferred bathroom reading."

Donovan gave a little snort.

"I figured you'd have a free subscription to some of those rags, as often as you've appeared in them," he teased. "Anyway, Carly handled the little Paris Hilton wannabe. She even tried to make friends with the ugly dog, but the little rat was just bad to the bone. Even a diamond dog collar couldn't make it look pretty. It was growlin' at its own shadow."

Shane had no problem picturing Carly reading Gabe's wife the riot act. Her crazy blue eyes would be wild in her agitation. Her breasts all perky as she stomped around reciting the signing bonus rules chapter and verse. He was getting excited just thinking about the two women sparring. Despite a Herculean effort during the past week to banish Dorothy from his fantasies, he hadn't been too successful.

"I missed a girl fight?" he asked reverently.

Donovan laughed. "Not quite, but *that* probably would have made *TMZ*."

"Damn." Shane slowed briefly to call to the Labrador retriever who'd been sidetracked from the jog when a passing scent caught his attention.

"Probably would have been a good fight, too. According to the office scuttlebutt, there's no love lost between Carly and the little bridezilla." Donovan bent down to massage his knee.

Shane lifted his T-shirt to wipe the sweat off his face. "How's that?" he asked through his shirt.

"Who knows," Donovan said as he stretched his leg. "Probably has something to do with her being jealous of Carly and Gabe. She practically accused Carly of purposely withholding his bonus because she had a thing for him."

"Carly and Harrelson?" His pulse, already racing from his run, ratcheted up a point or two.

Donovan looked at him out of the corner of his eye. "No," he said. "They're just friends. Carly was recovering from a serious burnout in a relationship. Gabe is more in touch with his feminine side. In fact, I'm surprised he even married, if you get my drift. Anyway, he was more like a confidant to Carly while she got over that crazy Italian soccer player she was engaged to. Guess Gabe's new wife is just the jealous type."

She wasn't the only jealous type, Shane thought. Not that he'd admit to being jealous; more like curious. The first opportunity he'd gotten after overhearing Carly's conversation in her office, Shane had searched the Internet for details about her former fiancé. The story played out like a soap opera within the European media, specifically the tabloids. Maxim Vicente charmed "Darling Carly" while having a secret relationship—and a child—with a married woman, eventually leaving Carly a month before the wedding. Unfortunately, the paparazzi painted Carly as an unstable victim, unable to hold on to her man.

"About you and Carly . . ." Donovan's sharp tone brought

Shane out of his reverie. Neither man had broached the subject of the incident in Carly's office the other day. Shane had hoped his friend would just let it lie, but apparently not. Donovan stood facing him, hands on hips, his interrogator's face clearly in place.

"There is no 'me and Carly,'" Shane answered. Trying his best to project nonchalance, he locked eyes with the former Marine, challenging him to say otherwise.

Donovan held his ground for a moment, before finally shaking his head and looking away. "Look, Shane," Donovan said. "What you do is your business. But Carly . . . she's been through a lot, you know? She comes across as all poised and sophisticated, but underneath, she's still pretty tender and raw. I just wouldn't want to see her hurt."

Shane tried not to wince at Donovan's words. Obviously, his friend bought into the public's perception of him. The implication that he would somehow hurt Carly rankled. People's opinions of him hadn't mattered before, so why were they becoming important now? And why did the idea of Carly being hurt—by him or someone else—bother him so?

"You ready to head back to your place?" Donovan asked.

"Yeah, I probably should get this guy a drink." Shane gestured to the large chocolate-colored dog lolling in the shade of a large tree, his pink tongue hanging out of the side of his mouth.

"A beer sounds good to me, too," Donovan said with a grin as he jogged down a side street.

Shane lived in one of the team's rental properties in the elite, gated community. The four-bedroom house sat on over a half an acre on a cul-de-sac at the very back of the neighborhood. He and Donovan navigated a maze of smaller row houses to get to the more exclusive area of the community.

"You're lucky you got a place in here, man," Donovan said as they rounded a corner. The tree-lined street was quiet in the early evening. "A few of the Blaze staff live in here and they say it's pretty quiet. I guess you'll be running into Carly in here, too."

Shane stumbled, but he was able to right himself without Donovan taking too much notice.

"Carly lives *here*?" he asked, the words escaping his mouth before he could temper his reaction.

"Yeah." Donovan looked at him sharply. "In fact, that's her place up ahead."

Shane looked farther down the street to where the object of his distraction stood gesturing to another man. The trunk of her Saab convertible stood open. It looked like she'd been disrupted in the act of carrying in groceries. The man was obviously offering to help haul in her bags, but Dorothy was having none of it.

"Shit!" Donovan swore, picking up his pace. Shane followed suit, his pulse beginning to shoot up again. He wasn't sure if it was from seeing Carly again or from Donovan's apparent concern.

The cloying smell of Joel Tompkins's cologne first alerted Carly to his presence behind her. *God, this guy is a pest,* she thought to herself as she turned from the trunk of her car to see him reaching in to grab a grocery bag. It went against her nature to be openly hostile to another person, but she was beginning to think today might be an exception.

She was still reeling over her encounter with Gabe's wife earlier. *That woman was a nutcase!* What could have possibly possessed Gabe to marry her? Okay, Carly *knew* why he had married her—for the publicity—but the little bridezilla obviously did not. Carly actually sympathized with Chloe; right up until Chloe accused her of being involved with her husband. The little scene in the lobby of the training facility had propelled Carly's pity into annoyance. Damn Gabe for sending the tabloid princess to do his dirty work anyway. The fight for his signing bonus was going to get messy, but Carly knew she had an iron-clad contract on her side.

Escaping her office early, she'd sought solace in a Pilates class at her health club. She'd been looking forward to an evening of kicking back with a glass of wine and watching *Downton Abbey* reruns on PBS. Instead, she was staring into the hooded, dark brown eyes of Joel Tompkins.

When she'd first met him, Joel had reminded her of a puppy. Eager and affectionate. Lately, however, he was becoming more persistent and clingy. More . . . menacing. He took the plastic grocery bag from her hand.

"I've got it," Carly said, pulling the bag back from him. Her gut was telling her not to give him any excuse to come inside her home.

"I insist." He pulled back, nearly tearing the plastic bag. A nervous laugh escaped as she envisioned the grocery bag rupturing and her jumbo box of tampons flying across the lawn. The lopsided grin he offered her in return made her shiver. *Were his teeth always that big?* Crap, now she was imagining him as a wolf, not a puppy. She nearly shrieked with hysteria at the low growl that seemed to be conjured up by her thoughts. The growl caught Joel off guard as well; he loosened his grip on the grocery bag and she quickly pulled it to her chest before it ripped completely.

"Is there a problem here, Carly?"

She looked up to see Donovan Carter standing, hands on hips, next to her open car trunk. A large brown Labrador retriever was insinuating itself between her and Joel, letting out another low growl as it sat possessively on Carly's feet. Joel looked from the dog to Donovan. A brief scowl covered Joel's face, but he quickly hid it.

"No problem here, dude. I'm just helping the lady with her groceries." He looked down at the dog. "Your dog's got a bit of an attitude, though."

"The dog's mine." Carly's head whipped around to see Shane standing on her other side, his arms folded across his chest, hands tucked under his arms. *Looking more menacing than Joel ever could.* She glanced down at the panting dog now lying across her sneakered feet. The dog thumped its tail as its eyes darted from her to Shane. Joel moved to grab the grocery bag again and the dog immediately came to attention, its growl fiercer than before. Taking a step back, Joel looked at the animal as if he might kick it.

"Hack journalism must not be paying well these days, Tompkins." Donovan stepped between Joel and the dog. "Now you're working as a bag boy?"

"I was in the neighborhood. We're friends, so back off, man." Joel was becoming increasingly defensive. It didn't help that Donovan now stood inches from his face. Carly thought she really should step in and defend Joel. He worked for the local television station, after all, and she didn't want any bad publicity for the team.

"That right, Carly? You two friends?" Donovan asked, his eyes never leaving Joel's face.

But Joel had become a pest. Maybe Asia was right: The only way to get rid of the guy was to be a little mean.

"No." Her voice shook a little. "Joel, we work in the same place. We are *friendly* to one another, but that's it. It really wouldn't be professional for us to have any other type of relationship. I'm sorry."

Jeez, she felt like a hypocrite. Not more than a week ago, her hands had been all over Shane Devlin, and he was one of the team's players! And two of the three men standing there knew it. She didn't dare turn around and look at Shane.

"You hear that, Tompkins? The lady doesn't need any help." Donovan backed Joel toward his car. Joel's face briefly clouded with anger. But, as before, he quickly masked it. When he looked up, he had become the overeager puppy dog again.

"Sure. Whatever. You can't blame a guy for trying." He smiled at Donovan as he pulled his keys out of his pocket. "She is pretty hot," he said with a wink as he slid into his car and started the ignition.

"Thank goodness." Carly let out a relieved breath as she absentmindedly stroked the broad head of the dog.

Donovan turned to face her as Joel drove off, the bass of the car's stereo thumping down the street.

"I don't trust that guy. I'm going to jog out to the guard

house and make sure he leaves. I also want to know how he
got in here." Donovan looked past Carly to speak to Shane.
"I'll be back in five."

As he jogged off, Carly tried not to think about being left
alone with Shane. He'd been remarkably quiet during the
exchange with Joel. It didn't seem to be in his personality
to resist an opportunity to strut his testosterone. She wondered if he was saving it up for her.

Stop thinking like that!

In the week since their encounter in her office, she had
done some serious introspection. This *thing* between the
two of them couldn't continue. Shane Devlin wasn't her type.
Sure, he was dark, brooding, and sexy as hell, but he wasn't
the type to stick around. And Carly had had a lifetime of men
who didn't stick around. She wanted more than that. She
wanted happily ever after, the kind that was quiet and out of
the public eye. Shane Devlin was *not* happily-ever-after material. She'd just gently but firmly let down Joel Tompkins—
and he hadn't gone postal on her. Now it was time to set things
straight with the team's new quarterback.

She looked up from her musing, still absently stroking
the dog's head, only to find the object of her thoughts had
silently lifted the remaining grocery bags from her trunk
and was striding toward the front door of her row house.
She let out a frustrated huff. Just moments ago, her instincts
were telling her not to let Joel Tompkins in her house. Those
same instincts were remarkably quiet right now. Alarm bells
should be going off, but her mind was silent as she watched
a pair of muscled thighs and a tight butt—perfectly displayed in running shorts—disappear through the door. The
dog rose and trotted after its master. At the steps, it paused
to turn its chocolate eyes to her.

She swore the dog was asking her if she was coming.

"Oh, all right," she muttered as she slammed the trunk
closed, following man and beast inside. This conversation
would be a lot easier if it didn't take place in her house.

Shane had already placed the grocery bags on the counter
of the kitchen by the time she and the dog arrived. He stood

silently, giving the room the once-over, and she suddenly became conscious of how small her kitchen was. His presence seemed to stretch the limits of the room. He'd been running, and she could see the sweat staining his shirt. His scent should have been offensive, but instead he smelled . . . good. Like a man. All man. As his scent permeated her nostrils, she could almost taste him. She had to swallow as she remembered the taste of his skin beneath her lips. Heat pooled low in her belly. Quickly, she turned away from him to regain her composure. Trying to distract herself, she reached up into the cabinet and pulled down an empty, plastic whipped topping container from a stack of twenty or so. *Great, now he knows I'm addicted to whipped cream.* Filling the makeshift bowl with water, she set it on the tile floor. The dog paused in its perusal of the baseboards beneath the breakfast stools to drink. For a few moments, the only sound in the room was the dog lapping up water.

"Look, Carly." Shane hadn't moved any closer, but his voice seemed to caress her. "Donny will be back any minute and we need to clear something up."

Carly turned to face him. She leaned a hip on the counter and raised her chin up a notch, waiting.

"About the other day in your office," he began.

"Let's forget it happened," Carly said quickly, standing up straight.

"It was a mistake." Shane said at the same time.

A mistake? She hugged her arms to her chest and willed the tears not to come. His words stung. For a moment, she was back in Italy. The press labeling her as pathetic, unable to hold on to a man. Why was it always her fault? Hadn't Shane initiated the kiss in her office?

"Whoa," Shane said, taking a step closer. "I wouldn't say it never happened, Dorothy. I'm pretty sure that was your tongue down my throat."

Seriously? He could call it a mistake, but she was supposed to be pining for more? No freakin' way. Carly rolled her shoulders back. She was not that gullible girl the Italian paparazzi had created. It had taken her months to get over

Maxim's betrayal, but she *was* over him. She could easily handle Shane Devlin.

"It's not like I'm lying awake nights dreaming of it," she said smugly.

She dared to look into his eyes. What she saw reflected in them surprised her. She expected to see arrogance. Instead, she saw hunger. And heat. That same look she'd seen in Cabo. With a little bit of loneliness mixed in. She turned away so he wouldn't see the tears that still threatened. Ripping off several sheets of paper towel, she threw them on the floor, stepping on them with her sneaker to wipe up the water the dog had slobbered. Shane sighed behind her.

"I'm sorry, Carly." It sounded as if he were speaking through his hands. "I'm not good at this."

She turned to see him run his fingers through his hair.

"What I want—what I think we both want—is to keep this professional. I don't have a very good track record when it comes to relationships. If I'm going to screw something up, I'd rather it not be with the GM's assistant. Especially if she happens to also be the coach's sister-in-law. As much as I'd like to explore whatever this is between us, it's just not a very good idea."

Honesty. That was not what she was expecting from Shane Devlin. She bit her lip to keep it from trembling.

"Even if she is hot," he finished softly. The grin he added nearly took her breath away. She knew she needed to say something. Something mature. But she couldn't trust her voice.

"So, we'll just be *friendly* to one another around the office," he forged on, repeating her words to Joel from earlier.

"Yeah." She let a slow smile escape. "That would be best."

He held out his right hand for her to shake. She went to take it, but pulled back at the last instant.

"I . . . don't think we should . . ." She stumbled over the words.

"Yeah, no touching," he finished for her. "I don't seem

to know how to stop once I start touching you," he whispered.

They stood there, not touching, for a moment more. The only sounds in the room were the hum of the refrigerator and the deep breathing of the dog dozing on the floor.

"I'd better go," he said finally. "Donny'll be looking for me."

Shane headed for the door, whistling for the dog as he went. Scrambling to its feet, its tongue still hanging out, the retriever happily followed him out of the house. Carly remained rooted to the kitchen floor. Being friendly coworkers was what she wanted. Wasn't it?

Six

The next four weeks went by quickly for Carly. Her usual duties assisting Hank in the Blaze front office had been fairly light, it being the off-season. Still, between monitoring Shane's media blitz and dealing with Gabe Harrelson's crazy new wife, Carly had very little extra time to help Lisa plan for her gala—which the team was cohosting—now only a week away.

Sitting cross-legged on the floor of Asia's office, Carly carefully stuffed engraved tickets into envelopes that she then neatly stacked in assigned piles beside her.

"I can't belief Gabe is giving the team such a hard time about his signing bonus," Asia said from her perch on the sofa behind Carly where she was monitoring media reports about the team on her iPad. "He's out for the season, if not for good, and it was his own fault. He's an idiot for going hang-gliding."

"Actually," Carly said, "Gabe hasn't been in contact with the team at all. Neither has his agent. It's just crazy Chloe. Between emails and phone calls, she's averaging fifteen rants a day."

"She's been very effective using the media, too. What do either of them need the money for? Gabe must be set for life and Chloe should be making a mint on the residuals from her days on that sitcom. According to *Daily Variety*, her show is broadcast every day on hundreds of stations around the world."

Carly brushed a strand of hair from her face. "Don't believe everything you read." It was an axiom she lived by. The matter of Gabe's signing bonus was beginning to annoy Carly, however. Chloe demanding money from the team just didn't make sense. Asia was correct; Gabe didn't need it. Most likely, the situation was a case of the young actress trying to kick-start her career through her marriage to a sports icon. Carly wondered if Gabe even knew of his wife's efforts.

Several times these past weeks, Carly had tried to contact the injured quarterback, but he wasn't returning her phone calls, texts, or emails. She thought they'd been friends. Gabe's sudden reluctance to talk was a mystery. Video of him rehabbing his injured hip in Southern California appeared on *TMZ* a few days ago, but there was no sign of his young bridezilla accompanying him. Carly thought back to the times Maxim had been injured, when she'd become invisible to the soccer star as he rehabbed his body to get back to the one thing he loved most. She almost felt sorry for Chloe. *Almost.*

"Well, at least our new quarterback is behaving himself. His interviews seem to be going well," Asia said. "You've done a great job running him through the media circus, Carly. I don't know what I would have done without you." Asia let out a hiss as she tried to maneuver her leg to a more comfortable position.

Carly jumped up from the floor to help her friend, adjusting the pillows beneath Asia's brace. "It really hasn't been too bad. I'm pretty anonymous among the sports press here in Baltimore, so no one even notices I'm there. It's kind of nice doing a job I'm comfortable with. I guess journalism is in my blood." Carly smiled down at Asia before resuming her place on the floor.

She was telling Asia the truth; working as a publicist again was kind of fun. Working with Shane wasn't too difficult, either. All she had to do was accompany him to his various interviews and stand back and watch. Shane was a natural at navigating his way through an interview. He was knowledgeable about the game of football and patient with those who weren't. His candor was appreciated by both the interviewers and the fans who called into the radio talk shows Shane appeared on. When questions got too personal, Shane expertly steered the conversation back to football. Carly couldn't help but be a little envious of such a well-honed skill.

For the most part, Shane was relaxed and charming during the interviews. Except when the questions were about his father. Whenever the topic shifted to Bruce Devlin, Shane's whole body language changed. He became tense and his answers more curt. The change in his demeanor was subtle, making it almost indiscernible to most people. But Carly had spent enough time with Shane these past weeks to pick up on the tension.

She was curious about Shane's relationship with his famous dad, but not enough to ask him directly. While the sexual tension still hummed between them, Carly and Shane managed to carry on the guise of "friendly coworkers" by keeping their interaction to a minimum. It was working just fine. So far.

"Oh, puh-lease! Like you could ever be anonymous with those looks." Asia's comment brought Carly back to the conversation. "I've had at least three calls this week alone from guys at the radio and TV stations asking who you are and if you're single," Asia practically snorted.

Carly jerked her head up. "Tell me you didn't let on who I am," Carly pleaded.

"No way!" Asia said. "You know I'd never do that, Carly. Besides, I finally got that dweeb Joel Tompkins reassigned. We don't need some other pest from the media creeping around after you."

"Thanks," Carly said with relief. "And thanks for taking

care of the Joel situation for me. It's been nice not to have to check around corners every time I walk around the building."

"No problem." Asia tossed her iPad onto the table next to the sofa. "Donovan said he wasn't getting a good vibe from the guy. It wasn't easy getting him out of here, though. Apparently, his grandfather owns the television station. Despite that fact, Joel doesn't have too many friends there. He obviously makes a habit of creeping people out. No one actually wants him working for them. It took some doing, but Donovan and I persuaded them to transfer Joel to covering the Orioles. Let him bother some baseball players."

"You and Donovan, huh?" Carly grinned. She carefully placed the last of the envelopes into a cardboard box. "Should I scratch the 'and guest' off his ticket to the gala?" she asked.

Asia smiled serenely. "He offered to take me. Obviously he's not afraid to be seen with an ungraceful, gimpy woman."

"Oh, puh-lease," Carly mimicked her friend. She stood and brushed off her pants and glanced at the clock on the Asia's desk. "Wow! Four thirty already. I promised to do Emma's hair for the dance tonight. I'll drop these off with Amy before I go. Is there anything else I can do for you before I leave?"

"You can answer a question for me," Asia said.

Carly gathered the box under an arm. "Sure, anything."

"Do you ever do anything for *you*?"

Carly looked at her friend quizzically, unsure of what Asia wanted her to say.

Asia reached out to grasp Carly's free hand. "You're always running around here doing for everyone else. Or at Matt and Lisa's doing for them or the kids. Even if Hank hadn't butted in on your trip to Cabo, you still wouldn't have spent it as a vacation. You would have been *doing* for Julianne."

When Carly didn't answer, Asia squeezed her hand. "All I'm saying is you don't have to do so much for everyone else. You can say no once in a while. Instead of trying to make everyone else happy, why not do something that makes you happy? You're allowed. The media won't crucify you. I promise."

"I am happy," Carly pushed out through her suddenly tight throat.

Asia stared at her a moment before finally releasing her hand. "Go. Make your beautiful niece look more beautiful. Just remember what I said, okay?"

"Sure," Carly said. It was unlikely she would forget.

In fact, Carly spent a restless night pondering Asia's words. Was she happy? Staring at the ceiling as sleep evaded her, she ticked off the things in her life she was happy with: Her family. Or her half sister's family, to be precise, definitely brought her joy. Lisa was alive thanks to her bone marrow, and Carly couldn't be more thrilled.

Money wasn't an issue, thanks to a generous trust fund left to Carly by her mother. In spite of that, Carly had a job she enjoyed, one that felt purposeful. It was certainly better than the life of a party girl the media expected of her. And she had friends. Carly had a few left who wouldn't sell her out to the paparazzi.

All that was left in the happiness department was her love life, which was currently not bringing her much joy. Carly tried to rationalize with herself that she wasn't necessarily *unhappy* with her lack of a love life, but her close encounters with Shane Devlin pretty much negated that argument. This thing—this pull—she felt for Shane made her aware that she missed the intimacy she shared with her former fiancé. Fortunately, she no longer missed Max.

Which left her where, exactly? A fling with Shane was out of the question for so many reasons. He was a public figure, for one; what's more, he was a professional athlete.

Maybe Asia was right. Carly should do something to make herself happy. She needed to start by actively searching for her Mr. Right. Only, thoughts of an accountant or podiatrist weren't exactly torching her body the way a single look from Shane Devlin could.

The following morning, standing next to a tangle of utility cords off to the side of the set of the *Good Day, Baltimore* show, Carly watched as Shane bantered with the program's perky female host during a cooking segment. To the amazement of the host, and everyone else in the studio, he was actually whipping up a plate of strawberry crepes. Shane laughed at something the woman said, his killer dimple appearing on one side of his mouth. Carly rocked back on her heels, his handsome smile nearly knocking her off her feet. He was definitely oozing charm this morning.

Shane was dressed in a Blaze golf shirt, which stretched handsomely over taut pectoral muscles and broad shoulders. He'd declined to wear the show's logo apron, instead draping a pink breast cancer towel over his right shoulder. His fashion statement did nothing to diminish his masculinity. Carly tried not to drool as his strong hands whipped the wire whisk in the metal bowl. Her stomach growled. She wasn't sure if she was hungry for the delicious-looking food or the more delicious-looking man.

"You certainly know your way around the kitchen, Shane," the woman said, slithering a little closer to him.

"I make it a point to be good at whatever I attempt, Cindy," Shane replied with a wink at the now blushing TV host.

He's definitely good at kissing, Cindy.

As if he'd read her thoughts, Shane looked up past the TV camera to where Carly stood and shot her a quicksilver grin. Carly felt her blush to her toes. She stepped back farther into the wings so as not to distract Shane. Or, more likely so she wouldn't run on camera, douse him with whipped cream, and lap him up.

Moving away from the glare of the bright television lights, Carly was forced to close her eyes momentarily, allowing them to adjust. When she opened them, she slapped a hand over her mouth to avoid interrupting the show with her shriek. Joel Tompkins was standing in the shadows, blocking her path.

"Hey there, Carly," he said quietly.

Carly tried to take a step back, but she was pinned in by a huge teleprompter. The only way to escape Joel was back across the live set where Shane's cooking segment was being filmed.

"Joel," Carly said, straightening her spine. Joel was a pest, but so far he'd been basically harmless. She could be nice for a few minutes. There was no need to panic.

Joel closed the space and reached over to push a piece of Carly's hair behind her ear. Carly flinched. "Please don't touch me," she said, trying not to let her voice betray her now quivering nerves.

"The Blaze's badass security dude isn't around to interrupt us. Maybe we can take a ride and grab some breakfast. Or something."

No way were they grabbing anything. Carly looked around for reinforcements, but everyone was still fascinated with Shane's cooking skills, their backs to her and Joel. She would not panic. They were in a crowded studio. Swallowing around the lump in her throat, Carly figured she could stall Joel until the commercial break. One look into his eyes, though, and she realized reasoning with him might not be easy. He was high as a kite. She was sure of it. Years spent at a prestigious boarding school for the rich and unwanted had exposed her to all kinds of addicts. Joel was exhibiting all the classic signs of the stoned.

Now, it was time to panic.

Just as she was about to speak, the alarm bell sounded, indicating the show was no longer live. People started to mill around and, not wasting an opportunity, Carly made for the set. Joel reached out and wrapped his fingers around her arm, but before he could do or say anything, a voice rang out.

"Tompkins! Get that teleprompter moved over to Studio B. Now!"

Joel hesitated, seemingly weighing his options. Carly pulled her arm from his grip. With a menacing smile, Joel grabbed the handle of the teleprompter. "Don't worry. We'll get our time, you and me. You'll see." And with that he left the studio.

Carly's stomach was no longer growling. It was rolling with waves of nausea.

Shane's megawatt smile dimmed along with the hot, tungsten studio lights. He'd outdone himself this morning. No one in the Blaze organization had better dare complain that Shane wasn't giving the media blitzkrieg his best. *Christ, they ought to give me a freaking Academy Award.*

Tossing the hand towel onto the countertop, he looked around the set for Carly. The show's host—Candy, Cindy, or whatever the hell her name was—rubbed her hip next to his, leaning across him to drag her finger through the bowl of whipped cream. A seductive smile on her face, she stuck her whipped-cream-laden finger into her mouth and sucked on it dramatically, her bright red collagen lips bulging.

Seriously, lady? Shane looked around the studio in disgust. He hated these television segments. Why did anyone care what he was like off the field? Wasn't his job to win football games? And where the hell was Carly? It was her job to run interference with the overly made-up television hostess. Usually, Carly jumped right in at the end of each interview, graciously but effectively untangling him from fans and interviewers and herding him out the door to his next gig. Right now, Candy-Cindy was being a bit too playful as she shoved her business card in the back pocket of his jeans, her hand lingering on his ass just a little too long.

"Call me if you want someone to show you around Baltimore, Shane," she said, tossing her hair for effect.

Shane gave her a noncommittal smile before quickly heading off the set to find Carly. She'd be hard to miss. Dressed for the spring weather, she'd arrived at the studio in a clingy blue dress, showing off toned, bare arms and legs. Normally, Carly wore her hair done up in some conservative style, but today she'd left it cascading down her shoulders. Every man with a pulse stopped to stare as she wandered about the set offering a cheery hello to the show's staff.

Shane wasn't immune, either. His pulse had been racing since he'd laid eyes on her earlier; the effort to keep their relationship strictly business was making him testy. In fact, these last few weeks as "friendly coworkers" had been torturous for Shane. As much as they both tried to will it away, the sexual tension still burned between them. By sheer will, Shane kept it professional. He couldn't afford any distractions. He had records to break.

Despite the daily punishment of looking but not touching, Shane was grateful for Carly's help "working" the media. In fact, he was a little in awe of her skill. Putting aside her tenuous relationship with the reporters, Carly managed to carry out Asia's media plan without any glitches, always remaining poised and professional. Her tactic seemed to be to kill them with kindness, ingratiating herself with everyone she met. Shane found himself looking forward to his scheduled interviews—if it meant he could spend time with Carly. The "no touching" rule was still in place, but he discovered that on the occasions when she gifted him with a smile, it was almost as good as a touch. Almost.

Searching the studio, he finally found her standing alone back against one of the movable set walls, her arms wrapped around her midsection.

"Hey, the Hostess with the Mostest was coming on to me with the whipped cream. You wanna go take her down? You know, one for the team?" Shane teased.

Carly looked up at him then, her blue eyes wide and frightened.

"Whoa, Dorothy, that was a joke," he said, bending down so he could peer into her face more closely. She was trembling. *Jesus!* Gently taking her by the elbow, Shane steered her off the set and out into a blessedly empty hallway.

"What gives?" he asked, reluctantly releasing her elbow. As soon as he did, she turned and buried her face in his chest. He wrapped his arms around her without conscious thought.

They stood there for a few moments, her taking deep breaths against his instantly aroused body, him slowly rubbing her back as he breathed in the distinctly sunshiny scent of Carly. His lips itched to brush over the top of her head, but he knew not to go there.

What the hell had happened to her in there? Had someone said something about her past? Her ex-fiancé? Whatever had happened, Shane was going to kill the offending sonofabitch with his bare hands.

Releasing a breath, Carly took a step back. She patted her hands against his chest—almost as if to assure herself he was real—before slowly raising her eyes to meet his. Instead of being wide with fear, they were know tinged with the same smoky passion he was sure was reflected in his own eyes.

God, he wanted to kiss her. Right there in the hallway of the Channel Three studios. At that moment, he didn't care about his career with the Blaze. Or about breaking Bruce Devlin's remaining records. All Shane cared about was sinking into her luscious mouth. Carly gnawed on her bottom lip and Shane would have kissed her had she not taken another step away from him. He fisted his hands at his sides to keep from dragging her back into his arms.

"Do you wanna tell me what's got you so upset?" Shane hadn't intended for the question to sound so terse, but he was feeling pretty charged up.

Carly took another step back, briefly glancing over his shoulder at the studio behind them. "It was nothing," she said, lifting her chin up a notch.

Nothing my ass. Shane arched an eyebrow at her, his hands now on his hips. "Carly . . ." he said. But she was backing away from him.

"I need to get my bag out of the station manager's office and you need to be back at the training facility for the mandatory conditioning session," she said as she backed down the hallway. "I'll see you back there." With a wave, she disappeared around the corner, leaving Shane standing there wondering—not for the first time with Carly—what exactly had just happened.

Kids were running amok in the Blaze offices. Shane watched from his table as Carly shepherded a group of toddlers through the Blaze commissary, clutching their tiny hands as another Blaze staffer dispensed frozen yogurt into cups for the kiddies. Their precious treat in hand, Carly led them to a table overlooking the Blaze practice field. The chairs—built specially for large athletes—were so enormous, she and her partner had to lift each child into a seat, their stubby legs dangling precariously above the floor. The sight looked as ridiculous as the time he and some teammates struggled to fit into the tiny chairs in a kindergarten class his former team had forced Shane to visit.

Leaning back on the two back legs of his chair, Shane took in the scene. Carly was dressed in khaki shorts and a fitted Blaze golf shirt, her hair neatly pulled back in some kind of braid. He hadn't seen her since the incident at the television studio earlier in the week. The remaining media commitments were national and Asia was handling them now that she was back at work full-time. Fortunately, the major sports writers focused most of their questions on the x's and o's of football, steering clear of his personal life. The final stages of the Blaze media campaign had been easy for him, in more ways than one.

Carly was all smiles dealing with the kids, handing out napkins and dispensing spoons and sprinkles. She looked like she was actually enjoying catering to the little ankle-biters. Shane wasn't much for kids. His agent, Roscoe, had a pair of twin boys aged somewhere between diapers and kindergarten. The few times he'd been around them, he'd ended up with some sort of food product or worse stuck to his clothing. Shane shuddered at the thought. Although, watching Carly gently stroke her hand over a little towheaded boy stirred something inside him. *Probably just feeling jealous of the little bugger.* Shane took a pull from his protein shake as Carly walked over to his table.

"Can I grab this chair?" she asked.

He shrugged his shoulders. "Sure. You running a day care now?"

"Well, after working with you for two weeks, how hard could an afternoon with seven preschoolers be?"

"Nice one." He saluted her with his drink.

Carly grinned at his compliment. "We do this most Fridays, especially during the season."

"You bring in kids to play? Here? During the season?" he said, not bothering to hide his shock.

"Not just any kids. Children of the players and coaches. We also have a family dinner on Wednesday nights. The coaches and players spend so much time here during the season that we try to give them an opportunity to see their families, too. It makes for a stronger team. One big, happy family."

In Shane's experience, families weren't generally happy, but he wasn't going to tell her that. She looked so proud of the concept that he figured it had to be her idea.

"It works pretty well, if I do say so myself," she said, notching her chin in the air.

Yep, definitely her idea. One thing he'd learned about her these past few weeks: Carly would do anything for her family. In fact, her life outside the office pretty much revolved around helping out her half sister, Coach, and their kids.

"As long as I don't have to play the family game," he said.

Carly tilted her head to the side, studying him for a long moment. "What's your problem with the concept of family?"

Shane thumped the front legs of his chair back down. "I don't have a problem."

Placing her palms flat on the table, she leaned in front of him, giving him an excellent view down her shirt. His groin grew tighter beneath his workout shorts.

"Okay, then, if you don't have a problem with families,

why do you clam up every time an interviewer asks you about your father? Or your brother?" she demanded.

Shane's eyes shot from her breasts to glare at Carly's face. He was so *not* having this conversation with her. His father was not up for discussion with anyone. Period.

Bruce Devlin might be his father, but he was not Shane's family. The man everyone was so interested in was on the upside of life again. He'd landed on his feet after conquering his addiction and was now regarded by many as one of the top coaches in college football. After dragging himself from the gutter, he'd found religion and was now leading his alma mater to bowl game appearances while lecturing at faith conferences for athletes across the country.

Further aggravating Shane, Bruce Devlin also managed to acquire a hot new wife half his age. A former Miss South Carolina, Lindsey Devlin was everything Shane's own mother had never been: beautiful, well educated, and possessing enough social graces to charm the shit off a man's shoes. Shane had taken an instant dislike to the green-eyed, statuesque brunette who was his father's young wife. The few times Bruce and Lindsey had invited him to visit when he was a teenager, Shane took every opportunity to demonstrate that his soul was beyond redemption—including propositioning his father's wife.

Looking back, Shane was ashamed at his childish behavior. Bruce and Lindsey—especially Lindsey—had treated him with extreme patience. She continued to invite Shane to family events despite his staunch refusal to attend. He chalked it up to her doing her "Christian duty." Making the effort to include Shane probably allowed her to sleep at night. He assumed his father was glad he stayed away so as not to poison the character of his other son.

The one Bruce Devlin stuck around to raise.

When Shane continued to glare at her, Carly stood up crossing her arms under those problematic breasts. "Seriously, Shane? Not even a smart comeback to my question?"

"I'll answer your question when you answer one of mine."

She annoyingly arched an eyebrow at him, refusing to back down.

"What was the problem at the television studio the other morning?" he challenged.

For a moment, he didn't think she'd answer. In fact, he was counting on her not answering and stalking back to her charges and leaving him the hell alone. Instead, she surprised him, sinking down into the chair next to his. He watched her, curious, as she picked up the wrapper from his straw and silently twisted it around her finger. After a quick glance over her shoulder at the little ones still enjoying their yogurt, she finally looked at him.

"That guy who was outside my home a few weeks ago when you and Donovan ran by—Joel Tompkins—he works at the station. He's very . . . eager . . . for a date with me, even though I've told him no a couple hundred times," she said.

From the look on Carly's face, Shane knew there was more to it. "What. Did. He. Do?" he demanded.

Carly took exception to Shane's tone, stretching back in her chair to put some space between them. The move made Shane angrier.

"I'm serious, Dorothy. If the guy's a problem, you need to let Donnie or Coach know. One of us can handle him."

Rolling her eyes at him, she let out a huff. "Donovan has already *handled* him. He and Asia had Joel reassigned from the Blaze complex, but Donovan has no jurisdiction at the television station, although he's tried." A chagrined smile quickly came and went from her face. "Donovan had him banned from my neighborhood. Now that I know where he works, I'll definitely boycott Channel Three. Problem solved."

Shane banged his head back on the wall behind him and closed his eyes in frustration. "I hadn't figured you to play the victim."

"Been there. Done that," she said quietly. "Don't worry, I don't plan to play the victim ever again."

Opening his eyes, he looked into her determined face. He sighed. "Just promise me you won't be a hero?"

A slow grin spread across her face. "I promise."

They sat there staring at each other like two idiots for who knows how long, until Asia hobbled up. She thumped something that looked like a seating chart onto the table between them.

"Just the two people I've been looking for," Asia huffed, pushing her crutches aside to slide into the other empty chair. "I need to finish this seating chart for the gala tomorrow night and you two are the last singles I need to seat."

Shane had bought his ticket for the thousand-bucks-a-head gala, but he hadn't actually planned on attending, so he really didn't care where Asia sat him. Looking at the faces of both women, Shane decided it was best to keep his planned no-show a secret.

"I'm sitting at the kids table," Carly said, pointing to a spot on the chart.

"Shocker," Asia said.

"There's a kid's table?" Shane asked.

"Yes, Shane, there is," Carly said. "Since this is a foundation for kids, Lisa and Matt want their children there for the fund-raising launch. They want to share the moment with their fam-i-lee." She shot him a cheeky grin.

"Yeah, and you'll be the babysitter." Asia rolled her eyes at Carly. "And, to make your evening more enjoyable, I'm putting the punter, Tom Rakowski, next to you since he's coming stag. Seriously, you guys are professional athletes. Why is it you can't get dates?" she asked, looking up at Shane.

"Kickers are dweebs," Shane said. Still, he was a more than a little bothered by the fact that the Blaze's punter would be spending tomorrow evening making nice with Carly.

"While you, Shane Devlin, have star quality. I'm putting you at one of the big spender tables. Most of the men are in their seventies, but their trophy wives will appreciate the view you bring," Asia said. Something about her tone gave Shane the feeling she might not be joking.

"Hey, why can't Rakowski man the cougar table?" Shane asked.

"Dweeb, remember?" Asia said, penciling something on one of the circles on the chart.

Carly laughed, her eyes sparkling at Shane.

"Or . . ." *What was he doing? He wasn't even going to the damn dinner.* "Carly and I could sit together and Rakowski can sit with the Richie Riches."

Both women stared at him.

"It wouldn't be like a date, really," Shane bumbled. "Just 'friendly coworkers' going to a team function together."

"So not a date, then," Asia said with a perplexed look. Carly continued to stare at him.

"Well, sort of like a date, but not. A safe date," Shane said.

"Ah, a *safe* date," Asia drawled. "Hmm. Well, Carly, what say you? Do I pencil the dweeb kicker at the money table, leaving Mr. Safe here with you at the kids' table?"

Shane tried not to shift uncomfortably in his chair as Carly just stared at him. If she said yes, he was going to the gala tomorrow night. He didn't want to go. So why did he desperately want her to say yes?

"Sure," Carly finally said. "It's a date. A *safe* date."

Seven

"Safe date, my ass," Shane muttered as he leaned against the bar.

Looking across the crowded ballroom, he was oblivious to its backdrop: a panoramic view of Baltimore's Inner Harbor. He didn't notice the glittering lights on the masts of the tall schooners moored beyond the windows. Or the sparkling centerpieces of black-eyed Susans and flickering tea lights neatly placed on the tables. All he saw was Carly standing in the center of the ballroom. She looked radiant.

From his perch, he watched as most of the men entering the gala stole a quick glance at her. Not that he blamed them. Her dress wasn't so much the "do-me" dress he had envisioned; it was better. It was made of some shimmering blue fabric that softly reflected the light, making her look like the ocean on a dark summer's night. He was sure that women would have another name for the color, but to him, blue said it all. It somehow wrapped around her body, highlighting her luscious curves, ending in a knot between her shoulder blades.

Her hair was loosely piled on top of her head. Not exactly

the neat little knot she wore to work every day. Tonight, wisps of hair escaped their sparkling clips and drifted down over her slender neck. Shane's fingers itched to pull the rest of her hair down and untie that knot holding her dress up. God, this had been a huge mistake. He should have stuck to his original plan and stayed home tonight.

"Jack Daniel's, neat," he said as the bartender came by to take his order. He really should order something for Carly, but he didn't know what she liked. He figured margaritas wouldn't go with the dress, so he ordered her a glass of chardonnay instead.

"You drinking the hard stuff tonight?" Donovan asked as he slid up to the bar next to Shane.

"I'm dressed like a waiter, so I thought I'd play the part this evening," Shane told him. "Carly's father wanted a drink, so I offered to get it for him. I'm sticking to my game plan of water with a splash of lemon." He really wanted a beer, but he needed to keep his wits about him where Carly was concerned.

"They both look pretty hot tonight," Donovan said a little reverently as he stared across the room. Shane turned to see Asia, walking tonight with just a cane, join Carly and her father, network news anchor Hugh Delaney.

"They do," Shane agreed. It seemed he wasn't the only one lusting after a Blaze employee. Only in Donovan's case, his relationship wouldn't be as complicated as anything between Carly and Shane. He tipped the bartender and both men headed over to their dates. Shane handed the drinks to Carly and her father.

He'd met Hugh earlier in the day, as the family gathered for appetizers and cocktails before the gala. His first thought was the television newsman seemed older than he appeared on TV. No surprise there. His second thought was he was an ass for treating Carly like the second or third string. Hugh acted as if his beautiful daughter were a friend of Lisa's, not a sibling. Sure, the guy was attentive to her, but in the way a parent might humor a neighborhood friend of their own child. One who came over for dinner most nights because he had no place else to go. It was a feeling Shane knew too well. And his gut burned at the thought of Carly being on the receiving end of it. The problem was, from what Shane could tell, Carly didn't seem to mind it. She smiled serenely at her father, picking up the morsels of attention Hugh threw her way as if they were treasured gems she'd string on a chain around her neck. Shane's hands balled into fists just thinking about it. She deserved better. Just as he had from his own father. Neither of them deserved to be treated like mistakes.

The governor entered the ballroom accompanied by the owner of the Blaze, and Hugh quickly excused himself. Asia and Donovan followed closely on his heels to do a little ass kissing themselves, leaving Shane and Carly alone. Or, as alone as they could be with three hundred or so other people milling about. Carly turned to Shane, taking a sip of her wine.

"I wasn't sure what you liked," he said, gesturing to her glass.

"This is fine," she said, taking another sip.

Man, he was an idiot. He was standing in the center of the room making inane small talk when all he wanted to do was tell her how beautiful she looked. The words were out before he could stop them.

"You look . . . amazing," he said.

A faint blush crept up her neck.

"Why thank you," she said, returning his compliment with a smile. "You clean up pretty nicely yourself, Devlin."

"Next time I'll remember not to put my jacket on the sofa before I put it on. It took me a half an hour to get the dog hair off."

"I think you might have missed one." Reaching over, she pulled a stray dog hair off his arm. He shoved his hands in his pockets to keep from taking her hand and holding it in his own.

"Beckett says hello, by the way." He rocked back and forth on his heels.

"He does?" Carly was beaming now. He wasn't sure who

moved first, but they began to stroll from the center of the ballroom. By mutual acceptance, they wandered to a quiet corner behind the dais. She stopped in front of the picture windows overlooking the harbor. As she turned to face Shane, the lights in Fells Point cast a halo around her head.

"I didn't figure you for having a dog. You don't seem the type to want the responsibility."

It was the truth, but her words struck a nerve. Once again, he found himself wondering why people's opinions of him mattered.

"Actually, he found me."

"Seriously?" Carly tilted her head to the side, awaiting further explanation.

"He belonged to a family in my neighborhood in San Diego. I'd see him outside playing with the kids when I went jogging. He was always coming up to me and jogging along until we got to the end of their yard. He really is a good dog. One day, I was driving by and noticed the family had moved. I guess I hadn't been paying too much attention because I didn't realize the house was on the market. Anyway, a few days later I found Beckett rummaging through my garbage cans. The family had just up and left him. I learned later that they had been foreclosed on. I guess they couldn't afford the expense of another mouth to feed."

"But leaving him to fend for himself, that's cruel!" Carly's eyes widened in horror.

"Yeah, well, the vet says it happens more often than you'd think. I meant to find him a home, a family with kids. He really seems to like them. But it's been six months and I haven't gotten around to it yet."

"Shane Devlin, you're never getting rid of that dog," she said with a knowing grin.

She was right, of course, her confident words touching something deep inside. Shane stood riveted, admiring her smile as the lights danced on the harbor behind her head. She took another sip of her wine and held his gaze.

"Aunt Carly!" Molly appeared out of nowhere, shattering the moment. "Mom says we need to find our table for dinner.

Can I sit next to you, *please*! I don't want to sit next to Grandpa Richardson. I think he took a bath in his Old Spice again, and if I have to smell it at dinner, I'll just puke!"

He watched jealously as Carly turned her beautiful smile to her niece, reaching over to gently cradle the girl's cheek, a move that instantly settled the girl down.

"Of course, pumpkin. Go ahead to table number three and pick out the seats you want us to sit in."

Molly left them at a gallop, weaving her way through the crowd to find their table.

"She's a bit of a drama queen, but she's a sweetie," she said with an apologetic grin.

"That's okay. I'm not that big a fan of Old Spice, either."

Carly laughed then. Really laughed. Shane nearly lost his breath at the sound. Unable to resist temptation any longer—he had to touch her—he held out his arm to her.

"Shall we?" he asked. Without hesitation, she wrapped her hand around his sleeve.

Carly really had to stop drinking. She'd guzzled a glass of wine already and was moving quickly through a second with dinner. Her nerves were a mess. It was bad enough to have to spend the evening doing the pretty with her father and his wife, but Julianne had wrapped her in some concoction that had most of the men ogling her all evening. Publicly flaunting her sexuality had been her mother's trick, not Carly's. As much as possible, she preferred to fly below the radar.

Then there was Shane. Oh my, he looked good in a tuxedo. If she were being honest, Shane looked hot even when he had on sweaty running shorts and a T-shirt. But when she laid eyes on him tonight, she nearly keeled over in her high heels. Most athletes looked like sausages stuffed into a tux, their necks too wide for the collar or their thighs bulging out of their pants. But not Shane. He looked like he just stepped out of a 1950s nightclub. And he was being sweet. Almost as if he sensed how stressed she was by having to spend the evening with her father and stepmother.

They were seated at a round table just next to the dais, surrounded by her nieces and nephew, Matt's parents and Penny, who was escorted by one of the team's crusty offensive line coaches. The dinner had been enjoyable with the old coach and Mr. Richardson trading stories, each more colorful than the next, until Penny and Mrs. Richardson had reminded both men that "little ears" were present. Shane seemed to be enjoying himself, too. The strain she'd perceived during that first dinner with the family not evident this evening. He joked with the older men at the table and paid equal attention to the kids. He and C.J. spent part of dinner discussing cars and football, C.J. apparently having left his surly demeanor at home. At times, Molly stood between Shane's and Carly's shoulders, watching as Shane played a game on her pink Nintendo DS.

"I wonder what's on the menu for dessert?" Mr. Richardson asked, patting his belly and winking at his grandchildren.

"Chocolate mousse cheesecake," Penny said.

"Aunt Carly's favorite!" Emma clapped her hands.

"With lots of whipped cream, I'll bet," Shane said softly. Carly quickly turned to glance at him. He was leaning toward her, his shoulder lightly touching hers. His forearms rested on the table as he openly grinned at her, that errant lock of hair tempting her to touch it. She blushed for the umpteenth time that evening. *Oh God, he had noticed all those whipped topping bowls in her kitchen.* Taking another sip of wine she shouldn't be drinking, she turned away from his knowing grin.

"Has anyone seen Molly?" Matt stood behind his son, looking around the table.

"She went to the bathroom awhile ago, Dad," Emma said.

"She probably fell in." Apparently her nephew hadn't left his attitude entirely at home. Matt lightly smacked him on the head.

"You promised me," he said through clenched teeth.

"I'll go get her," Matt's mother said as she rose from her seat, placing her napkin on the table.

"No, Mom." He stilled her with a hand on her shoulder. "The governor wants to meet you all. He's on his way over."

"I'll do it," Carly said, pushing away from the table. "I need to freshen up anyway. And, I've already met the governor," she teased him.

"Hurry back," he said. "Lisa wants to start the program soon."

Carly waved in acknowledgment and traversed her way through the crowded ballroom. No sooner had she made it to the main lobby when she spotted Molly. A woman dressed in a tuxedo played a ragtime tune on the grand piano in the foyer while Molly sat on a stuffed chair behind her, feet swinging in time with the music, her face buried in her video game.

"Molls," Carly said, stopping in front of her chair. Her niece looked up with a sheepish grin. "Your dad is looking for you. They're going to start the program in a little bit and he wants you back at the table."

Molly sighed as she turned off her game. "Do I have to? It's so loud in there!" But she was already standing, carefully tucking the game in her small purse. Carly smiled and brushed the girl's hair back over one shoulder.

"Sorry, pumpkin, but you've got to be a team player. Tonight's important to your mom." Carly tweaked her under the chin. "I've got to use the restroom. You go back to the table and make sure they leave me a big piece of cheesecake, okay?"

Molly suddenly reached forward and grabbed Carly in a fierce hug.

"Aunt Carly," she mumbled, her face buried against Carly's stomach. "Thanks for making my mom better."

Swallowing a lump in her throat, she leaned down to kiss the top of Molly's head.

"You're welcome," she whispered. "Now, get back in there!"

Her niece released her and, with a quicksilver grin, hopped back into the ballroom.

It took great effort to keep the tears at bay. Carly hurried to the restroom before anyone noticed. Glancing at herself in the mirror as she passed through the ladies' room, she was surprised by her reflection. The woman looking back at her was poised and beautiful. Not exactly how Carly felt.

The dress Julianne designed for her was exquisite. Dressed like this, she looked like one of the portraits of her English ancestors hanging in her late grandmother's estate. She wondered if her mother had felt the same way. By all accounts, Veronica had been quite the rebel, turning her back on her place in English society—on her family—to work as a foreign news correspondent. Carly's recollections of her mother were from the standpoint of a young girl. At times, Carly wished she could have known her as an adult. Perhaps she would have understood her better.

Really, what was she doing thinking of her mother? Molly's thank-you was turning her into a sap. She needed to pee and get back to the ballroom.

A few minutes later, she finished touching up the damage her unshed tears had caused to her eye makeup, then snapped her evening bag shut authoritatively.

"Get ahold of yourself," she whispered to her reflection in the mirror. "No more wine. Just coffee and cheesecake." She couldn't afford to be tipsy around Shane. He'd been playing Prince Charming all night; the safe date. But Carly was getting tired of constantly denying the attraction between them. She needed to get this night over with before she did something stupid. Something that might make her happy for tonight. But that type of happiness would only be temporary, she was sure of it.

Charging out of the ladies' room into the now empty hallway, she suddenly collided with a man standing directly outside the door. Two hands grabbed her bare forearms a little too tightly. Startled, Carly looked up into the eyes of Joel Tompkins. A very high Joel Tompkins. Quickly glancing around for someone to help her, Carly tried to yank her arms free, but Joel held her tighter. He smiled, his big white teeth a little too close for comfort.

"Well, well. Look who we have here." His breath reeked, causing bile to rise up in the back of her throat. She didn't know what he wanted. He certainly wasn't an invited guest. Especially dressed as he was in a Grateful Dead T-shirt, black cargo pants, and flip-flops.

"Damn, Carly. You look hot," he said, pulling her closer to him. "It's just you and me. Alone. Finally." Leaning in, he began to kiss her neck. Pressing her hands on his chest, she tried to push him away. Her breath came in quick staccato beats and she couldn't get enough air to speak. She barely managed a squeak when he bit her along the collarbone.

"Joel, let me go! You're hurting me!" She forced the words out. But he didn't seem to hear her. Panic spread through her body. Her heart was beating too quickly and her skin felt clammy. She opened her mouth to scream and he closed in. She gagged as his tongue swept through her mouth. Her struggle against him proved futile. So she resorted to the only option left to her: She bit his tongue. Hard.

"Oww," he cried, pulling away from her, wiping at his mouth. "What did you do that for?"

Carly wiped at her own mouth. "Joel," she said, her voice raspy and a bit unsteady. "Get away from me."

"But Carly, you want this. You want me." He moved toward her as she pressed her back to the wall. Clearly, this guy was delusional. Looking around quickly, she weighed her options as he reached out for her again.

Suddenly, Joel was no longer holding her and she slid down the wall. The sounds of fist meeting bone filled the air as a huge shape wrestled with Joel. She tried to stand, but she was afraid of getting caught in the melee. A low growl escaped one of the men as a head hit the wall. She wasn't sure if it was Joel or her rescuer.

"Shane!" Donovan grabbed at the huge body standing over Joel. "What the hell are you doing?"

She should have known it was Shane.

"You okay, sweetie?" Asia was sliding down the wall next to Carly.

Donovan turned at the sound of Asia's voice. He obviously hadn't seen Carly until that moment. His hands were in fists as he turned back to Joel's body slumped on the floor.

And then, as if things couldn't get any worse, the bright flicker of a camera flash went off in Carly's face.

"Let me see if I can get this straight," Hank Osbourne said. Carly was sitting in the office of the hotel's general manager. Lisa and Shane were crowded on either side of the sofa with her. The jacket of Shane's tuxedo was draped around her shoulders, but Carly still couldn't seem to stop shivering. Lisa gently rubbed a hand over Carly's back. Matt stood in the doorway like a sentry, his arms crossed over his chest. Hank paced the room, pinching his nose between his fingers.

"The quarterback whom we've paraded around Baltimore these past two weeks to dispel his reputation as a hotheaded, rebellious smart-ass just pummeled some guy unconscious in a downtown hotel," Hank said, his normally taciturn composure threatening to explode.

Shane shifted beside her. "It was one punch," he mumbled. "I swear I only hit him once and the jerk crumpled."

"That jerk, Devlin, is the grandson of a very powerful man in this city. His grandfather was sitting in the dining room with the rest of us. Now he's threatening to press charges," Hank yelled.

Surging to his feet, Shane got right in Hank's face. "I don't give a shit who that stoner's grandfather is! He was all over Carly. Guys like that . . ." Shane shook his head in disgust. "But I didn't pummel him. I only threw *one punch.*"

Matt grabbed Shane and forced him back onto the sofa, pressing a hand to his shoulder to keep him seated. Hank stood before them, hands on his hips pushing his tuxedo jacket open. Carly felt like she was in the principal's office awaiting expulsion.

"Hank, Shane didn't start this. Joel did!" Carly tried to intercede on Shane's behalf.

"Well, I guess we'll just see how the incident went down because apparently there's film at eleven," the GM ground out.

"Not again," Carly groaned, burying her face in her hands. Lisa wrapped her arm around Carly's shoulder.

Not for the first time in her life, Carly was in the wrong place at the wrong time when the media were watching. It was bad enough Joel had put his hands—and mouth—on her, but now the paparazzi could blow the incident out of proportion. What was it about her that the media found so fascinating? She'd already been run out of Italy and a job she liked by the actions of a man and the overzealous media he practically commanded. Surely it wouldn't happen again.

Worst of all, Shane was telling the truth. Joel *had* collapsed after one punch. Apparently he couldn't hold his liquor or his drugs. The facts would win out and the Blaze would probably be able to protect Shane. But who would protect Carly from the evening entertainment shows? She wasn't a celebrity, but by virtue of the fact that her mother and her former fiancé were, she had to suffer the media scrutiny. Well, she'd had her fifteen minutes of fame—and then some. The thought of enduring more made her sick.

"Hank," Lisa said. "Could we please not forget about Carly?"

Hank rubbed his hand over his head before crouching down on his knees in front of the sofa. "I'm sorry, Carly. Nobody should have to go through what you did with Tompkins. We'll make this right. The Blaze organization is a family, and we take care of our own." Hank took one of her hands and squeezed it gently. The warmth in Hank's eyes did a great deal to calm Carly's racing nerves.

Donovan hustled into the room. "The bartender told police Tompkins had three drinks in the hour before he confronted Carly. He also said Tompkins was pretty wasted when he arrived. Police are taking his statement now."

"Can the police ask for drug and alcohol tests while he's in the ER?" Hank asked.

"Already done," Donovan said.

"Good," Hank said. "That'll give me something to bargain with in convincing the grandfather not to press charges."

Donovan handed a disk to Hank. "Surveillance tapes. The hotel gave me the originals. Their security chief is a friend. Also, the photographer in the hallway is just a hotel patron. Asia convinced him that season tickets to the Blaze and a comp hotel room for every game were a better bargain than whatever the picture would be worth to someone else." He winked at Carly and she was finally able to breathe normally.

"Nice work," Hank said, pocketing the disk. "Let's hope my negotiations with the grandfather go as well. I suggest you two quietly leave the hotel. The media know something is up since the police were called, but I'd rather we control the spin on this."

They all stood and walked out of the office, Lisa's arm draped over Carly's shoulder. Hank was examining Shane's hand.

"Get some ice on that," he said. He walked over and gave Carly a gruff kiss on the cheek. "You get some rest. I'll see you on Monday." He made his way back to the ballroom, presumably to speak with Joel's grandfather.

Matt was next. He took Carly in his arms and brushed his lips over the top of her head before handing her off to his wife.

Lisa gave her a squeeze. "You call me if you need me. No matter what! Promise?" she demanded.

"I promise. Now go and wow them with your speech." Carly shooed her sister and brother-in-law away, offering them a forced smile as they left. Once they disappeared into the ballroom, Carly turned to Shane. Gently, he put his hand on her back and guided her over to the concierge desk. He reached for his jacket. Carly began to shrug it off her shoulders, but Shane pulled it closed instead.

"Huh-uh," he said, his warm breath stirring the tendrils of hair along her forehead. "I just need my valet stub." He reached into the breast pocket of the jacket, lightly brushing her bare shoulder. She took a calming breath as heat rose in her belly. Apparently not even being accosted by a drug-crazed creep could temper her body's reaction to Shane. He retrieved the ticket and put his hands on her shoulders, gently easing her down onto an upholstered bench tucked behind the concierge.

"I'll be right back. Sit. Stay," he commanded her. Carly raised her chin to stare at him, arching an eyebrow for good measure.

"I'm not Beckett."

"No, you're not." He leaned down to whisper in her ear, his lips brushing the sensitive skin on her neck. "You smell better." Shane smiled. And Carly felt her heart flutter. He was the same man who'd been charming her all night. Except now she was looking at him differently. He'd just put his position on the team in jeopardy so he could help her. She returned his smile with a genuine one of her own. He froze for a minute and she thought he might say something. Instead, he clucked her on the chin.

Carly slowly leaned back against the wall as she watched Shane walk away. He stopped to speak sternly to the hotel security guard who was following them discreetly and then left her there in search of the valet. She closed her eyes as she waited for him, her inner self telling her she could trust Shane. The prickling sense of fear she felt whenever she was around Joel wasn't evident when Shane was near. He'd come to her aid tonight. She hated that Hank was so ready to accuse him of being a bully, when Shane was really the hero in all of this. Heck, the man even rescued lost dogs. What would the media think of that? She smiled to herself. Yes, she could trust Shane to keep her safe. Too bad he wasn't the type of guy she could trust with her heart.

Eight

Shane was still seething as he held the passenger door to his Lincoln Navigator open for Carly. As elegantly as was possible considering the circumstances, she climbed up into the SUV, gathering the skirt of her dress up under her. The car wasn't exactly made for women in high heels and evening gowns, but he didn't like cramming himself inside a tiny sports car. He needed space. As he walked around to the driver's side, he ripped at his bow tie and unbuttoned his shirt collar. Enough of the monkey suit.

Climbing in beside Carly, his hands tightly gripped the steering wheel. He took a deep breath before glancing over at her. She sat with her eyes closed, her head leaning back against the headrest. *Man, what a night,* he thought as he looked out over the hotel's drive. He could have killed that bastard Tompkins. If Donovan hadn't come along, he very well might have. Thoughts of what might have happened if he hadn't gone looking for Carly made his palms sweat. He didn't even know why he'd gone looking for her, except that he missed her. Boredom had set in within two minutes of her leaving the table. Trying to calm his thoughts, he dragged in another breath.

"You okay?" Carly asked softly. He turned to look at her. The interior of the car was dark, but he could see her cheek silhouetted against the streetlights. Reaching over, he traced a finger along the spot on her shoulder where Joel had grabbed her.

"I should be asking you that," he said. "I don't think he left too much of a mark."

"I'm fine." Her battle cry for the past hour. She gave him another one of those fake grins she'd given to her sister and Coach. The darkness of the car's interior obscured her eyes. He desperately wanted to know if she was really okay.

"Let's just go home," she said. With a sigh, he started the car. He slid in a jazz CD and Carly once again rested her head against the seatback. She seemed content to just be in the car with him. He was astounded at how well she was taking the events of the past hour. Most women he knew would be hysterical by now, but not Carly. Growing up in a media fishbowl had obviously toughened her up. It was almost as if she were resigned to her fate. The thought made Shane's gut clench.

Braking for a red light, he looked over at her again. She was still leaning against the headrest, but her eyes were open and she was staring at him.

"Thank you," she said.

"We're not there yet. Don't thank me until you've arrived at your door in one piece."

Her lips curved into a soft smile as she gently shook her head from side to side.

"No. Thank you for earlier. For, you know, dealing with Joel."

Shane swallowed. God, she made it sound so simple. As if guys tried to force themselves on her and she needed rescuing all the time. His fists clenched more tightly on the steering wheel until his knuckles were white.

"Don't mention it. I have a reputation as a brawler, remember?" he quipped.

Gnawing on her bottom lip, she reached over to lightly caress his right hand where it rested on the steering wheel. He flinched as she grazed a bruised knuckle.

"Does it hurt?" she asked, quickly pulling her hand away. He hadn't flinched from pain, but he didn't bother telling her that. This was getting complicated. The sooner he got her home and got the hell away, the better. He needed his familiar safety net of isolation.

"No," he said as he lifted the bruised hand and flexed it.

"Hank won't sleep a wink until a trainer looks at it on Monday."

"It'll be fine by then. Don't worry."

The light turned green and Shane focused his attention back on the road. The only sounds in the car were the purr of the engine and John Legend's piano. His plans for a quick getaway evaporated as they reached her town house. She hadn't bothered to leave a light on. Silently, she sat staring at her front door. Shane would be a heel to let her go in alone after the night she'd had. Not to mention the coach would have his balls if he did. Getting out of the car, he walked around to help her out of the passenger side. She didn't say a word as he reached in the back to take out a foam container. Gently, he guided her up the steps and stood as she unlocked the door. Her hand didn't shake, which he supposed was a good sign. Turning on lights as he went, he guided her into the house. When he walked into the kitchen, he carefully placed the container on the counter. He turned to find Carly standing directly behind him, one hand still clutching the lapels of his jacket around her neck. She looked calmer, more like herself, here in the light of her kitchen. Definitely a good sign.

"What's in there?" she asked, gesturing to the container.

"Ahh," he said, pleased with himself. "Dessert to go." He opened the container to reveal a perfect slice of chocolate mousse cheesecake, complete with whipped cream and a raspberry on top. Carly's face lit up. A man can never go wrong giving a woman chocolate.

"Where did you get that?"

"I had the waiter box up your piece while I was getting the car. You seemed so excited about the dessert when you were talking with your nieces; I didn't want you to miss it." Shane also wanted to erase the look of vulnerability he'd seen on her face when he'd come upon Joel mauling her in the hallway. He was still coming to terms with the scene himself, and he could only imagine how Carly felt. No woman should ever have to go through what she'd endured earlier. Shane didn't regret punching the little prick. He'd have done it for any woman. The fact that it had been Carly getting attacked hadn't made his reaction any more intense. At least that was what he was telling himself.

"You didn't bring yourself a piece?" she asked. "I suppose I could be persuaded to share. After all, you did beat up a guy for me earlier." He absently rubbed at his chest in reaction to the pleasure flickering in her eyes. Despite everything that had happened this evening, the attraction between them still hummed. Common sense dictated that he leave her safely tucked away in her home with her dessert and get the hell out of Dodge.

"In that case, bring on the forks." Apparently, he'd left his common sense out in the car. Taking a seat on the bar stool at the end of the counter, he watched as she bustled around the kitchen, transferring the cake to a plate and grabbing two forks. She pulled two mugs from a cabinet.

"Would you like some coffee? It's decaf."

Hell no! He needed a stiff drink after the night he'd had. "Sure," he said instead.

She filled the carafe and turned on the brewer, then reached into the freezer and pulled out an ice pack.

"Here, put this on your hand. I'm just going to clean up a little while the coffee brews." She slipped out of his jacket and laid it carefully on the other bar stool. Shane's breath hissed as he saw the mark Tompkins had left on her neck. She followed his gaze and reached up to rub the spot.

"It doesn't hurt," she said. "Lisa must have put a whole tube of antibiotic cream on it." She disappeared upstairs somewhere as Shane unclipped his cuff links and rolled up his sleeves. As he looked around for a TV remote, he put the ice pack on his battered hand. Although given the way his body was reacting to Carly, he'd be smart to put it somewhere else. Of course, if Shane were really smart, he wouldn't be sitting in her kitchen.

Carly brushed her teeth for a full five minutes. Lisa had cleaned and disinfected the bruise Joel left on her neck while they were waiting for the police. But now Carly needed to get the taste of him out of her mouth. She really should take a shower and crawl into bed, but Lisa had been right, Carly didn't want to be alone. Shane Devlin was the last person she should be alone with, but her family was still at the gala. Certainly she could have a cup of coffee with the man without losing her head. Unclipping her hair, she brushed it out, removing the heavy sapphire dangle earrings as she went. She decided to leave the dress on. Shane was still in his tux, after all.

Shane had no trouble locating the remote to her TV and was watching *SportsCenter* when she came downstairs. When he saw her, he changed the channel to the cable company's jazz station. Pouring them each a cup of coffee, she took a seat on the opposite bar stool.

"Well, at least he didn't tear your dress," Shane said out of nowhere.

"Ohmigod! Can you imagine?" Carly laughed as she stirred cream and sugar into her mug. "Julianne would hunt him down and castrate him if he had!"

Shane chuckled as he took a sip of his coffee.

"How'd you and Julianne meet anyway?" he asked.

"Boarding school," she said wistfully. "Molly likes to think it was a scene out of *The Parent Trap*, but nothing could be further from the truth. The headmistress put us together because we had both lived mostly in Europe—Julianne's father is an ambassador—and we'd both recently lost our mothers. Aside from that, though, we had nothing in common. She is artistic—which is a polite way of saying she's a bit of a slob to share a room with. And she was the ultimate party girl in school. She knew everyone on campus and they all loved her. I, on the other hand, just wanted to bury my nose in a book and have everyone ignore me. I'd been homeschooled by my mom as we traveled around for her work, and boarding school was my first real exposure to the whole school experience." Carly took a sip of her coffee, her mind drifting back through the years.

"Julianne is a force of nature," she said with a grin. "She wasn't going to let me hide out in our dorm room. The other girls weren't as friendly, really cliquey. I was kind of the odd girl out with a very different life experience. The other girls weren't quite sure what to do with me and I didn't really have the social skills to stand up for myself. Julianne took me under her wing. I think I was her first pet project. She didn't care about what the other girls said about it. That's when I realized that Julianne was her own person and always would be. I've been devoted to her ever since."

"Your friend was speaking Italian in Cabo. One of the bartenders at the resort claimed she was from a mob family. Was he telling the truth?" he asked, a little in awe.

"No." She laughed. "Her brother is a U.S. senator! I think Julianne secretly wished she was a Mafia princess. Her way of dealing with her mother's death was to create a whole fantasy life. It's what makes her such a fabulous designer today."

Carly looked up from her coffee at Shane. His eyes were dark and contemplative. She almost asked him how he had dealt with his own mother's death, but given his track record of avoiding all conversations involving his family, she decided against it.

"It helped that we both bonded against our evil stepmothers. Her father remarried a twenty-seven-year-old flight attendant from Brazil. She's only a year younger than Julianne's brother. Can you imagine?" she asked.

"Is she hot?" Shane asked, a lopsided grin on his face. Carly rolled her eyes at him.

"Of course!" She laughed. "Why else would we hate her?"

"Hugh and your stepmother aren't hard to hate, either," he said. His face had hardened again.

"Yeah, well, you can't really blame them." It had become second nature to Carly to defend them. "They weren't exactly looking for another kid. They've mostly let me be."

Shane shook his head and huffed.

"What about your dad?" she asked in an attempt to change the subject. "Do you see him much?"

He stiffened in the chair. When he raised his eyes to her, they were black as night. Too late, she realized that her attempt to change the subject had only increased Shane's ire.

"No," he said. Draining his coffee, he set the mug down on the counter with a thump. "He's not a part of my life and I'm not a part of his."

"Why?" She regretted asking as soon as the word left her mouth. This wasn't a safe topic. She could feel it.

Abruptly standing, he paced a circle around her small living room, running his hands through his hair as he walked. When he turned to her, his face was taut with strain. He seemed to be debating something with himself. But then he spoke, his voice soft but lethal.

"The other day, you asked me if I had a problem with my dad."

It was a statement, but Carly heard the question implied within. She tried to swallow, her mouth becoming suddenly dry, not sure whether she should let this conversation continue. Her curiosity got the better of her, though, and she nodded.

Shane let out a brief snort. "The Bruce Devlin the media portrays is a fake. The real-life version is a rotten SOB who abandoned his family when they needed him the most." He paused to run another hand through his hair. When he spoke again, his eyes looked everywhere but at her. "My dad tried to escape the only career option open to him. He didn't want to spend his life as a coal miner. So he worked hard at the one thing he knew. He threw a ball."

Carly's body tensed as Shane spoke. She knew he and his father weren't close, but the vehemence in his voice was

a bit startling. She wasn't sure if she wanted to know the
reasons Shane obviously hated his father.

"I'm not sure how," he continued. "Luck, I guess, but he
got a scholarship at a small university. It was an hour away
from where he grew up, but to him it may as well have been
a continent away. He was the big man on campus from the
day he arrived. The dean of the school worked the media like
a Madison Avenue professional to get attention for my father
and the school. If they only knew what he would turn into."

Carly stifled a shiver at the force of his words. She was
familiar with Bruce Devlin's story, having read the synopsis
of the elder Devlin's best-selling biography when the team
was considering signing Shane. Clasping her hands in her
lap and waiting for rest of the story to unfold, she knew
Shane's version of events would differ from the book.

Shane's voice was a flat monotone as he continued.
"When my dad knocked up a local townie, the dean was the
one holding the shotgun at the wedding. My dad had enough
sense to do what was asked. He knew football was his only
means of escaping the life of all the Devlins before him."

As he began to pace again, Carly's hands gripped the
seat of the bar stool.

"He married my mother, but that was it. They were like
two kids playing house when I was born. He won the Heisman, got drafted in the top three picks, and promptly set my
mom and me up in a house in West Chester, Pennsylvania.
I'm not even sure he ever lived with us. He showed up for
photo spreads and Christmas card pictures, but not much
else. He was just going through the motions with us."

Shane looked at her then. She opened her mouth to speak,
but thought better of it. Her heart ached for the little boy
Shane had been. It was a childhood she could easily relate to.

"Yeah, I know what you are thinking," he said, his tone
clipped and bitter. "He was just a kid. But so was I. So was
my mother." His voice softened as he spoke of her. "She was
great. She took me everywhere. She did everything with me.
When I started school, I think it broke her heart to have me
gone all day. Of course, this was around the time my dad

blew out his shoulder. Instead of coming home, he began the drinking and the drugs. My mother got sick when I was in the second grade. She suffered through two years of chemo while my father boozed and snorted his way around the country feeling sorry for himself. He showed up a couple of weeks before she died."

"He seems to have gotten his life back on track now," Carly said softly. Shane whirled on her, his eyes angrier than Joel's had been earlier. Surprisingly, she didn't feel the same fear. Reining in his temper, he stared at her. Briefly, she glimpsed the vulnerable boy he'd once been, but then he tamped down the emotion.

"Yeah. Like your friend's father, he went and got himself a trophy wife and a new family." He didn't bother to keep the bitterness from his voice.

"Don't you ever see your half brother?" she asked. Carly couldn't imagine not having Lisa in her life.

"No," he all but sneered at her. "They keep the good child away from the bad seed."

"Oh, Shane," Carly said as she stood and walked over to him. She stopped inches from him, the tension rolling off his body in waves. Not trusting herself to keep from touching him, she wrapped her arms around her middle. They stood like that, toe to toe, staring at one another for several minutes before Shane closed his eyes, seemingly fighting his own inner battles.

"You know what I think, Shane Devlin?" she whispered. A muscle twitched on the side of his mouth as he opened his steely eyes. "I think the bad-boy persona you've cultivated all these years is just a ruse. A way to get back at your dad for hurting you. You'd like everyone to think you're a selfish jerk, but I know for a fact you're not."

His eyes hardened at her words and Shane stepped around her to pace her small living room.

"Wow, Carly," he tossed over his shoulder. "You've been reading your sister's psychoanalysis books. That's quite a diagnosis."

Lisa would have a field day psychoanalyzing Shane,

Carly thought as she turned to watch him pace. But she wasn't being fair. She hated when her sister analyzed her. Although something told her peeling back Shane Devlin's layers would be a much tougher challenge for Lisa.

Carly wanted to say she was sorry. Sorry for what he had gone through. Sorry for bringing the subject up. But she knew how empty the words would sound. She'd heard them too many times in reference to her own life. So she tried to steer the conversation back to lighter waters.

"Well," she said, clearing the coffee mugs. "Your story earns you sympathy, but you won't get the big box of tissues until it's been played out on the big screen and on cable every week."

Shane stood in the center of the room, hands on his hips. She'd startled him, she knew, but after a few seconds, he shook his head and laughed. The sound resonated throughout the small area. Carly crossed her arms under her breasts and stared at him. The action seemed to startle him more. He slowly walked over to her, the hunger returning to his eyes. Her breath hitched. He glanced down at the cheesecake on the counter beside her and a slow grin spread over his face.

"I go to all the trouble to snare you your favorite dessert and you haven't even touched it." He shook his head at her as he sat on the bar stool and speared a piece of the cheesecake with a fork.

Carly's mouth went dry again. Shane was waving the fork in front of her face until she had no choice but to open. The dessert tasted like sawdust, but the whipped cream was cool to her hot lips. She licked some off her lower lip. Shane swallowed. His knuckles were white where he gripped the fork. Reverently, he closed his eyes.

"Dammit, Carly," he whispered. "I'm so tired of avoiding this."

She took a step closer and stood between his knees, gently placing a hand on each of his hard thighs. His eyes shot open.

"So am I." It was as if another woman had taken over her

body. Carly knew she should not be getting involved with Shane, but she didn't care anymore. He was right; she was tired of avoiding the incredible pull between them, too.

He put his hands on her waist, his thumbs reverently caressing her hip bones.

"Maybe"—his breath fanned her ear as she swayed into him—"we should just go ahead and get it out of our systems. Then we can move on to being . . ."

"Friendly coworkers?" she finished for him, her lips tracing his jaw.

"With benefits," he said just before his mouth seized hers. When he swept his tongue in, she met it with her own, his erection jumping against her stomach. Like their previous encounters, the heat between them was almost instantaneous. She feverishly kissed him back, her hands dragging through his hair. His fingers fisted in the flimsy fabric of her dress as he bit her bottom lip. Suddenly, he tore his mouth away and rubbed his hands on her bare arms, pushing her back slightly.

"Carly." His voice was raspy as he struggled for control. Her arms tingled where he rubbed them. He leaned his forehead against hers as he caught his breath. "I've been fantasizing about getting you out of this dress all night. But right now, if I touch it, I'll rip it."

She smiled provocatively as she took a step out of his warm embrace. Her eyes never left his as she reached up behind her head and untied the knot holding her dress in place. His eyes followed the fabric as it slithered down her body and pooled at her feet. He stood as his gaze slowly traveled back up her body, taking in her silk stockings, the garter belt that held them up, and her lacy bustier. He let out a slow breath that came out sounding a lot like *holy shit*.

"That may be better than the dress," he whispered.

Stepping over the fabric lying in a heap on the floor, Carly trailed her fingers up his torso and began to undo the studs on his shirt. Strong fingers traced along the skin of her back, leaving a trail of heat in their path. She kissed his throat as she continued her task, slowly rubbing her lower body against him. His lips cruised over her shoulders. Carly winced as his mouth came in contact with the bruise Joel had given her.

"Jesus, Carly!" He jerked back, his hands dropping to his sides as if she'd burned him. "I shouldn't be doing this. Not after what that bastard nearly did to you tonight."

Carly fisted her hands in his shirt, trying to pull him closer. She didn't want to lose contact. Shane's face was drawn, a sheen of perspiration forming on his forehead.

"No," she begged. "Don't you dare stop now, Shane. I need you. I need to feel a man's hands on me. A man whose hands I *want* to feel on me. Please!" The last came out in a desperate whisper.

"God, Carly. The last thing I want to do is hurt you." But he'd stopped backing away. His eyes were more focused again. Their smoldering heat focused on her lips. She leaned back into the circle of his arms. With one hand, she cupped the back of his neck, bringing his mouth down toward hers. With the other, she cupped his still-throbbing erection.

"You won't hurt me," she said before kissing him. Contemplating the reasons she trusted this man so implicitly would have to be for another time. Carly just wanted to shut her mind off and lose herself in the warm body standing in front of her.

Whatever chivalrous objections Shane had were gone once she started kissing him. He shed his shirt in one easy move. Pushing down Carly's bustier, he gently bent her over the back of the bar stool, giving him better access to her nipple. As he wrapped his mouth around it, a breathy sigh escaped her and she lightly ran her nails down his muscled back. Heat pooled between her legs and her caresses became more urgent. He responded by taking a nipple in his mouth and sucking. Carly moaned, snaking a leg up the back of his thigh.

"Wrap your legs around me," he urged before taking her mouth in another deep kiss. Lifting her up, he carried her over to the sofa. Gingerly, he laid her down on her back, his mouth never leaving hers. She kept her legs wrapped around him, her hips grinding against his erection. She was so incredibly aroused that she nearly came as her body rubbed against his vibrating arousal.

Vibrating?

"Shane!" she cried as she pulled out of the kiss. "Oh. My. God!"

He jerked up on his forearms and reached into his pants pocket and pulled out his cell phone. Carly felt the blush spread from her face to her exposed chest. How embarrassing! She'd nearly climaxed because of his cell phone. She couldn't help it; a giggle escaped.

"And I thought you had magic power in those pants," she teased. Absently, he placed the cell phone on the photo shelf above their heads. A sly smile came over his face as he looked at her. A lock of hair hung in the middle of his forehead. His eyes deepened to a smoky gray.

"One of those girls, huh?" His voice was husky as he slid farther down her belly, his long legs hanging off the sofa's edge.

"Shane!" Her body was so tense, she jumped as his tongue cruised the inside of her navel.

Shane just shook his head and crawled lower. Expertly, he unsnapped her garters and skimmed a fingertip between her legs. Another moan escaped her. He dragged his tongue against her inner thigh; his five-o'clock shadow stung as it brushed against the tender skin. Her hips bucked at the pain and the pleasure of it. Pressing them back down with one hand, the other dipped between her thighs. Watching her intently, he slowly placed a finger inside her.

"Please, Shane," she said, reaching out to grab his shoulders. "Come back so I can touch you."

"Huh-uh," he mumbled. "You'll get your chance. Right now, I want to show you that the real thing is better than the toys." Grinning widely, he slowly lowered his chin, his eyes never leaving hers. With his finger he stroked her intimately, following it up with his tongue. Throwing her head back against the cushions, she gasped for breath as he tasted her with his mouth. She dragged her hands through his hair as his tongue pulsed inside her. He found her sweet spot and coaxed it with his tongue. Carly's back arched as she came, brilliant shards of light dancing behind her eyelids. He sucked harder and she heard a scream: hers. Her body was too satisfied to register any embarrassment.

"Oh God, Shane, that's amaz—Oowh!" The vibrating cell phone fell from the shelf, hitting her in the nose.

Swearing, Shane crawled up her body to lie on top of her. His erection throbbed against her thigh as he fished the phone off the floor. Turning the phone on to check the text, he sat up suddenly, Carly's legs scissoring his body. For a long moment, he stared at the phone, the blue light of its text screen shining on his face. Feeling the tension rising up in his body, she bit her lip. Her own body, languid from her orgasm, began to come to life again.

"Shane?" she asked gently, her hand stroking his arm. "What is it?" He didn't answer, continuing to stare blindly ahead. A slow knot of tension began to form in her back as she sat up more fully to caress his shoulder.

"It's my father." She almost didn't hear him, he spoke so softly.

"Bruce called you?"

"No." When he finally turned toward her, she caught a glimpse of true pain on his face. It was fleeting before his eyes became hard again.

"He's dead."

Nine

Troy Devlin sat in the sunroom of his parent's home watching the people milling about. He didn't think their house could hold all these people. They were eating and drinking as if nothing was wrong. He tugged at the collar of the Easter Sunday shirt Consuelo insisted he wear. Everyone else was dressed in black. Consuelo said it was okay for him to wear his light blue dress shirt and his blue blazer. She'd gone to Macy's to get him a new tie, though. It wasn't a clip-on or zipper tie, but a real tie. Except it had footballs and basketballs all over it. His dad would think it was cool. His mom would say he looked grown-up. Tears stung his eyes again. He needed to stop thinking of his mom and dad.

He looked back over the sea of black rolling through his parent's family room. They stood there, their plates heaped with food, chatting and shaking hands, trying to meet the famous people who'd come over after the funeral. Even his travel baseball team was here. They hadn't come to see Troy. His teammates had only come to meet some of his father's friends. Heck, they would probably drop him from the roster now anyway. Every kid on the team knew they'd only picked Troy because of who his dad is.

Was.

Randy Martinelli never let a practice or game go by without making some comment about Troy being a wuss. All because he'd cried the day the ball hit him in the eye. *Well, it had hurt!* His eye was black for nearly two weeks and the doctor said he had a hairline fracture in his eye socket. But all the guys on the team cared about was that he'd dropped the ball. And they'd lost the game.

Troy tried to convince his parents to let him play on one of the local city teams, but his dad would just say that he'd grow into his talent. Travel team was for elite players like Troy, his father would say. He was a Devlin, after all. Troy's mom would just give him a reassuring smile and tell him how handsome he looked in his uniform. But he'd seen the looks they would exchange when they thought he wasn't looking. He sucked at baseball—even worse than he sucked at football—and they all knew it. He wasn't like the rest of the Devlins. Not anything like his dad. Or his brother.

Glancing across the room, his eyes landed on Shane. He'd waited all these years to meet his famous big brother and there he was, leaning a hip against his mother's curio cabinet and scowling. His dad always said it would take something big to get Shane to come visit them. Well, he was right. Troy had been so relieved to see him yesterday he'd jumped into Shane's arms, so glad someone was there to take care of him. But Shane, the big jerk, must think hugging was for girls, because he couldn't wait to get away from Troy. He didn't seem all that sad that Dad was dead. Heck, Shane had barely said one word to him.

Slumping farther back against the wall, Troy tried to inconspicuously wipe away a tear. He couldn't believe his parents were dead. Two days ago they were flying to Ohio to meet a potential player. They never made it. Instead, the plane his dad was flying had some sort of engine trouble and crashed. The state trooper who'd come to the door said they died instantly. The officer got down on one knee, placing a big hand on Troy's shoulder, explaining everything in a soft, soothing voice. He probably thought it would make Troy feel better. It didn't. His parents were never coming back.

"Mister Troy?"

Furiously wiping another tear away, Troy turned to face Consuelo. Her eyes were as red rimmed and swollen as his. She gave him a wobbly smile as she brushed his hair off his face. Usually he didn't like when she tried to mother him, but today it was okay. She was the only mother he had left. He swallowed to keep the tears from coming back.

"Your grandmama, she wants you to come and say goodbye to some of the guests, okay?" Consuelo made everything sound like a question. Troy's dad would always make a joke about it.

"The cat threw up in your breakfast, okay?" his dad would tease. Or, "Your shoes, they have dog crap on them, okay?" Troy would always laugh. But not today. Taking a last swipe at his eyes with his sleeve, he stood up. He didn't want to stand around while his grandparents paraded him in front of the people who'd taken over his house. He just wanted everyone to get out. The sooner he got to bed, the sooner he could wake up from this rotten dream. *Surely, it was all just a dream.*

Consuelo's eyes were pleading with him. Troy sighed, resigned to not let her down. She'd been taking care of their family since he was five. Right now, she was the only other person in the world who was truly sad his parents were dead. His grandparents didn't seem too upset his dad was gone. According to his mom, they'd never forgiven her for marrying Dad because he used to do drugs and stuff. Mom told Troy that Dad needed her.

"It was the best thing I ever did," she'd say. "Because then I had you! And you and Daddy are all my prayers answered." It was how she ended their bedtime prayer every night, just before kissing Troy good night.

Gulping back a sob, he tried to summon up his best swagger, only to end up shuffling his feet in the direction of his grandmother holding court in the foyer. Following Consuelo across the room, he chanced a quick look out of the corner of his eye at his brother. No help there. Troy felt his shoulders slump a little more.

He wanted to pray to God for help, but he was kind of mad at Him right now. Nope, Troy was on his own now. Both God and his big brother had let him down. Troy resolutely let Consuelo steer him across the room.

Shane took a sip from his glass of iced tea as he watched the housekeeper lead the kid through the crowded room. He'd been crying, Shane was sure of it. The kid had been fighting back tears all day. Earlier, at the funeral, the kid hadn't shed a single tear. But when he thought no one was looking, the tears snuck out.

Shane's palms began to sweat as his mind wandered back to another funeral and another little boy who didn't dare cry; Shane hadn't wanted to give his father the satisfaction. Memories of Bruce hovering in the back of his grandmother's small living room played in Shane's mind. No one bothered to go near Bruce, taking his red eyes and swollen nose as a sign of profound sadness over his wife's death. But Shane had known the truth. His father didn't give a damn about his mother's death. Fooling them all, he'd stood bracing up the living room wall because he was stoned, the drugs and alcohol giving him the look of ravaged despondency. Bruce had been biding his time until all the guests left and he could raid his wife's jewelry box to finance his next fix.

Ten years later, Bruce confessed this sin in his sanctimonious tell-all biography that topped the best-seller lists for six months. He'd written that his biggest regret of that day was hawking his Super Bowl ring. Shane stopped reading at that point, hurling the book off his balcony into the Pacific Ocean.

Shaking his head to clear the memories, he bit down on a piece of ice, glancing at the kid over the rim of his glass. Bruce's son wasn't what Shane had expected. Not that he was an expert on kids, but Shane was sure Bruce's was small for his age. Unlike his Devlin brethren, he was light, with dirty blond hair and his mother's beauty pageant green eyes. They'd never met before, but that hadn't stopped the kid from flinging himself into Shane's arms when he'd arrived yesterday morning. The unexpected display of affection caught Shane off guard and it had taken a moment to untangle from him. The housekeeper standing guard glared at Shane, her mouth set in a grim line. She'd quickly maneuvered the kid back against her chest, her eyes mulish and protective.

Her possessiveness was still evident today as she reluctantly let her hand drop from the kid's shoulders, handing him off to his famous grandparents. The kid quickly shot her a despondent look before she shuffled off to the background once more.

"Something's wrong with that picture," Roscoe said from his perch on the stone fireplace hearth behind Shane.

"What makes you say that?" He took another swallow from his drink.

"I don't know. I just figure kids shouldn't look so uncomfortable around their grandparents." Roscoe pulled his buzzing BlackBerry from the pocket of his suit jacket. "It just seems unnatural, that's all."

Shane watched as the kid stood, wary, between his imposing grandparents. The grandmother wasn't your typical televangelist's wife. She lacked the overdone makeup and the teased hair. Instead, she looked like a society matron with her petite figure and perfectly coiffed, champagne-colored hair. It was easy to see where her daughter got her beauty queen good looks. Today, she was dressed in a somber but elegant black dress, a brittle smile pasted on her face, as fake as the bloodred nails gripping her grandson's shoulder.

"She doesn't strike me as the type to chase the kid around with a wooden spoon," Shane said, fondly recalling his skirmishes with his late grandmother.

"No," Roscoe grunted as his fingers tapped out a message. "She's more the broomstick type."

Shane raised an eyebrow at his friend. His silence forced Roscoe to look up from his BlackBerry.

"Troy doesn't seem to like them too much, that's all. He

seems nervous to be in the same room with them. A fact you might have picked up on had you spent more than thirty seconds conversing with him." Roscoe pushed his glasses back up against his nose, a gesture that always made Shane think he was being flipped off.

"I'm not good with kids," Shane said, turning his attention back to the foyer. "You've got more experience. You're a dad."

Roscoe snorted and glanced back at the screen in his hand. "I hardly think being the father of eighteen-month-old twins qualifies me to console a boy who's just lost his parents. It wouldn't be a stretch for you to relate to how Troy is feeling," he said.

"You know, Roscoe, sometimes you really piss me off."

"It's in my job description." Roscoe shoved his phone back in his pocket. "Before you go about firing me for the bazillionth time, I'm going to go track down Bruce's attorney and find out if we need to be present for the reading of the will. I'd like to get home tonight if possible." He strolled off before Shane could tell him to save his energy. He didn't want anything of his father's, even if he had left him something.

"Excuse me."

Three hundred pounds of solid Samoan stood to Shane's right. The lack of a neck and the beefy forearms identified him as one of his father's offensive lineman. Shane allowed himself to be impressed with Bruce's recruiting efforts. If the tank played with any skill at all, he'd make one a heck of an NFL player someday. Running a mammoth hand through the stubble on his head, the guy seemed to be trying to get up the courage to speak to him. Shane had managed to avoid signing a single autograph the entire day. Apparently, no one had told Tank this was a funeral.

"We were wondering what's gonna happen to Troy?"

Shane wasn't sure what stunned him more: Tank's question or the Mickey Mouse voice he'd used to ask it. It was a good thing the guy was big, because otherwise that voice would bring on a host of problems in a locker room.

"What Tiny's askin', man, is, are *you* gonna take care of Troy now?"

Tiny was obviously nicknamed for his voice, not his size. Shane looked past Tiny to the mouthy black kid who stood next to him. Definitely a ball handler. Shane had been around the game long enough to recognize a running back's demeanor. The two-carat diamond studs in each ear only solidified Shane's perception

Who was going to take care of Troy? Heck if he knew. Shane hadn't given the matter much thought. Truthfully, he hadn't given the matter *any* thought. He assumed that Troy would live with his grandparents now. After all, that's what Shane had done.

"I suppose his grandparents will take him in," Shane said.

"But, dude! You're his brother!" Shane turned to find a third player, the team's pretty boy, standing in the shadow of Tiny's other shoulder. Pretty Boy stuck out his hand and grinned.

"Evan Andrews. Defensive back. It's a real honor to meet you," he said. Shane didn't take his hand. Someone needed to tell Pretty Boy it wasn't considered an honor to meet Shane Devlin.

"E!" The mouthy one was obviously the leader of the trio. "He don't care who you are. He don't care about nobody but himself. Let's go, fellas. This is a waste of time." He sneered at Shane, the diamonds in his ears glittering as he turned on his heel and stalked off. Pretty Boy puffed out his chest to say something, but decided against it before following.

Tiny stared at Shane a moment longer, his baby face and small black eyes a well of sadness, before he tore his gaze away, shuffling off after his teammates. Shane's gut seized up slightly and, once again, he cursed the fact the opinions of others had begun to matter to him. Jeez, he needed to get something to eat. He turned to find Roscoe standing beside him, a plate of food in his hand, disappointment etched on his face.

"Here," he said, shoving the plate at him. "Eat this. Your black soul needs food."

Shane scowled at him, taking the plate. "Then can we go?"

Roscoe put one hand on his hip, running the other through his hair before releasing a deep breath in an exasperated whoosh.

"They're not going to read the will until tomorrow. Apparently it's the reverend's doing." He shrugged his shoulders. "But Bruce's attorney said you need to be present. It looks like neither of us is getting home tonight."

Shane stared down at the plate of food, his appetite forgotten.

"In that case, let's get out of here."

It took nearly fifteen minutes to make it through the crowd of mourners. Sensing his departure, the guests were quick to stop him and pass along a few words of condolence. Everyone from former NFL players to blue-haired ladies from the university's alumni society paused to tell him how sorry they were for his loss. Roscoe earned his paycheck by smiling and nudging him along before Shane could tell them he'd actually lost his father thirty years ago. They'd almost cleared the front door before being stopped by Lou Douglas, the president of the NFL Players Association. Lou was holding court in the foyer, one arm loosely draped over Bruce's kid's shoulder.

"Ah, Shane," Lou said, his booming voice echoing off the chandelier hanging in the alcove above his head. "I was just telling Troy here what a great ball player his old man was. He set a quite an example for young people today."

Come again? Shane could hear the blood roaring up the back of his neck to his brain.

"And I want both you boys to know that I am going to do everything I can to make sure your daddy gets a fair shot at making it into the Football Hall of Fame," Lou said proudly.

For a wiry, one-hundred-seventy-pound, five-foot-ten lawyer, Roscoe sure could move like a defensive back when the pressure was on. Shane wasn't sure how he managed it, but somehow Roscoe got them not only out the door but to the car without Shane punching Lou right on his fat kisser.

Not only that, but he'd called out a polite good-bye, ruffling the kid's hair as he hauled Shane's butt out.

"I really ought to pay you more," Shane said as he took another swallow from his bottle of beer. They had just polished off a plate of nachos and two sirloin burgers at the Old College Inn.

"That's what my wife says every day, dude." Roscoe leaned back against the vinyl booth. Even in the dimly lit bar, Shane could see the frustration in his friend's face. "Seriously, man, you've to get a grip on that temper of yours. I can't even imagine the public relations nightmare it could have been if you'd punched out the league's player rep at your own father's funeral. You keep this up, and I'm going to have to put that PR firm on retainer again."

Shane plopped his elbows on the table, resting his face in his hands. A prolonged sigh escaped as he ran his fingers through his hair.

"Yeah, I know. I can't afford to screw up this chance."

"It could be your last," Roscoe said, pouring salt in the wound.

Shane threw his head back against the high booth back and closed his eyes.

"It's just the hypocrisy of it all. It sticks in my craw," he said through a clenched jaw. "The world thinks Bruce Devlin is a saint. When all he ever was, was a bastard."

"That's always going to depend on where a person's sitting," Roscoe said. Shane's eyes flew open as he braced two hands on the table. Roscoe held a hand up to stop him.

"Hold on, Shane," he said. "I've been on the bad end of this argument way too many times to go at it again tonight. Yeah, your father treated you and your mother poorly. That fact is irrefutable. But you can't change the past. Bruce is dead. Stop letting him dictate your life."

Shane hated that Roscoe always made the same argument. He hated it even more that he was always right.

Snatching up his beer bottle, he chugged the remainder of it down. Bruce's death hadn't dulled Shane's hatred for his father one iota. It was a hatred he'd nurtured on his own for more than twenty years. He couldn't remember exactly when it had started. As a child, he'd been proud to have the Great Bruce Devlin as a dad. He was a professional athlete—a Super Bowl Champ. He'd wonder why his father didn't come home at night, but his mother always had an excuse. *Your father needs to concentrate on his game,* she'd say. *He'll come home after the season.*

But he never did.

Adoration and expectation led only to disappointment, which bred cynicism, eventually leaving him with a hatred that saturated Shane's bones. The emotion was embedded so deeply in his heart, it had become a part of him. It was the one thing that kept him going. It was also the one thing that kept him from fully living. Everyone had forgiven Bruce Devlin. Everyone except Shane.

"Like my father always says, 'you don't get to pick your family, so choose your friends wisely.'" Roscoe looked at his watch. "Speaking of which, I need to get back to the hotel so I can call home." He signaled for the waitress to bring their check. "How's Beckett doing with Darling Carly?"

Shane peeled the label off the beer bottle, not wanting to think about Carly. He hadn't slept the past two nights. And his restlessness had nothing to do with his father's death, either. It had been two days since he'd had his hands on her, yet he could still feel her; he could still taste her. Fate seemed to be stymieing him every time he touched her. Or maybe it was his conscience. He knew any kind of involvement with the coach's sister-in-law could lead to the end of his career. His brain just couldn't get the message to the other parts of his body.

They'd agreed to a one-night stand. One night of sex to get it out of their systems. Jeez, Carly had practically proposed the deal herself. He knew she'd honor the deal. Carly wasn't interested in a relationship with another jock—or the headlines that would surely go with it. Shane needed to focus all his energy on making the team. The sooner he got Carly to bed, or the sofa or the backseat of his SUV, the sooner she'd be out of his system. And they needed to ditch the cell phones first.

Shane refocused his attention to find Roscoe staring at him.

"I asked about Beckett. Shane, tell me nothing is going on with the coach's sister-in-law." He put a strong emphasis on the last two words.

"Nothing's going on," Shane said. It was mostly true.

"Good," Roscoe said, tossing a few bills on the table. "That would be an epic mistake. If you took anything away from that fiasco in San Diego, it's don't mess with team personnel or family. Your career couldn't handle another scandal like that. So keep your hands off her."

As they left the restaurant for the hotel, Shane didn't bother mentioning to Roscoe that he'd have an easier time of controlling his temper than keeping his hands off Carly March.

"I can't believe they let that jerk out of jail!"

"Me neither, Jules," Carly said into her cell phone. "But they didn't have much to hold him on. Besides, his grandfather owns the television station where he works and he has a lot of clout in this town. According to Hank, his grandfather has agreed not to press charges against Shane. Joel is going into rehab, so he won't bother me again."

"And you believe that?" Carly had to hold the phone away from her head. When Julianne got angry, she spoke quickly and loud.

"I don't have any reason not to," Carly said, tucking her feet beneath her in the Adirondack chair. She looked across her meager backyard at Beckett, his big head sniffing beneath the hosta plants surrounding the black maple tree growing against her fence. "His grandfather doesn't want Joel getting into any more trouble, either. It's not the best publicity for the station. Joel just needs a little help, that's all."

Julianne was muttering something in Italian on the other end of the phone and Carly braced herself for her friend's tirade.

"Look, honey," Julianne said. "Haven't the last few years taught you anything? You're too trusting of men. You can't keep going around living life like a doormat."

Ouch! No matter how many times she heard the same refrain from Julianne, it still hurt.

"If I want to be psychoanalyzed, Jules, I'll go see my sister, the professional."

"Oh, Carly. You know I love you. I just want you to be happy."

"This from a woman who spends her life lusting over a priest!" It was fighting dirty, but Carly wanted to prove she wasn't a doormat. At least not to her best friend anyway.

"Hey! You leave Nicky out of this!"

"Face it, Jules. You are in love with a man you can't have. Instead of dealing with that, you take it out on me."

Julianne was silent on the other end of the cell phone.

"I'm sorry, Jules. I didn't mean it. I guess I just got a little mad at the doormat thing. I really am happy, though. I wish you could see that."

"We're quite a pair, huh?" Julianne's question came out more as a hiccup. "You attract narcissistic bastards and I can't stop dreaming of St. Nicholas. It's pathetic. And Carly." Her voice cracked. "I do know you're happy. I guess I just don't like that you're happy living down there and not here in New York with me. The guy attacking you has me a little wigged out. I would just die if something happened to you."

"All you had to say was that you missed me, you idiot." Carly wiped a wayward tear from her eye.

Beckett wandered over, nudging his wet snout between Carly's hand and the armrest, forcing her to pet him.

"Oh, sweetie, do you miss your daddy?" She nuzzled the dog's nose.

"Are you talking to that dog?"

"I am," Carly cooed. Beckett's head lolled back as she rubbed behind his ears. "He really is kinda cute. A little sloppy with his food and water. And he snores like a freight train. But other than that, he's kind of nice to have around."

Julianne snorted. "You've just described my last boyfriend."

"As I recall, you didn't think 'Chad the Cad' was all that nice to have around," Carly teased as the dog tried to climb up on to the chair.

"Yeah, you'll feel the same about that dog. Just give it a few days. When's Dark and Mysterious coming home anyway?"

Carly shoved the ninety pounds of drooling dog off her lap and stood up, brushing tufts of brown dog hair off her yoga pants. She closed the glass door behind them as she went inside, checking the lock twice. Beckett trotted over to his water dish for a drink, sending as much water to the floor as into his belly.

"I'm not sure. The funeral was yesterday, but he texted me last night and said he wouldn't be home until sometime tomorrow. Something about the will." Beckett went over to the old comforter she'd thrown on the floor for the dog to use as a bed. He scrunched up the sides and lay down with a humph. Grabbing a towel from the bar stool, Carly bent down to wipe up the water he'd slopped on the floor. "If he doesn't come home tomorrow, I'll need to go back over to his place and get more food for Beckett."

"So what's his place like?" Julianne asked.

"I don't know." Carly switched the phone to the other ear so she could wipe under the cabinets. "I didn't get past the kitchen."

"Carly!" Julianne wailed. "What good are you? Didn't you want to check out his place? Aren't you curious about him? If it were me, I would have made a beeline straight for the bedroom and checked out his bed." No doubt Julianne would have. Carly stiffened at the thought of her best friend in Shane's bedroom.

"That's not nice." Carly silently berated herself for being a hypocrite. She'd thought about taking a look around Shane's house, too, but she wasn't going to admit it to her friend. "He just lost his dad. I didn't want to invade his privacy."

Julianne let out a huff. "Yeah, well, he sure didn't think twice about invading your private parts," she teased.

"Jules!" Carly's stomach tightened at the thought of Shane and his wicked mouth. He'd been right though, the real thing was so much better. Her knees got weak just thinking about it, forcing her to take a seat on the bar stool.

"I did get a good look at his kitchen, and I'm pretty sure he wasn't faking his culinary skills on *Good Day, Baltimore*. He has a lot of toys in that kitchen. I think he might even have a few you don't have." Carly knew this would divert her friend's attention back to a neutral subject. Julianne loved to cook. If she hadn't made it as a fashion designer, there was no doubt in anyone's mind that she would have had her own cooking show. She also hated to be shown up in the kitchen.

"I seriously doubt that," Julianne scoffed. "What does a football player know about cooking?"

Carly laughed. "Why, I believe it was the brilliant fashion designer Julianne Marchione who once said that all you need to be a good cook are the proper tools and a passion for food. Are you accusing football players of lacking in passion?"

"You tell me, Carly. You're the one swapping spit with the quarterback."

"So, are you still going to the race car driver's wedding next weekend?" Carly did her best to change the subject as she loaded her dinner dishes into the dishwasher. Julianne mumbled something that sounded like *chicken*.

"Yeah, I'm still going," she said with a sigh. "But I really wish you'd reconsider and go with me. I won't know a soul there and the bride's parents said I could bring a guest."

"I don't want to be your plus one."

"I'd do the same for you! The bride is a client. I don't even know why I am going at all."

"It might have something to do with the extra ten thousand dollars the Ricky-Bobby race car driver is paying you to be there in case something goes wrong with his bride's gown."

"Ha! Like I'm going to sew on a pearl that might fall off the woman's eight-foot train."

Carly grinned. Julianne would definitely sew on a pearl and anything else that fell off. Her dresses were like her children. *She'll probably be the only one in the church crying because of the gown, not the woman in it.*

"Well, you're getting a free trip to Sea Island," Carly reminded her. "Go and have fun. You deserve it."

"I guess I could call Chad the Cad if I get desperate," Julianne said. But Carly knew she wouldn't. Julianne was right; they were quite a pair. Both seemed destined to chase the wrong men. Carly puttered around her kitchen as Julianne regaled her with snippets of gossip from New York's fashion world. Before ending their call, they agreed to get together in New York before training camp began in a few weeks.

Later that evening, after showering off the sweat from her Pilates class and an evening run with Beckett, Carly stood in her kitchen setting up the automatic coffeemaker for the next morning. The laptop computer on her counter beeped, alerting her to an incoming message. She wandered over to check the email before she shut down the computer.

"If this is another email from Gabe's bridezilla about his signing bonus," Carly said to the slumbering dog, "I'm going to scream."

The email wasn't from Chloe. Carly's heart slammed into her ribs as she saw the name of the message's sender: Joel Tompkins. The message was brief, but it terrified Carly just the same.

We belong together. It's meant to be. You'll see.

She wasn't sure how long she stood there staring at the message. Her hands trembled as she quickly deleted it. Wiping it off the screen didn't stem the furious beating of her heart. She wrapped her arms around herself to keep from shivering. Forcing her arms to move, she reached for her cell phone. Who should she call? The police? Maybe she should have saved the message. She tried for a deep, calming breath. She'd call Donovan; he'd know what to do. She searched the phone's address book for his number as she bit her lip to keep it from trembling. Maybe she should call Matt? God no! He'd go ballistic. It was just an email, after all. She was safe inside her house. Besides, Beckett was here to protect her. She looked over to where the dog lay snoring, oblivious to her distress. Great!

Her breath was coming more evenly and her pulse had subsided to a reasonable rate. She didn't want to disturb Donovan at home, but she'd seen enough episodes of *Law & Order* to know she shouldn't wait until morning to let someone know about Joel's message. She'd just calmed down enough to make the call when the chime of her doorbell made her jump. Clutching her cell phone tightly, she looked over at Beckett. The dog lifted his head in confusion and was trying to rouse himself from his deep slumber. Apparently, he didn't realize it was his job to bark at the doorbell.

"No wonder your family left you!" she hissed at the dog as he stood and stretched.

Slowly, she walked to the foyer, her cell phone in her hand, one finger on the 911 button. Not bothering to turn on any lights, she figured she'd just peek through the side window and see who was on her front porch at nine thirty at night. If it was Joel, she'd barricade herself in the foyer powder room and call the police. Beckett padded behind her, his tail swishing in anticipation. Carly carefully peeked behind the cellular shade on the window and glanced outside. She released a deep shaky breath at the sight of Shane Devlin.

Ten

Carly flicked on the porch lights and threw open her front door. She was dressed for bed in plaid cotton sleep pants and a pink cami. She wasn't wearing any underwear. Had she not been so frightened over Joel's email, she might have thought twice about what she was—or wasn't—wearing before opening the door. Instead, she stepped outside, not bothering to hide her relief at seeing Shane standing on her doorstep, hands in his pockets, his face drawn. The cool night air and Shane's quirked eyebrow quickly made her aware of her outfit. Carly's cheeks burned as she nearly tripped over Beckett, who was dancing around Shane's legs. Dashing back inside, she pulled on the sweat jacket she'd left lying on the bench in the hallway, zipping it up to her chin. Shane and Beckett followed her in and she slammed the door behind them, securing the locks before turning to face him.

"Hey, are you okay?" he asked.

Leaning against the door trying to calm her still-racing heart, Carly drank in the sight of Shane. In the light of the hallway, he looked exhausted. His dress shirt and slacks were rumpled and his hair mussed. The lines on his face looked more pronounced. Rather than athletic, his posture screamed bone weary. The forlorn look in his eyes made him seem vulnerable. She was sure he hated appearing that way.

"No. Yeah. I mean, I'm just a little jumpy, that's all. I guess the other night is still getting to me." The residual panic caused her to babble.

Shane reached over and ran his knuckles down her cheek.

"It'll be okay," he said softly. "Just give it time."

It was all she could do not to turn her head and brush her lips against his hand. Instead, she took a deep breath, pushing away from the door. The man just lost his father. While she was grateful Shane's unexpected arrival distracted her from the panic of the email, one look at his face and Carly knew she couldn't burden him with her problems. She would worry about Joel's nonsensical email message tomorrow. For tonight, she'd do what she could to comfort Shane. After he'd rescued her at the gala, she owed him that much.

Beckett shattered the moment by shoving a stuffed goose into Shane's thigh. The toy made a honking noise and Shane grabbed for it, only to have Beckett run away with it.

"I bought him a few toys to play with," Carly said as they walked into the living room.

"A few?" he asked, gesturing to the basket of toys next to Beckett's makeshift bed.

"Did you know they let you bring dogs into the pet stores?" She took a seat on one side of the sofa, tucking her bare feet beneath her legs.

"You took my dog shopping?" The tone of his voice was incredulous as he sat on the opposite end of the sofa. He braced his forearms on his thighs as Beckett sat between his knees.

"It's not as if I had him neutered. It was just shopping. And, for your information, he liked it," she teased.

"That's the last time I leave you with a girl," he promised the dog.

Silence settled around them as Shane rubbed the dog's

ears. Carly couldn't help squirming as she remembered the last time they were together on this sofa. She chanced a look at Shane's exhausted face. His thoughts weren't as easy to read as he absently stroked the dog. Suddenly, Carly was imagining those same hands stroking her, and her pulse sped up yet again.

"Are you hungry? Thirsty?" she asked, springing up from the sofa. "I'm afraid the only thing I can make is an egg. Unless you want a Lean Cuisine," she called from the kitchen.

"Carly. It's okay." His voice sounded as tired as he looked. "A bunch of blue-haired ladies have been shoving food down my throat for three days. I'm good for right now."

"Oh." He must have heard the disappointment in her voice.

He sighed. "I'll have a drink if it'll make you happy."

Carly pulled a bottle of beer from the fridge and grabbed a glass from the cabinet, pleased Julianne had made her buy fancy beer glasses. She put the glass and a coaster on the table next to Shane and handed him the beer. He twisted off the cap and took a swig, ignoring the glass.

"It's diet," she said, babbling again. "Well, not exactly diet. Reduced carbs."

He leaned his head back against the sofa and closed his eyes, patting the seat next to him. "Sit down. You're making me nervous."

She didn't quite trust herself to sit next to him, so she chose the other end of the sofa instead. He briefly opened his eyes as she sat, giving her a half scowl—as if he realized her reluctance to be near him—before closing them again.

The only sounds were Beckett's heavy breathing and the hushed voices from the TV she'd left on upstairs. She thought for a moment that Shane had fallen asleep until he took a long swallow from his beer.

"So, how did everything go?" she asked when he finished.

He rubbed a hand over his face. "About like you'd expect."

Carly should have let it alone, but she desperately wanted

Shane to open up to her. The night of the gala, she'd glimpsed a vulnerable man behind the public persona of arrogant, isolated athlete he wore like a shield. He was a man who'd been abandoned by his father, and Carly knew firsthand what that feeling was like.

"Hank said the service was very nice," she pressed on.

Opening his eyes, he slowly turned his head toward her. His steely stare told her she was treading on thin ice.

"It was a lovely service, Carly," he said, his tone sarcastic. "The right reverend sure can put on a funeral. Even if the deceased is his own daughter."

"Well, I'm sure your brother appreciated it."

Leaning back, he closed his eyes again. "I'm sorry. I really don't want to go into this, Carly. My father never was my favorite subject."

"But what's going to happen to your brother now? He's what, twelve? Who's going to take care of him?"

He opened his eyes and looked across at her. Carly nearly flinched at the anger she saw reflected there.

"He's going to live with Lindsey's parents." His clipped tone stifled any additional questions Carly might have had about Shane's younger brother. Losing both parents had to be devastating for the boy. Shane had been nearly his brother's age when he'd lost his mother. Had he wanted guardianship of the boy, only to have his brother reject him like Bruce Devlin had? It would explain the anger and the pain in Shane's eyes. Carly's heart ached.

"I need to get some sleep. I just wanted to take Beckett off your hands before I crashed, that's all."

He was going to take his dog and leave. She didn't want him to. Not just because of Joel's email, either. The sexual tension that always seemed to hum around them crackled sharply in the air. But tonight it was more than that. Carly felt a powerful need to wipe out the haunted look in Shane's eyes, to do what she could to ease his sadness.

Shane stretched his arm across the back of the sofa, reaching for her hand. She took it and stood up, stepping over Beckett, now slumbering at Shane's feet.

"Come to bed," she said, tugging him up.

He stood, his eyes more smoky now.

"If I stay, Carly, there won't be much sleeping," he said.

"You'll sleep," she said as she switched off the lights. "Eventually."

Grabbing his beer, he followed her up the stairs.

Shane wasn't all that surprised when he saw the décor of Carly's bedroom. Whereas the rest of her condo was decorated in classic but comfortable Pottery Barn chic, her bedroom looked like one his grandmother's *Victorian* magazines had exploded in it. A massive bed with a curly iron headboard dominated the room. It was piled high with a fluffy white comforter and enough pillows for an entire team to sleep on. Miles of lace hung from the windows. He'd already figured out that Carly liked to hide her sexy, feminine side underneath her tailored, conservative exterior; her bedroom only validated his theory.

As he finished his beer, he watched in fascination as she unzipped her sweat jacket in a mock striptease and tossed it to the floor. With a coy smile, she leaned over to light the votive candles on a weathered oak chest beside the bed. Pulling his wallet from his pants pocket, he tossed condoms onto the bedside table. She quirked an eyebrow at him as she walked on her knees across the bed, tossing off pillows as she went. His cock jumped as he watched her breasts bounce while she maneuvered across the mattress. His brain was too tired to process all the reasons why this was the king of bad ideas. His body was worn down from lusting after her these past weeks. Maybe if he buried himself inside her, he could forget the last three days of his life.

He toed off his shoes as she reached him. Flicking her hair over her shoulder, she lifted her hands to unbutton his shirt. Her fingertips were warm against his skin and he couldn't stop a sigh from escaping. A smug grin curved over her lips as she pulled his shirttails from his pants, pushing the shirt off his shoulders. As he stepped closer to the bed, their bodies nearly touching, he watched as she slowly slid her hands between his T-shirt and the bare skin of his abdomen. He sucked in a breath as she tangled her fingers in the hair on his chest. When he felt her body tremble, he suddenly couldn't stand still any longer. Gripping her bare shoulders, he pulled her face to within a fraction of an inch of his. Shane needed to know if the game plan they'd set in place a few nights ago was still in play.

"Carly," he rasped. "This can't be anything more than sex. Are you still okay with that?"

"Yes. But you should know it's been a long time for me," she whispered.

Shane dragged in a ragged breath, willing his body to slow down. He leaned his forehead against hers, gently kissing her nose. He'd never been one to rush through, ignoring his partner. But he was having trouble tonight. He *needed* Carly. Badly. Not just to release the sexual tension simmering between them since they'd first met, but to forget the events of the last few days. To erase from his mind the look on Bruce's kid's face as Shane drove away. He was using her in every possible way and he couldn't make himself stop.

Carly's fingertips traced Shane's chest. "Shh," she said, lifting a finger to rub it along the worry lines on his forehead. "Stop thinking and get naked before I change my mind." Except she wouldn't change her mind. They'd been moving toward this moment for weeks now, and nothing was going to stop them tonight. She'd been frightened earlier and now she just wanted to be held. She wanted to feel the strength of a warm body possessing her, soothing her. Shane's warm body.

And Carly wanted to use her own body to comfort Shane. The look of pain and vulnerability she'd seen in his eyes the night Bruce died still lingered there tonight. It was a look she could relate to. Tonight, she didn't want either of them to be alone in the world.

Her hands drifted to his belt buckle, but he pushed her

back on her heels. Finally, his features relaxed, a lock of dark hair hanging down between his eyes. A boyish grin overtook his face as he pulled the T-shirt over his head, further mussing his hair. Carly couldn't help it; she licked her lips at the sight of his perfectly sculpted bare chest. He was gorgeous. Her skin grew hot as he slowly peeled off his pants, revealing a pair of long, muscled legs lightly dusted with hair. Heat pooled between her own legs as she took in the sight of the rampant erection straining his boxer briefs. Letting a deep sigh escape, she rose onto her knees and tugged off her cami, the fabric abrading the sensitive buds of her nipples.

"God, you're so beautiful," he whispered reverently. The seriousness of his statement and his perusal of her body brought a flush to her skin. Slowly, the corners of his mouth turned up into a wolfish grin. Carly felt her own lips curve into a smile as she watched the tension drain from his face. It felt good to know that here in her bedroom they could both leave everything outside. For one night, they could enjoy each other as two adults. She'd worry about everything else tomorrow.

The bed swayed as he knelt on it, his knees straddling hers, his huge hands sliding up the bare skin of her back. She arched into him, giving him access to her breasts. No further urging was necessary as he bent over a nipple, slowly running his tongue around it. His tongue was warm against her cool skin, and Carly moaned something unintelligible before pulling his head closer against her bare breasts. She felt his smile against her skin before he took the bud into his mouth and gently sucked.

Carly nearly shattered right then. She was wet and panting, becoming increasingly desperate for him to relieve the ache between her legs. Just exactly when she'd become so easy she'd have to delve into later. Right now, Shane was nibbling his way from one breast to the other, causing her to lose all conscious thought. Her hands were on autopilot as they cruised over his shoulders. As his mouth tugged at her other breast, she scored her nails down his back. Her fingers burrowed inside the waistband of his underwear, giving her access to his well-toned glutes. With one hand, she pushed the boxer briefs to his knees while the other reached around to stroke him. When she wrapped her fingers around the velvet skin, his body shuddered around her.

"Carly." His breath was ragged as he untied the drawstring of her sleep pants and pushed them to her knees. "I can't go slow. I want you too badly. I've spent the last three nights dreaming of being inside you." He pushed a finger inside her and she bit back a moan of pleasure. "God, you're so ready. I need to get inside you. I promise I'll try to bring you along with me, but if I don't, I'll make it up to you later."

Unable to find her voice, she stroked him again, gently squeezing this time. Growling, he pushed her back on the bed. She kicked off her sleep pants as he tossed his briefs onto the growing pile of clothes scattered on the floor. He sheathed himself with a condom before returning his attention to the sensitive nub between her legs. Heat pooled in her belly. Her hips began to writhe as his fingers sent fissions of pleasure through her core so intense it was almost painful. When she couldn't stand it any longer, Carly wrapped her legs around him, pulling him down into an openmouthed kiss. Their teeth scraped as he kissed her hard, slowly guiding his cock inside her. Her body offered up a brief resistance at the size of him.

"You're so tight. So sweet," he breathed into her ear before biting the tender lobe. At last, he began to move. She could feel his tension coiled tightly in the warm muscles bunched beneath her fingers. Shane thrust hard, then nearly pulled all the way out.

"Oh my God!" Her breath was coming in staccato bursts as her body stretched to accommodate him; the pleasure of it was exquisite.

He began to thrust again and again, taking a breast in his mouth as she matched his rhythm. Hitching her legs higher so her pubic bone rubbed against his, she locked her hands around his shoulders. Shane continued thrusting deep inside as the tension built in her body. Silently she begged the building orgasm to crest and release her as the heat within her core grew in intensity and spread throughout her body. Suddenly, a wave of brilliant ecstasy overtook her. She thought she shouted his name as her body convulsed. After dragging in a deep breath, her body went limp beneath him.

A pair of slightly dilated gray eyes looked down at her through spiked lashes. Her stomach tightened at the hunger she saw in them. Leaning on his forearms above her, Shane's body went still. The cords in his neck were stiff with tension; a sheen of perspiration clung to his chest. With her palm, Carly gingerly caressed his back from the base of his spine to his neck. Slowly, he bent his lips to hers and brushed a soft kiss over them. Then, he thrust hard one last time, throwing his head back as his body shook from his own release.

Eleven

Shane wasn't sure how long they lay there. He could feel the beat of her heart as it slowed to a more normal rhythm. The gentle stroking of her hands along his spine helped to bring his own heartbeat and breathing under control. He didn't want to come out of her yet; she was so tight and warm. But he knew he was too heavy, so he rolled over on his back, taking her with him. She breathed a contented sigh as she snuggled up against his chest, her cheek gently lying over his heart.

The blood returned to his brain, forcing him to realize the shitload of trouble he was in. Sex with Carly March was not what he'd been fantasizing about all these weeks. *It was more. So much more.*

Raking a hand through his hair, he tried to make sense of the situation. He'd had one-night stands before. But never with someone he'd have to face at the watercooler every day afterward. Most of the women he'd been in relationships with were hung up on the idea of dating a jock. A celebrity jock at that. Sex had been part of the bargain. But the

no-strings-attached proviso had been understood by all par-
ties concerned. He liked his life unencumbered.

The fact that he had struck such a deal with Carly—the
coach's sister-in-law and the GM's assistant—was crazy. He
was risking what was left of his career fooling around with
her. Not only that, but he felt more than a twinge of guilt for
using her. Something he'd never felt with other women.

Shane wasn't the type to bask in the afterglow, so he slid
out of bed, gently repositioning Carly on one of the many
remaining pillows before heading for the bathroom to dis-
pose of the condom. As he splashed cold water on his face,
he tried to rationalize away the guilt. Christ, he was tired.
That didn't help matters. It also hadn't helped that she had
practically thrown herself at him, coming to the door
dressed as she had. He should have gone straight home and
picked up Beckett in the morning.

Leaning against the vanity, his body tensed as he replayed
the evening in his head. She'd been upset by something when
he arrived; he'd sensed it. He'd assumed she was still jumpy
from the incident at the gala the other night, but Carly was
made of sterner stuff. She'd rallied quickly after the attack,
showing none of the hysteria he would have expected from
a woman who'd just been physically threatened.

It had to be something else. And it bothered him that he
needed to know what it was. That's when it hit him: This
connection between the two of them was more than sexual.
It was why the guilt nagged at him. He actually cared what
happened to her. Sex was sex. *Only this time it wasn't.* He
didn't have any room in the equation for caring. He needed
to focus all his attention on his game. On winning the starting job. But first, he needed to get out of Carly's house.

He stalked back into the bedroom to do just that, but the
sight of her on the bed halted him in his tracks. She lay right
where he'd left her: on her stomach, one arm draped over a
pillow allowing a rosy nipple to peek out. Her lush rear end
was partially covered by the sheet and her mane of soft
chestnut curls covered her cheek. His cock was apparently

doing the thinking again, because rather than leave, he climbed back into bed as she murmured softly. Bundling her up, he settled her in the crook of his arm, her warm breath fanning his chest. Forgetting he was trying to extricate himself from the situation, he brushed a kiss on top of her head.

"Thank you," he said, pulling the sheet more fully over them.

"Hmm," she mumbled. "I'm glad I could do something to make you feel better."

"So that was just pity sex then?" The words were out before his brain could remind him exactly why he didn't engage in pillow talk: he sucked at it. Shane felt her tense instantly. Slowly, she pushed the hair back from her face, rolling more fully on his chest so she could level her eyes at him, eyes that were now as blue as the Arctic Ocean. Her elbow jabbed him in the ribs, but he bit back a complaint; he'd said enough already.

"What did you say?" Her voice was as frosty as her eyes.

"Umm . . . it's like you said, you wanted to make me feel better. You work for the team. I'm sure no one in the organization will fault you for wanting to make the quarterback feel better." He sounded like an arrogant jerk, he knew. But the more he thought about it, the more this tack made sense. He wanted to sever whatever was between them. He seized on the idea of making her angry with him and ran for the end zone.

With a huff, she shoved off his chest, slamming her head back against the other pillow and snapping the sheet against her breasts. "Oh. My. God!" she railed at the ceiling. Somehow, it didn't sound nearly as gratifying as it did when she'd screamed it a few moments earlier.

"You are an insufferable, egotistical ass! You think that I had sex with you out of some sort of . . . of . . . *duty*?" She was flailing an arm around in agitation, and the gesture caused the sheet to drop lower, which gave him a nice view of her full breasts. Her skin was flushed and her nipples puckered. The sight was making him hard again.

"You have definitely taken a few too many licks to the helmet, Devlin, because they don't pay me enough for that." She pulled the sheet back up and pressed her arms tightly across her chest. "You're not the only one in the Blaze organization, Devlin. Maybe I needed a little comfort tonight. Did you think of that, huh?"

And just like that, the niggling feeling that something— or someone—had upset her earlier returned with a vengeance. Concern for her flickered in his belly, totally distracting him from honing in on her comment about not being paid enough. He reached over to caress her shoulder, but she pulled away.

"You jocks are all alike." Her voice had lowered, but her tone was still hard. "You all think the world revolves around you. You wouldn't even consider the fact that perhaps I might enjoy a little sex now and then."

He had to hand it to her. Most women would have either been crying hysterically by now or throwing his clothes out the window. But not Carly. She wasn't a drama queen. He rolled on his side to face her, propping his head on his hand.

"So did you? Enjoy it, I mean." His hand itched to touch her, but he didn't dare. He knew if he did, he wouldn't be leaving anytime soon. And the game plan still was to get out of there. Shane was just having a little trouble executing the play.

She shot him a quick look out of the corner of her eye. With a huff she returned her gaze to the ceiling.

"It was okay, I guess." She shrugged.

Okay? Shane inched closer, a grin tugging at the corner of his mouth. She wasn't going to give him an inch, and he had to admire her toughness.

"I seem to remember you screaming in the middle of it," he said, his mouth just an inch away from her bare shoulder. A shoulder he desperately wanted to nibble.

"It seemed like you could use some encouragement at the time," she said, examining a cuticle. He stifled a laugh.

"Are you saying I was a dud?" he taunted her. *She* had definitely *not* been a dud, and his body hardened just thinking about it. She tried unsuccessfully to suppress a shudder as his arousal nudged her thigh.

"Well, I made allowances for the fact that you were tired and you've been through a lot these past few days. But I'm not going to be singing your praises to my book club, if that's what you're asking."

A man's ego could only take so much. Ripping the sheet from her, Shane pinned her with a leg. She raised her hands to push him away, but he was too fast for her. Shackling her wrists, he pulled her arms over her head. Carly flinched slightly and he loosened his grip. The last thing he wanted was for her to feel threatened. She could get out of his grasp if she wanted, but he made an effort to tame her with his tongue before she tried. Reverently, he traced the outline of the areola on her breast. She shivered as he teased the nipple with his lips. His free hand cruised along the hollow of her waist to the curve of her hip and lower to the thigh.

"What do you think you're doing?" she asked breathlessly, most of the fight gone from her tone.

"I'm giving you something to brag to your book club about," he said before taking the nipple fully in his mouth and sucking. She bucked off the bed. Grabbing her fingers, he wrapped them around the iron headboard. With that done, he released her wrists so he could settle more fully between her legs. Using one hand he fondled her other breast while his other hand dipped between her legs. She didn't bother to take her hands from the bedposts as he explored her body.

"You know, we're reading the new Kennedy biography. It's really an interesting book. I don't think we'll have much time to discuss you." Her voice now was weak and raspy.

"After this, Dorothy, you'll wanna make time, 'cause I'm about to rock your world."

It was the last thing he said before burying his face between her thighs, his tongue invading the sweet, soft folds. He was going to lick her to oblivion. Sounds of her soft panting filled the room as her head thrashed from side to side. Her hands had shifted from the headboard to fist in the sheets. When she tossed a knee over his shoulder, his tongue delved deeper. He wasn't sure, but he thought she might have growled. Then she came, climaxing in long waves, her body convulsing around him. His cock jumped in anticipation. It was just going to have to wait because he wasn't finished. Glancing up over her dewy, limp body, he saw her eyes were closed, but a smile graced her flushed face. Once again, he lowered his head between her thighs. She didn't have enough energy to stop him.

"Oh, Shane!" She grabbed at his hair, her hips thrashing. "I can't! You can't! Please . . ." She was gasping for air now. He chuckled as he licked her. When he found the nub and sucked, she came again with a silent scream. He kissed the inside of her thighs before raising his head.

His body ached now. It wasn't going to be denied. He crawled up over her and her mouth gaped open as she caught sight of him.

"Oh," she breathed. But she spread her legs wider as he sheathed himself with a condom.

"Huh-uh," he said as he rolled her over on her stomach. He tucked a forearm beneath her slick belly and pulled her backside against his erection. She gasped as he slid into her warm, tight body. He thrust deeply and she instinctively ground her hips against him. Then he was lost. Pumping in and out, he fondled a breast with one hand and her sex with the other. The sounds of her moaning with pleasure filled the room, spurring him on as she thrust back against him. Over and over he pumped into her until he could feel her body begin to tense again beneath his. Her muscles squeezed around him and, with a guttural groan of his own, he followed her into oblivion.

Carly's body, glistening with sweat, slumped over her knees as she fought to control her breathing. Leaning over her back, he kissed the knots along her spine. When he reached her neck, he buried his face in her hair and waited for his heart to slow down. He took a long moment to breathe in her scent: citrus and sex. Laying her down on the pillow, he covered her with the blanket.

This time when he returned from the bathroom, there wasn't any decision to be made about whether he would stay or not. Crawling under the frilly comforter, he wrapped his arms around her languid body. She pressed her back against his chest, their legs tangling together. He felt his cock twitch again as it made contact with her warm bottom.

"Seriously?" she gasped.

He couldn't help laughing. "Professional athlete," he said, nuzzling her neck. She shuddered.

Then, he couldn't help but ask, "So, what's the verdict with the book club?"

"I'm pretty sure you deserve your *own* book," she said reverently.

He snaked his arm around to allow his hand to gently palm her breast as he closed his eyes. "You promised me sleep," he mumbled into her hair.

"Umm." She relaxed against him, her breathing soft and steady.

He fell asleep trying to remember the last time he'd felt so comfortable.

Sunlight streamed through the plantation shutters when Shane awoke. It took him a moment to become fully conscious of where he was. The citrus smell permeating the fluffy pillows and the sound of a blow-dryer in the other room reminded him that he'd spent the night with Carly. His sluggish body reminded him he was still exhausted. Unfortunately, one part of his body was wide awake and at full attention.

The blow-dryer stopped and he watched through slightly closed eyes as she quietly slipped out of the bathroom and headed for the walk-in closet. She was dressed in a pair of skin-colored panties that looked like skimpy shorts and a matching push-up bra. He groaned as the rest of his body caught up with his morning woody.

"Oh, you're up." Startled, she turned from the closet door to face him. She held a towel in her hand but didn't bother to cover herself. Pulling himself up to lean back against the pillows, he placed a hand behind his head and just enjoyed the view.

"Well, part of me is up, anyway," he said with a grin.

He watched as her eyes roamed over him, but she remained where she was, crossing her arms under her breasts. The gesture made him want to bury his face between them. His body got harder as he sucked in a breath.

"C'mere," he said, patting the bed.

"No," she said with a swing of her head. She looked like a goddess standing there, shards of sunlight sneaking in through the shutters and reflecting off her hair. "I have an early morning meeting with Donovan and I need to get dressed."

"It's still early." The clock beside the bed said seven thirty-five. "Besides, I happen to know you're easy and I can set you free in no time. You know you want to," he teased, giving her a lopsided grin as he reached out a hand to her.

After last night, Shane knew she liked sex. He also knew she liked sex with him. Hopefully it would be enough to get her back in bed this morning.

"Unfortunately, you didn't pack enough protection. Impressive as the stash in your wallet was." She was walking toward him now, which he took as a good sign. She stopped beside the bed and he traced a hand softly over the skin at the curve of her waist. Reaching inside her panties, he skimmed a fingertip over the birth control patch there. Moving lower, he traced his finger through her curls before slowly burying it inside her. Her back arched as she gripped his wrist.

"You have access to my medical file. You know I'm clean," he said as he continued to finger her while he pushed off the sheet with the other hand. She moaned as she caught sight of him. Biting her lip, she pushed his hand away. But instead of retreating, she crawled across his thighs, straddling him, the lacy fabric of her panties tickling his skin. She smiled wickedly as she ran her hands down his chest, trailing her nails across his nipples. His breath came out in a hiss as she bent her head to kiss his belly. A cascade of damp hair hid her face as she moved lower. Before he realized what she intended, she'd taken him in her mouth. He tangled his hands in her hair as he pressed his head back against the pillows. She ran her tongue along the length of him and his breath hitched as she wrapped her lips around him more fully. Cool hair brushed the hot skin of his belly as her round bottom bopped rhythmically.

"Carly!" he bellowed, pulling her up by her hair so she lay across his chest. He was close to the edge. With another sinful smile she wrapped a warm hand firmly around his cock. She tongued his nipple as she stroked him to climax with her hand. He swore as he came in a rush.

She busied herself by using the damp towel to wipe him off.

"Get some sleep." She brushed a kiss over both his closed eyelids as she pulled the sheet over skin that still burned from her touch, tucking him in like a little boy. He watched her retreating backside through half-closed eyelids, but he couldn't summon the strength to call her back. She disappeared into the bathroom as he drifted off into oblivion.

When he awoke several hours later, Beckett sat staring at him, a stuffed cow clenched in his jaw. At the first crack of Shane's eyelids, the dog's tail began to wag frantically, the cow mooing as the dog bit down on it in his excitement. Beckett squirmed closer as Shane became more alert.

"Okay, buddy, I'm getting up," he said as the dog dropped the cow and tried to scramble up on the bed. "Off, you beast! She may love you now, but I guarantee she'll never let you come over again if you get dog hair all over her bed. What time is it anyway?" he asked as he threw his legs over the side of the bed. Shane absently patted the dog's head as he looked at the clock: eleven fifteen. With a groan, he stretched, feeling rested for the first time in days. He glanced at the bedside table and saw the note Carly had left him.

Beckett's been fed and put out. Fresh towels are in the bathroom. Coffee's in the carafe in the kitchen. Lock up when you leave. C

Shane smiled as he picked up the key chain. It was a miniature beach sandal with *Bethany Beach* written in rainbow ink on the heel. Most likely a gift from one of her nieces, he thought, because it didn't fit Carly's personality at all. But after last night, he wasn't really sure what her personality was: the straight-arrow conservative administrative assistant or the sex kitten in the white-hot lingerie. One thing he was sure of: one night with Carly March wasn't enough. Trying not to delve into that too much, he stumbled off to the shower.

Twelve

Carly squinted at the bright sunlight as she and Donovan stepped out of the courthouse. It had taken the better part of the day, but they had accomplished their mission.

"You're doing the right thing," Donovan said as he slid on his sunglasses. Carly dug in her purse to pull out her own.

"It's just a piece of paper, Donovan," she said as they climbed down the steps onto West Pratt Street and walked the half block to the parking garage. The sun was warm on her skin, but she still felt chilled. Three hours in the air-conditioned courthouse cooling her heels waiting for the judge had left her a bit frosty. "I'm not sure what kind of deterrent it will be." The judge's pointed questions and insinuations that she was somehow asking for Joel's attention hadn't helped her demeanor.

"I know that was rough, Carly. But a restraining order gives you a little more leverage if he does anything else." Donovan's words sent a shiver up her spine. He gently gripped her upper arm as he led her to his BMW. "The judge's order covers the training facility and your neighborhood. He can't

leave you any more flowers or gifts at home or at work. All
he needs to do is send you another unwanted love note via
email and he is in violation of the restraining order. Because
you went to the trouble of getting the RTO, anything he does
that might otherwise have been considered a misdemeanor
can now be treated as a felony."

"It wasn't a love note," she grumbled.

He opened the car door and she slid in, the sun-baked
leather warming her legs. Despite it being nearly ninety
degrees outside, she couldn't seem to get warm. Donovan
walked around the car and took off his suit jacket before
climbing behind the wheel. The German engine purred to
life when he turned the key and a blast of air flew from the
air vents. Carly shivered again. Wordlessly, he adjusted the
vents away from her.

"What if the restraining order has the opposite effect?"
she asked, staring out the windshield at a family of tourists
making their way from the aquarium, a stuffed whale under
the father's arm as he held a sleeping toddler with the other.
"What if it makes him angry and he does something else? I
mean, he was pretty spaced out at the gala." She finally
braved a look at Donovan. His rich brown eyes softened as
he took her hand in his.

"Not gonna happen, Carly." His voice was like velvet as
he stroked her palm. "His grandfather won't be pleased when
he finds out about the restraining order and he'll probably
have him in rehab tonight. I'm sorry you had to put up with
all the humiliating questions from the judge, but the laws
against stalkers aren't always that black and white. Like I said
before, you did the right thing. Everything will be fine now."

Carly tried to give him a reassuring smile as he released
her hand and pulled out of the parking lot. But she didn't feel
reassured. And deep down, she didn't think Donovan did,
either. She had the feeling he was as frustrated as she was,
he was just a lot better at maintaining his cool. Carly also
knew he'd never let anything happen to her. He was playing
it by the book with the law, but she was aware of the efforts
he'd put in place at the team's training facility and within her

neighborhood. The security guards at both places had received a severe briefing from Donovan earlier in the day.

Leaning her head against the seat's headrest, she closed her eyes as Donovan maneuvered through the late-day traffic mix of commuters leaving the city and tourists on foot. She knew he was right; she needed to get the restraining order, but it didn't make her feel any better. The laws surrounding stalkers were loose and open to interpretation by the presiding judge. Aside from the assault in the hotel, Joel hadn't done anything she could prove constituted stalking. Yes, he'd been leaving her red roses for weeks now. On her desk chair, her doorstep, the windshield of her car. No note ever accompanied the flowers, but she knew they were from him. He'd always ask her if she'd found them, usually in front of another reporter or insignificant Blaze personnel. The roses had stopped appearing since the altercation with Donovan and Shane outside her home several weeks ago.

There had also been that time Joel followed her home, but was he a stalker? His grandfather had downplayed the incident in the hotel as a by-product of his drinking problem—a result of a troubled youth. Maybe his grandfather was right; he wasn't dangerous, just a pest Carly should feel sorry for.

Only, she didn't feel sorry for him. What she felt was fear.

It was a feeling she wasn't familiar with. As a child, her mother had put her in harm's way numerous times. But Carly had never felt frightened. Perhaps she'd been too young to know she should be scared. Later in life, after the death of her mother and then her grandmother, she'd felt lonely and apprehensive, but never true fear. Life had toughened her up. Why, then, was she succumbing to fear now? The email last night hadn't been overly threatening, but it had set off alarm bells. She said a silent prayer of thanks for Shane's unexpected arrival on her front porch the night before.

At least thoughts of the previous night were helping to warm her up. She told herself that she should be ashamed of using Shane that way. But after Joel's email, she hadn't wanted to be alone and he was a means to an end. Of course, she knew she was lying to herself. Carly wanted him as much as he wanted her. Had they not been interrupted several nights before by the news of Bruce Devlin's death, their fling would have been over and done with. So what if last night he was using her to forget the tragedy of his father's death? She'd been able to offer him comfort in the only way he would accept it. What she had with Shane last night was just that—sex. Incredible sex, but nothing more. It was what they both had agreed to.

Besides, Shane wasn't happily-ever-after material. But there was nothing wrong with enjoying herself while she waited for Mr. Right. Except, of course, for the fact that it really didn't bode well to be fooling around with a football player. Hadn't she learned her lesson where professional athletes were concerned? Carly let out a soft sigh. Her wicked side would have to be happy with one night of hot, steamy sex for now. She couldn't risk her job—or her heart—with anything more.

Donovan interrupted her thoughts. "I have to let Hank know about the RTO, but I'll let you handle telling the coach."

"I'm not telling Matt!" Carly whipped around to face him as they pulled into the parking lot of the training facility. "He's got too much on his plate right now. My sister is finally feeling better and they're leaving for a family vacation next week. I don't want them worrying about me. Besides, you said everything will be fine now. You did mean that, right?"

His lips were set in a grim line as he jerked the car into his assigned parking space at Blaze headquarters. He turned a stern glare on her, which probably worked when he as in the military but was having little effect on Carly. She didn't flinch, only raising an eyebrow at him. Donovan let out a slow hiss before speaking. "I guess it's your call. But when he comes at me with a baseball bat, I'm hiding behind you. Got it, gorgeous?"

She manufactured a bright smile. "You'd better be glad this is a football team, then," she teased. "Thank you, Donovan. For understanding. And for your help today." Leaning across the center console, she placed a soft kiss on his cheek.

"It was nothing. I'm just doin' my job." But she swore he

blushed underneath his dark skin as an aw-shucks grin lit up his face. The chill finally left her body as the late afternoon sun bathed the parking lot with warmth.

"Did you know that more than one million women are victims of stalking every year?" Asia asked. The two women were walking to Carly's office after Asia intercepted Carly and Donovan when they returned from the courthouse. Carly picked up on the meaningful glance the two exchanged, but she couldn't get a word in edgewise to interrogate Asia on it. Frankly, she'd rather discuss what was going on between the team's media rep and its security chief than listen to statistics on stalking.

She'd had enough for one day.

Unfortunately, Asia obviously spent the day surfing the Web and wasn't going to be denied her press briefing. Trying to tune her out, Carly flipped on the lights of her office, stopping short when she spotted the rose on her desk chair. But this wasn't Joel's usual red rose. It was a beautiful Oceana rose, a brilliant peach color, with baby's breath wrapped in the plastic. Asia stopped in midsentence, following Carly's gaze.

Spying the rose, Asia reached for the phone. "I'm calling Don," she said.

"No!" Carly said. Something was different. Forcing her feet to move forward, she picked up the delicate blossom with shaky hands. A note lay beneath it. When she saw her key chain lying beside it, her body relaxed and she allowed a smile to spread over her face. "It's okay, Asia. This isn't from Joel."

"You have multiple stalkers?"

Laughing now, she read through the note.

Dinner tonight. My place. S.

He'd signed it with a big *S* similar to the way she'd signed her note to him this morning.

"Nope, just a friend." She lifted the rose to her nose and sniffed, hoping to restore her equilibrium.

Asia crossed her arms across her chest. "Spill it, girlfriend."

"Sure, when you tell me everything that's going on between you and Donovan," Carly said, aiming a smug smile at her friend.

Asia turned on her heel and left as quickly as her cane could carry her.

"That's what I thought!" Carly called after her with a laugh. She couldn't wipe the smile from her face now if she tried. Shane's note had resurrected the happy afterglow brought on by a great night of sex. Her day at the courthouse was pushed to the back of her mind as her body hummed with thoughts of Shane.

She shouldn't see him again. They'd agreed to one night—and what a night! There was no harm in a little dinner, though, Carly rationalized. A girl had to eat.

Two hours later, Carly pulled into Shane's garage and parked her car next to his. She'd called him earlier and they'd agreed not to advertise her presence at his house. Too many Blaze employees lived in the neighborhood and could recognize her car. She knocked on the mudroom door.

"It's open! Come on in," he called from inside the house.

Beckett greeted her with a slobbery tennis ball as she emerged into the kitchen. Something was sizzling on the industrial-sized stove. Butter and garlic, from the smell of it. She brushed her fingers over Beckett's head as Shane turned from the pot he was stirring.

He looked delicious, dressed in a pair of ancient Levi's, worn out in all the right places. A T-shirt advertising a San Diego microbrewery stretched perfectly over his broad, sculpted chest. His feet were bare and his hair damp as if he were fresh from the shower. Turning from the massive cooktop, he tossed a dish towel over his shoulder, greeting her with his now-familiar wolfish grin. Tingling began in the pit of her belly.

"Hey there," he said, his voice husky as his eyes took in her dark blue suit like a man who knew exactly what she wore underneath it—which he did. "I hope you're hungry."

It was all she could do not to lick her lips. She stepped out of her high heels and slowly strolled across the kitchen, stopping inches from him. She could feel the heat of his body—or was it hers? A little sigh of satisfaction escaped her mouth at his indrawn breath when her hands came in contact with his taut abs. Slowly, she slid her hands up his chest before wrapping them around his neck. The look in his eyes told her everything she wanted to know.

"I'm starving," she whispered before pulling his lips down to meet hers. Her resolve to keep tonight dinner-only evaporated as quickly as the steam escaping the pot on the stove behind them. She lost control of the kiss instantly as Shane devoured her mouth, his tongue pressing in and exploring all of her. It was a heady sensation, his kiss. One her body couldn't seem to get enough of. Somehow his hands had already found their way beneath her skirt, but he stopped kneading her bottom long enough to reach behind him to turn off the gas.

"I planned on eating right away, but I guess we can enjoy some appetizers first," he said, kissing the side of her mouth. Then he lifted her and she wrapped her legs around him, her skirt riding up to her waist as his hands continued to caress her backside while he carried her to his bedroom.

"So, where did you learn to cook?" Shane looked across the table at Carly. She'd pulled on one of the dress shirts he'd left by his bed when he unpacked earlier that day. The wrinkles in the shirt and her rumpled hair made her look as if she'd just tumbled out of bed—which she had. Her skin still held a trace of pink and her blue eyes sparkled against the blue of the shirt. Spearing another bite of sea bass with her fork, she waited for him to answer.

"The Food Network." He fiddled with the stem of his wineglass as he watched her enjoy the grilled fish and pasta.

"Seriously?" she asked.

"Rachael Ray, Sandra Lee, and food. What's not to love? Besides, a guy's gotta eat. If you can read and follow a recipe, you can cook." He took a sip of his wine.

She laughed. "It figures. I'll bet you love Giada, too."

"Hey, I've been told my linguini in clam sauce is to die for." He watched as she speared another piece of fish. She closed her eyes as she chewed and swallowed, a look of bliss on her face.

He could watch her eat all night.

Shane was glad she enjoyed the food he'd prepared. Thankfully, she wasn't one of those women who counted every calorie, analyzing every morsel before putting it in her mouth. And her body was none the worse for wear in spite of it. His hands and mouth had covered every inch of her over the past twenty-four hours and he could testify to the fact that she was luscious and firm in all the right places. He'd frequently seen her working out in the gym at the training facility, so he knew she wasn't careless about her body image, just not obsessed with it. It was one of the things he liked about her.

"What are you thinking?" she asked, dragging his thoughts back to the present. Crossing her forearms on the table, she leaned her breasts on top of them, giving him a great view down the front of her—his—shirt.

He smiled. "I was just thinking that it's nice to eat with a woman who actually enjoys food. No whining about a special diet or stressing over the ingredients."

"Ah." She leaned back, picking up her wineglass as she did so. "You mean those anorexic/bulimic Hollywood types you date. I'll bet it's a drag having to use laxative as the main ingredient of every meal," she teased as she took a sip of wine.

He laughed with her. "Yeah, well. I gave up cooking for women."

She raised an eyebrow in question.

He saluted her with his wineglass. "I made an exception for you." Relaxing, he leaned back in his chair, stretching out his jean-clad legs, crossing his bare feet at the ankles.

"I feel so honored." She smiled at him. "Do your team-mates know of your culinary talents?"

"Most of the guys on my old team did. I would cook for the offensive line a lot. They were big into ribs and Mexican. No one teased me about it, if that's what you're getting at." *Not if they wanted to eat.* "You ever cook for the soccer player you were engaged to?"

He wasn't sure what prompted him to ask. By virtue of his celebrity status, she knew everything about him. Shane wanted to even the score and know more about her love life. He didn't want to examine why he even cared, but he did.

"Not that often," she said. "I know my way around the kitchen, but I'm not that big into cooking. The kitchen was always Julianne's domain."

She'd deftly shifted the conversation off her fiancé, but Shane wasn't going to let her leave the subject.

"Tell me about him."

A long silence stretched as Carly toyed with her wine-glass and Shane tried not to look like her response was important to him. Except it was.

"Max is a lot like Julianne: passionate and demonstrative and very Italian," she finally said. Her words were spoken softly in a voice tinged with melancholy. "It's easy to get caught up in his larger-than-life personality. It was also easy to drown in it. I thought I could handle it. And everything that went with it."

Seeing the sadness reflected in Carly's eyes, Shane felt like a jerk, wishing he'd let her change the subject when she'd attempted to.

Carly chewed on her bottom lip before continuing. "I think he liked the idea of marrying a woman who was as notorious as he was in the tabloids. It ensured he'd always get the media attention he thought he deserved. I was stupid and naïve enough to believe he loved me for who I was as a person, not as a personality."

Shane forced himself to keep his body relaxed when inside he wanted to hit something. "The guy didn't deserve you." The words didn't adequately express the feelings swirling around in his head, but he didn't know how to deal with those, so he kept it simple.

Carly smiled sadly. "I'm just happy he followed his heart before we both made a big mistake."

Shane stared at her. *Surely she isn't that forgiving?* "Yeah, he lives happily ever after and you're made the scapegoat by the paparazzi. Somehow I don't think that's fair."

"I learned a long time ago that life isn't fair, Shane."

He shook his head. Was it possible this woman had thicker skin than he did?

"So now you're spending your life waiting for an accountant or a podiatrist? Or was it an actuary and a proctologist?" Shane teased, trying to steer the conversation back to a lighter topic.

Carly's eyes grew wide and her mouth formed a perfect *O*. "You *were* eavesdropping outside my office that day!"

He shrugged, giving her his best Devlin grin.

Carly shook her head in exasperation with him. "I've learned to be careful who I date. Most guys either want to save the little girl they saw in the movie about my mother. Or, they're after my aristocratic title and the trust fund that comes with it."

"Not me," he drawled. "I just want you for your body."

She buried her face in her hands. He couldn't tell if she was laughing or embarrassed. When she lifted her head, her eyes were shimmering. She took a deep breath.

"About that, Shane. We really need to talk."

"Ugh. That has to be the most dreaded phrase in the female vocabulary," he said, sitting up in his chair and leaning across the table. "Let's not analyze this, Carly." He took her hand, resting his palm against hers, intertwining their fingers. "Let's just live this. I'm not going to kiss and tell and neither are you. We both know this isn't forever. It's just two people enjoying each other. When it's over, it's over. Let's just take it one night at a time. Okay?"

Pulling her hand to his mouth, he placed an openmouthed kiss on her palm, enjoying the feel of her shiver beneath his lips. Neither one of them was immune to the other's touch. She nodded, nibbling on her bottom lip as she did so.

Together, they finished what was left of their meal and cleaned the kitchen. The intimacy of the domestic scene should have unnerved him, but it didn't. Carly stood beside him at the sink, barefoot and naked underneath his shirt, her hip brushing his thigh. They washed and dried the dishes while talking about their similar, dysfunctional childhoods. They laughed over stories of boarding school. They talked about their favorite foods: she craved Thai; he loved Mexican. Their favorite music: he liked grunge rock—Pearl Jam and the Red Hot Chili Peppers; she was a Top 40 girl who loved the international artists. Both loved Springsteen. He'd seen him five times; she'd seen him three. Before he knew it, the kitchen was spotless and darkness had fallen in spite of the summer solstice. She leaned against the kitchen counter looking sexy as hell with her hair covering one eye.

"I really should get going. You have to be up early for mini-camp tomorrow." She didn't say it with much enthusiasm. Shane knew it wouldn't take much persuading for her to stay. Sliding his hands under her shirt, he wrapped them around her waist. At the same time, he nudged her with his hips so her back was against the stainless steel refrigerator. With two fingers, he pushed her hair to one side, giving him access to her neck.

"Sure you don't want to stay for dessert?" His tongue trailed along the soft skin below her ear.

"I really shouldn't," she whispered. Her body was saying something else as it came to life beneath his roving hands. Reaching behind her into the fridge, he pulled out a can of whipped cream. A squeak barely escaped her lips as he shook the can.

"You sure? I got fat-free."

Her skin betrayed her again as a blush crept from her chest to her forehead.

"Only if we can work it off first." She licked her lips.

"Your wish is my command, Dorothy."

Thirteen

Carly woke early the next morning. Shane's house sat secluded at the back of a cul-de-sac and they had forgotten to draw the shades before going to sleep. The long June days began early and sunlight spread out over the bed. A muscled leg hung outside of the sheet. His breathing was steady and deep with sleep, giving her a moment to take in her surroundings.

The house was a large contemporary. He'd filled it with comfortable, rented furniture, but it had the feel of a monastery. With the exception of the kitchen, there wasn't one picture or personal effect evident anywhere in the house. The walls were bare. The tables lacked any knickknacks. She wanted to believe the sterile environment was because he'd only lived in the house for a month, but she knew better. Shane Devlin was the ultimate loner. His house was a reflection of his personality. She doubted he'd ever lived any differently. Sadness crept into her heart as she thought of the anger he still held on to.

Slowly, she rolled over onto her side so she could leisurely take in his face, relaxed and boyish in sleep. His body was beautiful. She thought of how that body had merged with hers last night and heat rose from her toes to the pit of her belly. Shane was a powerful lover. Playful at times, focused and intent at others. Tuned into her needs, he never left her wanting. But he took as much as he gave. The man sleeping beside her was dangerous to her senses. Dangerous to her heart.

The intimacy of their dinner last night shook her more than their lovemaking. Perhaps it was their similar life stories that bonded them together. It was more than just sexual chemistry, she knew. That's what scared her. He would have no trouble keeping things on a physical level. Could she?

Reaching over, she traced a finger along his chest, trailing it down along the line of hair at his belly and lower. Mumbling to himself, he blinked his eyes open. With a slow, dazzling smile he rolled over on top of her. She wrapped her hand around him and he covered her mouth with his. The shrill ringing of the telephone startled them both.

"This is starting to get old," he growled. "For crying out loud, it's six fifteen in the morning."

"Don't answer it." She tried to pull his hips back in contact with hers.

He swore as he looked at the caller ID. "It's the guardhouse." He snatched up the phone. "Yeah?"

Carly winced as his warm body rolled off hers. He sat up on the side of the bed. She trailed a finger down his spine.

"What?" he bellowed. He stood, searching for his clothes. Tucking the phone between his neck and his ear, he pulled on a pair of jeans over his naked butt. "Are you kidding me? Sure. Fine. Send him here." He slammed down the landline phone before grabbing his cell off the nightstand, swearing under his breath.

"Shane? What is it? What's going on?" Carly sat up, clutching the sheet to her bare chest.

"It's the kid." He pounded the buttons of his cell phone.

"What kid?"

"Bruce's kid!" he all but shouted.

"You mean Troy?" she asked incredulously, taken aback by his reaction. "Your brother?"

Finally bothering to look at her, he pierced her with a menacing glare. "Yeah, *that* kid." Shane stormed out of the bedroom, yelling into his cell as he went. "I know what time it is, Tif, just put him on the phone," he demanded as he stomped down the stairs.

And just like that, the sympathetic lover of the past two nights was gone and the Devil of the NFL was back. Carly flopped back down onto the bed listening to Shane argue with someone on the phone. He'd gone into the kitchen so she couldn't make out exactly what he was saying, which only heightened her curiosity about who he'd called. Staring at the ceiling, she took a few deep, cleansing breaths. Obviously, there would be no returning to the bliss of five minutes earlier. One thing she knew for sure: she needed to get some clothes on before his younger brother arrived. Things were difficult enough to explain without a preteen boy finding her naked in his brother's bed.

It only took a few minutes for her to brush her teeth and pull back her hair. They'd showered together last night after their adventure with the whipped cream. She'd grabbed her gym bag out of her car afterward, which, thankfully, had clean clothes in it. A pair of yoga pants and a modest V-neck T-shirt would have to do. Her sneakers were next. She was shoving yesterday's clothes into the bag when the doorbell rang. She didn't want to intrude, so she kept herself busy by tidying up the bedroom. Turning on the TV was out—she might miss something important going on downstairs.

Standing in the doorway she strained to hear the voices. Shane and the voice of a boy were easily distinguishable, but she heard other voices as well.

Several other voices.

Curiosity got the better of her and she made her way to the top of the stairs. After all, Shane hadn't actually told her to wait upstairs. Maybe she could slip out to the garage without anyone noticing. But then she'd miss the action.

What if Shane wanted her there? Somehow she doubted that. She wasn't exactly sure *what* she should do. Her feet were already moving before she could make up her mind.

The voices were louder now, interspersed with the sound of Beckett's paws clicking on the tile floor. He was obviously more excited than his owner at this morning's company. Carly couldn't see the boy clearly from this vantage point, but he obviously hadn't come alone. Three other men were with him. They were large, one of them as big as some of the players on the Blaze. One wore a college T-shirt. If she had to guess, she'd say they were players from Bruce Devlin's team.

No way this was going to go well.

Silently, she climbed down the last few steps and rounded the corner toward the kitchen. Hanging back in the shadows, she tried to get a better look. Troy Devlin stood near the French doors in the breakfast area. His brilliant green eyes shone with unshed tears behind a pair of wire-framed glasses. His dirty blond hair had a bad case of bed head. She guessed he was about Molly's age. He still hadn't grown into his gawky body, but the boy was going to be a lady-killer one day.

Troy was beyond tired, his eyes red rimmed with dark bruises beneath them. But even exhausted, he held his chin in the same defiant way his brother often did. From his stance, he looked as if he'd come to do battle with Shane.

Beckett seemed to sense the tension in the kitchen. The dog parked himself on Troy's toes, panting frantically at everyone else in the room. Carly empathized with the wounded look in the boy's eyes. That feeling of being alone in the world was a familiar one. What's more, Shane was well acquainted with that feeling, too. Surely he'd have some compassion for his brother?

Beckett outed her as soon as she slipped into the kitchen. Jumping from Troy's feet, he galloped over to bury his nose in her crotch.

"It figures," Troy's voice squeaked. "You didn't want me here so I wouldn't mess up your sex life. Is this the latest bimbo of the week?"

Well, alrighty then. Clearly, the boy had been reading from the same manual on obnoxious behavior as her nephew.

"Hey!" Shane yelled at the boy, causing him to flinch.

The big football player cuffed Troy in the back of the head. "Mind your manners," he said in a voice higher than Troy's.

Inhaling a deep, cleansing breath, she stepped farther into the room. Something wasn't right here. Whether or not it was her business, the boy standing across the room was hurting and she wasn't leaving until he was taken care of. It was impossible to interpret the look Shane flung at her: anger, frustration, perhaps even a bit of confusion. Too late now. She was in this mess whether he liked it or not.

"You must be Troy," she said, trying to infuse a little cheer in her voice.

The boy just stared at her, his chin betraying his bravado with a slight tremor. "Yeah, that's me."

"And you are?"

She turned to look at the source of the question. Besides the big Neanderthal standing with Troy, there were two other players. One was a handsome all-American blue-eyed blond who had poster boy written all over him, and the other a sculpted African American with diamond stud earrings that probably cost more than her car. His expression was surly, like the tone of his question.

Shane answered before she could. "Your worst nightmare." His tone was soft but lethal. "She's assistant to the Blaze GM. So if you buffoons are thinking about playing in the pros someday, I'd watch your mouth and your step. I'm sure you broke any number of laws on your little escapade last night."

Carly forced herself not to roll her eyes at Shane's statement. She wasn't sure what constituted a "little escapade" or whether any laws had actually been broken, but she'd get to the bottom of that later. Fairly confident that these three hadn't seen the inside of a law book, she played along with Shane. It was his house, after all.

"Kidnapping comes to mind," she said. Mr. All-American went pale, while the big guy nervously shuffled his feet. The walking DeBeers advertisement only sneered at her. He probably had a defense attorney on retainer. "Ain't nobody been kidnapped," he said.

Shane's cell phone rang, shattering yet another climactic moment.

"I'll take this in the office. Keep an eye on them, Carly."

Shane's attitude was beginning to really annoy her. He ignored Carly's defiant glare as he snapped open his cell phone. "What have you got, Roscoe?" he said as he left the room.

So, he was talking to his agent. Something wasn't right here, and now was the time to get the truth. She looked over at the boy. He was dead on his feet, one hand stroking Beckett's big head, the other gripping the back of the chair.

"You seem to have made a new friend," she said, gesturing to the dog. "Would you like to give him his breakfast?"

The boy's eyes darted from her to the dog. Beckett looked up at him, swishing his tail across the floor. Troy gave him a ghost of a smile back. "Sure," he said.

Carly showed him where the dog food was kept in the pantry, scooping up the dry food and handing it to Troy to deposit in Beckett's dish. True to form, Beckett inhaled the food in thirty seconds flat.

"Dang, that dog eats faster than Tiny," the all-American said with a laugh. The big guy had to be Tiny, because he responded with an indignant, "Does not."

His belly full, Beckett bounced around the room with a tennis ball in his mouth. It was answer time.

"You can take him outside if you'd like, Troy," she said. "He likes to play catch."

"Sure, whatever," Troy mumbled as Beckett danced in front of the door.

Tiny went too as dog and boy disappeared into the backyard.

"Okay, why don't you two tell me what's going on?" she asked. "Let's start with your names."

The two exchanged glances. After some sort of nonverbal communication, they turned to Carly.

"Dante Stuart, wide receiver." Carly had to stifle a laugh. The boy sounded like he was doing his cameo intro for *Monday Night Football*. He'd probably been practicing in the mirror since he was six.

"Uh, I'm Evan Andrews," the all-American said. "We aren't really in any trouble, are we?"

"That depends." She leaned a hip against the counter. "What exactly have you done? Why did you take Troy from his grandparents and bring him here?"

"He asked us to!" Evan answered, as if the reason were simple. "Tell her, Dante. Troy wants to be with his brother."

She glanced out the window as Beckett ran circles around Troy and Tiny. "His life as he knew it has been upended," she said softly. "I doubt he really knows what he wants right now."

"He knows he wants to be with his brother and not those crazy folk," Dante said.

"I doubt his grandparents are crazy," Carly said. She tried to remember if she'd done any research on Shane's stepmother. She'd been a beauty queen, but other than that, she couldn't recall anything unusual about Lindsey Devlin's family.

"Oh, but they are," Evan said, his voice earnest. "I don't mean any disrespect for religious people and all that, but Troy's grandparents are a little nuts. They said Troy has to stay home and be tutored because they don't want him associating with certain *elements*, if you get my drift." Evan's voice rose in pitch as he be became more indignant. "They told Consuelo, Coach's housekeeper, to go back to Mexico. She isn't even *from* Mexico; she's from Guatemala! She's legal to be here! She works for the university. His grandma wants him to sing and pray at their church every night. I'm telling you, it's just not right for a boy like Troy to have to live that way."

"Surely it isn't that bad," she said, but a nagging feeling had begun to form deep in her stomach.

"It is that bad," Dante hissed. "He's got nobody else. The lawyer said we can't keep him. We asked. He'd be better off

with us than those people. And better than living here. But
the lawyer says we had to bring him here."

"Lawyer? What lawyer?" The nagging feeling was blos-
soming into a full-grown knot.

"Coach's lawyer. It's what Coach and Mrs. D wanted.
For Troy to live with Shane," Evan said.

"What?" Carly was suddenly light-headed. Surely she
hadn't heard him correctly. Rubbing her temple in an effort
to stem the drumming there, she looked from one boy to
the other.

"Lady, you need to keep up," Dante said. "Coach's will
said Troy had to live with his brother. It don't matter if the
grandparents want Troy or not. That's not what his mama
and daddy wanted. And Troy don't want to live with them
anyways. He wants to be here. Not sure why, though. That
jerk don't want Troy," he finished with a mumble.

In an effort to steady herself, Carly wrapped her fingers
around the edge of the granite countertop. Were they telling
the truth? Bruce Devlin had named Shane as Troy's guardian? And Shane had foisted his brother off on the boy's
grandparents. It wasn't hard to reconcile with the Shane
Devlin everyone knew. But not with the Shane Devlin she'd
come to know over the past few days.

Of course, *that* Shane Devlin might only exist in her
dreams.

"I'm not sure what there is to eat, but help yourselves.
I'll be right back." It wasn't her job to play hostess, but she
didn't care anymore.

She barged into his office just in time to see Shane turn
his cell phone off. He swore as she closed the double doors
and leaned back against them, trying to get a handle on the
emotions thrumming through her body. Anger was winning,
but disappointment was running a close second.

"What?" he asked with a scowl.

"I'm just trying to figure out what's going on."

"You should have stayed upstairs." He got up to pace
menacingly around the room.

Her body wasn't numb enough to absorb the pain of his

comments, but she was a glutton for punishment, so she stumbled on anyway. "Too late."

"It's going to take a few days to sort this whole mess out. His grandparents want to have custody and that's fine with me. I just have to get it all finalized." He ran his hands through his hair as he settled against the edge of the desk.

"From what I've gathered, Bruce's wishes were that Troy live with you."

He shot off the desk like a rocket. "They only left me the kid as a joke, Carly!" he shouted. "They just put my name down as guardian to fill in a blank when they were making out their will, never thinking it would have to be executed."

"Are you sure about that?" It was like spearing a wild animal; he roared back after each jab.

"What do you care, anyway?" He stood inches from her, effectively pinning her to the door. His eyes were dark with an emotion she couldn't make out and his face was hard. "I'll have this all sorted out before the season. That kid won't affect my play in any way!"

Carly was finally, blissfully numb. "That's all you care about, isn't it, Shane? Your stupid football career! You don't give a crap about that boy out there! My God! Is there not a compassionate bone in your body? Don't you remember what it's like to lose a parent and feel all alone in the world?" Her breath was coming fast and raspy, as if she'd just sprinted a mile. She would not cry! "Well, I do! That boy just lost both his parents. He's scared and he's alone and *you* are one of the few people who can relate to that. Instead, all you care about is a stupid game." Her words were coming out in gulps now, as she realized she'd been drawn in by yet another selfish athlete. How could she have let it happen again?

"I thought you were different," she whispered. "But you're going to punish a kid for all the horrible things your father did to you. How could I have been so stupid?"

She wrenched around to open the door. But before she could escape, he pressed his body flush against her, sandwiching her between him and the door. His breath was warm against her neck. God, she hated him right now! She hated herself more for how her traitorous body still responded to his.

"Don't, Carly, please," he pleaded. "I don't want to remember. Is that what you want to hear? I don't want to have to relive that time in my life again. I can't. And I don't want to be responsible for my father's kid."

"Well, you are," she said, choking down a sob. "And your father's *kid* is your *brother.*"

As he buried his face in her neck, she felt his body tremble. She wanted it to be from anger, but she was afraid it had more to do with that ever-present attraction.

"I need your help, Carly, please," His lips brushed the back of her neck as he spoke and her knees nearly buckled. Her body reacted to his touch and it disgusted her.

"Can you do something with him today while I try and straighten this mess out? I need to be at mini-camp in an hour. I can't think about football with all this hanging over my head." Shane's voice was a whisper as he pleaded with her. "Remember that little speech you gave about the Blaze being a family? Well, I need that family now. Please?"

Her body tensed at his words. She pushed away from the door and, thankfully, he released her. Carly turned to face him, finally sure her face and body would give nothing away.

"I don't care about your football career and I'm not doing it for the team," she said, pulling the door open. "But I'll do it for Troy."

Fourteen

Chaos reigned in the Richardson kitchen as Carly absently pushed food around on her plate. The sound of sausage sizzling in the frying pan competed with ESPN on the television. Penny stood at the griddle flipping pancakes as she chatted animatedly with their guests: three hungry football players and an exhausted, forlorn little boy. The older boys sat together at the table with C.J., their conversation a series of grunts as they devoured breakfast faster than Penny could serve it. Molly sat at the breakfast bar absently swinging her leg as she nibbled on a piece of sausage and peppered Shane's little brother with questions. *How old are you? What's your favorite TV show? Do you play any sports?* Troy was too well mannered to ignore her, but his responses were quiet and brief. Penny made a point to ruffle the boy's hair or rub his back as she shuffled between the stove and the table as if she, too, sensed the boy's desolation.

Carly basically had acted on instinct bringing Troy and his friends to her sister's home. The boy needed some TLC, and who better to provide it than her sister, a professional psychologist, and Penny, the ultimate mama bear. The three football players weren't hard to convince, either. She thought the opportunity to meet an NFL head coach would be attractive to them, but it was their devotion to Troy that ultimately swayed them. Clearly, the college students were fond of Troy and would do just about anything to see him happy.

It was also obvious the three had been close to Bruce Devlin and were nearly as devastated by his death as Troy was. On the short ride to Lisa's, Troy dozed off while Tiny shared with Carly whispered stories of how Coach Devlin had impacted his life and those of so many of his teammates. She was having difficulty reconciling the icon he described with the demon Shane portrayed his father as.

"So, exactly how are you involved in all of this?" Lisa asked quietly, not that anyone else could hear their conversation over the din in the kitchen.

Carly looked up from the pancake she'd been pushing around on her plate. "Leave it alone, Lisa."

Not that her sister would. Lisa had a spidey sense well honed through motherhood and years of professional training. Her sister couldn't resist probing. It was in her DNA. Carly sighed, wondering if her sister could just be grateful she'd been handed her first client for her fledgling grief-counseling practice.

"Well, were you out for a jog at six thirty in the morning when you saw Troy arriving at Shane's?" Lisa continued to dig.

So much for her being grateful.

"I just want to know what's going on," her sister continued when Carly remained mute. "Why is Troy here and not in Florida with his grandparents? You can't just dump a kid and the Three Amigos on my doorstep and not expect me to want answers, Carly."

"His grandparents were supposed to take him to Florida today. Troy doesn't want to go or to live with his grandparents. He wants to stay with Shane," Carly said tersely.

"And how does Shane feel about that?" Lisa asked, employing her best psychologist's voice.

Carly felt her eyes fill with unshed tears. She wasn't sure

who she was more angry or upset with: herself or Shane. How could she be so attracted to a man who would refuse a relationship with his only living family? A kid who'd just lost his parents, no less. She shivered at the thought of Lisa not reaching out to her when Carly was a young teenager in boarding school. If Lisa had ignored her as Shane planned to do with Troy, Carly wasn't sure she could have made it through the whole ordeal with Maxim and the media circus that followed.

Yet the man she'd come to know over the past few weeks wouldn't abandon his younger half brother. At least, the man she thought she knew. It was almost as if Shane Devlin had two personalities: the Devil of the NFL and the kinder, gentler version he kept hidden from everyone else. She hated that she was so disappointed in him because clearly it meant she wasn't doing such a good job keeping their relationship simple.

Lisa reached out and gently squeezed Carly's hand.

"Bruce wanted Troy to live with Shane. He went so far as to stipulate it in his will. But Shane doesn't want him," Carly finally managed to whisper.

As the shock registered on Lisa's face, Carly wiped her own eyes. She needed to get herself together and dressed for work. Mini-camp started at noon and she needed to figure out a plan for dealing with Troy and his friends. She wouldn't ignore the boy even though his brother wanted to. Lisa would help, but she'd demand her pound of flesh from Carly, seeking information about the exact nature of her relationship with Shane. Information Carly did not want to share.

An escape route arrived as Emma waltzed down the stairs dressed in a Mickey Mouse T-shirt and shorts so short, they were indistinguishable under the shirt. Lisa opened her mouth to warn her teenage daughter they had guests, but Molly beat her to it.

"Look, Em, college boys!" Molly shouted gleefully.

With a shriek, Emma retreated up the stairs as C.J. and Molly barked with laughter. The boy who'd introduced himself as Evan leaned back in his chair to get a better glimpse of Emma scrambling back to her bedroom.

"Whoa! How old is your sister?" he asked C.J.

Penny whacked him on the head with a dish towel. "Too young for the likes of you, buster!" she said. "Now, if you boys are finished, bring your plates into the kitchen. This isn't a restaurant."

Molly jumped down from her stool and grabbed for the remote control. An argument followed between her and C.J. over what channel the TV should be tuned to. It was a daily occurrence in the Richardson household. Lisa interceded before the inevitable tears began.

"Hey!" she yelled. "Molly, why don't you and Troy go downstairs to the playroom and watch TV down there?"

Molly stomped out of the room, pulling Troy with her. "We have a Wii. Do you wanna play?" Her voice trailed off as they headed down the stairs.

"Do you have Xbox?" Evan asked.

"What do you think?" C.J. said, and they headed after Molly and Troy, Dante following behind. The big Samoan boy stayed to help Penny with the dishes, much to her delight. While Lisa dealt with the kids, Carly made her escape upstairs.

She kept some work clothes and essentials in the guest bedroom for nights when she watched the kids. Lisa found her there a few minutes later. Carly mentally sighed as her sister sat on the bed and watched her pull a suit out of its dry cleaner wrapper. Obviously, Lisa wasn't giving up.

"Do you have a camisole I can wear with this?" she asked, trying to distract her.

"I could dig one up," Lisa said, reclining back against the headboard and crossing her arms in front of her. "If I get some answers."

"Now I see why you're such a good psychologist. You're annoyingly persistent." Carly realized the futility of avoiding her sister's questions and sat down on the bed with a thump. "Shane didn't know what to do with him. He's freaking out about mini-camp starting today and winning the starting job. As if that's the most important thing in life. His agent is looking into changing the custody codicil of the will. The grandparents want to raise Troy, apparently. But the process could take a couple of days. I said I'd help out. Hank would want me to. For the team."

"Well, of course, you're just doing your job," Lisa said as she picked at a loose thread on the comforter. The room was quiet for a few moments as Lisa employed her psychologist skill of waiting a patient out. It was a skill that really annoyed Carly. Probably because it always wore her down.

"I was there when Troy showed up." Carly's back was to Lisa, so at least she didn't get to see the look of disappointment on her sister's face.

"So you just happened to pop over at the crack of dawn with coffee and donuts?"

Slowly, Carly turned her head at her sister's sarcastic tone. "No. I never left after dinner. Are you happy?"

"Are you happy?" Lisa asked, once again employing her best psychologist voice.

"Ugh!" Carly moaned, flopping back on the bed. "Please don't use your psychobabble on me! You know I hate it when you do that."

Lisa unsuccessfully bit back a small smile. "How long have you two been dating?"

"We're not dating," Carly said. "It's just sex." Carly closed her eyes, bracing herself for a rant from her sister.

Instead, Lisa surprised her with a simple question, still using her best psychologist voice to ask it: "And how long has it been 'just sex'?"

"Just last night. And the night before." Carly continued to avoid Lisa's eyes, staring at the ceiling instead.

"Ahh," Lisa said.

Carly grabbed a pillow and clutched it to her face before screaming into it.

"Did you have to take a class in that?" she asked as she threw the pillow across the room.

"A class in what?" Lisa asked, not working very hard to suppress her grin.

"The condescending *ahh*," Carly said. "It's so annoying."

Lisa did smile now. "It's not meant to be condescending. My apologies."

Carly desperately wanted her sister to tell her that she was an idiot for making the same mistake twice. That she had awful taste in men. But Lisa remained frustratingly mute.

Carly let out a heavy sigh. "I thought he was different. Different than Maxim. With Max, I always knew it was about the publicity." Carly turned her head to stare at a startled Lisa. "I'm not stupid. I knew I was being used to keep Max's name on the cover of the tabloids. But Max made me feel so needed and, in his own stupid way, loved. Aside from you and Julianne, no one had ever made me feel that way before."

Lisa reached over and intertwined her fingers with Carly's as they lay side by side on the bed.

"And let's face it," Carly continued. "It was kind of nice living the rock-star life. Except for the paparazzi, of course. And, up until a few nights ago, I thought the sex was great."

Lisa turned her face toward her sister, arching an eyebrow.

"American football wins," Carly said with a blush and smile. "And that's all I'm saying on the subject."

"Ahh," Lisa said again.

Carly jumped from the bed in frustration. "Will you stop that!" She threw the pillow at her sister. "It's over anyway. It wouldn't have worked. He plays on the team I work for. The media would eat me alive if I fell for another jock. Besides, Shane is incapable of a relationship of any kind," she said solemnly. "It's better to find that out now, than later on."

"What makes you think he's incapable of a relationship?"

"Great, that's the part you want to discuss. You couldn't just agree that I should stay away from him because of who he is?" Carly thrust her hands on her hips, staring down at Lisa in challenge.

"Okay, fine," Carly huffed and slumped back down on

the bed when Lisa continued to stare at her without answering. "It's the whole thing with Troy. Just because Shane has a boatload of abandonment issues over his father, doesn't mean he should take it out on a twelve-year-old boy."

Lisa again arched an eyebrow at her.

"I've read some of those articles you've emailed me," Carly said curtly.

A chuckle escaped as Lisa sat up and curled an arm around Carly's shoulder.

"Do you honestly think Shane couldn't have a relationship with either Troy or you?" Lisa asked, giving her sister a gentle squeeze.

Carly shook her head slowly before letting it drop to her chin.

"You know what I think?" Lisa said, cupping Carly's chin and lifting her face up. "I think the reason you're so upset by Shane's treatment of Troy this morning is because you *do* believe Shane is capable of a relationship. Hmm?"

"You said you wouldn't psychoanalyze me."

"You're right." Lisa laughed as she stood and pulled Carly up with her. "You need to get to work and I have a house full of college boys to entertain. I think I'll try to get Troy to sleep today. I'll talk to Shane this afternoon and see if he wants Troy to stay here for a few days."

"Don't do him any favors, Lisa. I told him I'd help, but only because I wanted to help Troy, not Shane."

"Try not to be so hard on Shane," Lisa urged. "He's struggling to come to terms with his father's death, too. No matter what he says."

Carly gave a little snort as she pulled a pair of heels out of the closet.

"I speak from experience when I say having a half sibling show up out of nowhere can be . . . well . . . a little unnerving," Lisa said.

Carly swung around to face her sister, her eyes wide and her mouth forming an *O*.

"Give him some time to work through his emotions, Carly, before you paint him with the same brush as Maxim.

Shane hasn't had that many positive relationships in his life. He might surprise you yet."

"Did you hate me when you found out about me?" Carly's voice trembled as she asked the question.

"No!" Lisa said as she pulled Carly into a tight hug. "And I don't think Shane hates Troy."

"Is that your professional opinion?"

"Yes, it is," Lisa said with a smile.

Carly desperately wanted to believe her sister. She wanted the scene she witnessed this morning to be a reaction to the grief Shane wasn't prepared to deal with. Not an indication of the man he actually was. The alternative meant she really needed to examine the type of guy she was constantly attracted to.

Troy slid under the big down comforter. He hated sleeping during the day. He didn't need a nap. Naps were for babies. He was getting sick of people treating him like he was in kindergarten. His parents had just died. He could take it like a man. Unfortunately, the manners his mom had drummed into him for the past twelve years kept kicking in. It was easier to just smile and do what he was told.

Penny said he could watch TV if he wanted. Penny was nice. Her pancakes tasted a little like the ones Consuelo used to make, except Consuelo would put sprinkles on them when his parents weren't home.

Penny wanted to give him a hug, he could tell, but he wasn't ready to be hugged by anyone. He brushed a tear off his cheek. He missed his parents. He missed Consuelo. He wished his grandmother hadn't sent her away. Consuelo didn't have a cell phone or a car. How would she find him?

Troy snuggled a little deeper under the covers so Penny wouldn't see his nose start to run. She closed the blinds so the room was almost dark. Quietly, she walked around the bed and put the remote on the table beside it.

The lady who'd been at Shane's house this morning—Carly—turned out to be a lot more welcoming than Troy's brother. She didn't try to baby him or touch him like every other lady who'd been around him since his parents died. Instead, she'd made him program her number into his cell phone.

"Whatever you need, whenever you need it, wherever you are, you can call me, okay?" she told him. "You're never alone as long as I am around."

Then she'd taken them to the Richardsons'. She said they were her family and he could rest there as long as he wanted. Troy wished they'd taken the big dog with them, but apparently he belonged to the butthead. He could care for a dog but not his own brother. Carly must have thought Shane was being a jerk, too, because she didn't even say good-bye to him. *Good.* His brother didn't deserve a girlfriend who was so nice. And pretty.

The Richardsons seemed like a nice family. They teased each other a lot, but it didn't seem like they actually meant it. Troy had always wanted to have more brothers and sisters to hang out with. Instead, it had just been him and his parents. Now it was just him. He dragged in a deep breath and tried not to think about what happens to kids nobody wants.

Molly was in the hallway arguing with her mother. Troy liked Dr. Richardson. She smelled like a mom and she had a pretty smile—the kind that made you feel like she'd keep you safe always. His stomach hurt as he realized his mom would never smile at him that way again.

The voices grew quieter and Troy tried not to think of his parents as he listened for his new friend. Molly was okay—for a girl. Even now, she was trying to get her mom to let him rest on the sofa in the playroom so they could play Wii some more. He didn't hear what Dr. Richardson said because they'd moved down the hall. But he could tell Molly was the persistent type. Maybe if he just laid here and watched TV, she'd get her mom to change her mind. He really hoped so, because he didn't want to be alone.

He turned on the TV and Penny reached over to push the hair off his forehead.

"You're so much like your brother," she said.

What a bunch of crap! He didn't look like that a-hole, Shane. Not at all. Troy looked like his mom. Everyone said so. Shane Devlin was a dick and he hoped he never had to see him again. His stomach clenched again. Troy really had thought his brother would be different. When Shane left his parents' house late the other night, Troy was sure he'd be back the next day to take him to Baltimore. But he never showed up. Instead, his grandparents told him he was going to Florida with them. Troy didn't want to live with them. And, deep down, he knew it wasn't what his parents would have wanted.

He needed a new plan, but his mind was really tired and it was hard to think. Maybe if he just watched a little TV, his stomach would stop hurting. Tomorrow, he'd get Tiny to take him to find Consuelo. She could take care of him until he was eighteen. He didn't care what that stupid lawyer said. No way was he going to live with his grandparents. And if his jerk-faced brother didn't want him, he'd live with Consuelo.

If he could find her. He gulped back a sob. Why was this happening to him? How come his brother didn't want him? This all had to be a bad dream. Maybe if he went to sleep, he'd wake up back in his own house. With his mom and dad and Consuelo.

Penny quietly shut the door as she slipped out. Troy tried to concentrate on the Nickelodeon show he'd seen a thousand times before, but his eyes kept drifting shut.

Fifteen

Later that night Shane slipped into the Jacuzzi in his master bath and wondered how life could spiral out of control so quickly. His day had been a nightmare from beginning to end. The ninety pounds of petulant twelve-year-old boy the three stooges deposited on his doorstep early that morning proved to be just the beginning.

Once he'd finally arrived at camp, the hordes of media wanted to delve into his feelings about the loss of his father. Shane didn't bother telling them his feelings for Bruce Devlin weren't fit to print. Keeping his answers short and sweet, he tried steering the questions back to football.

By mid-morning, he'd finally made it to the practice field. It wasn't his best showing. His timing was off and he couldn't quite find his receivers as quickly as he would have liked. Fortunately, everyone cut him a little slack, and Shane wasn't above using their sympathy to his advantage. He figured it was about time Bruce Devlin played a positive role in his career.

"Things will go better tomorrow," he said as much to himself as to his teammates as they trotted off the field.

Unfortunately, his stint on the practice turf proved to be the highlight of his day.

Lisa Richardson stood on the sidelines waiting for him. Dressed casually in khaki shorts and a golf shirt, a pink ball cap covering the stubble of hair growing on her head, she smiled as he came near. But thanks to the ball cap, he couldn't tell if the smile reached her eyes. Carly had taken Troy and his posse to her sister's home earlier that morning. Shane wasn't sure what reason she'd given Lisa for Troy being with her. But since the family jewels were still firmly attached to his body, he figured whatever excuse she'd given, it didn't include details of her sleeping arrangements the night before. Or the night before that.

"I'm so sorry for your loss, Shane," Lisa said, falling in step beside him.

Fiddling with the helmet he was holding, he pondered how to best get to the locker room without insulting her. He'd pretty much had it with people's condolences for the day.

"Thanks," he mumbled.

Lisa was having no trouble keeping up with his stride. He slowed a little, realizing he couldn't escape the inevitable. Obviously, she'd honed her skills during her marriage to Coach.

"You and Troy seem to be holding up well," she said as she came to a stop, strategically blocking the entrance to the locker room. "In case you're wondering, Troy is sleeping at our house. He was exhausted."

Her tone put him on the defensive. He wasn't wondering where the kid was. He'd known Carly had left him with Penny. C.J. told him as much when he and Troy's posse arrived at the training facility for lunch. This was some kind of test, he could feel it. She was baiting him to see how he'd react.

He put on his best Boy Scout smile. "Thank you for that," he said. "I wasn't expecting him to arrive this morning. I appreciate everything you and Penny have done for us. It's been a rough couple of days." Playing the sympathy card was becoming easier. He didn't feel like puking when he invoked it anymore.

Lisa cleared her throat. "As a professional counselor, I want to encourage you to seek grief counseling, Shane. The team has people on retainer who can help you through this."

Is she kidding? Grief counseling! He wasn't grieving. The only thing he felt about his father's death was aggravation. This whole thing with Troy's guardianship had thrown off his concentration. He needed to get his head back in the game. Furthermore, he needed to get Troy out of Baltimore and firmly ensconced with his grandparents. What he didn't need was a grief counselor.

"Thank you, Dr, Richardson. I'll definitely look into that," he lied. The sooner he got into the locker room, the better.

He wasn't sure, but he thought he saw a smirk pass over her mouth before she harnessed it. "Good," she said. "I'm afraid it won't be as easy with Troy. Of course, you could both go to therapy together."

Shane felt his whole body tense. He knew where she was going with this and he didn't like it. He'd survived the loss of his mother without the help of a shrink. If Troy couldn't, then his grandfather the reverend would be the one to counsel him.

"Thank you, ma'am," he managed to squeeze out of his clenched jaw. "But where Troy will be living hasn't been settled yet. His grandparents would like him to live with them. I'm sure they'll have some idea how to handle his grief."

"Ahh. I see," she said, crossing her arms underneath her breasts. Her tone implied she didn't see at all. The coach's wife tilted her chin up at him in the same belligerent way her sister did. Shane didn't like it from either one of them. "In that case," she continued, "perhaps you want to leave Troy with us until the situation is resolved? We have plenty of room. That way, you'll be able to get through the next couple of days of mini-camp without being distracted."

Damn, she was tricky. Tossing out the perfect solution to his problem, she waved it in front of his face like chum before a shark. But he couldn't take it. He knew it. And so did she. Pasting a smile on his face, hoping it didn't come off too much like a sneer, he took a step toward the locker room. "That's very gracious of you. But I think it's best if he stays with me until we get things settled. But I appreciate the offer."

She gave him a cheesy smile of her own. Yep, she'd been testing him. And he didn't care if he'd passed or not. He slipped past her into the locker room before she could answer.

Hours later, he was regretting giving in to his conscience. His cell phone rang, snapping him back to the present. He flipped the phone open as he slid farther into the warm water.

"Roscoe, where the hell have you been all day?" he snapped, instantly regretting his tone. His agent was the one person who'd always been there to save his ass. Shane needed an ally to help sort out this mess Bruce had left for him.

"When will you get it through your head that you're not my only client, Devlin?"

"When you stop charging me like I am," Shane teased, trying to lighten his tone.

Roscoe chuckled. "You get the family discount, dude, so quit complaining. How's the hip?"

It hurts like hell! But Roscoe didn't need to know that. "Great. No problems," Shane said, trying not to slosh the water.

"Really? So you're in the Jacuzzi at ten o'clock at night because you feel great?"

Shane sighed and sunk into the heat, not bothering to muffle the sound of the water.

"Seriously, dude, do you have hidden cameras installed in here?"

"Hmm, nice idea, but you're just not that interesting," Roscoe joked. "It's just plain intuition. I've known you too long."

"I've had a stressful day. I'm just trying to relax before hitting the sack."

"Is Troy asleep?"

"Yeah, Beckett has appointed himself babysitter for the night."

Shane was amazed at how quickly the dog had attached himself to the grieving kid. Beckett had provided a nice buffer earlier in the evening. What little conversation the two had was centered around the dog's care and feeding. It helped Shane to stay detached from the kid. It was best for both of them. Except now, all he could see was the kid's red-rimmed eyes and his trembling lip, a look of complete desolation on his face. Shane's chest tightened as he remembered that aching feeling of abandonment. He thought those feelings were long buried. Damn Bruce for making him live through them again.

"How'd you manage to shake the boy's posse?" Roscoe asked.

"It wasn't easy. Tiny didn't want to let him out of his sight. But the other two were getting restless to get back to campus. Evan had a hot date and Dante needed to polish his jewelry," Shane joked. He took a swig of mineral water.

"From what I gathered, Tiny was a fixture at Bruce's place," Roscoe said. "He didn't get home often, so he spent his holidays with Bruce, Lindsey, and Troy. He's probably pretty shaken up about their deaths. It would explain his attachment to Troy."

"Yeah," Shane said, remembering the devastation on Troy's face when Tiny and the others drove off. He took another swallow of water. "Well, I'm sure his grandparents will let him invite Tiny for Christmas."

"Don't count on it." Shane sat up in the Jacuzzi, not liking the ominous sound in Roscoe's voice. "Look, Shane, this situation isn't going to resolve itself quickly. I finally got a hold of Dave Shapiro, Bruce's lawyer, late today. He's adamant that Bruce and Lindsey wanted you to have guardianship of Troy. Apparently, Lindsey was estranged from her parents since the time she married Bruce."

"Can you blame them?" Shane quipped.

Roscoe sighed. "The grandparents were allowed to see Troy once a year, but only in Pittsburgh. He was never allowed to travel to the church's compound in Florida. Shapiro says he can't in good conscience facilitate Troy living with his grandparents. He said to tell you that you'll have to take him to court to contest the will."

Shane sucked in a breath. "Christ! Is this guy serious?"

"Oh yeah, he's serious, Shane. And from some digging I did today, he may be right to keep the kid from the grandparents. They are teetering near bankruptcy. Bruce had a six-million-dollar estate from sales of his motivational book. He and Lindsey weren't very careful setting up the trust. You're probably right that they didn't plan on dying young. Nobody does. They hadn't gotten around to naming a trustee yet. The money goes with Troy for his guardian to use for his care. According to Shapiro, there's nothing to stop the grandparents from pouring it all back into the church. The same church that keeps them living the elite life, I might add."

Shane closed his eyes and swore. He didn't like the queasy feeling forming in his stomach.

"Apparently, they've already dismissed the nanny or housekeeper or whatever Consuelo was. Shapiro says she was in his office yesterday, distraught to be separated from Troy. She'd begun to file her retirement papers with the university, so she could travel with Troy to his grandparent's home."

"So now what?" Shane asked the question even though he didn't want to know the answer.

"Now you have to decide if you want to contest the will. It will be a long, protracted process, Shane. And I don't have to tell you, you won't come out smelling too pretty," Roscoe said.

When Shane didn't answer, he continued. "There are other options. Troy has enough money to live well. You can hire someone to look after him full-time. Consuelo, perhaps? You wouldn't have to alter your lifestyle too much."

Shane found the situation ironic. When his mother died, Bruce Devlin was a homeless junkie. Shane was sent to live on welfare with his grandparents in their double-wide trailer. Troy could afford to live in a palace anywhere in the world.

"Not an option," Shane said firmly.

Shane wanted to believe his staunch refusal was about him concentrating on his career, on breaking Bruce's records. But that was only part of the truth. A very small part. If he were being honest with Roscoe, he'd tell him he didn't have the emotional arsenal to help the kid. What did Shane know about raising a kid, much less nurturing him? He certainly didn't know a thing about love. His mother checked out when she got cancer, and his dad . . . well, it was common knowledge how that turned out. You had to be loved to give love, and Shane had no experience with that. But Shane wasn't going to admit that to anyone.

"What's with you, man? Do you sleep in a coffin or something?"

"If I did, you'd have already read about it in the tabloids."

"Stop being a smart-ass and talk to me, Shane," Roscoe pleaded.

When Shane didn't answer, Roscoe sighed wearily. "Fine," he said. "Keep your phobias to yourself. The other option is boarding school. He can afford the best."

Boarding school. Carly had gone to boarding school, and she'd turned out okay. In fact, the two of them had shared a few laughs last night over her tales of classic dorm pranks and late-night escapades. Christ, had it only been last night since they'd been together? His nerve endings hummed and his body tightened up at the thought of her. Maybe she'd help with the whole boarding school process. She had promised to help out with the kid. Then again, maybe pigs would fly. The tightness in Shane's chest ratcheted up a notch as he recalled the look of utter regret in her eyes this morning.

"That sounds like the winner," Shane said. "How long will it take to get him into one?"

Roscoe let out an exasperated huff. "I really have no idea. I'll get someone working on it tomorrow. You are planning on letting Troy have some say in where he goes, aren't you?"

"It depends on how black my heart is tomorrow," Shane said sarcastically.

"You've got a freakin' screw loose, you know that?" Roscoe asked. "You're punishing an innocent kid for the way your father treated you."

"I don't pay you to analyze me, Roscoe. Just find a school for the kid."

Roscoe let loose a few obscenities before hanging up.

Shane snapped the phone closed and placed it on the tile floor surrounding the Jacuzzi as he leaned his head back against the wall. Roscoe was the second person today to accuse him of punishing Troy for Bruce's sins. Carly was the first.

Closing his eyes, he could still clearly see her angry face right before she stormed out of his office. It was better this way. It was easier to break it off if she was angry at him. He never should have gotten involved with her in the first place. Hell, a few weeks ago his life had been so simple: make the team, become the starter, and break Bruce's remaining records. The starting job wasn't guaranteed. Just today, he'd had to share reps with an undrafted rookie from Idaho. Potato Head had youth on his side, but Shane still knew the game better than any quarterback.

Fooling around with the coach's sister-in-law, though, likely jeopardized not only his status as starter but also his spot on the team. Yeah, it was definitely better to have her hating him. It seemed something positive had come out of the mess Bruce had left him, after all.

Shane hefted himself out of the Jacuzzi and toweled off. Wrapping a towel around his waist, he went down to the kitchen to set up the coffeemaker for the next morning. On his way, he paused at the door of the guest bedroom to check on his uninvited guest. The kid was sleeping peacefully, one arm tucked under the blanket and the other gripping a tattered pillow he must have brought from home. His eyes were puffy and his cheeks tear stained, but he was finally sleeping peacefully.

The kid hadn't said much when Shane retrieved him from the Richardsons'. Penny was as unhappy as his posse to let him out of her sight. One hard look from Shane, and she'd bit back whatever she'd wanted to say. Apparently all women associated with Coach couldn't wait to give him a piece of their mind.

Beckett lay sprawled across the foot of the bed. The dog opened one eye as Shane passed, but didn't bother to get off the bed. *Traitor.* Shane closed the door and headed to the kitchen.

As he stood at the sink filling the coffee carafe, his mind drifted back twenty-four hours. He could still feel Carly's hip pressed up against his as they stood side by side washing dishes. For the life of him, he couldn't remember ever washing dishes with another woman, much less enjoying it. Hell, most of the women he dated had so many food hang-ups they wouldn't be caught dead in a kitchen. But the previous evening with Carly was more than just a night of sex. He'd let his guard down with her, and that could only lead to disaster. Women like Carly wanted more than Shane was capable of giving. He just wasn't genetically programmed for a lasting relationship with anyone.

Flicking off the light, he padded barefoot up the stairs trying to shake off the memories of last night. When he reached his bedroom, he yanked off the towel, tossed it on a chair, and climbed into the king-sized bed. The scent of Carly's citrus perfume clung to the pillow. For a split second, he contemplated changing its case before succumbing to temptation and curling his face into the pillow.

He'd been a fool to get involved with Carly. But he'd been unable to ignore the sexual pull she had on his body. The look of contempt she gave him this morning hadn't done too much to lessen the pull, but at least whatever they'd shared had ended quickly, with her seeing his flaws for what they were. Heck, he'd never pretended to be anyone other than who he was. Carly March was like all the rest of the women who thought they could change him and were disappointed when they couldn't. Only this time, Carly's disappointment stung.

A blast of cool air hit Troy in the face as he came into the locker room. It was a hot June day, more than ninety degrees, and he'd spent most of it outside on the practice field watching Shane in mini-camp. The air-conditioning felt good on his damp skin. He grabbed a bottle of water from the cooler and slid down the wall to sit on the floor, rubbing the bottle over his face before guzzling its contents.

The last couple of days had been like a dream come true for Troy. After Shane's initial shock when Troy had surprised him at his house, he thought his brother would send him immediately back to his grandparents. But Shane had instead surprised Troy, letting him tag along to the training facility. The first day, Shane kept him on the field with him, telling the reporters to leave them both alone. It was cool how the reporters wanted to talk to them. It made Troy feel important. They wanted to ask questions about their dad, but Shane said the reporters should respect their privacy and not distract practice. So, Troy stood on the sidelines, ignoring the media and watching in awe as his brother threw one perfect spiral after another.

Clearly, Shane had gotten all the athletic genes and that's why Troy was such a klutz. But he was okay with it because his big brother was a superstar who was finally paying attention to him. His mom and dad would be so happy. Troy shook off the numbness that threatened to overtake him whenever he thought about his parents, refocusing on the good times he shared with his brother these past few days instead.

That first night, Shane and his friend, Donovan Carter, took him to get burgers. The three then played a few rounds of mini golf at a local ice cream stand. Donovan teamed up with him so they could beat Shane. Troy couldn't remember a night being more fun.

Yesterday went the same as the one before. C.J. Richardson recruited Troy to work as a ball boy, toweling off the sweaty footballs and trotting onto the field with Gatorade for the players. Afterward, Shane invited C.J. over for steaks and to watch *Gladiator*. Troy's mom would never let him watch that movie. He swallowed a huge lump as he thought of his mom and how much he missed her. But he had his brother now. He was so happy he'd talked Tiny into bringing him to Shane's house. Things were going great.

Until Troy had ruined it.

He really needed to learn to keep his mouth shut. Last night, while they were cleaning up and getting ready for bed, Troy asked Shane if he had an Xbox. Everyone has one. Especially rich sports stars. Surely Shane had one somewhere.

"Nah," Shane said. "Those things rot your brain."

Troy laughed because that was what his father always said. "You sound just like Dad," he'd joked.

Only Shane didn't think it was funny. He just stared at Troy for a long moment, looking a little scary. Then, he snatched up Beckett's leash, snapped it on the dog's collar, and yanked him out of the door for a walk. Troy waited up awhile, but when Shane didn't come back, he crawled into bed and tried not to cry.

He'd waited all his life to meet his brother. He wanted Shane to like him. He desperately needed them to be a family. Without Shane, he had no one else. And now he'd gone and blown it. When he woke later that night, Beckett was back and laying on Troy's feet in the bed, snoring softly. At least Beckett still liked him.

This morning, Shane told Troy they'd be going to his cabin in western Pennsylvania the next day. Troy wanted to ask questions about the cabin, but his brother was back to grunting at him. When they arrived at the training facility for mini-camp, Shane told him to stick with the other ball boys and to make sure he drank plenty of water. Troy wanted to believe Shane was concerned about him. But more likely his brother didn't want Troy dropping dead of heat stroke because it would interfere with his precious practice.

All Shane cared about was football. He didn't even seem to care about girls. Troy thought all sports stars cared about girls. But, except for that first morning, he hadn't seen any women hanging around. Maybe that's why Shane was so mad at him. The girls wouldn't come over if Troy was there. But Troy could be polite and all. He could make himself scarce if that's what Shane wanted him to do.

Even Carly was ignoring Shane. At first, Troy thought maybe she lived with Shane. That would be okay. She was really pretty and nice. And, she was Molly's aunt. Molly said Carly was really cool. But Molly had looked at Troy funny when he'd asked if Carly was Shane's girlfriend. Then Molly had laughed. Maybe Troy was wrong. Maybe Carly was just there that morning to borrow some coffee or something. After all, she didn't look like she liked Shane at all. She always smiled at Troy when he saw her in the commissary or around the practice facility, but she never looked at Shane. Except when she thought no one was looking. Then she stared at Shane, but her eyes were really sad when she did it.

Just then, C.J. walked into the locker room, a blast of hot, sticky air following him in. He had a bag of footballs slung over his shoulder and was mumbling into his cell phone. He wasn't paying attention to where he was going and Troy quickly scrambled to his feet to avoid being stepped on. Troy didn't want to get C.J. mad at him, too. C.J.—all the Richardsons—were nice to him. C.J. treated him like any of the other ball boys, overlooking the fact that he was smaller and younger than the other kids. He didn't smirk or laugh when Troy threw the football even though they both knew he threw like a girl. Like Shane, C.J. had been given all of his father's athletic genes. Troy liked him in spite of it.

"Hey, Short Stuff," C.J. called from the equipment room. "Let's go get some ice cream in the commissary."

Okay, so he didn't like being called Short Stuff, but Troy's friends were few and far between right now, so he'd take what he could get.

Sixteen

The hot afternoon sun beat through the commissary's giant windows, warming Carly's bare legs, which she'd stretched out on the chair in front of her. In deference to the record heat, she wore a floral wrap skirt and sleeveless linen blouse to work. One slide sandal hung precariously from her foot, its spiked heel dangling off the side of the chair. She dipped her spoon into a bowl of frozen yogurt and sighed as the cool chocolate slid down her throat. Mini-camp had wrapped up earlier in the day and a quiet calm had now settled over the training facility. After the hustle and bustle of players and media the previous week, she was amazed at how quickly the place had cleared out.

"I thought this week would never end," Asia said from her seat beside Carly.

She glanced over to where her friend sat. Asia's neck arched gracefully as she lifted her closed eyes toward the sun streaming in the window. "It's amazing how a controversy over who is going to play quarterback can rally the media."

Carly sucked on her spoon, wishing Asia hadn't brought

up the subject of the Blaze quarterback. She'd spent the last
couple of days trying not to think of him. Unfortunately,
Shane was everywhere she turned. Avoiding him in the flesh
had been easy. She simply stuck to her side of the training
complex. It was harder to avoid him when she closed her
eyes, though. At night when she slept, she could feel his
hands exploring her body. Carly dreamt about his greedy
mouth as it made love to her. His smell still permeated the
thick comforter on her bed. She could taste his skin . . .
Argh!

Carly ripped the spoon from her mouth and stuck it in
the bowl of half-eaten yogurt. Yanking her feet off the chair,
she slid closer to the air-conditioner vent. Fantasies of Shane
were wreaking havoc with her internal body temperature.
In spite of her resolution to keep her distance from all things
Shane Devlin, she found herself asking Asia about him.

"Isn't Shane the starting quarterback?"

Asia's body never wavered from its relaxed position. "Not
necessarily."

Obviously, she needed to pay more attention to how
American football was played. She didn't want to examine
why the thought of Shane not playing for the Blaze suddenly
bothered her. "But I thought he was supposed to replace
Gabe."

"You really know nothing about how this game works,
do you?" Asia asked, her tone incredulous.

"I grew up in Europe, remember?"

Asia huffed, closing her eyes once more. "There are no
guarantees in this game, Carly. Hank brought Devlin in
because he needed a strong veteran at the position. But he
drafted a rookie quarterback the very next week. It's anyone's
guess who'll replace Gabe," she said with a shrug of her
shoulders.

Well, wasn't that ironic. Even if he behaved, Shane still
wasn't guaranteed a starting gig. No wonder he was so
obsessed with mini-camp. It still didn't explain—or excuse—
his behavior regarding Troy, however. She hadn't spoken
with Troy since that morning she'd left him with Lisa. She'd

seen him on the practice field with Shane, however. His brother practically used the boy as a human shield to get past the media each day.

She stood up and stretched, tossing her unfinished yogurt into a trash can. Asia rose next to her, gathering her cane as she did so.

"I guess I'd better get my stuff together so I can make my flight," Asia said as both women headed across the room.

"What time are you leaving?"

"I'm on the eight o'clock flight to L.A. But I need to get home and grab my bags first. What are you planning to do with your free time?"

It was a sad commentary on her boring life, but Carly had no real vacation plans. Julianne was headed to her NAS-CAR wedding for the weekend. Matt, Lisa, and the kids were leaving shortly for two weeks of much-needed family time at the beach. All week Lisa had been pestering her to join them, but Carly was looking forward to some downtime herself. She meant to take advantage of a quiet office to get everything ready for the next season.

"I've got a lot to do here," she lied. "I need to help finalize the logistics for the team's away games so Hank won't have to worry about that when he gets back." Which was the truth, but there wasn't much involved with that other than reviewing the package the travel office had already put together. She'd probably spend most of her free time brooding over the hard-bodied, steely-eyed quarterback on the Blaze payroll.

Jeez, she was pathetic. The man had the emotional capability of a newt. Everything about him screamed "not long-term material." She wanted to smack herself in the head. Hadn't she already learned her lesson about professional jocks? She needed to exorcise Shane Devlin from her mind. And from all her body parts.

Which was easier said than done. She kept trying to tell herself the attraction was only physical, but she'd discovered these past few weeks that he hid a lot behind the persona he presented to the public. There was something very vulnerable about Shane. A vulnerability that kept nagging at her chest and wouldn't go away.

Her anger with Shane's attitude toward Troy had subsided over the past several days. Carly didn't need her sister's clinical psychology degree to realize he didn't have the skills to deal with all the turmoil in his life—much less accept a brother he barely knew. But Troy was still living at Shane's. That had to mean something.

"You just keep a careful eye out for that Joel Tompkins," Asia said, interrupting her musing. "He's trouble. With or without a restraining order."

"I haven't heard a peep out of him in a week. I'm sure his grandfather convinced him to go to rehab. It'll be fine now," Carly said as she caught sight of C.J. and Troy entering the commissary.

"Well, just the same, Carly, you keep an eye out, okay?" Asia said. "In my experience, creeps like Joel don't hide under their rocks for long."

Carly nodded, unsure how to respond. She'd just begun to be less skittish about the situation with Joel, but Asia's concern caused Carly's nerves to twitch.

"Good girl," Asia said, giving her a quick hug. "I've got to go or I'll miss my plane. See you in two weeks," Asia called as she hobbled out to her office.

Turning back to the cafeteria, she watched C.J. and Troy head for the ice cream bar. Both were red faced and sweaty as each grabbed for a plastic bowl.

"Hello, boys," she said with a smile. "You both look like you could use something cool to eat."

"Yeah, well it's like ninety-five degrees out there, Aunt Carly. We all don't get to sit around in the AC all day." C.J. made it sound like it was a hardship shagging balls for his father's team, but she knew he loved it. Carly smiled, refusing to let her nephew's surly demeanor get to her.

"What?" he asked, eyeing her suspiciously.

"Nothing," she said, reaching up to pat his cheek. "You just look so cute all mussed up."

"Jeez, Aunt Carly," C.J. said as he pulled away from her

touch, his face even redder now. "You're blocking the ice cream."

Troy smiled broadly at their exchange, hero worship shining in his eyes. Carly grinned back at him. "Are you enjoying camp, Troy?" she asked. She really should avoid the Devlin brothers, but it was nice to see Troy not looking so ragged around the edges. Besides, he wasn't the brother who constantly sent her pulse racing.

He pushed his glasses up against the bridge of his nose and gave her a lopsided grin. "Yes, ma'am."

When both boys had filled their bowls to nearly overflowing, they sat at one of the round bistro tables. Not waiting to be asked, Carly hooked her foot around the leg of a chair and pulled up to the table to join them. Much as she hated to admit it, she was dying to know what was going on with Shane. Troy was the most likely source of that information.

"So," she began as she watched C.J. tuck into his bowl. "Do you and Shane have any big plans for the next few weeks?" *Really, what was the sense of beating around the bush?*

Troy's chin dropped to his chest as he stared at his ice cream. C.J. nudged her with the toe of his Nike. She looked over at him and he shook his head slightly. She glanced at Troy. He fidgeted with his glasses again.

"We're going to some cabin for a while," he said softly.

"Well, that sounds cool," C.J. interjected. She felt a rush of love for her nephew. Clearly, he was trying to make the trip sound exciting. "Maybe you can go fishing and stuff." He actually made it sound like he thought it would be okay to be out of cell phone range somewhere.

"Sure," she added enthusiastically. "You and Shane could get to know one another better." C.J. shot her the "are you really that dumb?" look he normally reserved for his sisters. Troy sunk lower in his chair, if that were possible.

"I guess so," he mumbled.

"Hey, you could always come to the beach with us," C.J. said around another mouthful of ice cream. A hopeful look appeared in Troy's eyes, but it vanished just as quickly. He sat up in his chair.

"That would be great, but I think Shane likes to go to the mountains to clear his head before the season," Troy said. "My dad told me once that he goes there every year. We used to invite him to come visit us in Pittsburgh, but he never did."

Bruce invited Shane to come visit? Now that was interesting. From what Shane had told her, his father had pretty much shut him out of his new life.

"Well, if you change your mind, you're always welcome at our beach house. Crap, I'm getting a brain freeze!" C.J. said. Not surprising, given the way he was shoveling ice cream into his mouth.

"Stick your thumb on the roof of your mouth!" Troy said.

Carly left the boys laughing about brain freezes while she pondered the information she'd just wheedled out of Troy. Shane was taking his brother with him to his cabin. A week ago, she was sure he'd ship his little brother to his grandparents as soon as he got the chance. Was it possible Shane was finally putting aside some of his animosity for his father? Maybe Lisa was right; Shane just needed some time to come around to the idea of having a half brother. Surely, once they'd spent some time together, he'd realize being Troy's guardian wasn't so bad. Perhaps it would all work out for the best.

For Troy, anyway.

As for Carly, her relationship with Shane was over and done with. If you could call it a relationship. It was really a one-night stand. Well, actually a two-night stand, but that was just semantics. It was over, whatever *it* was. She was just having trouble convincing herself to be happy it was over.

It was nearly five o'clock and the hallways along the training center were deserted. Shane didn't bother to hide the slight limp in his gait. He'd just spent a half hour in the whirlpool and now he was hoping to find a trainer to administer some ultrasound to his painful hip. The coaches had already left, and with a little luck, he could find a member of the training staff who wouldn't talk. His hip hurt, but he could play through the pain. The coaches didn't need to know a thing.

The tap-tap-tapping of heels along the tile floor alerted him that someone was coming around the corner just before she plowed into him. He wrapped his arms around Carly, steadying her before she could fall.

"Oh!" she said. The skin on her bare arms was soft and warm beneath his fingers. Her familiar scent filled his nostrils. She brushed against him as she tried to regain her balance. His cock sprung to life beneath his cotton gym shorts.

"Hey, Carly," he said, his voice a bit huskier than he would have liked.

She lifted her eyes up at him and a blush began to creep up her neck to her face as she tried to take a step back. He let her body break contact from his, but he kept his hands cradling her elbows. He'd missed touching her. Hell, he'd missed *her*. He was out of his depth handling a grieving twelve-year-old. It was too painful reliving emotions he'd long since buried. More than once these past few days, he'd wanted to just talk to her, watch her smile, kiss her.

"Oh," she said, biting her bottom lip. "Umm, if you're looking for Troy, he's in the commissary with C.J."

Shane hadn't been looking for the kid. He'd just texted him and knew he was with C.J. But he wasn't going to tell Carly that. Hell, she probably thought he should be with the kid 24/7 right now. Besides, she'd just lecture him about his fraternal responsibilities again. Not that he didn't like the way she looked all hot and bothered.

"He was telling me about the trip you two are taking to your cabin in the mountains. Troy seemed excited. It'll be good for you both," she said, her voice laced with enthusiasm.

Ah, hell. It seemed he was going to get a lecture anyway. The earnest expression on Carly's face was nearly his undoing. She thought everything had been worked out, when in reality nothing had changed. It was just delayed. He had to stop her before she got the wrong idea about his relationship with Bruce's son. She'd only be disappointed again with what she thought was his lack of emotional depth. Better that she not know what really scared Shane.

Fortunately, he knew the perfect way to distract her. Pulling her into an empty training room, he closed and locked the door behind them.

"Does this mean you're not mad at me anymore?" he asked, backing her up against the door.

"Shane!" she whispered, her eyes round in her beautiful face. He wasn't listening. The overpowering need for her that should have burnt out several days ago overtook whatever logic existed. Pressing his body against hers, he took her mouth in a ravenous kiss. Her mouth was soft and warm just like he remembered. It tasted like chocolate. He fully expected her to resist him—probably with a knee to the jewels—she'd been so angry with him the other day.

But he was wrong again.

After the briefest hesitation, she kissed him back with the same ferocity. Her fingers found his hair as she gripped his head. Shane's hands slid beneath her full skirt and they shook as his fingers came in contact with bare leg.

"You're not wearing underwear!" he breathed against her neck.

"Am too," she whispered in his ear, just before her teeth nipped at the lobe.

"This I gotta see," he said. Lifting her at the waist, he carried her over to the training table while her lips feasted on his neck. He flung her skirt up around her stomach and set her down on the end of the table. She leaned back on her elbows, exposing herself to him, a saucy grin on her face. All the breath left his body at the sight of her. He flopped down on the rolling stool so he was at eye level. A sexy scrap of hot pink lace formed a triangle between her legs. He hooked her knees over his shoulders and wheeled in for a closer look.

"The only thing that could make those sexier would be if they're edible," he said, his eyes never leaving the prize.

She gave a husky laugh. "They're Hanky Pankys and they are definitely *not* edible."

"God, you have amazing skin. I missed the taste of it."

He leaned in to run his tongue along a small purple bruise that he had left on her inner thigh the other night. She trembled beneath his lips, a hiss escaping hers.

"Shane, we shouldn't be doing this. Especially not here." Too bad her voice lacked any real conviction.

She tried to unhook a leg from his shoulder, but he held her tight. He didn't want to stop. If she'd objected when they first entered the room, he might have been able to walk away. But she'd kissed him back, stoking the fire inside him with her own roving hands and mouth and her breathy moans. Shane didn't want her coming to her senses now. He just wanted her to come. So he pushed away the pink lace and sent his tongue in to pleasure her.

She sighed softly, but instead of pulling away, she kicked her stiletto sandals to the floor so she could wrap her legs around him. He licked and sucked until she was shaking.

"Shane, you have to stop," she said, her voice husky and sexy as hell. "I'm going to scream and everyone will know we're in here."

There was no way he was going to stop. His hunger for Carly was insatiable. Focused on possessing her, Shane continued what he was doing. One hand massaged her bottom while the other reached below the table and grabbed a rolled-up towel.

"Here," he said, tossing the towel at her. "Shove that in your mouth." He glanced up at her incredulous face. Her eyes were the deep blue color that happened when she was aroused, but there was annoyance there, too. The annoyance turned him on and he returned his mouth to between her thighs. Before she could get a protest out, he found the little nub and sucked on it. She moaned loudly before stuffing the towel in her mouth. Shane might have tried to prolong his feast, but he was excruciatingly hard and he didn't want to waste time. He needed to get inside her.

She came quickly, a series of spasms rocking her body. Normally he would have taken his time to pleasure her again or at least kiss his way out. But he couldn't chance her becoming too alert. Standing up so quickly he sent the wheeled stool spinning across the room, he dropped his shorts and his boxer briefs to his ankles and entered her.

Both her eyes and mouth flew open. The towel was now clenched in her hands. As he stared at her without moving, a slow grin of pleasure covered her mouth and her fingers reached for the hem of his T-shirt. Yanking him on top of her, she wrapped her legs around his bare butt as she clenched her warm muscles around his throbbing erection. Groaning, he found her mouth for a kiss. Their tongues tangled as he thrust into her. Carly rose to meet him, running her hands in his hair. There was no way of holding out any longer. Tearing his mouth away, Shane threw his head back in a silent scream as he came.

As he buried his face in her hair, Shane waited for their breathing to return to normal. Inhaling deeply, he tried to capture her scent. The smell of her no longer lingered on his pillows and he realized he missed it. If he was being honest, he missed everything about Carly. God, he was turning into such a sap.

Carly marched toward her office, a still-grinning Shane Devlin trailing behind her. How could this have happened? One minute, she was minding her business, and the next, Shane was chewing through a fifty-dollar pair of thong underwear. Where was her self-control? Why couldn't she resist this man? The one man she ought to say no to.

She huffed softly to herself.

He chuckled behind her.

Carly wheeled around. "It's not funny! This is my workplace! *Our* workplace!" she said, her voice a hoarse whisper as she whipped her head from side to side making sure no one was in the office to hear them.

"Okay," Shane said, lifting his palms up in a defensive position.

"And why are you following me to my office?" she snapped. "There is so *not* going to be a repeat performance in there!"

"Calm down, Carly," he said, his just-had-sex smirk still gracing his lips. "You were a little unsteady on your heels when you bolted back there. I just wanted to make sure you made it back to your desk okay."

His smug teasing infuriated Carly more. "I've said it before and I'll say it again: You arrogant jocks are all alike!"

"Hey, don't put me in the same category as your ex," he said.

Carly saw anger flash in his eyes and it caused her own ire to die down a bit. It wasn't fair to take it out on him. Sure, he'd initiated their encounter in the training room, but she hadn't done a thing to stop him. Instead, she'd joined right in, enjoying the interlude as much as he had—maybe more.

She tucked a strand of hair behind her ear. "I'm sorry," she whispered.

He reached for her then, but she backed away into her office. "Please, Shane. Let's just stick to the original plan and keep this professional from here on out."

When she looked up into Shane's face, his eyes were thunderous. Confused, she took another step back before Shane shoved her aside. "What the hell is this?" His voice took on that lethal tone her brother-in-law frequently used on the sideline.

Carly turned toward her desk.

A rose, ripped from its stem, was lying on her chair. Underneath it were photos of her with Shane at the gala and with Donovan walking arm in arm into the building. Shane reached for the photos and a note fell to the floor. Carly picked it up. The handwriting was neat and clear, but the tone was vicious.

These men don't love you the way I do. You were
meant to be with me. You WILL be with me.

The note was unsigned, but she knew who had written it. Her hand trembled as she frantically looked around her.

"Joel was here," she said, trying to force the words out of her suddenly dry mouth. Carly gripped the side of her credenza to steady herself. Shane was rapidly dialing the phone.

"Donovan Carter!" he demanded, only to slam down the receiver a second later. Rifling through her drawers, Shane pulled out a folder and stuffed the photos inside. "Give it to me," he said as he pried the note from Carly's trembling hand. "Come on." He wrapped his strong fingers around her wrist and dragged her from her office. Desperately, she tried to keep up as her heels tapped along beside the squeak of his Pumas on the tile floor.

They found Donovan sitting on a bench in the weight room, a towel hanging loosely around his shoulders. If he was startled to see them, his face didn't show it. As if he sensed something was wrong, his detective's mask slid firmly into place.

"What's going on?" he asked, although the look he shot at Shane told her he'd already taken in their rumpled appearance and knew exactly what had been going on moments earlier.

Shane moved to speak, but Carly cut him off. "I need to talk to you," she said as she yanked her arm free of Shane's death grip. He glared at her as she rubbed her wrist. "Joel left me another note on my chair. Donovan, he was in the building."

"What?" Donovan was standing now, his cell phone already out of his pocket. "When?"

"I'm not really sure." She pulled the folder from Shane's hands. Shane drew his lips into a tight line as he crossed his arms in front of his chest and rocked back on his heels. "He left this on my desk. And another rose. It was . . . it was torn apart." Her voice had a slight tremor to it now. She took a deep breath to control it.

Donovan took the folder and glanced at the photos. "When did you find these?" he asked.

"They were there when I went to my office a little bit ago." She rubbed at her wrist again. It didn't hurt. Her skin was just cold and she missed the warmth where Shane's fingers had been.

"When were you in your office last, Carly? I need to know when Joel was in the building," he demanded.

"Um, I don't know," she hedged. "Asia and I stopped in the commissary for a snack right after the four o'clock press briefing."

Donovan looked at his watch. "That was over an hour ago. Where did you go after the commissary?"

I stopped to have hot monkey sex in the training room with the idiot standing next to me! "I don't remember. I sat with C.J. and Troy for a little bit. I got sidetracked on the way back."

Donovan looked at both of them. His eyes said he didn't believe her, but at least he didn't voice his doubts out loud. He barked at someone on his cell phone. Carly glanced over at Shane, who had his game face on.

"I need to get that rose and anything else he might have left and take it over to the Baltimore PD," Donovan said. "I've got my people going over the surveillance tapes to see how and when Joel got in the building."

"You don't think he's still here?" The waver was back in her voice.

Donovan looked at Shane before he answered. "No, I don't. But maybe you should head home with Coach tonight."

She glanced at the clock on the wall behind him. "He's already left. Lisa was supposed to pick them up fifteen minutes ago and they were leaving directly for the beach." Of course, if she hadn't stopped for a quickie in the training room, she could have caught her family before they left.

"It'll be okay, Donovan. I'm sure Joel is long gone." She tried her best to sound convincing. "I'm just going to pack up for the day and go home."

"Like hell you are," Shane said from beside her.

"Excuse me?" She slowly turned her head to face him. He was still standing with his arms folded across his chest looking as if he ruled the world.

"I'll make sure she gets home safely, Don," he said, ignoring her.

Donovan looked from one to the other. It was clear he

didn't like the idea of Shane taking her home, but apparently he liked the idea of her going home alone less.

"Fine," he said, and both men headed for the door.

"What just happened here?" she called after them, refusing to move from the room.

"Carly." Shane's tone was softer now, but still firm. "He's right. Until we know where Tompkins is, you shouldn't be left alone. Let Don do his job and get the police to pick him up." He walked back over to her and lifted a hand to gently caress her cheek. "Come to dinner with Troy and me. By the time we get home, the police will have Joel in custody for violating the restraining order."

Carly stifled a shiver, unsure whether it was caused by Shane's touch or her current situation. She hated having to rely on someone else for safety. But she hated what Joel was doing to her more. Truth be told, she was a little spooked to go home alone. She only wished Shane wasn't the one acting as her bodyguard. But he said Troy would be with them. Dinner with the Devlin brothers would definitely be a distraction from Joel's note. Surely Shane would keep his hands to himself with his brother around. He'd better. Because it was obvious she couldn't keep her own hands to herself.

Three hours and a glass of wine later, Carly drove into her neighborhood as night began to fall. Shane had taken her and Troy to Little Italy for dinner. The food was delicious—what little bits she managed to get down. It didn't help that Shane was back to being his moody, arrogant self, grunting monosyllables throughout the meal. She tried to ignore him, instead listening to Troy babble about minicamp and C.J.—the boy was in awe of everything her nephew did—and Beckett, his new best friend. Troy was a sweet boy, much like C.J. at that age.

When dinner was over, they headed back to the training facility to pick up her car. Troy begged to ride home with her and Shane seemed relieved to be rid of him. He headed home to walk Beckett while she and Troy stopped off at

Santoni's for ice cream. Rather than eat it there, they'd decided to grab a couple of pints of Ben & Jerry's and bring it home.

"Carly?" Troy said as they pulled into the neighborhood. "Dr. Richardson said your mom died when you were younger than I am. Like nine or something."

"Yeah," she said, cringing a little because she really didn't like to discuss her mother's death. It might be therapeutic for Troy, but Lisa was better at the psychobabble than she was.

"She said that movie *Death in a Sandstorm* is about your mom."

"Yep." She waved to the guard as she drove through the main gate.

"That's gotta be so cool," he said.

"I guess." She never knew what to say about the legend her mom had become as a result of a blockbuster movie immortalizing her life and death.

"Do you still miss her?" he asked quietly. "I mean, does it ever go away?" She glanced over at him as she pushed the garage door opener. His eyes were red behind his glasses again and he bit his bottom lip as he waited for her to answer.

Pulling into the garage, she put the car in park and cut the ignition. As she leaned her head back against the headrest, she let out a long sigh.

"Yeah. I miss her sometimes. I wish I could have known her better. She was just always Mum to me, you know? That fearless reporter in the movie was the part I never got to see. But it does get better, Troy. It's just going to take some time."

She looked over at him as he brushed away a tear. "Oh, sweetie," she said, gathering him up in her arms. "It's going to be okay. You'll see. You're lucky. You have people who want you. My grandmother and my father didn't even know I existed until my mom died. You have your grandparents who know and love you. And Shane. And all of us here. You're gonna be just fine."

"My grandparents don't want *me*. They just want my money. I heard them talking the night Mom and Dad died.

They want to use the money to help people with their ministry. I don't mind helping people, but it still doesn't seem right somehow. I mean, would they still want me if I were poor? They barely even know me." Troy sniffled against her. "And Shane, he definitely doesn't want me," he said.

She suspected that last part might be true, but she wasn't about to add to the boy's sorrow. It was surreal how this little boy's life could be so similar to hers. Those feelings of being lost and alone in the world still lingered despite the fact that she had her own home, her own job, and her own money. It was that sense of belonging she kept searching for. And she thought she'd found it here in Baltimore with her sister Lisa's family and her job with the Blaze. But it still felt precarious, as if it could be ripped away from her at any moment. She wondered if that feeling would ever go away.

Shame on Shane for making this boy feel so vulnerable. She gave Troy a gentle squeeze. "He doesn't want anybody," she said, brushing a kiss over his hair. "He thinks he's too cool to need anybody. He's just a big butthead."

Troy giggled into her shoulder.

"Hey," she said, holding him away from her. "Our ice cream is melting. Whaddya say we eat it before the butthead shows up to take you home? He should be here any minute."

They were both laughing when they entered the kitchen. But when Carly turned on the overhead light, she stopped dead in her tracks. The sweet smell of roses reached her nostrils at the same time her eyes took in the mess in her kitchen and living room. Mutilated flowers were strewn everywhere. It looked as if wild animals had been let loose inside. Photos were ripped from frames, their glass scattered about the floor. Pillows and cushions were slashed, pieces of stuffing still floating in the air.

She gulped for air as her breath froze in her lungs. The plastic bag holding the ice cream slipped from her numb fingertips.

"Who did this?" It took her a moment to realize that Troy

was echoing her thoughts. Except Carly already knew who'd done it. Joel Tompkins.

Troy took a step farther into the house before she grabbed him tightly by the arm, pulling him behind her.

"No, Troy." She was amazed she could find the breath to speak since her chest felt like it might explode. "Get outside." Dragging him into the garage, she shoved him back into the car. With shaky hands, she jammed the keys into the ignition.

"Get out my cell phone," she ordered, tossing Troy her purse. Backing out of the garage, she parked the car down the street and he handed her the phone. With trembling fingers, she dialed 911.

Seventeen

Shane worked off some steam as he and Beckett jogged the last mile to Carly's. They'd run a two-mile loop through the back of the neighborhood. He figured he'd arrive at her house just as they were getting home after their dessert of ice cream. Surely, the kid could manage to walk a mile back to his place. Hopefully it would tire him out and he'd go right to bed. Shane had had enough of listening to him gush at Carly for one night. Not that Shane could blame the kid. Obviously, he had a major crush on her.

Well, so did a couple other guys, including one psycho sportswriter.

Shane had checked with guards at the gatehouse when he drove in to make sure Joel hadn't attempted to enter the neighborhood. Both men assured him they knew to alert the police if they spotted his car. He'd texted Donovan fifteen minutes ago, but still no reply. Hopefully, the police had already picked Joel up. Just the same, even with the added security of being in a gated community, Shane would make sure her place was locked up tightly before he left.

His cell phone vibrated. Digging it out of his pocket, he

recognized Donovan's number on the caller ID. Great. They'd finally picked up Tompkins. But he never answered the call because as he rounded the corner next to Carly's house, he spotted three police cruisers, lights flashing, parked in front.

What the hell? They were going out to eat ice cream. They weren't supposed to be back yet. Beckett trailed behind him as he sprinted toward the house, ignoring Donovan's call.

Shane pushed through the half-open front door, the dog following him in. The place was a mess. Police technicians were moving about dusting for fingerprints and putting things in plastic baggies. Beckett trotted over to where the kid stood talking to a man wearing a rumpled suit. The guy was jotting something in his notebook and chewing on a plastic coffee straw.

"Shane!" the kid said as Beckett planted himself firmly on the kid's feet.

The cop in the rumpled suit looked up at Shane. His mustache was as raggedy as his clothing.

"Who're you?" he asked without removing the straw.

"He's my brother, Shane Devlin."

Rumpled Suit's eyes lit up in recognition as Shane clamped his hand on the kid's shoulder.

"What happened?" Shane asked.

"I don't know. It was like this when we got here." The kid's glasses magnified his eyes, huge with what was either fear or bravado. Probably both.

"Did you see anyone in or around the house when you came in?" The cop directed his question at the kid. Shane's gut clenched and his palms began to sweat. Whoever did this could have been here when they'd walked in. The guards at the gate either hadn't been doing their job, or Joel was a lot more determined than they'd all given him credit for. He raked his fingers through his hair and sucked in a deep breath.

"No. Carly wouldn't let me go past the kitchen. Once she saw the mess, she took me back to her car. She drove to the corner and we stayed there until you guys came." The kid looked from Shane to the cop. "You guys got here really fast."

"You did the right thing," the cop reassured him.

"Where's Carly?" Shane asked. The kid pointed behind him, stepping out of the way as Shane reluctantly let go of his shoulder. Carly sat on the bottom step of the stairs leading to her bedroom. Another detective stood over her, gently questioning her. His suit wasn't rumpled. In fact, he looked like he'd just stepped off the cover of *Menswear* magazine. He was young and fresh faced, and a dead ringer for Matt Damon. From where he stood looking down at Carly, he had a great view down her blouse, which he seemed to be taking full advantage of.

Shane crouched down between her and the cop's shiny wingtips.

"Hey," he said softly as she looked up at him. The same blue eyes that had shone with passion earlier in the day were now blank. Her lower lip was swollen and pink from where she'd been biting it. It stood out against her pale skin. Her hand trembled as she brushed her hair over her shoulder.

"I'm sorry, Shane." Her voice was soft. "I wouldn't have brought Troy here if I'd known . . . if I'd known . . ." She was unable to finish her sentence.

Damn, he never should have let them come home by themselves. If anything had happened to them—either of them . . . Shane pushed the rest of the thought from his mind. His heart was racing just thinking about what he wanted to do that creep Tompkins. But he needed to reassure Carly right now. The look on her face was scaring the hell out of him.

He reached up to cradle her cheek. "Are you kidding? He'll be talking about this for years. Don't worry about him. You're both safe. That's all that matters."

The cop cleared his throat as Beckett nearly knocked Shane off his haunches. The dog buried his face in Carly's lap and she wrapped her arms around him, resting her cheek on his big head. Shane stood up, eyeing the cop who was looking between Shane and Carly.

"You guys were supposed to pick up Tompkins hours ago. What the hell happened?" Shane maneuvered the cop farther away from Carly.

"Baltimore PD is trying to serve the arrest warrant now, but the guy is pretty slippery. We don't even know if Tompkins did this," Pretty Boy said slapping, his notepad against the palm of his hand. Shane was so exasperated he was about to rip the notepad from his hands when Donovan strode into the room, his cell phone pressed to his ear. He ended the call when he saw Shane. The vibrating in Shane's shorts stopped at the same time.

"I just got here," Shane said by way of explanation.

"What have you got?" Donovan asked the two detectives.

"Looks like your run-of-the-mill house trashing," Rumpled Suit said. "The perp wasn't on the premises when the patrol officers arrived. The sliding glass door was jimmied. Pissed-off ex-boyfriend, maybe?"

Boyfriend? Was this guy kidding? Shane wanted to lunge for the cop's neck, but Donovan stepped in between them, which probably was a good thing since half the occupants of the room were armed and stupid.

"Chill out, Devlin!" Donovan barked at him, shoving him toward a wall. "I got this!"

Shane sucked in a few deep breaths. Donovan slowly pivoted around, both hands on his hips, his tone razor sharp.

"Joel Tompkins is a stalker who has violated a standing restraining order twice today. He has never been or never will be a boyfriend of Miss March's. He illegally entered her office and her home, destroying personal property. He's a criminal with an arrest warrant outstanding. Do I make myself clear?" Rumpled Suit chewed a little harder on his straw as Donovan stared him down.

"Until we get prints back, we can't confirm Tompkins even did this," Pretty Boy reiterated. "And it's standard operating procedure in these types of break-ins to ask about any relationships the victim may have. You'd be surprised how often that occurs."

Stepping away from the wall, Shane clenched his hands

into fists of frustration. "Hey, we're on the same side, here," the detective said, eyeing Shane. "We want to catch the guy who did this as much as you do."

"Joel was here." Carly's soft voice interrupted them. "Don, he was in this house. I know it."

Donovan ran a hand over his bald head. "Yeah, Carly. I know. His car was in front of his place when they went to serve the arrest warrant, but he wasn't home. His roommate let them in and they searched the place and found a rental car receipt. Apparently, he's been driving around in a rental van while avoiding his apartment all week. They put a BOLO out with the new information. The guards only knew to stop him by the make of his vehicle. I've got someone checking the surveillance tape and the logbook at the guard shack right now. We should know when he was here." He crouched down in front of Carly, placing a hand on her knee. "They'll get him tonight, Carly. Don't you worry."

Carly chewed some more on her bottom lip before managing a nod for Donovan.

"If this was Tompkins," Rumpled Suit said, holding his hands up before either man could argue with him, "we need to make sure we document this mess and get any evidence to the district attorney's office. It'll help make your case stronger when the patrol officers pick him up."

"I appreciate it," Donovan said, shaking hands with both detectives before they walked away. Donovan stood with his back to Shane and Carly. He clasped both hands behind his head and took a deep breath. His suit jacket pulled against his back, revealing the bulge of his gun. Shane stepped forward, pulling Donovan out of earshot of Carly.

"Since when do you wear a gun?" he asked Donovan quietly.

Donovan pinned him with another of his military tough-guy looks. "Since I went with the cops into that perv's apartment thirty minutes ago," he whispered. He rubbed a hand over his face. "Shane, this dude is sick. His apartment was filled with pictures. Pictures of Carly. Pictures of her mom and the actress who played Carly in the movie. It was like a shrine."

He didn't think it was possible, but Shane's whole body tensed further.

"I'm no shrink, but it's obvious the guy's got some crazy obsession with Carly. It's quite possible he's under the delusion she has the same feelings for him. Seeing her with you seems to have set him off." Donovan gestured toward the mess around them. "Because now, he's one pissed-off crazy dude."

"You should have let me beat the crap out of him when I had the chance." Fury—and a little bit of guilt—ripped through Shane's body. He wanted Tompkins locked up and out of Carly's life for good.

"We'll get him," Donovan said. "Hopefully tonight, but maybe not until tomorrow or the next day. In the meantime, she needs to get out of here. Preferably, out of town for a few days. Asia left for L.A. earlier or I'd send her to stay there. I need to call Hank and see if the team has a place she can stay."

"She can come home with us." Until he spoke, neither one noticed the kid standing behind Shane. With his arms crossed over his chest and the patented Devlin look on his face, he faced Shane without flinching. "If you say no, then I'm stayin' here with her." Something stirred in Shane's gut; he wasn't sure if it was annoyance or pride. Whatever it was, the kid wasn't budging.

Shane dragged a hand through his hair, mussing it further. "Yeah, she can come with us." It wasn't the best idea. The look Donovan threw him confirmed it. But there was no way was he letting her out of his sight again tonight. "Tomorrow, I'll put her on a plane to New York to see her friend. Hopefully the cops will have found Joel by then and he'll be behind bars."

Donovan continued to stare at him, his hands on his hips beneath his suit jacket, until he finally nodded.

Turning away from Donovan, Shane motioned for the

kid to take Beckett. Carly looked up at him as she released
the dog. The vacant look he'd noticed on her face earlier
was still there. Gently he pulled her up off the step. "Come
on, Dorothy, let's get you packed."

They navigated past a pair of officers who'd been gathering evidence upstairs. With their work finished, Carly was
free to take what she needed before leaving. Shane heard
her ragged intake of breath as she caught sight of the mess
in her bedroom. It looked as if Joel had touched everything
in her drawers. Anger was beginning to overtake the fear in
Carly. "That little creep!" she said, lifting a ripped pillow
off the floor and clutching it to her chest.

"Why don't you grab what you need from the bathroom,"
Shane said, gently maneuvering her out of the room. "I'll
throw some things in a bag. You can get new clothes tomorrow." Treating it as if it were still intact, she carefully laid
the ripped pillow on the corner of the bed before slowly
shuffling to the bathroom.

Shane spotted her gym bag in the corner. It was empty
except for a pair of sneakers. Clothes were strewn everywhere throughout the room. *What had the guy been doing?
Trying it all on?*

Shane stuffed the bag with shorts and shirts and a pair
of jeans. When he got to the lingerie, his hand froze. Most
of it was in tatters on the floor. It looked like the pervert had
shred it all. He swore for the umpteenth time as he fingered
a scrap of lace. Reaching in the back of a drawer, he pulled
out a pair of serviceable cotton bikini panties. Definitely
not her normal repertoire, but they'd do in a pinch.

"Carly?" He zipped up the bag. "How's it going in there?"

When she didn't respond, he threw the bag over his shoulder and followed her into the bathroom. "Holy shit," he
swore again. Joel had left no room untouched. A plethora
of obscenities were scribbled in lipstick on the mirror. Shane
felt his anger ratchet up a notch—if that was even possible.
Fear had paralyzed Carly again. She stood, white knuckles
clutching the vanity, staring at the word *whore* smudged

across the center of the mirror. Grabbing her toothbrush and some hair bands, he threw them in the quilted floral bag he'd found in the linen closet. Anything else she needed, she could pick up at a drugstore later. "Come on," he said, taking hold of her arm.

"No!" She wrenched her arm free and snatched up the lipstick off the vanity, snapping the top on it. Pulling open the draws, she whipped out hair brushes and lotions, tossing them in the bag. Her movements were manic. When he caught sight of her eyes in the mirror, they looked unfocused and wild. "I can do this," she muttered.

He had to hand it to her; she wasn't going to give the jerk any power over her. But she was straddling the line of hysteria and he wasn't sure he could deal with the aftermath if she crossed it.

"Hey!" He grabbed her by the shoulders, forcing her to face him. It took a moment for her eyes to focus. When they did, he raised his hands to cup her face. "It's okay. *You're* okay. This is all just stuff. Leave it." He brushed a kiss across her hairline.

"That's easy for you to say," she mumbled. "That was a thirty-dollar tube of lipstick he ruined."

He grinned, feeling a stirring of pride at her surging resilience as he let his lips linger on her forehead. "Let's get out of here, Dorothy. Toto and the Munchkin are waiting for us downstairs."

It took nearly two hours and several minor miracles to get Carly out of her house, back to his place, and settled into his bed. The first obstacle was Carly's refusal to leave her home looking like a war zone and occupied by police. Donovan turned on his ten-thousand-megawatt smile, assuring her that he would lock up and make arrangements to have it cleaned. Next, the pretty-boy detective wanted to know how to reach her for further questioning. Donovan explained their plan for her to go to New York for a few days.

"I can't go to New York!" she cried. "Julianne's not home. She's at a wedding this weekend." The kid wasted no time piping in, inviting her to join them on the trip to the cabin.

Now, instead of one uninvited guest to his pretraining camp retreat, Shane had two.

Once they'd finally gotten home, the issue of where Carly would sleep cropped up. Troy was occupying the guest room, leaving Shane's room and the sofa as possible places for her to land. Despite his reputation—and a burning desire to get another glimpse at her pink Hanky Panky thong—Shane played the role of gentleman and called dibs on the sofa.

There was another debate about where Beckett would sleep: The kid thought Carly would feel safer with the dog in the bed. Carly wouldn't hear of it. "Beckett is your new friend," she told him. Shane finally got both kid and dog to bed and headed off to a much-needed shower. When he emerged from the master bath ten minutes later, the lights were out in his bedroom and Carly lay sprawled across the bed. Light from the bathroom illuminated her long legs, uncovered except for where his well-worn Chargers T-shirt hit her mid-thigh. One arm lay across her belly and the other was slung over his pillow. As he reached for a pillow, her eyes flew open.

"Stay with me," she whispered.

Despite the fact that his body began revving up for action the minute he'd seen her long legs stretched across the sheets of his bed, he knew what she'd been through the last few hours. "You sure?" he had to ask. She nodded and he flicked off the bathroom light, crawling into the bed next to her. Fortunately, he was wearing cotton sleep pants and a T-shirt because he didn't think he could withstand skin-to-skin contact without making the moves on her. As soon as his head hit the pillow, she crawled on top of him, one leg pinned against his thighs, her hand tightly gripping his T-shirt as she burrowed into his shoulder.

"Hold me," she said, her breath warm against the bare skin at his neck. Tremors shook her body as he wrapped an arm around her, pulling the blanket over top of them with the other hand. Shushing her, he gently stroked her back, stifling a groan as he soothed her to sleep. It was the first time he'd had a half-naked woman draped boneless across him without doing something about it.

But something had changed inside him tonight. He had put not only the kid in harm's way, but Carly as well. The fear he'd felt as he raced into her house scared the hell out of him. He was responsible for Bruce's son, and no matter what the circumstances of the guardianship, he vowed to himself in the now quiet bedroom to make sure nothing ever happened him.

Or to Carly. For once, he wasn't even considering the ramifications to his career if something happened to her. He just knew he had to keep her safe at all costs. He tried to tell himself it was just because he felt a strong connection to her physically. Deep down, though, he knew it was something more.

She snuggled closer and his body jumped in response. Sainthood was not something he aspired to. But tonight, Carly needed to feel safe, so he'd do his best to hold his baser instincts in check. It was definitely a new experience for Shane.

Eighteen

Shane was an idiot. *A freaking idiot.* He had two weeks to get himself rested and ready for training camp. As he'd done every other season, he had planned to spend that time relaxing, fishing, and boning up on his playbook at his cabin in the Allegheny Mountains. Alone.

Instead, he was playing babysitter and nursemaid to a chatty twelve-year-old and a very distracting, sexy woman who should be three hundred miles away writing up new rules about how tightly a player's cleats should be tied. A long-suffering sigh escaped as he hefted four plastic bags filled with groceries onto the stainless steel countertop. The place was still a bit stuffy, but Carly was walking around the great room opening up the French doors to the A-frame cabin's deck, letting in a light breeze. The sounds of Beckett barking and the kid laughing only added to Shane's growing disgust with himself.

"This place is gorgeous."

Shane looked up across the industrial-outfitted kitchen and into the great room, which was open to the two stories above, to where Carly stood. She reached up to run her fingers along the mammoth stone fireplace. *She* was gorgeous. The fragileness in her eyes had faded as the day wore on, but he knew she was still edgy. The smiles she'd doled out to the kid were stiffer than her usual, easy grins. Still, she was a tough one, he'd give her that. The decision to bring her along had been instinctive. He couldn't leave her in Baltimore, but he should have sent her to the beach where her sister and Coach could watch out for her and he wouldn't have to battle his lusty thoughts.

Yep, definitely an idiot.

"When you said a cabin, I was expecting something a bit more . . . rustic. And definitely smaller."

Shane silently unpacked the groceries, letting Carly have a one-sided conversation. He knew he was being a jerk, but he didn't care. Last night had been long and sleepless for him. He wasn't used to sharing a bed with a woman without sex being involved. Carly spent most of the night clinging to him as she drifted in and out of a fitful sleep. He'd spent most of it hard despite trying to conjure up images of the Golden Girls in a Victoria's Secret catalog. Nothing worked. He was tired and mean from fighting off his desire to sink into Carly every time she laughed at the kid or bent over to pat Beckett.

"How long have you had it?"

He jumped at the sound of her voice. She'd joined him in the kitchen and was pulling bottles of water out of their case, loading them in the huge Thermador refrigerator.

How long had he had a serious case of the hots for her? *Since the moment I laid eyes on you.* He was pretty sure her question was about the cabin, though.

Shane gave up ignoring her. "I grew up a couple hundred yards down the side of the mountain. My grandparents had a prefab house—you'd call it a trailer—that couldn't be hauled up to this spot. My grandmother always liked to picnic up here, though. Grandpa dragged an old redwood picnic table up here so we could eat dinner in 'God's kitchen,' as my grandmother referred to it." He pulled apples from a plastic bag and tossed them next to some bananas in a fruit bowl.

"That sounds nice," Carly said as she paused in front of the open fridge.

"It was a pain in the ass." He wadded up the plastic bags and tossed them in a drawer. Carly gave him a hard look as he grabbed the cardboard case and began to break it down for recycling. "It's a long way to carry a supper up and back every night," he said in response to her look. "After I signed with the pros, I built this place for them."

Leaning against the stainless steel fridge, she crossed her arms beneath her breasts and grinned at him. Before she could get the words out, he stopped her.

"Don't say it was sweet of me," he practically growled at her. "My success was as much theirs and they needed a home. I didn't do it to be *sweet*." He watched as she bit back a grin. "My grandmother didn't live to see it finished. And my grandfather, he just kind of existed here for three years after she died."

He'd shocked her, he could see it in her face. Pushing away from the refrigerator, she unwrapped the paper towels, placing them on the decorative rack under the counter.

"So, no one uses it anymore?" she asked, her back to him.

"Roscoe and his family use it to ski during the winter," Shane said as he dumped a bag of tomatoes into the colander in the sink. "He uses it to entertain clients, sometimes."

"And you?"

He rinsed the tomatoes under the water. "I come here this time every year to regroup before the season."

"Alone?"

She'd taunted him once too much. Before he knew what he was doing, he had her pinned against the door of the refrigerator. "Yes, alone," he said against her neck. "No women. No distractions." He breathed in the citrus smell of her hair. "You're a distraction, Carly."

Jesus, he was as bad as Tompkins, using his body to force himself on a woman. He pulled back a couple of inches so he could look into her face. What he saw in her eyes wasn't the terror of a woman being ravaged by a man twice her size, but heat. Sexual heat. Her breathing was as ragged as his as she chewed on her bottom lip.

"You shouldn't be here," he said through clenched teeth.

Snaking her hands around his neck, she pulled his head down. "I know," she said before her lips met his. Her mouth was soft and warm, and Shane wasted no time returning her kiss. The tension of holding his body in check the previous night and all day drove him on as his hands roamed her body and he devoured her mouth. He couldn't get enough of her, ready to take her against the cool stainless steel.

Carly pulled away from the kiss, flinging her head back against the refrigerator door with a moan. Shane's mind shut down as his aching body took control, his lips cruising a path along her slender neck.

"There was a rental car place back in town," she said, breathless. "I can go there and get a car. I'll go to New York and wait for Julianne to come home."

It took a moment for her words to sink in. It took a moment longer for Shane to get his runaway libido back in check. "No," he said, his tone rough. What was she thinking? What were they both thinking? "You're not going anywhere until Tompkins is in custody." Reluctantly pulling back from her, he looked at her again. Her face was flushed and a purple mark was forming on her left shoulder. Christ, he was behaving like an animal. Taking a deep breath, he placed his hands on her shoulders, massaging them gently. Tears shimmered in her eyes and her body began to get that limp, rag-doll feel again.

"I can't stay here with you." She gulped back a sob. "It's just too tempting to crawl inside you where it's safe." Her body shuddered with another suppressed sob.

Safe. Shane was fairly certain no other woman had used that word to describe him. As flattering as some men might think it, he wasn't feeling too safe around Carly right now. Not to mention the idea of being responsible for her—and the kid—contributed to his bitter mood.

"Does Coach know you're here?" Maybe thinking of the

ramifications of them being alone together would cool them off.

She nodded slowly. "It's okay," she said, her voice nearly a whisper. "I . . . I told them I came to keep Troy company. They know you aren't exactly thrilled with having him around."

Great. Not only did she care more for the other Devlin, but he'd forgotten that the kid was within earshot. He and Carly had been thirty seconds from being naked on the counter and Troy could have walked in on them at any moment. Shane sighed and touched his head to her forehead. The sound of Beckett's toenails scratching on the tile floor gave them enough warning, however. He let his lips trail along her hairline as she pulled free of his embrace.

"Saved by the Munchkin and his beast," he muttered as she scrambled across the kitchen. Beckett bounded into the great room with the kid at his heels.

"Guess what? There's a huge fire pit outside. Can we start a fire and make s'mores?" The kid's voice reverberated throughout the open house as he began rummaging through the remaining grocery bags. "I thought we got marshmallows."

"Hey!" Shane yelled, sounding a bit like the father he never knew. "I'm making dinner first." Beckett scrambled for cover as the kid froze with his hand in the bag. Shane turned to the sink and drenched the tomatoes again so he didn't have to see the kid's lip start to quiver. Christ, bringing them here had been the king of bad ideas. But the thought of either one of them being out of his sight rattled him, too. He was tired, horny, and hungry. Two of the three weren't even his fault. The drive to the cabin had taken twice as long it should have because the other two occupants in the car thought they were starring in a *Vacation* movie.

"We have to stop at Cracker Barrel for breakfast," the kid had said, apparently forgetting the two bowls of cereal he had devoured an hour earlier. "We always stop there when we are on a road trip. Every family does. It's, like, a tradition or something." Shane wasn't sure, but he thought the kid might have ended on a sob.

Sensitive to the kid's delicate emotional state, Carly had wasted no time agreeing to his suggestion. "Well," she'd said, "seeing as how I've never been on a family road trip, I think it would be fun to stop. Since it's tradition."

Shane had glared at her across the front seat, but said nothing. Hell, he'd never been on a family road trip either, but that didn't mean he wanted to waste an hour sitting in a restaurant with all the rest of the summer's vacationers. It was a battle he wasn't going to win, in spite of the fact that he was driving.

So they'd spent half the morning eating a second breakfast while Carly and the kid tried to outdo each other shoving golf tees into a wooden triangle. Shane had actually been lulled into relaxing a little until the grandmotherly waitress who brought the bill commented on what a beautiful family they made. The kid had nearly started blubbering on the spot as the tension coiled even tighter in Shane's belly. *They weren't a family* he'd wanted to shout to the entire restaurant. What they were was a trio of castoffs who nobody wanted. Even the dog was a stray.

The trip to the Walmart had been another exercise in torture. The kid had kept asking if there were any games or things to do at the cabin. Yeah, there were things to do, but not for a twelve-year-old. UNO cards, a backgammon set, comic books, and enough food to nourish an entire Pop Warner football team made it into the cart. Apparently, cookies and candy made all things better for kids.

Carly had done some shopping of her own, replenishing her mutilated underwear wardrobe with a package of white cotton bikini panties. Watching her place it on the conveyer belt along with some toiletries she was purchasing, Shane had wanted to rip the package out of her hands. No, he'd wanted to rip Tompkins's face off, but that wasn't possible.

By the time they'd arrived at the cabin, Shane was close to spitting nails. And he was taking it out on the kid. Yeah, he'd just lost his parents. Roscoe and Carly weren't about to let Shane forget that point. But hell, Shane had been two years younger when his mother died and his father disappeared. And he'd survived just fine. There was no reason to mollycoddle the kid.

"Can I help?"

Shane turned to see him standing at the kitchen island, Carly's arms draped around his shoulders. "Be nice," she mouthed at him from over the kid's head. Well, at least he wasn't crying and he did want to help. Shane put the colander on the island and pulled a knife and cutting board out of the drawer.

"Here," he said. "Slice these up while I brown the meat for the pasta sauce."

He hesitated before slipping out of Carly's embrace. "Okay," he said. Shane watched from the corner of his eye as the kid carefully picked up the knife and held it to the tomato, nearly slicing the tips of his fingers off in the process.

"Jesus!" Shane jerked the pan off the burner and moved back to the island, startling the kid into dropping the knife as his lip began to quiver again. "Don't you know how to slice a tomato?" Shane barked.

Carly shot him a disapproving glare from where she stood uncorking a bottle of wine, looking as though she wanted to poke him in the eye with the corkscrew. The kid bit his lip and lifted his chin up a notch. "No," he said, hands on his hips. Shane stared at him for a moment before picking up the knife. "Com'ere and I'll show you how to do it without needing a trip to the emergency room." The kid stepped back up to the counter and slid under Shane's arm. Shane demonstrated before positioning the kid's fingers on the knife and around the tomato. "Nice and easy so you don't mutilate it." Cautiously, the kid sliced a piece of the tomato before looking up for approval. Shane nodded and went back to stove. The kitchen was silent except for the sizzle of the meat frying in the pan.

"We didn't do much cooking at home," the kid said softly.

"Your mom didn't cook?" Carly's voice drifted in from the dining room where she was setting plates on the table.

Shane pulled out a hunk of mozzarella and placed in on the counter to be sliced.

"Nah, Dad said Mom couldn't bake her way out of an EasyBake oven." Troy chuckled. "It was a really good thing we had Consuelo."

Carly handed Shane a glass of wine and gave him one of her honeyed smiles that, for the first time today, actually reached her eyes. Pulling out a plate, she wandered over to the island to arrange the tomatoes and cheese. The scene was so domestic, Shane almost shuddered. And, for the millionth time that day, he reminded himself what an idiot he was.

Nineteen

The house was dark. Rummaging around trying to find her purse, Carly swore as she stubbed her toe on one of the overstuffed chairs in the great room. She'd been getting ready for bed when she heard her cell phone ring. Finding a light switch proved almost as impossible as finding her phone. Relief flooded her body, however, when, after finding her purse behind a cushion, she listened to the voicemail message Donovan had left.

"The police scored a lucky break and arrested Joel during a random drug sting tonight. I guess this is one time his being a junkie works in our favor," Donovan said. "He's in custody and his arraignment is scheduled for the morning. The DA says it's likely he wouldn't see the outside of a jail cell until his trial begins and that could easily take months. I'll call you from the courthouse tomorrow. You can sleep tight now, Carly. It's over."

Carly released a relieved sigh and it felt like she'd taken her first normal breath in twenty-four hours. Turning to return to her room, she collided with Shane as he came up behind her. A nearly naked Shane.

He gripped her elbows as she laid her palms on his bare chest. His warm body was still hard with the tension that had seemed to consume him the entire day. He didn't want her there, she knew that. Yet he'd brought her along anyway. It seemed he was once again her knight in shining armor. Carly gave herself a mental shake. Shane wasn't happily-ever-after material, she reminded herself. He'd just been in the right place at the right time. Again. Try as they both might, they seemed powerless to resist the strong attraction pulling them together.

"I'm sorry if my phone woke you," she said. It was dark in the room, with only a shaft of light from the moon shining in through the high windows illuminating the shadows of Shane's face. His face was hard, showing no reaction to her apology. "The police finally arrested Joel. He's in custody."

He released a heavy sigh. "Good," he said, pulling her body in contact with his. Two things became immediately apparent to Carly: Shane was potently aroused and she didn't stand a chance of sleeping alone tonight.

"I can go back to Baltimore now," she said as his lips found that spot on her neck that always turned her knees to Jell-O.

"I'm pretty sure the rental car place is closed," he mumbled against her skin.

"Tomorrow then," she breathed as her hands trailed along the taut muscles of his back. "I shouldn't be here distracting you."

"It's a little late for that," he said as he placed an open-mouthed kiss beneath her ear. Carly moaned softly before he shushed her.

"Little ears," he said, motioning to Troy's room.

Somehow he managed to get them to his bedroom where they both quickly shed their clothes. His hands and mouth were not gentle on her body. But Carly didn't care. Much like that first night they'd slept together, she knew he was using her body to deal with emotions he couldn't deal with on his own. And she was using him, too. Despite the fact that Joel was finally in custody, she needed to feel safe again.

As much as she didn't want to admit it, Shane's strong body possessing her gave her that feeling—and something more.

Lying next to his slumbering body, Carly stared at the ceiling. Tomorrow she would leave. First thing in the morning she would call the rental car company. Maybe she'd head to the beach. Or to New York to wait for Julianne to come home. Either way, she needed to get as far away from Shane Devlin as she could. Something happened when she was around him. Obviously, she couldn't control it. They needed to stick to the original agreement of a brief fling. Things were getting too complicated. She was becoming way too attached to the feeling of security being with Shane somehow provided her. And she was really scared of the "something more" she felt.

The decision before her was simple. All she needed to do was execute it. She fell asleep, her plans firmly made.

The rental car had arrived the next morning, but it was already late afternoon and she was still trouncing around the woods outside the cabin with Beckett and Troy. *So much for her plans to hightail it out of there as soon as possible.* She told herself she'd stayed because of Troy. The sight of the rental car brought tears to his eyes and a tremor to his mouth. He was still grieving the loss of his parents. A fact his older brother seemed oblivious to. Shane's moodiness may have eased as a result of their marathon in his bed the night before, but his attitude toward his brother hadn't softened one bit. Someone needed to serve as a human buffer between the Devlin brothers. She'd grown attached to Troy, and the boy was still too fragile to leave alone with his brother. She was staying to make sure he got the love and attention he needed.

It was only a half-truth, of course. And she knew it. Carly could no more step away from the sexual pull that was Shane Devlin than she could give up breathing. Despite knowing nothing was ever going to come of their relationship, she remained at the cabin.

She wasn't sure how Shane spent his day, but he'd done his best to avoid her and Troy. When they arrived back at the cabin, he was standing at the island in the center of the huge kitchen, chopping vegetables. His hair was damp from a recent shower and he was dressed in a pair of cutoff jeans and a worn Dave Matthew's Band T-shirt, his feet bare. He looked up when they entered, but remained silent. If he was annoyed about her staying, he was careful not to let it show.

"Whacha' makin'?" Troy asked, he and Beckett making a beeline for the counter.

"Salsa," Shane said. "We're having Mexican for dinner."

Carly glanced at the three place settings on the table. Unlike Troy, Shane hadn't acknowledged the arrival of the rental car that morning. Not that she expected him to wave her out the front door, but he'd been pretty adamant about her distracting him from whatever preseason rituals he meant to go through at the cabin. It seemed he'd changed his mind—at least for tonight. She wasn't delusional enough to think he wanted her there for any reason other than to keep Troy entertained and out of the way. Fine with her. Keeping an eye on the boy was Carly's main reason for staying, also. Or so she kept telling herself.

"Can I help?" Troy asked.

Shane didn't look up from the tomatoes he was chopping, but his hand on the knife hesitated a second before he spoke. "Wash up first."

Troy scampered over to the sink.

"And the dog needs to be fed," Shane said.

"I'll do it," Carly said. Shane arched an eyebrow at her before she disappeared into the pantry to scoop some food for Beckett. Yep, it was a good thing she'd stayed, she congratulated herself. Things between Troy and Shane were already working themselves out.

"What have I told you about holding the knife?" Shane yelled.

Then again, maybe not.

———————

"Why are you still here?" Shane's breathing was ragged as he stilled himself inside her. Carly released a deep sigh, opening her eyes. They were inches from his and he could just make out their vibrant blue color. Passion shimmered there. And something else he chose to ignore.

It was midnight and they were naked in his bed. Her rental car had arrived promptly at ten that morning, but she hadn't left. Tompkins was in custody and there was no need for her to hide up in the Allegheny Mountains with him anymore. Not that he was complaining. She'd kept the kid occupied all day, and now, well, now he was enjoying the other major benefit to having her here.

"Because," she said, forcing a groan from him by clenching her muscles.

But he was stronger and wanted answers even though he had a feeling he wouldn't like them. Burying himself deeper, he leaned down to take a nipple in his mouth. "Because, why?" he asked, blowing on the sensitive skin and causing her to squirm beneath him. She gasped softly as he toyed with the nipple and repeated his question. "Why?"

"Because you're mean to Troy," she whispered.

"I am not! I'm being nice to him."

Obviously, Carly disagreed. She sighed—this time not with pleasure—and gave him a haphazard roll of her eyes. He wanted to argue with her, but the more she squirmed beneath him, the more desperate he was to finish. He picked up his rhythm again and her expression went from incredulous to blissful in ten seconds flat.

"So what you're saying," he said with a satisfied grin as he moved over her, "is that you are here for the kid and not for this."

"Yes!" she nearly screamed as he drove into her, making her come. "Oh, God, yes!"

He wasn't sure whether it was in answer to his question or not. But it didn't matter. With a groan, he followed her over the edge. "Liar," he mumbled against her ear as he collapsed over her.

It took several minutes for their breathing to return to normal. Rolling onto his back, he gently tucked her into the crook of his arm. She was quiet, but he knew she wasn't asleep yet. Her fingers glided over his chest, finally stopping over his heart.

"This was only supposed to be a one-night fling," she finally said, her breath softly caressing his skin.

He tucked a hand beneath his head and stared at the ceiling. "Uh-huh." Suddenly, he was regretting bringing up the subject. It had just been his ego talking earlier, wanting affirmation that he was more important to her than a twelve-year-old boy. He'd left the door wide open for "the relationship discussion" and he had no one to blame but himself. The thing was, his theory about getting over his sexual attraction to Carly in one night was a bunch of crap. Hadn't he figured that out the first night he'd had her?

Instead, sex with her was addictive. And not just the sex. Everything about Carly made him want more. More of her unguarded smiles. More of her casual caresses. More of her laughter. More of her. But in return, she'd want more of him. More than he was capable of giving.

He played with her hair and tried to defuse the situation by turning on his Devil-of-the-NFL charm. "We could always renegotiate our original agreement to cover the rest of the off-season." That way, they could continue as they were, but he'd have an out in two weeks when training camp started.

She rolled onto his chest, leveling her face with his. "Oh no you don't," she said. "If you want me to stay and help with Troy, you just have to ask. You don't get to use sex to sweeten the deal. I told you when he arrived I'd help him. But not because I want to sleep with you. That's insulting."

Something flickered within his sternum as she spoke. He wasn't sure if it was triumph or panic. Theirs was only a temporary relationship, the only kind Shane did. When the season started, he needed to focus all his energy on playing. It was the only way he knew to be successful. Yet the thought of not having Carly around made him break out into a sweat.

"This," she said, waving a hand between them, "this . . . is amazing."

The flickering in his chest became a drumbeat.

"But," she continued, her soft voice sad, "it isn't going to be more than it is right now. You're a total commitment phobe, I get that, Shane. And I've already survived a relationship with a superstar athlete. One which I have no desire to repeat."

The thing in his chest became a rock now as he watched tears fill Carly's eyes. He hated what her ex-fiancé had done to her. Almost as much as he hated her putting them both in the same category—the one labeled *jackass*.

"What I don't get," she said, "is why you can't try to have a relationship with the only family you have in the world. It's not like you can't relate to what he's going through."

Shane had no trouble identifying the feeling in his chest now. It was anger. He was really getting sick of everyone assuming he was the best person to care for the kid just because they'd had similar life stories. Nothing could be further from the truth.

"No!" she cried, slapping a hand on his chest. "You don't get to be mad, either. You've fooled the rest of the world into believing you're some independent, tough guy, but not me. Don't sell yourself short. I know you're capable of having a relationship with your brother."

He closed his eyes so he wouldn't have to look into her stormy ones. She thought he was capable of a relationship? Was she crazy? Carly had no idea how wrong she was. His mother had been so distraught that her husband no longer loved her, she hadn't bothered to fight her cancer. She hadn't bothered to stick around for the one person who did love her—her son. His father had been no better. He'd gone on to have a happier life with the son he'd actually wanted.

Carly's warm tears fell onto his skin, making him tremble. She had it wrong. He wasn't incapable of relationships;

he was just incapable of being loved. Raising Bruce's kid would only prove that. The kid would abandon him for someone else eventually. Hell, if given the choice, he'd probably pick Carly as his guardian. Not that Shane could blame him. And not that it wouldn't hurt just a little.

She gave a frustrated huff at his silence before rolling off and putting her back to him. Shane opened his eyes and stared at the ceiling. Carly certainly made it sound as though their relationship was casual, but that didn't matter. She had hopes and aspirations about him forging a bond with the kid. He knew he was going to get hurt in the end no matter what.

Carly refused to let Shane's ambivalence about Troy dampen the boy's adjustment to life without his parents, even though her heart was telling her she was entering dangerous territory. Her feelings for the Devlin brothers were complicated. She wanted to protect them—both of them. From each other and from the hard knocks life had dealt them. Something inside Carly couldn't let either of them go until they'd forged a relationship together. The problem was, the more committed she became to that idea, the more committed she became to them.

As the days passed, Shane seemed to relax, spending more and more time with her and Troy. Each day fell into a familiar pattern. In the mornings, he and Troy would argue about something they'd seen on *SportsCenter* as they prepared breakfast in the kitchen. Shane allowed Troy to help more and more with the cooking, unaware that the action only fueled the boy's hero worship. While Shane worked out after breakfast, Troy cheerfully cleaned up, chattering to Carly about what he and Shane were cooking for dinner or the game films they were going to analyze later. In the afternoons the three of them took Beckett and hiked through the hills surrounding the cabin. At night, they all played cards or made s'mores in the fire pit.

Afterward, in bed, Shane and Carly played their own

games. She was grateful he had relaxed back into the teasing lover he'd been before. It was easier to handle her feelings toward him when the sex was lighter, more playful. There was a vulnerable man behind the loner's mask he wore for the world, but she knew if she delved too deeply, he'd pull back. Just as he'd done the other night. His refusal to let her in had stung too much, sending up alarm bells of her own. She needed to be able to walk away unhurt, and she couldn't do that if she let him too close to her heart.

Later that week, Carly returned from the farm stand in town to find the house empty. Troy had mentioned wanting to go fishing, so Carly loaded up a basket with some cookies she'd picked up while she was out and headed down toward the stream. The sound of voices, deep in conversation, reached her before she made it to the water. She smiled as she realized that, in less than a week, Shane had gone from grunting monosyllables at Troy to actually engaging him in a conversation. As far as she knew, Shane still hadn't uttered the boy's name, but he was slowly making progress.

"At least I don't suck at fishing," she heard Troy say.

"There's not much to suck at with fishing," Shane said as he cast his line out into the pond at the mouth of the stream. "It's mostly luck."

Troy grunted. "I suck at most sports."

Carly stood still, obscured by a maple tree, and watched as the two fished. Shane waded up to his ankles in the water, his torso bare to the sun, a pair of worn Levi's hugging his thighs. Shiny Revo sunglasses glinted against the sun. Troy stood on a flat rock, barefoot, dressed in shorts and a T-shirt, with a Blaze ball cap shielding his eyes. He held his fishing pole perfectly still. Beckett snored softly from where he lounged in the sun farther downstream.

"Not everyone can be a star athlete," Shane consoled the boy.

"Yeah, well, I didn't get the Devlin genes."

Shane gave a little snort before turning to look at Troy. "That's nothing to be disappointed about."

"Says you. You're a professional athlete. And so was Dad. I can barely throw a ball ten feet."

"There's more to life than being a professional athlete, kid."

"Now you sound just like Dad."

Carly held her breath, unsure of how Shane would react to the comment. She watched as the muscles in his back tightened briefly before he relaxed, turning his attention back to his fishing pole and the pond.

"Maybe because your dad had a point."

"Yeah, but both of you are really great at sports and I totally suck at every one I try. I'm an epic failure."

Shane coughed, or chuckled, she wasn't sure. "Look, your dad, he was a freak of nature. As far as I know, most of the Devlins sucked at sports. Your dad had a gift and he used it to get as far away from the life that was his only option. Sometimes that little bit extra—like a need to escape—can make a person's drive that much greater. I'm pretty sure it was that way for your dad."

"If it was a fluke, then how come you can play?"

Shane didn't bother hiding his laugh this time. "I was too stubborn to let anyone tell me I wasn't good enough. I had something to prove."

They were silent for a few moments, serenaded by the cicadas and the gurgle of the stream where it met the pond. Before Carly took a step, Shane spoke again. "Look, just because you aren't an all-star in Little League or soccer or whatever, it doesn't mean you suck at sports or anything else. You're a good kid. Real smart and okay to have around. You can do whatever you want in life. And as long as you're a good person and do your best, you'll succeed." Reaching over, he grabbed the cap off Troy's head, ruffling his hair. Troy beamed at him as Shane replaced the cap. "Now, shut up or the fish won't bite."

Carly brushed away a tear and tried to control her breathing. With shaking hands, she realized the scene she'd just witnessed solidified the gnawing feeling hovering in her

belly for the past few days. She was in love with Shane
Devlin. Try as she might to prevent it, it had happened. Once
again, she'd fallen in love with the wrong man. A man
everyone—including himself—thought was incapable of
love. As overjoyed as she was at Shane's evolving relationship with Troy, she was frightened to death of her feelings
for Shane. How had this happened? Was it possible he could
change? Would she even want to stay and find out?

Later that night, wrapped in the cocoon of his slumbering
body, Carly wanted to blurt out her feelings for him. She
desperately wanted to know what his reaction would be. Lisa
had been right; Shane just needed a little time to get to know
Troy before realizing he could let the boy into his life. The
budding relationship between the two brothers gave Carly
hope of a future for her and Shane.

The only thing keeping her from telling Shane she loved
him were thoughts of Maxim. The feelings she felt for Shane
were different from those she'd once believed she felt for
Max. Still, she'd poured everything she had into her relationship with him, only to have him leave her for another woman.
The question keeping her awake tonight was, did she have
the guts to risk being rejected again?

Twenty

Beckett carried a three-foot stick up the slope of the hill, the kid shrieking with laughter in chase. Shane smiled as dog teased boy. He'd meant what he'd said yesterday. He was a good kid and Shane had gotten used to having him around. Sure he was a little chatty, but he was smart and some of what he said actually made sense. The red-rimmed eyes and the quivering lip had all but disappeared. Not that Shane could blame him. He'd just lost both parents, for crying out loud. But he wasn't as much of a pain as Shane thought he would be. In fact, this week had been much more relaxed than any he could remember.

Glancing ahead, he saw the other reason this trip had been so enjoyable. Scrambling up the hillside in tight white jean shorts, Carly's wiggling body never failed to arouse him. She laughed as Troy chased Beckett out of sight. Shane stopped beside a tree, taking in her long legs and wavy hair that felt like silk on his skin at night. As if sensing his wayward thoughts, Carly paused, peering over her shoulder to look at him questioningly.

"Come here," he said, leaning his back against an ancient walnut tree.

She hesitated, looking ahead to where dog and boy had disappeared. With a sly grin she turned and jogged back down the hill, careening into him at the last minute. He wrapped her in his arms as her body came in contact with his.

Shane took her mouth in a hungry kiss. She responded immediately, pulling her body in closer, allowing him greater access to her mouth. Christ, did she realize how much he needed her? How often thoughts of being with her consumed his day? It was a feeling that should have burned out by now or at least cooled. Instead, his desire for Carly seemed to grow stronger each time he touched her.

Shane knew she'd stayed to make sure the kid was okay, but he also knew the other reason she'd stayed. Her body came alive beneath his hands and it seemed to trigger a corresponding urgency within him. When he was inside her, he felt something he'd never felt before. Something undefined but . . . good. *Damn good.* He loved being inside of her. In fact, he loved everything about her.

Holy crap, where had that come from?

Shane pulled out of the kiss, staring down at Carly's face. Her breathing was labored and her eyes took a minute to focus, but when she finally looked up at him, his gut clenched.

"Shane, I . . ." she said, still breathless.

"Hey, you guys! Someone's here!" Troy's voice carried down the hill.

Carly bit her lip, pulling out of the embrace. Shane stared at her a moment longer, trying to harness feelings that seemed to be pulling him in a direction he'd never been before. This was getting complicated. He needed to think.

"You guys!" Troy called again, Beckett barking happily in the background.

"We're coming," Shane answered. He looked again at Carly, but the look he thought he'd seen was gone. "You'd better lead the way. It's probably a Girl Scout selling cookies and I'm likely to scare the hell out of her in my current state." Laughing, she grabbed his hand, tugging him up the hill. The position gave him an excellent view of her shorts. "On second thought, you'd better walk next to me," he said with a groan as he pulled up beside her.

If the sounds of toddlers squealing didn't calm his aroused state, the sight of a black Jeep Cherokee parked in the circular driveway did.

"Shit," Shane mumbled, spying Roscoe sitting on the long wooden front steps of the cabin. Carly had obviously seen him first, quickly slipping her hand from his in response to Roscoe's angry glare.

Beckett barked while the kid chased one of the twins across the lawn as Roscoe's wife, Tiffany, chased the other. "Beckett won't hurt you," the kid said, not realizing that to the twins, having someone chase them was their favorite game. Carly stopped well short of the front steps, pretending to take in the chaos.

"I thought that at least *she'd* have more sense." Roscoe didn't wait for them to get inside before voicing his disapproval.

"Leave her out of it," Shane said, stomping up to the porch steps.

"It's a little late now. Jeez, Shane, you've still got to get through training camp to play this year. She's the coach's sister-in-law, for crying out loud. And the GM's assistant! Did you not learn anything in San Diego?"

"It's not what you think," Shane said, barely keeping his voice from a yell. His hands were in fists and he was sorely tempted to leap up the steps and throw Roscoe over the railing. It wouldn't take much more to push him to do it, either.

Roscoe had the nerve to laugh. "Give me a break, Devlin. I've known you too long not to know exactly what this is." He put both hands up as Shane started toward him. "Hey, you don't pay me to be your moral compass. Just to clean up

the mess afterward. And my rates will be the same when
this one needs mopping up, too."

"Wow, Shane, your agent is as much of an egotistical ass
as you are."

Shane spun around to look at Carly standing beside him,
her arms mutinously crossed beneath her breasts as storm
clouds formed in her eyes. He felt a pinch of pride as she
stood up to Roscoe—who *was* being an egotistical ass—but
he hated that she felt she needed to defend herself. And he
wasn't that happy she'd essentially called him an egotistical
ass, as well. He thought they'd progressed beyond that.

"There won't be anything to mop up," she said, notching
her chin a bit higher. Shane stepped in front of her, essentially cutting her off from Roscoe's glare. From now on,
Shane would be the one doing the defending.

"I said leave her out of it, Roscoe." As grand gestures
went, it was pretty lame.

Roscoe arched an eyebrow at him. "Huh, that's interesting," he said, offering up a smirk.

Carly huffed behind Shane.

"What are you doing here anyway?" Shane asked.

"Boarding schools." Roscoe thumped a large manila
envelope that lay on the step beside him. "If you want the
kid settled before camp starts, you need to do a little song
and dance. The application process can be a lengthy one,
but some schools are interested in waiving the procedures
with the right amount of incentives. He'll need to go on
interviews next week."

"Boarding school?" the kid said from where he stood
on the front lawn, Beckett at his feet. "You're sending me
away?" The agony in his voice sent something flickering in
Shane's belly.

"Ahhh, for crying out loud, Shane! You didn't tell him?"
Roscoe swore. Shane looked at the kid. His lip was quivering
again and tears filled his eyes. Hell. He'd royally screwed
this up. Shane stepped away from the porch, but the kid
wasn't waiting around. With a sob, he took off down the hill.

"Troy!" Shane yelled, sprinting down the steps after him.

Carly shoved what she could into the gym bag
Shane had packed her clothes in the week before. In the bathroom she tossed her toiletries into a plastic grocery bag, not bothering to collect her toothbrush from Shane's bathroom. God, she'd been a fool. Despite knowing who and what Shane Devlin was, she'd fallen in love with him. Worst of all, she'd almost blurted it out to him earlier. Well, better off ending it before she got in too deep. As if she could fall any deeper.

"What the hell are you doing?"

She turned to see Shane filling the doorway, that menacing look back on his face. Letting her eyes drink him in one last time, she zipped up the gym bag.

"I'm doing what I should have done the day Joel was arrested. I'm going home."

"Carly," he said, his voice softening, but not his posture. "Don't listen to what Roscoe says. He's an idiot."

"No. As far as I'm concerned, the only idiots here are the ones standing in this room. And your lawyer is right. *I* should have known better."

"Don't do this." He'd moved closer without her realizing, sliding his hand over the one she had tightly gripping the handle of the bag.

Gathering her courage, Carly forced a smile as she lifted her face to him. "I have to do this. This was supposed to be just about sex. But I lost sight of that. I . . . I thought that maybe there could be something more. But I was wrong." Taking a deep breath, she licked her dry lips, trying to steady her voice. "You're not even capable of a relationship with your own flesh and blood. It would be impossible for you to love . . . to have a relationship with me."

He reached out to touch her, but Carly backed away. "Are you saying that you feel something for me?" he asked.

Great. Leave it to him to latch on to the love word. She hadn't meant to say it, but maybe it would work to her advantage and drive him away. After all, it sent most men running for the hills, didn't it?

"No. I mean, maybe. If we kept this up I might," she said, sliding her purse to her shoulder. "But I'm a grown-up and I can control my feelings, so don't get all hinky on me. I'm going back to Baltimore so you can concentrate on getting ready for the season. That is your main priority, isn't it? Shuffling Troy off to boarding school and getting rid of all the *distractions*? Well, I'm saving you the trouble. Now you have no excuses not to secure your precious starting job."

Avoiding any eye contact, Carly hefted up her gym bag and walked past Shane to the door. She tried to swallow but her mouth was like cotton, and her eyes ached from holding the tears at bay.

As she made her way to the front door, she heard the sound of the twins chortling in one of the bedrooms, their mother trying to get them down for a nap. Roscoe sat in one of the wooden rockers on the front porch, a beer in his hand. Pushing through the screen doors, Carly spied Troy dragging his huge duffel bag across the lawn to her rental car, a distressed Beckett following behind him.

"Take me with you, Carly," Troy said, his voice wavering. "Please." Carly's heart broke a little more as she looked at the boy's distraught face.

"Great." Shane's voice came from up on the porch. "A full-scale mutiny." When she turned, he looked like the mutinous one. "You're not going anywhere, Troy."

Twice now he'd called Troy by his name. She only wondered if he realized it was too late. Troy shoved his glasses against his nose defiantly as he glared up at his brother. "I don't need you." Leaving his duffel beside the car, he stormed up the steps to grab the large envelope Roscoe had left on one of the tables. "How many schools did you contact?" he asked the lawyer.

"Ten or eleven," Roscoe answered, his voice sounding amused.

"Are any of them that boarding school in Southern California? You know the one like on that TV show?"

Roscoe was grinning widely now as he slowly rocked the chair back and forth. "No, I didn't check that far away."

"Oh, for crying out loud!" Shane complained.

"I've got lots of money, though, right?" Troy didn't bother with Shane, instead directing his questions at Roscoe.

"Tons," Roscoe said, clearly enjoying the boy's tactics.

"Good." Troy flashed him a smirk. "Then I really shouldn't need to have anything more to do with you," he said, turning to Shane. "After all, I can do and be whatever I want, right?"

Shane's stance hardened a bit, but he didn't argue with Troy. Offering up a slight nod, he watched silently as Troy sauntered back down the stairs and loaded his duffel in the backseat of the car. "Good, I'll be sure and let you know where I land," Troy said with a cheeky grin.

Which meant Carly was obviously going to have to do something with him. Sighing, she watched as Troy gallantly loaded her bag into the car next to his. Roscoe chuckled on the porch as Shane stood on the steps, arms crossed and hands tucked under his armpits. That errant lock of hair blew in the slight breeze, but otherwise his face was expressionless.

"I'll take him to the beach. Lisa may be able to talk some sense into him," she said softly.

"Fine," was all he said. Troy reached down to wrap his arms around Beckett's big head as Carly made her way to the driver's side of the car.

"Troy," Shane called before they got in the car. Carly flinched at the sound of Troy's name coming off Shane's lips. Striding down the steps, Shane stopped beside Beckett.

"Your parents would want you to go to boarding school." His voice was quiet as he looked at his brother. "Your mom and dad didn't really intend for you to be left with someone like me. Hell, they didn't even like me. I'd be a horrible influence on you. They didn't know what they were doing."

Troy looked at him a moment before straightening his shoulders and pushing up his glasses again. "No. They didn't know what they were doing. They thought that all that stuff about you being the Devil of the NFL was just an act, a way to get attention. Mom always said that you just needed to be shown love before you could give it. Dad, *our* dad, always said he was so proud of you. Because you'd made something out of yourself in spite of his attempts to screw your life up."

Tears welled up in Carly's eyes, but Shane's face was like granite as Troy continued. "He always used to pray that one day you'd be able to forgive him for abandoning you. That you'd learn to understand that he was just a mixed-up kid himself. We celebrated your birthday every year and Dad kept a scrapbook with every article he could find about you. So yeah, you're right. They didn't know what they were doing. And I'm glad they'll never know the real you." With a pat on Beckett's head, he climbed into the car.

Carly stood frozen, looking over the roof of the car at Shane's emotionless face. *Say something,* she begged him. Instead, the silence surrounding them was deafening. The ache in her heart grew more severe as the gist of Troy's words sunk in. It took everything she had not to go to Shane and offer him comfort. Instead, with limbs so shaky she wasn't sure she could stand, she got behind the wheel and started up the car. Beckett whined as the car started to pull away.

"Don't forget to feed the dog," Troy yelled from the open passenger window. When he turned to face forward again, tears were streaming down his face. "Butthead."

Shane wasn't sure how long he stood there. He wasn't even sure if his heart was still beating. He couldn't seem to feel anything. Beckett turned his head to look at him, a sorrowful look in his big brown eyes. After a moment, he lay down in the gravel drive, plopping his head on his paws with a deep sigh. Breathing deeply himself, Shane forced his feet to move him back up the steps as the sounds of Carly's tires on the gravel faded away. Christ, he needed a drink. Several, in fact.

Roscoe sat rocking in the wooden rocker Shane's grandfather had made for his grandmother.

"What do you think is so goddamned funny?" Shane asked as he reached the shade of the porch.

"Oh, I'm just marveling at genetics. I mean, it fascinates

me that the two of you could grow up in completely different ways, yet still have personalities so similar." Roscoe chuckled. "The kid definitely has a set of Devlin balls."

With a snarl at his lawyer, Shane pushed through the screen doors, headed for the liquor cabinet. Digging in the back, he pulled out a dusty bottle of Scotch.

"Hey," Roscoe said from behind him. "I thought we weren't going to open that until you won the Super Bowl?"

"According to you, that's never going to happen," Shane said as he twisted off the cap and splashed a liberal amount into a glass.

"Devlin, don't be an asshole," Roscoe said, taking a seat on the sofa. "You pay me to watch your back. You know as well as I do a fling with the coach's sister-in-law is not the best idea if you want to make the team. Especially a team as morally out there as the Blaze. You say you wanna play football, break your father's records, and win a Super Bowl. You can't do that while messing around with the princess of the tabloids."

"Do you really want me to hit you?" Shane's voice resonated through the open room.

Roscoe laughed. "Dude, I'm feeling a little sorry for you right now, so I might let you have the first punch."

Before Shane could reach him, Tiffany hissed at them from the balcony above.

"That's enough, you two. Stop behaving like the twins. Who, by the way, I am trying to get to sleep. If you want to act like kindergartners, go outside and roll around in the dirt with the dog." She disappeared into one of the bedrooms. The sounds of the twins wrestling faded as she closed the door.

"It still turns me on when she bosses me around like that," Roscoe joked as he stepped around Shane to pour his own glass of Scotch. "I do owe you a free hit, though."

"What are you talking about?" Shane asked, wiping spilled Scotch off his hand.

"You don't remember?" Roscoe slid down into one of the overstuffed chairs beside the hearth. "I gave you a shiner the day I told you I was going to ask Tif to marry me. You deserved it, by the way."

Making his way to the opposite chair, Shane sat, trying to recall the exact events of that day. They'd been sailing, he, Roscoe, Tiffany, and some aspiring starlet whose name he couldn't remember. It was late afternoon and they'd just docked in the marina. Roscoe, a little wasted from a day of drinking in the sun, told him that he planned on marrying Tiffany in a Vegas ceremony later that night.

Shane was just trying to protect his friend when he suggested Roscoe give it a day or two. After all, she was a no-name model who he'd known for less than a week. At least, the conversation had gone something like that. Obviously, Shane might have added a little more graphic detail and colorful language because before he knew it, Roscoe laid him out flat on the wooden decking of the boat dock.

"Nah, I don't remember," he lied.

Roscoe gave a disbelieving snort. "You said I couldn't possibly fall in love with a woman in one week. As if you were an expert on love. Hell, judging by events today, you wouldn't know love it came up and bit you on the ass." He held a hand up as Shane balled his own hand into a fist. "All I'm saying is I love my wife more today than I did eight years ago. I can't explain it and I can't deny what it is. Maybe you have feelings for Darling Carly—"

"I don't," Shane interrupted him, desperately wanting this conversation to end.

"Yeah, like you'd know if you did. You're so busy shoving any feelings you have down that black hole where your heart is supposed to be. Jesus, Shane, that kid made *me* want to cry today. You can't possibly say you don't feel anything."

Shane glared at him. He didn't want to think about or discuss his feelings with anyone.

"No, of course not," Roscoe went on. "Because that would interfere with your grandiose plan to knock your father's name out of the record books. You do realize your old man is dead? He's not going to notice whether his records are broken by you or not. This obsession of yours is consuming you. One day you're going to wake up and wonder where your life went."

Abruptly, Shane stood, sloshing more Scotch on to his hand. He didn't have to listen to this. Picking up the bottle, he walked toward his office behind the kitchen.

"Don't drink all that," Roscoe called after him. "If you get too drunk, we'll be stuck eating Tiffany's tuna casserole for dinner."

"Great," Shane mumbled. He was well aware Roscoe didn't marry the voluptuous model for her culinary skills. "Beckett," he called out the screen door. "Come in the house. They're not coming back." The dog lifted his head to look down the road before laying it back down with a huff. "Suit yourself," Shane muttered as he entered the office he'd been using to study game films.

Placing the bottle on his grandfather's antique desk, he sat in the leather chair behind it and pulled out the bottom drawer. Inside was a steel strongbox. Shane placed it on the desk along with his glass. *Jeez, this day was a mess.* His body was sitting in the office, but he felt like his insides were lying in pieces on the gravel drive. Slowly, he opened the strongbox. Inside were old photos, report cards, and newspaper clippings. Things his grandmother had collected for him throughout the years.

Gently, he placed on the desk a picture of him on his first day of school with his mother, a sad smile on her face. Most of the photos in the box were of him and his mother. Digging down to the bottom, he found the one he was looking for. A photo of a laughing three-year-old perched on his father's shoulders. Bruce's eyes were obscured by a pair of Ray-Ban sunglasses, but his smile was a happy one. The smile on Shane's face looked eerily like Troy's.

Could Shane have been wrong about his father after all these years? The man in the photo was barely twenty-four. Bruce had been thirty-one when his wife died. The same age as Shane was now. Yet his father had always seemed so much older to him. Taking a swallow of Scotch, he felt it burn the whole way down. At least he was beginning to feel again. Perhaps that might not be a good idea.

Tossing the photo back into the box, he pulled out a worn manila envelope. Carefully, he dumped the contents onto the desktop. A rainbow of crayoned artwork and invitations fluttered out. He picked up a worn paper decorated in red and green glitter and read the letter scrawled in red marker:

> *Mom says if I pray real hard, you'll come for*
> *Chrismas. I asked Santa to bring you in his sled.*
> *Please come!*

It was signed in big letters: TROY. Shane looked at the pile of birthday invitations and cards his brother had sent him over the years. Had Troy spent his birthdays and holidays waiting for him? Just like Shane had done all those years with Bruce? He tried to swallow the lump that sat like a boulder in his throat. Cradling his head in trembling hands, Shane tried to figure out how he could have gotten everything so terribly wrong.

Twenty-one

Carly walked along the lengthy deck crossing the dunes between the beach house and the gazebo facing the Atlantic Ocean. The laughter of children mingled with the sounds of gulls and the rough surf. She handed Lisa a glass of lemonade, then plopped down on the wooden bench opposite her, the ocean breeze blowing her hair around her face.

"I'm used to the harem of girls materializing around C.J. each day, but I wasn't expecting the group of boys that seemed to have found their way to this end of the beach," Carly said before taking a swallow of her drink.

Glancing down at the beach, Lisa saw the familiar bikini-clad teenage girls angling for her son's attention, but she looked surprised by the four teenage boys bantering with Emma. "Good God," she said. "Matt is going to blow a gasket when he gets wind of this."

Carly chuckled softly and looked farther toward the shore to where Molly was busy burying Troy in the wet sand. "The resiliency of children never ceases to amaze me," she said.

Lisa followed her gaze to the younger children. Matt and her sister had been concerned when Carly arrived at midnight three nights ago with Troy asleep in the car, his eyes still puffy and his cheeks tearstained. Both were relieved she'd weathered the whole mess with Joel Tompkins. But aside from that, thankfully they hadn't pried too much.

Carly told them about Shane's decision to send Troy away to boarding school. Troy was remarkably hardy and, despite the sudden loss of his parents nearly three weeks before, he seemed happy and content to be absorbed into the Richardson family. All three kids were enjoying spending their evenings exploring potential boarding schools on the Internet, picking ones in the most exotic locations so they could go visit Troy throughout the year.

Carly's heart broke each night as she listened to the boy's muffled sobs as he went to sleep, though. But he seemed to be facing life a little better during the days. Unfortunately, she couldn't say the same for herself. She was angry at herself for losing her heart to Shane. Her eyes had been wide open and he'd never promised anything more than he'd given her. Carly still thought he was capable of more, but she couldn't fight that battle any longer. Not if she wanted to stay whole.

"You'd never know what he'd been through these last weeks," Carly said, her eyes still focused on Troy.

"You had a lot to do with helping him cope with his grief," Lisa said.

A wistful smile formed on Carly's mouth before she took another sip of lemonade. "Yeah, well, I was just doing what I could to help out," she said quietly. "He hasn't exactly got anyone else."

Leaning forward on the bench, Lisa took Carly's hand. "Legally, he does. Shane is coming to get him tomorrow."

Carly was startled by the information, nearly dumping her drink down the front of her.

"I just got off the phone with him. Apparently, he wants to be involved in Troy's life."

Damn her sister for being so perceptive. Lisa didn't need to pry because she'd already guessed Carly's feelings. She knew the news would shock Carly.

It was more than shock rolling through Carly, however. It was a stinging sensation somewhere in the vicinity of her heart. *Shane is going to make a real attempt at a relationship with Troy!* The idea should make her ecstatic. For Troy, at least. And it did. A little. But her selfish side couldn't help but be hurt that Shane didn't have enough love to go around to make a go of it with Carly.

"That's wonderful," Carly said. And she meant it. She really did. "Remind me to be somewhere else when he breaks that news to Troy." It was a strain to keep the pain from her voice, but her sister would pounce at any show of vulnerability. "As a matter of fact"—Carly wiped at the droplets of condensation that had dripped from the glass onto her bare thigh—"I probably should head up to New York for a few days. I promised Julianne I'd come visit."

"You can't avoid him forever."

"I'm not avoiding Shane or anyone else," Carly said, swinging her legs up on the bench. "I just don't want to be in the middle of this anymore."

"Carly," Lisa said, reaching across to touch her sister's leg. "It isn't the end of the world if you fell in love with Shane."

Carly whirled on her, swatting away a tear from her face. "Says you!" *So much for hiding my vulnerability from my sister.*

"Oh, honey," Lisa said.

"Don't you dare psychoanalyze me!" Carly sobbed, glad for the strong breeze that carried their conversation away from the kids playing, oblivious on the beach. "I know I was stupid for falling for him. I know I shouldn't have done it. But I did it anyway."

"Honey, you can't always decide who you're going to fall in love with," Lisa said, using her soothing but annoying therapist's voice. "Life doesn't always work the way we want it to."

"No? Well, at least I should have known better. I've made the stupid mistake twice now!"

Moving over to the bench where Carly sat, Lisa draped

an arm around her shoulders. "Stop it. You're going to make mistakes in life. Everyone does. It's part of living. Your mom made mistakes. God knows our father made mistakes. They made one big one that I'm thankful for every day. But their mistake isn't your fault. Your life has a purpose. I'm a walking testament to that." Lisa reached up to wipe her sister's eyes as her own tears streamed down her face. "But that's not the reason I love you so much. I love you because you are my sister. The only one I've got. And I'll love you whatever mistakes you make. So will Matt and the kids. Because that's what we do."

"You're right, Doc," she teased, reaching to brush her thumbs over the tears on Lisa's cheeks. "I know I have to take risks to find that one special someone. Going into it, I knew Shane could never be that guy. And it turned out exactly like I thought it would. Fortunately, without the paparazzi feeding frenzy this time," she said with smile. "I guess I'm just disappointed because, at times, I saw glimpses of a Shane who might be capable of more. Only I don't think he knows he has it in him. He's spent his whole life not counting on anyone for love and acceptance. He doesn't know how to give it in return. And it hurts me to see him so alone."

Lisa smiled with pride at her sister. "You could always give it a shot and see what happens."

Shaking her head, Carly looked toward the shoreline where Troy and the other kids were playing football. "No, I think Shane had best concentrate all his efforts on Troy. He might not have it in him for two relationships." She grinned. "Besides, I don't think I could handle getting in any deeper. If it hurts this much now, I can't imagine what the pain might be in the future. You can call me a coward, but I like to believe I'm being a realist. Besides, I'm holding out for an accountant or a podiatrist, remember?"

"*Coward* is not a word I would ever associate with you," Lisa said as she took Carly's face in her palms. "You're the bravest woman I know."

"Yeah, well, this brave woman is heading to New York before Shane arrives, just the same."

The ocean breeze felt good on Shane's face as he climbed the stairs beneath the Richardsons' beach house to the deck above. The morning was clear and warm, promising to be the perfect summer day. Beckett hesitated at the top of the stairs, briefly contemplating exploring the interior of the house before the sounds of kids laughing caught his attention. With a bark, he bounded down the long deck leading over the dunes to the shoreline. Moments later, Shane heard the squeals of Beckett's name as the dog found his way to the sand. He listened carefully for Troy or Carly's voices, but he couldn't make them out in the breeze.

"Devlin."

Shane turned to find the coach standing in the doorway behind him. His chest bare, he wore a pair of board shorts and flip-flops, a Blaze ball cap on his head.

"Coach." He hadn't been looking forward to confronting Troy or Carly, but from the looks of it he should have worried a little about Matt Richardson, too.

Sliding the door closed behind him, the coach walked over to the railing and picked up a can of spray-on sunscreen from a bucket there. Letting the silence stretch, he sprayed his torso and then his long legs before turning the can on his feet.

Shane decided it was best to plunge right in. "I appreciate . . ." It was a bad decision.

"No, Devlin, I don't think you *appreciate* anything," the coach said, slamming the can back into the bucket. "You sure as hell don't appreciate what it means to be a part of a family or to have someone depending on you. You'd better start learning what it is to appreciate folks—especially your teammates, because I don't have room for a quarterback who's only thinking about himself. I don't have to respect you to have you lead my football team, but you'd better respect your teammates or you'll be wearing a headset and holding a clipboard all season. Lisa says you're here to make it right with Troy." He laughed bitterly. "Well, don't expect it to go easy with him. We didn't tell him you were coming, but he's figured it out now." He gestured to the beach where Beckett had cut Troy from the herd of kids playing and the pair was heading away from the beach house. "You're gonna have to catch him first."

"Shit," Shane swore as he headed along the deck toward the beach.

"And Devlin," the coach said from where he followed closely behind him. Shane was forced to stop so he could turn and face him. He got right into Shane's face. "While I *appreciate* everything you've done to help with Tompkins, whatever is going on with you and Carly is over. Do I make myself clear?"

Shane would wager his last jock strap Carly hadn't given Matt Richardson specifics about their affair. But a guy like Richardson didn't need to be told anything. His instincts on and off the field were legendary. "Clear," Shane said through clenched teeth before turning to jog after Troy. If he didn't hurry, boy and dog would be halfway to New Jersey by now.

The mid-morning sun made the sand hot beneath Troy's feet. He walked over to the shoreline, joining Beckett as the dog romped through the water. Man, he was glad to see Beckett. Panting, the dog trotted along faithfully beside Troy as he walked away from the beach house.

His butthead brother was a different story. Carly must have known he was coming because she took off for New York earlier that morning. With a fierce hug for Troy, she'd told him to call her every day, and they'd both cried as she left. But now he was mad at her because she'd left him alone to face the butthead.

Man, it was hot. He should have grabbed a bottle of water before he'd taken off. Or some money, he realized as he passed a vendor selling ice cream from a cart he pushed down the beach. Beckett gave a happy woof and Troy looked behind him. The butthead was gaining on them with his stupid long legs. Shane stopped to buy a bottle of water from the ice cream cart. Troy's mouth got drier as he waded farther into the surf.

"You gonna try and swim away from me?" Shane called from behind him. Beckett galloped off to run in circles around Shane's legs. Gulping from a bottle of water, he held one up to Troy. "It's hot out here. Aren't you thirsty?"

Yeah, he was thirsty. But he would die before giving his brother the satisfaction.

"Come on, Troy, are you going to walk all the way to the Delaware Bridge?"

"Maybe," Troy said as he turned on his brother. "She left because you were coming!" he yelled at him.

That stopped Shane in his tracks. "Who?" he asked.

"Carly," Troy said, storming in his brother's direction. Beckett danced between the two as if it were a game. "She went to New York this morning. Probably so she wouldn't have to see you!"

Shane looked out across the ocean, his lips drawn in a grim line. Troy couldn't make out the look in eyes behind his sunglasses.

"I'm sorry about that," Shane said softly.

"Are you?" Troy yelled, running forward and grabbing the second bottle of water from Shane's hand. "You were mean to her. You can be mean to me all you want, but you shouldn't be mean to Carly." The bottle's cap was stuck and Troy couldn't get the water open. Shane took the bottle, setting his on the sand and opening Troy's with the hem of his shirt. Snatching the open bottle back, Troy guzzled the water.

"Easy," Shane said. They both stood with their feet in the surf, facing each other. Beckett wandered off to chase a seagull.

"I picked a school," Troy said, wiping his face with the cool water bottle.

"Did you?" His brother actually sounded interested. *Butthead.*

"Yeah, it's in Switzerland. C.J. said the girls would be really nice there."

The butthead smiled behind his sunglasses. "Ahh. I hadn't figured girls into the prerequisites for a decent school. But that's really good thinking."

"Carly promised to take me there. She's going to Italy for the fall to work with her designer friend, so she'll be close."

"She's left the team?"

"Yep. I heard her tell Coach and Lisa last night. She said it was just a courtesy position anyway. Now that Lisa is better, she didn't need to be in Baltimore taking up an unnecessary job. So, she's going to Italy."

Troy watched as Shane turned to the ocean, running his hand over his jaw. Beckett dropped a piece of driftwood at his feet and Shane threw it for the dog. "Well, if this school in Switzerland is a safe place and a good school, I guess you can go there. But I have another option for you to consider."

"I thought you said I could make my own choices," he said accusingly. Troy wanted to be near Carly and now his butthead brother was going to ruin that, too.

"You can. I just have another option to put on the table." Shane turned to face him. "I spoke with the headmaster at the school in Baltimore where C.J. and Emma go. He said there's a spot in the sixth grade. But you'll have to meet with them tomorrow to interview and take some tests."

"Is it a boarding school?" Troy wasn't going to allow himself to get his hopes up.

"No. That's the one drawback. You'd have to live with me. I wouldn't want you to come home to an empty house, so you might have to go to the Richardsons' and stay with Penny some days. At least until Consuelo's retirement papers come through from the university and she can live with us."

Troy tried to gulp in some air. He bit his lip to stop it from quivering. "Consuelo would live with us?"

"Yeah, except I do the cooking when I'm home. She'll be retired, after all."

Troy hurled himself at his brother. Shane caught him as

Beckett jumped at them, nearly forcing them both into the surf.

"You really want me to live with you?" Troy cried into Shane's shoulder.

"Only if that's what you really want to do. I have it on good authority I can be a butthead sometimes."

Shane lowered him back down to the sand as Beckett danced between them.

"We've got to call Carly," Troy said. "She can come home now. We can all live together. Like at the cabin."

"Whoa," Shane said. "I think for right now, we should just keep it us guys and maybe Consuelo, okay?"

He should have known it wouldn't last. His brother was turning back into a big butthead again.

"But I saw you. You always looked at her funny when she wasn't looking. And you kissed. I know you feel something for her," Troy argued.

Rubbing the back of his neck, Shane looked out into the ocean.

"Yeah, but *something* isn't always enough. Not for a woman like Carly. She deserves . . . everything."

"But she'll go to Italy." Troy's lip quivered.

Wrapping an arm around Troy's shoulders, Shane guided him back toward the beach house. "She'll come back. Her family is here. And you're here."

They walked in silence for a while, Beckett darting in and out of the water in front of them.

"What made you change your mind?" Troy finally asked.

"I guess it was the things you said about your dad," Shane replied.

"He was your dad, too!" Troy pulled out from under Shane's arm, shoving his glasses against his nose to hide the tears that were forming again.

"Yeah, he was. But not in the same way he was a dad to you. I don't blame him for that anymore, though. He couldn't help some of the things that happened in his life. He was young and he made some mistakes."

"He loved you," Troy sobbed.

"I'm gonna have to take your word for it, kid," Shane said, putting a hand on Troy's shoulder and squeezing. "It's too late now to go back and change things. I never got the chance to make it work with Bruce, but that doesn't mean you and I can't be a family."

Troy wiped his nose on the hem of his T-shirt.

"I'm pretty sure I'm supposed to tell you not to do that, but I'm going to ease into this big-brother parenting thing slowly."

With a laugh, Troy fell into step beside Shane, Beckett jogging ahead.

"I'm not all lubed up with sunscreen and I'm starting to fry," Shane said. "Walk a little faster, will you?"

Twenty-two

"I'm glad you chickened out about Italy," Asia said, stirring sugar into her iced tea.

"I didn't *chicken out*," Carly answered a little too defensively as she pushed a pickle around her plate.

She and Asia were sitting in a small sandwich shop on the Upper West Side of New York City. The Blaze were in town for their final preseason game against the Giants that night. Asia had arrived before the team to ward off any last-minute media glitches, and Carly was glad to have an hour or two to catch up with her friend before the frenzy of the game later.

"It's just that Troy wasn't going to Switzerland, so I really didn't need an excuse to go to Italy any longer." *Thank goodness!* The relief she felt at the thought of not having to brave the European paparazzi was palpable. She was glad things had worked out the way they had.

Carly texted or video-chatted with Troy daily. The pain of losing both parents still lingered, but he was excited about his new life with his brother. It wasn't hard to be happy for him—and Shane, who'd finally been able to commit to another person. She would be petty to resent that Shane's commitment wasn't to her. But her heart still ached. Carly missed the Devlin brothers. Both of them.

"Lisa tells me you're working with her foundation now," Asia said. "You know, you can do that from Baltimore. You don't have to stay here in New York."

Carly smiled at her friend. No doubt her family and Troy had put Asia up to this. Working with Lisa's foundation had been a natural transition after spending a few weeks with Troy. Months ago, the idea of setting up places where kids could go to talk, play, or just hang out with other kids who'd lost a loved one seemed like just one of Lisa's pipe dreams—a reaction to her own brush with cancer. But reliving her own experiences with childhood grief through the eyes of Troy awakened something in Carly. Finally, her life had a cause she could rally behind.

Working with her sister was an added bonus. She'd come to New York and convinced Julianne—who'd also lost her mother at a young age—to open up her client list. Together, they'd raised nearly two million dollars over the summer months.

"Hank even said you can work from your old office," Asia prodded. "We really miss you, Carly."

"But the big money is here in New York."

Which was a lie. She could raise funds from just about anywhere. But until her heart mended, she needed to put some distance between herself and Baltimore. Even if it meant not seeing her family or Troy as often as she'd like. "Besides, I'm only a three-hour train ride away. Lisa and Emma were up last weekend shopping. And I'll see the rest of my family tonight."

"Don't forget your Blaze family."

If Donovan had shared any details of her fling with Shane, Asia wasn't saying. But the look she gave Carly said she knew a lot. "Troy hasn't stopped talking about seeing you again."

Carly couldn't hold back her grin. It had been four weeks since she'd left him at the beach house. She couldn't wait to

see Troy, either. His brother, not so much. Hopefully he'd
be too wrapped up with chasing his father's records to even
notice she was there.

"Shane finally won the starting job," Asia said with a sly
smile, as if reading her thoughts.

Taking a sip of her drink to push down the lump in her
throat, Carly shrugged her shoulders. "That's great. I hope
it works out for him and the team."

Asia laughed. "Girl, you've still got it bad for the guy."

Carly wiped her mouth in a futile attempt to hide her
blush.

"If it helps," Asia said, "he's been the well-behaved big
brother. So far, he hasn't used the boy to troll for dates. At
least, not that I know of."

Both women laughed as Carly threw her napkin at Asia.

"Changing the subject," Asia said, her voice now serious
as she sat up in her chair. "Do you have to come back for
Joel's trial?"

"Hopefully, he'll take the plea agreement he's been
offered and I won't have to." Carly had tried not to think of
Joel these past weeks, but the district attorney wouldn't let
her. Joel's grandfather had finagled a deal whereby Joel
awaited trial at a minimum-security rehab center in Vir-
ginia. Maybe he'd get help with his drug habit and be reasonable enough to take the deal the DA was offering. She
wasn't looking forward to facing him in a courtroom.

Carly didn't have time to dwell on thoughts of Joel because
Asia's cell phone vibrated on the table. "Showtime," she said.
"It's time you and I headed for the Meadowlands."

Shane spied her in the crowd surrounding the
visitor's locker room as the team was disembarking the bus
and heading into the stadium. Hordes of media, Blaze personnel, and hangers-on milled about, but Carly was easy to
spot. Looking sexy as hell leaning against a cement pillar,
she wore a pair of skinny jeans, sandals, and a white jean

jacket. Her hair was shorter, just brushing her shoulders. And her face looked thinner underneath the tan she'd acquired since he'd seen her last.

Moving in to get a closer look, he stood obscured by his own cement pillar. Tension drew her beautiful face tighter than normal, but Shane couldn't make out her eyes. Her eyes would tell him what she was really feeling. With sweaty palms, he adjusted his garment bag on his shoulder, trying to avoid being jostled by the other players as they entered the locker room. Several of them called out to Carly as they went past. The smile she had pasted on her face suddenly lit up as Molly squealed her name. Shane watched as the young girl threw her arms around her aunt's neck and Carly buried her face in Molly's hair. Troy stood behind Molly, and when Carly noticed him, she pulled him in for a tight embrace. That familiar gut clench grabbed Shane as he watched her brush her lips across Troy's forehead. Curling an arm around each child, Carly beamed, finally giving him a glimpse of her eyes. His heart pounded in his chest as he saw her smile reflected in them.

C.J. materialized from among the frenzy, standing at Carly's elbow. Shane watched as the boy, hands in his pockets, forced himself not to react to seeing his aunt. Smiling, Shane sympathized with C.J.'s struggle between boyhood and manhood. The boy hung back trying to look cool while still desperately wanting the same effusive greeting his sister and Troy received. *Me too, dude,* Shane wanted to say to him.

Weeks ago, Carly had confided to him about how hurt she was with C.J.'s distance. But Shane could clearly see the boy wasn't distant at all. His adoration of his aunt was easily recognizable—especially to someone who felt the same way. She didn't wait for her nephew to come to her. Releasing Troy, she pulled C.J. in for a brief kiss on the cheek, retreating quickly so as not to embarrass him. Once again, Shane's stomach clenched. *Christ, he was jealous of two boys!*

Unaware that his feet were even moving, Shane made his way toward them. The rest of the team was in the locker room, getting ready for the game. He should be there, too. But, as usual, whenever Carly was around, other parts of his body took over.

"I'm so glad you're not going to Italy," Molly was saying, twirling herself in and out of Carly's embrace. "Will you move back to Baltimore?"

"No, sweetie," Carly said. "I'm going to help your mom out with her foundation. There's a lot to do here in New York. But I plan on coming to C.J.'s first football game next weekend."

"Don't make a special effort on my account," C.J. said, carrying the cool act a bit too far.

A wisp of her new, shorter hair clung to her chin and Shane's hand itched to brush it back off her face. But if he touched her, he knew he wouldn't be able to stop with a hand to her face. At last, she noticed him standing there.

Trying not to stand around like an imbecile, Shane forced himself to speak first. "Carly," was all he could get past his dry mouth.

"Hey," she said softly, tugging the hair behind her ear.

"Shane, Carly is coming to Baltimore next weekend," Troy said. "Maybe she can come over for dinner? We are taking a Japanese cooking class and we need someone to practice on," his brother explained to her proudly.

Arching an eyebrow, she smiled at Troy but managed not to commit to anything. "You don't say?"

"Yep. And you can come see Beckett, too," he went on. "I know he misses you a lot."

"He told you that?" she teased, fiddling with the collar of Troy's shirt. Shane shifted his stance as her innocent gesture led to not-so-innocent thoughts of her fingers on him. His reaction to this woman would never change. He should be in the locker room right now getting his head ready for the game. Not standing in the hallway dreaming of all the things he wanted to do to Carly's body. And all the things he wanted her to do to him.

"You got Molly, Aunt Carly?" C.J. interrupted Shane's thoughts. "Dad said I couldn't leave her without handing her off to you directly. I need to get inside and start checking the gear."

Yeah, inside the locker room. That's where Shane needed to be, too. He started backing up in that direction.

"I got her," Carly said to C.J. "I'll take her to the family lounge after the game."

"Shane, can I go with them to get dinner?" Troy asked.

"You just ate at the hotel!" Molly said.

Carly laughed. "Teenage boys have to be fed every twenty minutes, Mols. Or else they get cranky."

"Someone should tell C.J. that because he's *always* cranky," Molly said.

Placing an arm around both kids' shoulders, Carly smiled up at Shane, her delicate eyebrow lifted in question.

One look at her face and Shane couldn't remember what the kid wanted. "Huh?" he asked like the idiot he was.

"Can I go with Carly?" Hell, Shane wanted to go with Carly. He wanted to touch her, to kiss her, to bury himself inside of her. "Yeah, sure," he said. "I need to get inside and start warming up." As if he wasn't warm enough already.

"Congratulations, by the way," she said as Shane turned toward the locker room door. "Asia told me you got the start-ing job. I'm glad it all worked out the way you wanted it to." She bit her bottom lip gently before giving him one of her fake smiles. The kind that didn't wipe away the sadness he saw in her eyes. For a moment he stood there staring at her as she walked away with Troy and Molly. "I'll send Troy back down with one of the coaches from the spotter's box," she called over her shoulder. The team's second bus arrived and players and coaches hustled past him into the locker room. But Shane just stood there, trying to shake off the tightness in his chest.

He didn't remember finally making his way to his locker. Mechanically undressing, he pulled on his gray gym shorts and sneakers to warm up in, all the while trying to get his mind off Carly. His body burned for her. Not just sexually, though. He ached to feel her body snuggled up next to his. To hear her laughter. To smell her hair. He needed to get his head focused on tonight's game plan. He'd worked too hard to get the starting job in the first place. Carly was a distraction he couldn't afford right now.

But that look in her eyes still haunted him. She'd fallen in love with him, he knew that. Not to brag, but so had a lot of other women before her. Only, he hadn't felt anything when he'd let them down. Not like the feeling of numbness taking over his body right now. Since the moment he'd laid eyes on Carly March, she'd been like an intoxicating drug he couldn't wean himself from. Groupies threw themselves at him all throughout the past month's training camp. Just yesterday, at Troy's new school, a mother of one his classmates propositioned Shane. Yet not a single one stirred his blood like Carly had—and obviously still could.

"Get your head in the game, Devlin," he muttered to himself, whipping a Blaze T-shirt out of his locker.

"You always talk to yourself before a game?"

As Shane's head emerged out of the shirt, he looked over at Donovan standing beside him, a wide-eyed grin on his face. Dressed in his corporate security uniform of suit and tie, he looked like a fish out of water in the locker room of half-dressed men, not that he seemed to mind. "Man, I am in an NFL locker room on game day," he said, his voice laced with a childlike glee. "I still have to pinch myself every game."

His exuberance was contagious, allowing Shane to finally relax, taking in his surroundings for the first time that evening. "After a while, they all look the same," he said to his friend. "The real fun is out on the field before the game starts. Come on." Shane slapped Donovan on the back as they both made their way to the tunnel leading out to the playing field. Before they exited the locker room, however, a breathless C.J. stopped them in their tracks.

"Good. Found you." He bent at the waist, gasping for air. "Can't. Find. Carly."

"She took Molly and Troy to dinner," Shane said. But something in the boy's eyes forced a shiver down Shane's spine. Donovan must have seen it, too, because his demeanor sobered at once.

"No," C.J. said, shaking his head violently, still trying to force air into his lungs. "Asia said they never came up there. They're not answering their cell phones, either."

Shane's whole body tensed as the boy continued to huff. "C.J., what's the matter?" he asked quietly.

"Joel Tompkins," he said. His breath was coming more normally now, but his face was ashen and his hands shook slightly. "I saw him near the tunnel."

"You sure?" Donovan asked, his tone all business.

"Yeah." C.J. swallowed. "It was him. He had on that ratty Florida Gator's ball cap he always wears. He walked away real quickly when he saw I'd spotted him."

Donovan and Shane didn't hesitate before heading for the door, C.J. at their heels. "Guys!" C.J. called. "He's wearing a blue windbreaker. And he's got a gun. I saw it." Shane glanced at the boy's face. It was contorted with a mixture of fear and rage. The three of them charged down the hallway, Donovan shouting orders into a walkie-talkie, as a multitude of nightmares flashed in and out of Shane's head.

Twenty-three

Carly shivered involuntarily. The sweltering heat from the hot August day had not diminished with the onset of evening, but she felt cold to her core. Struggling to keep her breathing even, she shoved trembling hands into the pockets of her jacket. She tried to think over the loud hum of the huge generators necessary to run the stadium. Unfortunately, she couldn't come up with one rational thought—not since she'd felt the cold metal gun barrel pressed to her side minutes earlier.

It seemed like hours ago when she, Troy, and Molly went walking arm in arm through the stadium concourse. Both kids were trying to talk over one another as they recounted their exploits in the hotel pool earlier in the day. The next thing Carly knew, Joel Tompkins was behind her, his warm, sticky breath wafting on the back of her neck, making her flesh crawl in warning. Before she could react, he grabbed her arm with one hand, shoving the pistol nearly into her kidney with the other. He hauled her into a utility elevator at the end of an empty hallway. Since she still had her arm linked with Molly's, she and Troy were dragged along, too.

The elevator descended several floors before its doors opened into a deserted area beneath the stadium. Their loud footsteps echoed on the concrete corridor, drowning out the sounds of the exuberant crowd milling about far above. Joel quickly scanned the hallway before shoving them into a darkened utility room beside the steam generators. He flicked on the fluorescent light. The room was small, with a broken stadium chair in the corner and a metal file cabinet and card table against the wall. The smell of old cigarette smoke lingered in the air, but it was apparent the room was seldom, if ever, used. Certainly not on a game day.

No one would look for them here, Carly thought desperately.

"Damn it, why do you always have one of those kids with you?" Joel whined, slamming the door securely behind them and waving them deeper into the room with his gun. The surprise of seeing him must have numbed her brain, because she was reacting in slow motion. Giving herself a mental shake, she reached out, grabbing Troy and Molly, shielding them with her body. Her first priority was getting the kids to safety.

She only had to look into Joel's eyes to know he was high. *Sky high.* He looked even more manic than he had the night of the gala, if that were possible. Carly tamped down a shiver. Wishing for Lisa's soothing, therapist's voice, she tried to reason with him.

"Joel," she said over Molly's sniffles. "Molly and Troy don't need to be here, do they? This is between us."

Before Joel could acknowledge her, Troy shot out from behind her, yelling, "I'm not leaving you with this druggie!"

Joel was frantically pacing the room, trying to get a connection on his cell phone. He'd ignored Carly, but Troy's outburst got his attention.

"Hey, you shut up! She doesn't belong to you," he shouted at Troy, waving the gun around as Carly pulled the boy back behind her. "I've loved her since she was a little girl. She's my Darling Carly."

Trying to process Joel's words, Carly pushed out a breath

as nausea rolled through her stomach. Joel stepped in front of her and her body froze. He lifted a hand to her face before pulling it back without touching her.

"I'm sorry I messed up your house," he said, tears pooling in his eyes. "But you weren't being very nice to me." Anger quickly replaced the tears, almost as if he were a toddler in mid-tantrum. "You were a very bad girl with Devlin. But he's not going to have you anymore."

Carly flinched as he turned away, once again fixated on his cell phone. Troy shot forward, starting to say something, but Carly slapped a hand over his mouth, shaking her head. She pushed Troy back and, placing Molly's hand in his, took a step toward Joel.

"Joel, what do you want?"

He spun around, his face confused, as if he'd totally lost focus. But then the tears returned and this time, he did touch her. Carly held her ground.

"I want to take care of you, Carly. To protect you like your mother didn't. Veronica died and left you alone in the world. But I'm here and you'll never be alone again. You'll be safe with me." Taking his hand from her face, he placed it over his heart, his face the picture of sincerity.

Had Carly not been so frightened, she might have laughed at the irony of the situation. Obviously, Joel had bought into the dramatic portrayal of her in that stupid movie about her mother. It was true; her mother's death had left her with a constant need for security and stability in her life. But what he wasn't seeing were the events that came after the movie credits rolled. Carly knew she was a strong woman who clearly could survive whatever life dealt her. She'd found her sister and become a part of a family. And she'd finally found her niche helping other kids survive the same type of trauma. If she was lucky, she might even find someone to share her life with. Someone who loved her back.

But she had to get them out of there first. Joel claimed to want to keep her safe, but looking into his crazed eyes, she really wasn't feeling that way. She steeled her spine and gently caressed the arm he held the cell phone with.

"Who are you trying to call?"

"Keith," Joel said. He stared at her hand where it made contact with his sleeve. "He's our ride out of here."

Carly willed her hand not to tremble on his arm. As much as she wanted to get him away from the kids, the idea of going off with two stoned maniacs scared the heck out of her. She needed to act fast.

"I have a car." She willed her voice to sound convincing. It was the only option. "We don't need Keith." She stepped closer to Joel, forcing herself to look directly into his eyes. Biting the inside of her cheek to steady herself, she tried not to let his stare unnerve her. "We don't need the kids. Leave them here. They'll just slow us down."

Thankfully, Troy and Molly remained quiet as Joel anxiously looked between them and Carly. "They'll tell," he said, sounding like a toddler again.

"No, they won't," she said in reassuring voice. She tried maintaining eye contact. If she could just keep him focused, she might be able to pull this off. "They'll do what I say." At least she knew Molly would. Troy was a bit of wild card. He clearly saw himself as Shane's surrogate: her White Knight. Still, it was her only option.

"So let's go." She took a step toward the door, but Joel grabbed her wrist, pulling her against him.

"Tell them to stay," he said, waving the forgotten gun in her face. "Or I'll take care of them myself."

Carly shuddered. "I won't go with you if you hurt them, Joel."

They stood like that for a few minutes. Finally, the expression on his face swung back to whipped puppy as he slid the gun into the waistband of his jeans.

Letting out the breath she was holding, Carly turned toward both kids. "Molly, Troy, you both need to stay here until the game ends. I mean it."

Neither one said anything. Molly eventually nodded as she stepped closer to Troy. The look on Troy's face was pure Devlin defiance.

I love you, Carly mouthed over her shoulder as Joel hauled

her out the door. She prayed they'd stay at least long enough
for her to get Joel out of the stadium. Breathing a sigh of
relief that Troy and Molly would be okay, she let Joel push
her into the elevator. She'd only have a few minutes ride to
formulate a new plan.

"Surveillance video has them in a service elevator
at portal G nearly ten minutes ago," Donovan said as they
raced through the crowded stadium. Their progress was ham-
pered by the fans milling about on the mezzanine grabbing
a bite to eat and a beer before heading for their seats. "It
could have stopped on one of three possible floors. We'll
have to do a floor-by-floor search," he said.

Shane jostled his way between two oversized Giants fans,
causing one to spill his beer. "Hey," the guy bellowed, but
Shane pressed on. He had to find Tompkins and stop him
before he did something to Carly. Or Troy. *Christ*, the creep
had a gun on the two most important people in his life. If
he wasn't so frantic, he might have taken a moment to realize
the enormity of that thought. Shane actually *had* people in
his life. Two, in fact. Two people he cared about more than
anything. Well, technically he didn't have Carly in his life,
but he'd remedy that as soon as he killed Tompkins.

"Over here!" C.J. yelled from a few yards ahead. Donovan followed on his heels as they turned right into a shallow
hallway. Four security guards followed.

"We'll take the lowermost floor," Donovan ordered the
guards. "You four split up on the other two floors. Search
every space. He could have them anywhere."

The elevator doors sprung open and Molly charged out.
Tears streaming down her face, she threw herself into her
brother's arms. "Oh, C.J.!" she cried.

"Molly! Are you all right?" C.J. asked as he got down on
his knee to hug her. She nodded into his shoulder.

Shane checked the elevator for any signs of Carly or Troy.
"Molly, where are they?" he asked. His relief at finding Molly
quickly evaporated. Dread settled like a rock on his heart.

With another gulping sob, Molly lifted her head. "She told us to stay there. But Troy said we had to go after them. I didn't want to go, but I didn't want to stay there alone."

"Stay where?" C.J. asked.

"Go after them where?" Shane asked at the same time.

"Whoa," Donovan said, crouching down on his haunches. "Molly, baby, start at the beginning, okay?"

Shane didn't want to start at the beginning. He wanted to get to the end where Carly and Troy were safe in his arms. He plowed his fingers through his hair as he listened to Molly.

"We were walking on the concourse. Troy wanted nachos." She sounded annoyed, as if Troy's nachos had led to this. "And then Joel was there and he was pulling us into the elevator. He was really mad we were with Aunt Carly." Molly gulped another sob. "He had a gun." This came out in a whisper.

"Told ya," C.J. said.

The idiot did have a gun. Shane squeezed his head in frustration. They needed to find Tompkins. Now.

"Then what happened, Molly?" Donovan prodded.

"He said Aunt Carly was his. Not Shane's." She tossed an accusing look at him. Shane's chest felt like it was going to explode. "Aunt Carly talked him into leaving us there. She told us to stay, but Troy wouldn't. He said he had to save Aunt Carly." It was hard to make out what she was saying now because she was crying so hard. The pounding in Shane's head joined the pounding in his chest. Leaning down to look at Molly, he dreaded her answer to his question.

"Where's Troy now?" He had to push the words around the lump in his throat.

Molly's lips trembled as she tried to form the words. "He went after Joel."

Shane couldn't ask another question because all the breath had left his body.

"Do you know where they went, Molly?" Donovan asked, his voice annoyingly calm.

"To Aunt Carly's car."

Both Donovan and Shane shot to their feet.

"VIP parking," Donovan barked to the waiting security guards. "Where is it?"

"Portal B. It'll be faster if we cut through the concession loading dock," one answered as they moved as a unit into a jog.

Shane didn't wait for them. He took off at a sprint.

It was a good thing Carly's body was numb. Otherwise, she'd be unable to endure the last few minutes with Joel. The corridor leading to the loading dock was crowded with food vendors preparing for the game, forcing them to hide in a secluded cubby behind a narrow wall. They had a clear view of their escape route out to the VIP parking, but Joel was too preoccupied with feeling his way around Carly's body to make the next move. Apparently, he took her capitulation back in the storeroom to mean she was willing to be with him in *every* way. The touch of Joel's tongue in her ear coupled with the stench of stale beer seeped into concrete should have made her faint.

Fortunately, she remained upright because she needed to move this along. The farther she got him away from Molly and Troy, the safer they would be. Maybe they'd already gotten help. Part of her wanted them to stay put, while another part hoped they'd found someone to rescue her.

Shane, perhaps. He'd been her rescuer before and she wished he were here now. But he was probably already suited up for the game. Carly stepped away from Joel's roving hands, causing him to stagger a bit.

Concession workers were still moving about, but there were fewer of them than before. A still-stoned Joel seemed oblivious and needed a little prodding. Her plan was to get him to her car where she could try to make a run for it. It wasn't great, but it was all she had.

"Joel," she said. "We need to get to my car before somebody sees us, remember?"

Almost as if she'd changed the channel on a television, Joel's demeanor shifted back to belligerence. He quickly looked around. "Yeah, let's get out of here."

He grabbed her elbow and they walked arm in arm into the hallway, the gun pressed to her side under her jacket. If anyone looked closely enough, they'd see it, but she wasn't that lucky. Everyone in the busy hallway was like an ant, minding their own business, gathering food to take elsewhere.

Ten yards from the doorway, the hall was deserted. They were sidestepping a pallet of shrink-wrapped hot dog buns when Joel's phone rang. He couldn't hold the gun, answer his phone, and maintain the grip he had on her arm. Shoving her against the wall, he released her and answered the phone.

That's when Carly spied Troy following behind them. He stood behind a six-foot-tall rack of CO_2 canisters. He put his finger to his lips. *Oh, God! What if Joel saw him? And where was Molly?*

Stay back, she mouthed to him, hoping Joel was too pre-occupied with his phone to see. There was no time to wait until the parking lot. Carly had to run now and lead him away from Troy. She couldn't risk Joel hurting him. With both hands she shoved Joel away just as he answered the phone. He tripped slightly over his feet, allowing Carly to slip under the arm holding the gun. She took five strides before tripping, face first, onto the pallet of hot dog buns.

"Bitch!" Joel dropped the phone as Carly flipped on her back, struggling to get up. Joel knocked over the rack of CO_2 canisters, sending them careening to the floor near where Troy stood. Carly looked for Troy, but she couldn't see past an angry Joel bearing down on her.

The door behind him opened, and a man with a gun stood silhouetted in the doorway. Carly didn't have time to pray for him to be one of the good guys. Things were moving in slow motion again. Joel's gun was leveled at her head. Out of the corner of her eye, she saw Donovan holding a gun trained on Joel.

"Don't even think about it, Tompkins!" he growled.

"You won't take her away from me!" Joel shouted as

Carly tried to burrow deeper amongst the buns. She started to call out to Donovan that Troy was nearby when . . . *Ooof!*

Dead weight landed on Carly, knocking her breath out, just as a gunshot rang out.

Carly tried to suck in a breath, but a man was lying across her, pressing her deeper into her cushion of buns. A very big man. One that smelled and felt achingly familiar.

Shane! The gunshot! Oh please, don't let him be shot. Or dead! She tried to gather air into her lungs as her hands traveled over Shane's body feeling for holes or blood or anything. Her right hand landed on his heart. It was beating. Strong and fast. *Thank God!*

Donovan yelled "Clear!" and Shane began to move. He pushed himself up on his hands, locking his elbows and staring down at her.

"Are you all right?" they both asked at the same time.

Carly bit her lip and nodded as his eyes roamed her body, checking for damage. He sank down onto his elbows. With one finger, he gently traced her chin. "Did Tompkins do this?" She must have a bruise where Joel had pressed the gun barrel there earlier.

"It doesn't hurt," she whispered. Her eyes stung from holding back tears.

"Christ, Carly," he murmured as he sank into her, his warm lips taking her mouth in a fierce kiss. The kiss was aggressive and overbearing and not the least bit gentle, but she didn't care. She reveled in the weight of his body, strong and hard, pressing hers into the soft bread. Running her fingers through his hair, she opened to him, letting her tongue slide against his, reacquainting her mouth with Shane's. Oh, how she'd missed this. Missed him. She didn't care if all he was offering was comfort. She soaked it up like dry soil soaks up rain after a drought. She wouldn't think about him going home tomorrow, leaving her heart in pieces. Right now she just wanted to crawl inside him and bask in the safety that was Shane. And she was in the arms of the man she loved. There was no point in thinking about tomorrow. Better to enjoy the here and now. Molly was safe. Troy was . . . *Troy!*

Twenty-four

Kissing Carly wasn't helping his already elevated heart rate, but Shane didn't care. He'd almost lost her. He could still see Tompkins's gun pointed at her head. Leaping between her and a bullet was exactly the dumb-ass thing Donovan thought he'd do, but Shane couldn't regret it. Carly was safe and whole lying beneath him. Exactly where he wanted to keep her. Only not on a pallet of hot dog buns. With half of the stadium's security force watching. Reluctantly, he pulled out of the kiss. Touching his forehead to hers, he waited until their breathing settled. Her hands moved from his hair to his jaw. He pressed a kiss into her palm.

Joel was whimpering in the background, crying about being shot in the leg. Hell, if Shane had been the one shooting, the guy wouldn't be around to cry.

"What the hell do you think you were doing?" he asked finally. He knew right away it was a stupid time to bring it up. Her body tensed and her blue eyes, still bright with unshed tears, snapped to his face. "Donovan and I could have taken him. That was a stupid thing to do! He could have killed you!"

"Well, I'm not dead, am I?" she hissed as she shoved him off her. "And pardon me for not knowing Crockett and Tubbs were on the case!" Donovan snorted somewhere behind them. Slapping his hand away, she struggled to get off the slick pallet of shrink-wrapped rolls.

Shane hopped to his feet; he wasn't letting her walk away again. She went to push past him. "Troy!" she called, and Shane's heart went to his throat.

"Where is he?" she asked, shoving him aside.

Donovan snapped to attention along with the security guards milling about. Joel continued to cry from his spot on the floor, but Carly stepped over him.

"Troy was here?" Shane asked in disbelief.

She stepped over spent CO_2 canisters lying on the ground. "Yes, he was behind this."

"Got him," Donovan said from behind the rack. Shane leaped over the overturned rack to find Troy buried under several of the heavy canisters. Donovan was checking his pulse as Carly knelt beside him, tears in her eyes.

"I didn't see Molly with him," she said.

"We already found her," Donovan reassured her. "She's fine."

"EMTs are on their way," someone said behind him.

Carly pushed Troy's hair off his forehead. "He's out cold," she said.

"Looks like one of these bad boys hit him in the head," Donovan said, gesturing at the canisters.

"Troy," Shane said as he crouched beside him. Lifting one of his hands, he gave it a squeeze. "Hey, wake up, buddy. You did it. Carly's here and she's safe." He looked over at the woman he knew he couldn't live without while holding the hand of the boy he wouldn't live without. There were tears in his eyes, but he really didn't care who saw them.

"Sweetie, please, wake up. Shane needs you." Carly's whispered plea was nearly his undoing. Did she not know *he* needed *them*? Her and Troy.

The police and the EMTs arrived like the cavalry. Joel was howling now as they cuffed him to a gurney. Donovan waved one of them over to look at Troy.

"What have we got here?" the EMT asked just as Troy's eyes fluttered open.

Carly let out her breath as she bent down to kiss his cheek.

"Hey there, bro. Glad you could join us," Shane teased.

"Head hurts," Troy breathed. Shane made room for the paramedic, shifting to stand behind Carly, resting his hands on her shoulders. Troy winced as his head was checked over.

"He's gonna be all right," Shane whispered, his words a reassurance for Carly as much as for himself. "You're both gonna be all right."

Carly placed a hand over his and squeezed.

"Aunt Carly!" Molly shrieked as they arrived at the team lounge inside the stadium. Shane had carried Troy there as soon as the EMTs said he could be moved. Donovan had summoned the team doctor to take a look at him.

Molly launched herself at Carly, hugging her tight. C.J. stood behind her, a wide smile on his face. It had been a long time since C.J. had graced her with one of those smiles, and Carly smiled back.

"You're okay!" Molly cried. "I was so scared when Joel took you away."

"I'm fine, sweetie. Thank you for being so brave back there. I'm sorry I had to leave you."

"It's okay. Troy and I knew you were only trying to protect us." Like most kids, Molly recovered quickly. Carly was relieved to see it. She hated that she had put her and Troy in danger. Looking over at Troy beside her, she reached out her hand to grab his. Shane stood beside the two of them. He placed his own hand over theirs and squeezed.

A flurry of people rushed into the lounge, including Matt. Carly quickly pulled her hand away.

"Would someone mind telling me why I wasn't informed a nutcase held my family hostage?" Matt bellowed in his take-no-prisoners coach's voice. Molly ran into her father's outstretched arms.

"Things happened very quickly, Coach." Donovan's voice

came from somewhere behind her. "We had to hurry to neutralize the situation."

Matt had just opened his mouth to say more when Hank Osbourne materialized behind him. "A job well done, Mr. Carter," he said, placing a mollifying hand on his coach's shoulder. "Only minor injuries, I hope," he continued, surveying the scene around him.

"Our boy sustained a nasty conk on the head. My guess is he's concussed." Dr. Mittal, the team's elderly physician, was examining Troy with a small flashlight. "He'll need a CT scan and maybe an MRI to be on the safe side. I'd recommend a night in the hospital for observation since his vision is still foggy and he was out for several minutes." He glanced up at Shane, who nodded his concurrence. The doctor pulled out his phone to notify the EMTs.

Matt pulled Carly into the circle of his arms, Molly squeezing in beside her. "You're both okay?"

"We are now," Carly said, but her body had begun shaking uncontrollably and her teeth were chattering. Pulling away from Matt, she felt as if she might faint. Before she could hit the floor, Shane had scooped her up and was carrying her to the sofa opposite Troy. Dr. Mittal hurried over and was checking her pulse while the others crowded around.

Carly inhaled a deep cleansing breath.

"I'm fine," she said as the doctor felt the back of her head. "I just felt a little faint, that's all."

"Trauma can certainly cause someone to faint," the doctor said. "Of course, there are a multitude of reasons why a woman of your age would faint. Might there be another reason, Carly?"

Huh? Was he asking what she thought he was asking?

C.J. chuckled. "Whoa!"

"No!" she replied to the doctor.

Matt took another step closer. "Carly?" he asked, concern written all over his face.

"No!" she said a little more vehemently.

Shane shifted her in his arms, separating her from the

crowd surrounding them. The position allowed her to see his face more fully. He almost looked as if he wanted it to be true. Tears sprung to her eyes. Had she known for sure she wasn't pregnant, she'd wonder, since she seemed to tear up at the drop of a hat.

"No," she croaked. Shane brought his face to within inches of hers, grasping her hand at the same time.

"You're sure?" he asked softly. "Because I wouldn't mind. In fact, I'd be thrilled."

Carly swallowed the lump in her throat, gently shaking her head. Had he been serious? It was enough for Carly to wish she were pregnant.

"I almost lost you," he continued in that same hushed tone so only she could hear him. "It's taken me all my life to realize I don't want to be alone. Because of you, I gave Troy a chance and now I don't want to live without him. And neither of us wants to live without you. The life that I never thought I deserved, that I never thought I would have, is right here with you and Troy. And some wack job with a handgun almost took that all away from me. He almost took *you* away. What I'm trying to say—in my own sorry way—is I love you, Carly. And I want to spend the rest of my life with you."

He pressed a finger to her lips, which was okay because she was too stunned to form any coherent words anyway.

"Hush," he said. "Drink this." He reached behind her for a glass Donovan had brought over from the bar. "You're shaking like a leaf. We can talk about this later. Privately. I just needed to get that off my chest before something else happened to mess it all up." He brushed a kiss across her forehead as he handed her the glass.

"I was going to give her this," Dr. Mittal said, walking over with a syringe. "But that works, too."

"Devlin." Uh-oh. Matt playing overprotective brother-in-law was worse than his take-no-prisoners coach mode. She had to give Shane credit, though, he didn't flinch. Ignoring his head coach behind her, he cupped her face with both hands.

"I meant what I said. Every word of it," he said as he

gently brought his lips to hers for a brief but very meaningful kiss.

"Man, this is getting good!" C.J. said.

"C.J.!" Matt, Carly, and Shane said at the same time.

"Oww!" Troy mumbled, covering his ears.

"We need to get this young man out of here," Dr. Mittal ordered. The EMTs arrived. They carefully placed Troy on the gurney, ready to wheel him to the waiting ambulance.

"We'll finish this discussion later." Shane dropped another quick kiss on her lips before rising to follow Troy out.

"Where do you think you're going?" Matt demanded. Carly couldn't tell whether Matt was still in coach mode or brother-in-law mode, but either way, he looked like he wanted to kick Shane's ass across the room.

"I'm not letting him go to the hospital alone. I'm the only family he's got." Shane stood toe-to-toe with Matt, a situation that couldn't possibly end well.

"I need you here calling plays."

"Matt! It's only a preseason game," Carly said, nearly spilling the untouched Scotch. "Troy needs him more than you do."

The two men didn't take their eyes off one another as the rest of the room looked on in silence. "He stays, or he loses the starting position."

Carly shot to her feet. "That's not fair!" she cried. "Matt, stop being a jerk!"

"Don't, Carly," Shane said softly. "I know what I have to do." Stepping past Matt, he called over his shoulder. "Tell the Potato Head to have a good game."

The room was silent as he left.

"How could you?" Carly said, her voice trembling with anger. Her legs gave out again and she sank down onto the sofa.

Matt rubbed his hands through his hair and sighed. "Carter, will you see that my daughter and my sister-in-law get to the owner's box without incident? And make sure they stay there the entire game."

Donovan cleared his throat. "A couple of the local police

want to ask them both a few questions. I need your permission for them to speak with Molly."

Gathering Molly in his arms again, Matt pressed a kiss to the top of her head. "If it gets too much for you, Mols, you tell Aunt Carly you want to stop, okay?"

Molly nodded against his chest.

"That's not all," Hank said, his eyes on Carly. "There are scores of media out there wondering what's going on."

Carly swallowed deeply, eyeing the glass of liquor. "It figures."

"Let Asia handle it," Matt said, tersely.

"No, Matt." Carly had had it with him bossing everyone around. "They won't let it go with just a statement. They'll hound me for days. It's okay. After what I just went through with Joel, what's a little dustup with the paparazzi, right?" Carly forced a smile at the four men surrounding her like a group of warriors. She was alive. Joel was gone. And Shane loved her. Her smile became genuine as she realized she actually could face a room of reporters.

C.J. placed an arm over her shoulders, giving her a gentle squeeze. "Atta girl, Aunt Carly," he whispered before placing a kiss on her cheek.

With a decisive nod, Hank and C.J. headed out of the room. Matt stopped at the door, asking over his shoulder, "Do you love him, Carly?"

"A lot more than I love you right now," she answered belligerently.

He turned his head and winked at her. "As it should be."

"*Oooh!*" Carly tossed a pillow at him as he walked out of the door.

The game was in the third quarter by the time Carly made it to the hospital. Fortunately, the New Jersey detectives hadn't asked too many questions. The occupants of the owner's box were a different story, however. Everyone present wanted to know the details. Carly had spent an agonizing twenty minutes on the phone with Lisa reassuring her that she and Molly were fine. Molly was happily ensconced at the stadium, reveling in the attention. Earlier, Donovan relayed the news that Troy had sustained a concussion but no other head injuries. As Dr. Mittal predicted, he was being kept overnight in the local hospital for observation.

Carly knew where she needed to be.

Slipping into the darkened room, Carly stood inside the door, taking in the scene. Both Troy and Shane were lying in the hospital bed. With one hand propped behind his head and his feet crossed at the ankles, Shane's oversized body didn't look too comfortable hanging over the edge. The football game played on the TV with its sound muted, its light illuminating their faces. Troy's eyes were closed. Shane touched a finger to his lips before sliding off the bed. Tucking his hands in the pockets of his shorts, he stopped in front of the door, leaving a foot of space between them.

"Hey there," he whispered.

"Hey yourself." Carly bit her lip, unsure why she was so nervous. "How is he?"

"Fortunately for him, he inherited the hard head of the Devlin men." He laughed softly. "His ears will ring for a few days, but he should be fine otherwise. He doesn't remember anything after lunch today, but the doctor said that should come back slowly."

"It's probably better he doesn't remember."

"And let Molly have all the glory? No way. He needs details to be the big man on campus at school."

It was Carly's turn to laugh. "I brought your overnight bag," she said, placing the bag on an empty chair.

"They let you in the locker room?"

"I still have friends on the team. Mr. Potato Head threw two interceptions for touchdowns in the first quarter."

"Yeah, how 'bout that," Shane said, a slow, sexy grin crossing his face. He didn't seem too concerned about his starting job at quarterback.

"I caught the press conference before the game," he said. "That had to be hard for you, letting the media have a go at Darling Carly." He reached over and ran his knuckles down her cheek.

"Actually, you're the one getting all the press. You'll be happy to know the Devil of the NFL is now officially a hero. Hank couldn't be prouder."

Shane laughed again as he put his hand back in his pocket. Carly wanted to hear his laugh over and over. Every day. She also wished he would take his hands out of his pockets and touch her again.

She wrung her hands, unsure what to say. "Shane, about before," she began softly. He took a step forward, but still didn't touch her.

"Were you . . . were you serious?" she asked.

"About which part?" he whispered, taking another step closer so his body was nearly flush with hers. She could feel the heat radiating off him. The scent that was uniquely Shane's thrilled her senses. It was a comforting smell and it gave her the courage to continue.

"All of it. Especially the part about the baby?" His hands left his pockets as she spoke, creeping around her waist to pull her closer.

"Every word," he breathed into her neck. "*Especially* the part about the baby."

She turned her mouth toward his. "Even those three little words?" she spoke against his lips.

"Even those three little words," he said before sealing his mouth to hers. Carly pressed her body against him, opening her mouth to his kiss. This was what she wanted. This man. This life. Forever.

Breaking the kiss, she cupped his face with her hands. "I love you, too, Shane Devlin."

"About time. You might have mentioned that fact after I jumped between you and a loaded gun," he teased.

"About that." She wrapped her arms around his neck. "You do realize that by purposely engaging in such reckless behavior, you are in violation of the team's code of conduct."

"Huh." He began nibbling her neck, nearly causing her knees to buckle. "Do you have a specific punishment in mind?"

"Hey!" Troy groaned from the bed. "Get your own room, why don't ya. You're grossing me out here."

Shane raised an eyebrow. "Babies turn into twelve-year-olds eventually. You wanna reconsider?"

"No way. You made a verbal declaration in front of witnesses. I'll overlook your penchant for creating a media frenzy with everything you do as long as I get babies. Lots of babies." She leaned in for another kiss.

Troy laughed from the bed behind them. "Potato Head just threw another pick six. I'd say your starting job is secure for opening day, bro."

Breaking the kiss, Shane rushed over to the bed to catch the replay. Carly followed, letting him pull her onto his lap as he sat in the recliner beside the bed.

"This is the only starting job I need, kid," Shane said as he reached across to gently ruffle his brother's hair. Carly smiled as she snuggled in closer. She really should tell them Matt was punking Shane earlier. Maybe later. Right now she was enjoying being part of a family. Her very own family.

Epilogue

Carly fingered the Irish lace adorning the bodice of the magnificent wedding gown hanging in the master bedroom closet of Shane's cabin. *Her wedding gown!* The ornate dress was a work of art. Julianne had crafted the gown uniquely for her, and every detail spoke volumes about the designer's love for Carly. Stepping back, she brushed away a tear as she reread the note her best friend sent with the gown.

"Hey, I hope those are tears of joy."

Shane's voice startled Carly as she shoved the note into her jeans' pocket. Turning quickly, she spread her arms wide in an attempt to shield the dress from his view.

"Shane! It's bad luck to see the bride's gown before the wedding!"

He smiled his trademark grin, the one that never failed to make her body temperature rise. Softly, he closed the door and turned the lock before strolling toward her, his eyes telegraphing his intentions quite clearly.

"Nah. That old wives' tale says it's bad luck to see the bride *in* her dress before the wedding." He gave her a slow wink. "And, if you believe those old crones, the poor schmucks who go on that wedding dress show to help their fiancées pick out their dresses are destined to end up with shriveled jewels."

Carly bit back a smile as she stepped out of the closet and pulled the door closed behind her. "I don't care about the semantics. You're supposed to be surprised when I walk down the aisle tomorrow." It was difficult to keep a stern tone in her voice when her body was humming with pleasure. In less than twenty-four hours, she'd be married to the gorgeous man prowling toward her.

They met in the middle of the room, the king-sized bed looming behind them.

"I promise to be in awe when I see you standing at the chapel door." Shane gathered her in his arms. "I may even be drooling, but only because I'll be thinking about what's underneath that dress."

Carly smacked him on the chest before realizing her mistake. He winced, sucking in a hiss.

"Sorry!" She nuzzled his bruised chin, the result of a nasty hit during a rough game the night before. Carly and Shane were taking advantage of a rare weekend off during the season, squeezing their wedding in after a Thursday night win over the Blaze's rival in Pittsburgh. The ceremony was being held in the small mountain chapel where Shane's grandparents had married. The reception for the fifty or so guests would take place at the cabin, the peaking fall foliage serving as a spectacular backdrop.

Carly snuggled into the haven that was Shane's chest. Since that very first night in Cabo, she'd felt safe in his arms. Protected. And now, loved. She'd been searching her entire life for a place to belong. Someone to belong to. With Shane—and Troy—she was now complete. She belonged to two special guys and they belonged to her. Carly couldn't have been happier.

"Please tell me those tears don't mean you've changed your mind," Shane whispered against the top of her head.

The vulnerability in his voice forced Carly to pull back

and look up at him. Gone was the cocky bravado he normally wore to face the world. Instead, his eyes were wary, with tension lines bracketing them. His smile disappeared into a grim line.

Carly reached up to cradle his jaw. "No!" She stretched up on tiptoes to brush her lips over his in a soft kiss. "Absolutely not."

He touched his forehead to hers, letting out a sigh of relief. "Good to know. But you still look sad."

"Not about marrying you, Shane. Never." She kissed him again. "I'm just sad that Julianne won't be here. Ever since I was thirteen years old, I've pictured her standing beside me at my wedding."

"We could postpone until after the season is over. Or until after her baby is born."

The tense way he held his body and the strain in his voice told her it was costing him a great deal to make the offer. If it were possible, Carly felt her love for him grow even deeper. She wrapped her arms around his neck and closed the gap between their bodies.

"No way, Devlin. You're marrying me tomorrow whether you like it or not."

His relief was immediate. Dropping his head to her shoulder, he placed an openmouthed kiss on her neck.

"Thank you," he murmured.

"I just wish she'd talk to me. Tell me what's going on. She's pregnant—on bed rest! And she won't tell anyone who the father is. I don't even know how it happened."

Shane pulled back, arching an eyebrow at her. "Do you want me to give you a tutorial?"

Carly stifled an eye roll and then licked her lips as she caught a glance of Shane's eyes. They were smoldering again.

"I'm serious, Shane. As far as I know, she wasn't seeing anyone last summer. Other than our trip to Mexico, she didn't go on any photo shoots or vacations. The only place she went was to a client's wedding. That big celebrity wedding for NASCAR driver Chase Jennings. But she didn't mention

meeting anyone there. In fact, she was pretty mum about the
whole weekend."

"Which should tell you something right there." He
pushed a lock of her hair behind her ear, gently tracing his
fingers along her neck.

"Hmmm." Carly tilted her head into his caress as she
thought for a moment. Shane was right; Julianne had been a
little too evasive about the events of the wedding. But it was
also around the time Carly was preoccupied with Joel's
threats and her evolving relationship with Shane. Guilt
nipped at her as she realized she might have been too caught
up in her own life to recognize Julianne's distress. Could she
have conceived the child with someone at the wedding? If
so, who?

"Hey." Shane gave her a gentle shake. "If this is going to
worry you so much this weekend, why don't you ask Connelly about that wedding? He and Jennings are friends.
They're both from the same small town in North Carolina.
Hell, for all I know, he might have been one of Jennings's
groomsmen. Maybe he saw Julianne with someone."

"Connelly" was Will Connelly, the captain of the ominous
Blaze defense. Known by fans and media as "William the
Conqueror," the linebacker was a behemoth, fierce competi-
tor on the field, but a cerebral man of few words away from
the game. Carly doubted he would have even noticed Julianne
at the wedding; the two were so opposite of one another.

She looked up at her future husband. This weekend was
about him. *About them.* Shane was very understanding of
Carly's relationship with her best friend. But she wasn't going
to take advantage and ruin this once-in-a-lifetime event stew-
ing over the mystery that was Julianne's unexpected preg-
nancy. It would hurt not to have Jules standing beside her
tomorrow, but Carly couldn't dwell on her absence. Her
friend had said as much in her note, demanding Carly not
worry and just enjoy her special day. Which was exactly what
she intended to do. She'd get to the bottom of Julianne's crazy
life next week.

"No need to involve Will," she said, pulling Shane's head

down for another kiss. "I'll just ask Julianne. Even if it means I have to go to Italy and drag it out of her."

Shane stared at her, awe reflected in his eyes. "You'd really brave the paparazzi and go back to Italy?"

"I think I've already established I'd take on the crazy media for the people I love."

He grinned down at her, his hands roaming her back before landing with a squeeze on her butt. "Hmm. Yes, you did. Remind me again, did I properly congratulate you for that effort?"

"You do know my sister is going to make you stay at the hotel tonight?"

His grin grew wolfish. "Yeah, another old wives' tale about it being bad luck to see the bride—with or without her gown—on the wedding day. We poor grooms are cursed with rotten luck if you listen to those old biddies."

Carly laughed as she slid her hands along the waistband of his jeans, relishing his quiver as her finger met warm skin. "I know one groom who's going to get very lucky *before* his wedding."

Shane cradled her face in his hands. "Dorothy," he whispered, "I'm the luckiest man alive just having you agree to spend your life with me. A year ago, my life was all about chasing some damn numbers, showing up my old man. Then you and Troy came along and showed me just how totally screwed up my priorities were. Now I'm playing football because I love the game. But not as much as I love you and Troy. You're my world. And no old wives' tale is going to take that away."

And then he proceeded to show her just how lucky *she* was.

Turn the page for a preview of
Tracy Solheim's next novel

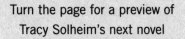

Coming in December 2013
from Berkley Sensation!

Paternity.

The word reverberated inside Will Connelly's head, pummeling his temples until they began to throb. He clenched his jaw firmly in place, at the same time willing his knuckles to release their death grip on the leather chair. It was an effort to appear unfazed despite the fact the supposed purpose of the meeting had taken a one-hundred-eighty degree turn. If ever there was a time for Will to put on his game face, this was it.

The United States senator sitting across the conference table was sadly mistaken if he thought he was a match for Will's trademark inscrutable stare. There was a reason he was known as "William the Conqueror" throughout the NFL: Will Connelly tore through offenses relentlessly, all the while wearing a stoic expression that caused many an opponent to declare that the Pro-Bowl linebacker had ice water running through his veins.

The men seated on either side of him, however, weren't as practiced at remaining cool. Both shifted uneasily in their chairs.

"Come again?" Roscoe Mathis, Will's agent, wasn't one to sit patiently while someone railroaded his client.

The senator's smug grin didn't waver, his gaze fixed on Will. "I said that Mr. Connelly might want to rethink his position as the national spokesman against deadbeat dads. He's been named the father in a rather . . . extraordinary paternity request."

"Now just wait one minute, Senator," said Hank Osbourne, the general manager for the Baltimore Blaze and Will's other companion. Often referred to as the "Wizard of Oz" around the league because of his ability to quickly turn a team into a contender, Hank's demeanor was normally as cool as Will's. But his current tone implied his temper was on a short leash today. "You march us up to Capitol Hill, supposedly to ask questions about an alleged bounty scheme your committee is wasting tax-payer dollars investigating, and then you surprise my player with some cockamamie paternity suit? What kind of game are you playing here?"

The senator lunged forward in his seat. "Correction, Mr. Osbourne. I didn't invite you or Mr. Mathis here for this meeting. This business involves a personal matter between him"—he shot a finger at Will—"and me."

"Your summons was rather vague," Roscoe argued. "We assumed it involved this witch hunt into Coach Zevakos's career."

Will's body tensed at the mention of Paul Zevakos, his former coach at Yale. After college, the coach took a defensive coordinator position in the NFL, bringing Will along as an undrafted rookie. Without Zevakos championing him, Will might never have seen a professional gridiron, much less become one of the league's most elite players. And now the world expected him to turn on his former coach.

Like hell he would.

Senator Stephen Marchione sank back into his padded leather chair. Somewhere near forty years old, the well-respected politician likely didn't have a daughter old enough to interest Will. And married women were off limits in his book. Will relaxed slightly, confident that a mistake had been made. Extremely careful in his personal life and monogamous to the women he dated, he took precautions to prevent children. He had to. No child should be subjected to the childhood he'd endured.

A ripple of unease crawled up his spine, however, as he remembered a sensual encounter the night of his best friend's wedding. But that had been nearly a year ago. If she'd conceived a child, she'd have made her claim long before today. Besides, the woman was Italian or French, the designer of the bride's wedding gown. It was unlikely she and the senator would cross paths. Reassured, he pretended aloofness by adjusting the cuff of his suit jacket as he waited for Marchione to continue.

The senator pinched the bridge of his nose and sighed. "You're right. Congress shouldn't be wasting time and money investigating professional sports. That's for the leagues to police. But I'm in the minority and this is politics. Connelly, you don't want to testify against your old coach and I can impede the committee from forcing you to do so. For the time being. In return, I need you to do something for me." He eyed the men seated beside Will. "Something I think both of us would like to keep private."

For the first time since entering the ornate conference room, Will spoke. "They stay." He wasn't sure what the senator was up to, but he wanted his agent and his boss as witnesses in case something went awry.

"Suit yourself." Marchione pulled a file folder out from the portfolio in front of him.

"Hold on." Roscoe pointed to a white-haired gentleman in a dark suit seated behind the senator. He was the only person to accompany Marchione to the meeting. "We'd like some assurances from your staff that whatever this is about, it'll remain private."

"That's Mr. Clem," the senator said. "He represents the child."

The room was silent for a moment while the men processed that statement. Will's temple throbbed harder as he realized another kid had been born a bastard. Just like him.

The senator's face was chagrined as he slid a photo across the table. Will's breath hitched as he caught sight of the alluring woman in the picture. Laughing, bright amber eyes dancing, she stood among several brides who towered over her curvy, petite frame.

Apparently, the senator did know the bridal gown designer.

Will silently contemplated the photo as his pulse ratcheted up several notches.

"I take it you recognize my little sister." The senator's voice sounded almost apologetic. "She designs under her mother's maiden name, J. Valencia. But her real name is Julianne Marchione."

He could feel the eyes of all the men in the room on him. Will was embarrassed to admit he and his mystery lover hadn't exchanged names. Hell, they'd barely spoken at all. His palms began to sweat as he pondered the ramifications of his one and only one-night stand. In the world of professional sports, men and women hooked up all the time, no strings attached. But not Will. He'd born the shame of being the consequence of a one-night stand all his life. "Your sister didn't offer her name, Senator," he bit out. "In fact, she gave the impression she spoke little English."

Marchione winced as he leaned back against his chair. "Julianne is multilingual. But since she's as American as I am, she's perfectly fluent in English." He sighed. "She has a bit of a flare for the dramatic sometimes."

Will pushed back from the table and stalked to the picture window behind him, turning his back to the men in the room as he wrestled with his composure. The spring sunshine illuminated the Capitol against a bright blue sky, but he didn't notice the postcard picture in front of him. His brain was scrambling to make sense of the meeting.

"Does that flare for the dramatic include seducing a multimillion-dollar athlete to be her Baby Daddy?" Roscoe earned his enormous salary with that one question.

"My sister is a lot of things, but she is not promiscuous!"

Roscoe gave a snort. "Forgive me, Senator, but in this

business, women aren't always what they seem. Not even little sisters."

Will leaned his forehead against the warm glass of the window while Roscoe and the senator argued behind him. He dared not join in because in his heart, he wanted to believe the woman—*Julianne*—hadn't been a conniving seductress. Everything about that night lingered in his memory as a mystical, erotic fantasy. One he relived often in his thoughts, each time wondering if the encounter had been real or imagined.

He didn't have to wonder anymore.

The wedding reception had been over for several hours. A summer storm pummeled the coastline of Sea Island, casting the resort into an eerie darkness despite the fact it was still early evening. Will remembered an overwhelming feeling of restlessness. Being back among his childhood friends always made him feel that way. Despite their friendship and the acceptance of their families, Will always felt like an outsider. His best friend, Chase, had married his longtime sweetheart that morning. Will's other friend, Gavin, was off somewhere with his fiancée. And, once again, Will was alone.

He'd left his room to fill his ice bucket when he saw her wandering the hall, still dressed in the knockout red dress that had every man at the wedding doing a double take. She'd tried to remain unobtrusive throughout the event, but she was hard not to notice with her curves and that luscious mouth. She stopped a few doors from him, fumbling with her key card. Her door wouldn't open and she mumbled something in Italian. Will wondered if she'd been drinking more than just the club soda he'd heard her order throughout the day.

"Here, let me try." He'd been raised in the South, after all.

Startled, she nearly dropped the key card. Will caught her hand and a jolt of electricity shot up his arm. At the time, he attributed it to the storm churning overhead. He tried the card unsuccessfully.

"You must have put it too close to your cell phone in your

purse." He carefully handed the card back to her. "These things demagnetize easily. They can fix it at the front desk."

A savage bolt of lightning suddenly lit up the floor-length window behind Will, illuminating her face. She wasn't drunk, she was terrified.

"Hey." He gently took her elbow. "Why don't I walk with you downstairs to get this fixed?"

She said something that was a jumble of English and Italian, but he had no trouble picking up the gist: She hated storms. Just as they turned toward the elevator, another crack of lightning hit, knocking out the power and enveloping the hallway in blackness. She let out a little squeak and dug her fingernails into Will's arm.

"Change of plans." He maneuvered her back toward to his room, where the door was propped open by the security lock. The blue glare from his laptop screen provided enough light to guide her over to the king-sized bed. As he eased her down, her eyes locked onto the storm outside the window. Lightning streaked across the dark sky. Will crouched in front of her, gently laying a hand against her cheek. "Shhh," he tried to reassure her. "It's gonna be okay."

Her stare darted between him and the storm raging on the beach, fear still paralyzing her face as she fingered a cross around her neck. There was no hope for it. Will lay down on the bed and gathered her in his arms, gently stroking her back.

At this point, things got hazy.

He wasn't sure who kissed who first, but when their lips met, something ignited within them both. She tasted of coffee and smelled of tropical flowers and he couldn't seem to get enough of her. Their clothes melted away, giving Will's hands and lips access to warm, soft skin. When he entered her that first time, she welcomed him, wrapping her legs around his hips and bringing him to near perfect ecstasy.

The thunder and lightning were winding down the second time they made love, her fingers and mouth torturing his body before he found his release. The third time he took her, the storm had dissipated outside but continued to rage on between them as the electricity he'd felt in the hallway reached a fevered pitch. Will had never felt such an intense connection with any other woman.

Until she called out another man's name while climaxing. And then the condom broke.

When he woke the next morning, she was gone, the battered beach the only evidence of the previous night's storm. Will's psyche was as ravaged as the shoreline. His mystery lover had checked out of the hotel and disappeared without a word. As it turned out, she might have taken a lot more from him than a little piece of his ego.

Will took a deep breath and grabbed at his tie to loosen the stranglehold it had around his neck. He needed air. Roscoe and Hank were standing when Will turned to join them.

"You can't leave!" Mr. Clem threw his body in front of the double doors. "That boy needs you!"

Will felt his chest constrict. *A son. I might have a son.*

"Mr. Clem." Roscoe's voice sounded miles away as the world spun around Will. "We're not acknowledging anything without a paternity test."

"We don't have time for that!" Mr. Clem slammed his fist against the door as his face turned scarlet.

The senator slapped both hands on the table in frustration. "She doesn't want you to acknowledge the baby! She doesn't want a red cent from you. You never even have to see him."

Rage swarmed through Will as he rocked back on his heels. What the hell was going on? Who was this woman? If the boy was his, there was no way Will wasn't going to acknowledge him or be a part of his life. A very big part.

Hank stepped in front of the senator, getting right in his face. "I'm going to ask you this one more time, Senator. What kind of game are you playing?"

"It's not a game. My sister never wanted Will to know about the baby. Her plan was to raise him herself. In Italy.

But things have changed. Julianne needs your help." The senator pleaded.

Will barely heard Mr. Clem over the roaring in his ears. "She doesn't want your money!" the man practically wailed. "She wants your blood!"